Praise for T. R. Napper

"An incisive and self-assured voice in near-future fiction. One of those writers with an effortless grasp of the highs and lows of human nature. Always a joy to read."

Adrian Tchaikovsky, Arthur C. Clarke and Hugo Award-winning author of *Children of Time*

"A couple of years ago, I said I couldn't wait to see where T. R. Napper's science fiction would take me next. Turns out, it was worth the wait."

Richard Morgan, author of *Altered Carbon*

"Brace yourself, this is the future, but not as you remember it… it's more badass."

Pat Cadigan, Arthur C. Clarke and Hugo Award-winning author of *Synners* and *Fools*

"T. R. Napper shows true genius in his storytelling, with a compelling plotline, noirish setting, and characters of true depth."

Kaaron Warren, author of *The Underhistory*

"This is one hell of a read. T. R. Napper is back on his quest to be the reigning successor to *Burning Chrome*, *Altered Carbon*, *Synners* and *Ghost in the Shell*. And it's definitely working. *The Escher Man* gripped me from the very first scene and never let go. This is the new face of cyberpunk."

Yudhanjaya Wijeratne, author of *The Salvage Crew*

THE ESCHER MAN

T.R. NAPPER

TITAN BOOKS

The Escher Man
Print edition ISBN: 9781803368153
E-book edition ISBN: 9781803368160

Published by Titan Books
A division of Titan Publishing Group Ltd
144 Southwark Street, London SE1 0UP
www.titanbooks.com

First edition: September 2024
10 9 8 7 6 5 4 3 2 1

A CIP catalogue record for this title is available from the British Library.

Printed and bound by CPI Group (UK) Ltd, Croydon, CR0 4YY.

To Kazuo Ishiguro, a realist of a larger reality.

And to my son, Robert. This is the third book I've dedicated to you, but I love you and I'm not going to stop. Even when you become a teenager, and find the whole thing embarrassing. Especially then.

A Note on Foreign Language Usage

By English-language convention, character names do not use diacritics or tone markings, nor do country names. However, all other foreign words use diacritics or tone markings where appropriate, except where a non-native speaker is using them (because the speaker is not using tones). This may sound a little complicated, but I swear you won't even notice.

PART ONE
The Memory Hole

The palest ink is better than the best memory.

– Chinese Proverb

1

People would try to do one of three things when I was about to kill them: bribe me, beg me, or pretend they didn't know me. A bribe could be any number of things, but it was usually money. The rational proposal that their counteroffer was of greater value than what I'd been paid for the hit. Begging was usually an emotional reference to family – I've got three kids to feed, I love my wife – that sort of inconsequential bullshit. Chances were, if it got to the point where I was paying them a visit, they hadn't made family the most important thing in their life. The last was ignorance, feigned: I don't know you, I've never seen you before – like it's all a simple case of mistaken identity.

I never understood that one. Bribe me, beg me, but don't bullshit me.

The guy looking up at me was trying to do just that. Fred 'the Rake' Bartlett: westerner, Former United States, business suit, crumpled now with blood on the dark grey lapel. He had a full head of brown hair that probably wasn't natural and he was smaller than you'd think, given his occupation. The product in his hair held it neatly in place, even after the beating I'd given him.

His apartment was far more tasteful than anticipated. I was expecting oversized gold throw cushions, monogrammed bathrobes, maybe a large painting of a tiger eating its prey. The usual gangster bullshit. But his place was surprisingly understated. Minimalist white-and-red furnishings, brass fittings in the kitchen, nondescript art on the walls. Down one corridor I'd glimpsed a door with the letter *S* on it, sparkling with glitter.

The floor-to-ceiling windows provided a generous view of the city: the mammoth, bulging structures of the casinos draped in their eternal neon. The hard perpetual rain that drew a thin veil over it all. Macau – that steaming, throbbing gambling mecca; the dark underbelly of the Chinese Dream; the gaudy, glittering, and unapologetic face of its power.

Bartlett was seated with his back to the windows, dripping blood onto his white lounge. He was a nobody, really – a middle manager in an ice-nine drug cartel who had been fool enough to try cutting in on Mister Long's territory. The memory of dinner, two nights ago, was burned deep:

Alone, eating chilli clams sautéed in beer, fresh-baked bread on the side and a large glass of whisky, straight up. The clams were real, so the dinner was expensive, but someone in my line of work ain't saving for retirement, as a rule. The two small rooms of A Lorcha were cosy, friendly, and filled with the tantalising smells of baked seafood and crisp soy chicken. Conversations in Cantonese and Mandarin and Portuguese washed around me while I dipped the fresh bread in the clam sauce and savoured the reason this was my favourite spot in town.

The front door opened and a short guy (who I later learned was Fred Bartlett) *sauntered over, cigarette dangling from his lips, a goon on either side of him. He had a gun in his belt that only I could see from this angle, sitting at a small table in the back corner of the second room. The guys with him were big shouldered: one Filipino, one white. The white guy had a shaved head and teeth that glinted metallic blue – a nano-alloy affectation wannabe gangsters had* taken to implanting lately. The Filipino wore a white fedora and the calm, coiled stance of a professional fighter.

Bartlett had this grin on his face that made me want to break a chair across it. He said: "Endgame Ebbinghaus, in the flesh." He made a show of looking me over. "I guess I thought you'd be more intimidating. Solid titanium limbs, tattooed skull, a dick that shoots flames – that sort of thing."

I slugged half my whisky and said: "I have no idea who you are. And the woman who takes the reservations here is more intimidating than you."

The grin stayed on his face, though it strained a little. He took a drag on his cigarette, blowing the smoke out through his nose. "I have a feeling you'll remember me after this," he said, and pulled the pistol from his belt.

I'd looked down the barrel of enough guns not to get too flustered by this one, but it's never a pleasant experience. Quiet rippled through the restaurant as heads turned to watch. A table of three got up slowly to leave; one of the goons pointed at them and made them sit back down. Everyone else sat stock-still.

So, yeah – I've looked down enough barrels to know there's one thing you never do: hesitate.

I threw the table up with both hands, the edge slammed into Bartlett's wrist, making him fire a shot into the ceiling. I followed in one smooth motion with a straight right to the man with glittering teeth, using the full force of the augmented joints in my shoulder and knees as I rose with the punch. His head snapped back and he crashed into the table behind as he fell.

The Filipino was already moving, kicking low. I checked it. He flowed smoothly into a high kick. I stepped back; the blow didn't come close.

I smiled at him. He didn't like it.

He came at me hard, as expected, I moved inside to meet his

charge, ducking and ramming my elbow into his face. The Filipino staggered, I grabbed him by the collar before he could fall and hefted him above my head, easily. The titanium sockets in my arms clicked and whirred softly.

I paused to savour the moment while Bartlett scrambled for his gun and patrons gasped or screamed or quietly cried. I laughed, though I'm not sure why, and then hurled the Filipino, knocking Bartlett backwards and over a chair. But the blow didn't hit square, and the runt had sufficient adrenaline and panic coursing through him to pick himself up and fly out the front door.

I didn't bother following him. Men that careless were easy enough to track down, and my main concern at that moment was finding a new spot for dinner.

I surveyed the mess. The Filipino groaned, but stayed down. The white guy was out cold, marinating in the beer and garlic prawns from the table he'd taken with him on the way down. I walked over to where the manager, a short Portuguese woman, was standing behind the bar. Her usual expression was harried and stern, with a touch of you-must-be-fucking-kidding-me when confronted by an atypically stupid customer. But now her mouth was parted in shock, and she had this look on her face like she was seeing me for the first time. I got that a lot.

I was mildly disgusted at myself for the scene I'd made, but outwardly I kept my face hard as carved wood as I threw a bundle of currency onto the counter.

I said: "I seem to have spilt my dinner. This is for the mess, and the meals of the patrons here whose evening I interrupted."

She took the fat roll of yuan and weighed it in her hand, then eyed me. In Portuguese, she said: "[We don't have any associations here.]"

"This isn't the start of one," I replied.

"[We can handle security just fine.]"

"Lady, I'm just here for the clams."

She thought it over, lips pressed together, then closed her hand around the money. When I lingered, her familiar temperament returned: "[Well don't just stand there, clogging up my bar with all that shoulder and chin.]" She nodded at the door. "[Get out of here.]"

"I'll see you next week."

She eyed the two thugs groaning on the ground, the splatters of red wine and broth on tablecloth and wall, and the shocked customers whispering emergency calls into their cochlear implants. "[Better make it two.]"

Hard to credit the tough-guy grin and trigger-happy disposition with the beaten-down, pleading little creature here in front of me now. But that is always the test of the mettle of a gangster: how they face death. Most failed in my experience – they begged or wept or wet their pants, and I went ahead and killed them all the same.

Bartlett wiped away the blood from his mouth, his hand shaking. "I don't know what you're talking about," he said, his voice higher than I remembered. "I'm not a drug dealer. I'm a nanotech designer at Baosteel Technology."

"You're saying you don't remember me?"

"I've never seen you in my life."

I seated myself opposite on the tasteful white-and-red faux-leather lounge. I nodded at him, impressed. "Comfortable."

He kept giving me the scared shitless look.

I said: "You should have left town while you could."

"Huh?" His pretence of confusion was very convincing. Imminent death has inspired some of the great acting performances, and Fred was angling for Best New Talent at the Shanghai Film Festival.

"It's always the most logical response. You mess with the wrong people here, you're dead. Macau is the most unforgiving town on Earth. Indifferent, too – just swallows you up into its black bottomless maw, and not a shred remains. Not even a memory.

Everybody knows this, yet everyone believes this somehow doesn't apply to them. So here you are, sitting in your nice apartment, trying to disbelieve the bullet that's about to enter your brainpan."

His eyes were wide open. When he spoke he made sure to verbalise each word, slowly. "Mister. I've never seen you before in my life. I swear."

I placed the pistol on the armrest, pulled a packet of Double Happiness cigarettes from my pocket, and tapped one out. I lit it, snapping the heavy lighter shut, and drew the biting nicotine hit into my lungs. I sighed through my nose, blowing out the smoke. "Cigarette?"

"No I…" He took a deep breath. "Are you really going to kill me?"

"You've been in this business as long as me, Bartlett. I'm going to paint that nice view behind you with your brains."

His lip quavered, tears welled. I shifted in my seat. I'm not sure why, but seeing a grown man cry made me more uncomfortable than beating one to death. When the first tear rolled down his cheek I stood up, stepped over, and slapped him.

He looked up at me, eyes glistening, hand at the spot where I hit him.

I held out the pack. "You need a cigarette."

Bartlett cleared his throat, then took one, hand shaking. I lit it for him. He inhaled deep, sucking on that stick like he was giving head to the last moment of his life. Then he started coughing, hard, as though it was the first time he'd smoked. At first I thought he was faking it, that maybe he was looking for a chance to grab at my pistol. But his face went bright red, so I sat back down and let him cough it out. He did so, colour in his face abating with the shaking in his hands. He took another drag, coughed a little, but not too much this time.

"Have mercy. I have a family – a daughter," he croaked.

"Shouldn't have brought them into this."

"*Please.*"

"I am a man of violence, Bartlett. I don't care about your children. I don't care about your woman. I don't care about that irrelevant sideshow you call a life. I'm not even going to remember you tomorrow, and the way this world is, nobody is going to remember you long after that. Violence is the language of these streets, and I am merely the calligrapher's pen. There's no mercy here Bartlett, no negotiation, no compromise, no way out. There's just this." I showed him the gun, side on. "Now, I have rules when I do this. The first is to tell you why you're going to die. The second is to give you a minute for a drink or a cigarette, while you make your peace with the world. Enjoy it."

He started to argue again.

Irritated, I shot him in the forehead. The windows behind were painted with blood and brain matter, as promised. I sat there and finished my cigarette, the air thick with smoke and gunpowder. I felt flat as I looked at the body. Mild disgust, at the man's weakness I guess, and nothing more. Nothing more.

2

I sat on the glimmer bike at dusk under the deep shadow of the cemetery wall. The air was hot, fecund, so rich in this town it could be mistaken for something rotten. Rain was coming. When it wasn't here already, it was always on its way. I kept the mirrored visor of my helmet down as I watched the little girls cross the crossing: white dresses, big red kerchiefs around their necks, hair in pigtails. A level of cuteness so absurd and un-self-aware it made even me smile a hidden smile.

Jian waited at the other side of the crossing, watching the children approach. My heart tightened in my chest – even after everything – as it did every damn day. Her bare arms were like pale jade in the low light, the smile on her face warm and easy as she bent down, and two of the girls in the parade of tiny children ran to her. Kylie, my angelic child, her face alight and more beautiful even than her mother, laughing as Jian picked her up. Seeing her, the tightness in my chest twisted until it hurt, as it did every day, as well. The other girl was younger than Kylie – Jian's new child with her new husband. I didn't know the little girl's name. But I didn't feel angry or bitter, like I was supposed to. All I had was this deep dull pain, this old familiar ache of wanting that girl to be my girl, too.

I gripped the handles of the bike hard, the leather of my gloves creaking. Not mine and they never will be, because I am a violent man.

I gunned the glimmer bike, shooting out between slow-moving automated cars, the solar particles coating the bike scintillating, even under the roiling grey-clouded sky. I swerved, barely missing a Chinalco delivery truck, the big C-little c insignia looming large as I flashed by.

Further and further from the school and those beautiful children, my pain anonymous behind the reflective visor. Over the roar of the bike no-one could hear me scream.

3

"Endgame. Come in, mate." Wangaratta Nguyen slapped me on the back and led me into one of the hotel rooms at the Grand Lisboa. Porkpie hat, always smiling, hands big and strong enough to crush a man's throat easy as blinking. He was the only other Australian I knew in Macau. Often we'd drink whisky down on the foreshore, eat fresh-grown mussels with garlic and butter, and talk about the white sand beach at Bondi, how it felt under your toes. That big sky country, blue and limitless, where the Macau skyline was cramped and grey. Manufactured, where Australia was raw and fierce. They had their architectural triumphs here, sure, but sometimes you'd wonder if these were what you consoled yourself with once the wilderness had been consumed.

We talked and tried to remember, and remind each other, how it was back home. And once the reminiscing was done, we'd go find a dingy pool hall and pick a fight with local gang members. Always a good night, with Wangaratta.

We entered a three-room suite with canary yellow walls stencilled, for no apparent reason, with black elephants. Mister Long sat at a mahogany table, eyes closed, no doubt watching his c-feed. He wore a tight, white, stiff-collared silk shirt that accentuated his slender, too-perfect body. His face was smooth, buffed clean of lines and wear and emotion. His lips were painted red, his heart another colour entirely. Some people would look at Mister Long and think he was twenty-five years old; I knew he was closer to fifty.

On a lounge nearby sat Chrome Linh Phu. Purple eye shadow and matching lipstick, short dark hair, she was wearing a black singlet and her default anger. Tattoos twisted up each arm, depicting the serpent designs of her first gang in Shanghai. The slender tails started on each wrist, twining around as they disappeared under her top, before reappearing on the other side, the heads ending on the top of each hand. The design could be mistaken for a snake, if not for the thin beard of spikes that lined the long, slender jaws of each creature. Holotype ink had been used to edge the scales deep blue, creating a shimmering effect when she moved her arms, as though the serpents lived. The eyes atop each hand burned a fierce blue.

There weren't many people in Macau I'd hesitate raising my fists against, but Chrome Linh Phu was one of them. She moved so fast when she fought, her opponents didn't even know when or where they'd been cut. She'd just walk away and three minutes later they'd find themselves dead, bled out on the steaming polycrete of some anonymous back alley.

Wangaratta announced to the room: "Endgame here to see you, Mister Long." He turned, winking at me as he did so, and left.

I stood, feet shoulder-width apart on the thick cream carpet, while the two ignored me completely. Chrome cleaned the action on her sleek needle pistol while Mister Long mumbled under his breath, talking with whomever it was he could see in three technicoloured dimensions on the back of his eyelids. The only word I heard him murmur was the incongruous *happy*.

I pulled the pack of Double Happiness from my pocket and tapped one out, grabbing the cigarette with my lips.

"No smoking," hissed Chrome, her eyes flashing. "How many times I got to say?" Linh's English was excellent, though whether from learning it in Vietnam, or being raised in an English-speaking country, no-one knew. I thought I heard a touch of Australian in it, but she'd told me I was an idiot when I'd once asked.

I snapped shut my lighter, put the unlit cigarette behind my ear and said: "I don't remember you ever saying it."

Her mouth twisted into a whisper of a sneer before she returned to working on her gun. It was a look she often gave me: somewhere between disappointment and contempt. The latter I got. The former was harder to figure.

For a few more minutes I stood there, waiting while Mister Long mumbled, Chrome cleaned her gun, and I thought about the cigarette sitting behind my ear. Finally, Mister Long opened his eyes and gave me the look he always gave when we talked – like he saw right through me, knew everything turning over inside my head. It was a feeling I just couldn't shake. "[Mister Ebbinghaus.]"

"Mister Long."

He held out his slender hand, palm open. "[Your memory pin, please.]"

Mister Long was a mainlander and, as such, spoke only Mandarin. I couldn't sing, play an instrument, or learn another language. Just wasn't in my skill set. So I relied on the translation from my cochlear implant. It ran a couple of seconds behind the pace of conversation, making any non-English speaker seem badly live-dubbed to my eye, their lips not matching the words pumped into my ears. My lack of aptitude at Chinese never worried me that much, what with the implant and all, but it seemed to rub a lot of people the wrong way. Once I was running security at one of Mister Long's cocktail functions when a white guy wearing a silver-grey Xiong original suit and matching fedora, thinking I was one of the guests, acted appalled when he realised I couldn't speak Mandarin. He proceeded to lecture me about the crudities of cochlear translation and the nuances of cultural resonance –

whatever the fuck that was – I was missing by not knowing the language. I leaned in close and asked him how hard it would be for him to *resonate* the different tones with all his front teeth missing. He smiled, then un-smiled when he saw the look on my face, then stuttered and walked away.

Wangaratta had me remove my memory pin before entering the suite. I handed it over to Mister Long. He unfurled a flexiscreen flat on the table and whispered into it. The surface came to life with scrolling, soft glowing green icons. He placed the pin in the centre of the screen, the icons begun swirling around it, the pin the eye of a digital storm.

"[Your new memories will take two minutes to upload.]"

I nodded.

He placed a green glass vial on the table across from him. "[Miz Phu will fix you a drink while you wait.]"

Chrome Linh allowed irritation to cloud her features for half a second, then rose and walked over to the bar at the side of the room.

"Single malt, straight up," I said.

Mister Long and I looked at each other while she made the drink.

The red on his lips glistened. "[Effective as always, Mister Ebbinghaus.]"

I shrugged.

"[Take a seat.]"

I sat opposite as Chrome Linh placed a tumbler in front of me, filled with vodka. I eyed the drink and then the enforcer. She looked back, her mouth a thin line of disdain, and returned to the lounge and her pistol.

Mister Long indicated the glass with his eyes. "[Drink up.]"

I picked up the glass vial, unscrewed it, and used the eye dropper inside to put three drops into the vodka. The drops glistened golden yellow as they fell. I knocked back the booze in one hit. It was just after breakfast, so only my third drink of the day. My head spun, but not too much, and left a metallic aftertaste in my mouth, but that subsided quick.

I pulled the cigarette from behind my ear, tapped it on the table. "Anything else?"

He blinked at me. "[No. Your pin will load the new memory while you sleep. A day or two and it will encode. I'll have something new for you in a week.]"

I waited.

He blinked at me again, then directed his voice at Linh: "[Miz Phu.]"

Chrome rose slowly and walked over, reaching into the back pocket of her black, faux-leather pants. I tensed, but all she pulled out was a brown envelope. She threw it onto the table in front of me. I picked it up – the weight felt about right – and put it inside my leather jacket.

I got up from my seat and walked to the bar. I looked over my shoulder at Mister Long and said: "You want anything?"

Mister Long stared back, looking at me with the disinterested contempt I usually reserved for barflies begging for change. He said: "[Sobriety. At breakfast time.]"

"Come now," I said, grabbing a bottle of expensive single malt and pouring myself a triple. "A pusher shouldn't be so squeamish around drugs as mild as this."

"[I'm not some common corner drug dealer, Mister Ebbinghaus.]"

"That's true," I said over my shoulder as I poured. "You're a *superb* drug dealer. The best."

The backing for the bar was mirrored and I glanced up as I said it, hoping to see Mister Long show a flicker of annoyance at the jibe, and expecting Chrome Linh to rise from her seat and threaten me. But she just smiled, which seemed strange. Mister Long gave nothing away, as usual.

I looked away from them and back at the mirror, drink in hand, and found myself fixed on the guy staring back at me. He didn't seem so familiar these days. Big shouldered and big jawed, sure, that hadn't changed. But there were lines of purple under each eye, courtesy of the booze and the memory drugs and the sleepless nights. The once-magnificent dark hair now receding and a long scar that ran straight down near my right eye that, right then, I couldn't recall receiving. But the eyes, most of all, were unrecognisable. Flat, distant, without spark; blue eyes that once attracted attention for their rarity, now washed out. The eyes of a stranger. They were like the waters of Macau's outer bay: nothing lived there anymore.

I downed the drink, still looking back at myself, and poured myself another.

I turned to Mister Long and leaned back against the bar, holding up the glass in one hand. "I'm not complaining, not at all. I'm just a junkie looking for a fix. Glad, that I've come to the right place."

He watched me, in silence, red lips shining in the dim morning light. Mister Long's skin was young and perfect, but his eyes were old, so old, filled with the ancient cruelty of this city. Even I couldn't hold those eyes long.

"[You're right,]" he said, finally. He plucked my pin up from the now-quiet flexiscreen, holding it in his palm. "[So drink, Ebbinghaus. The most powerful drug of all: the dreams I dream for you.]"

4

I took the elevator down, the floor of it a gleaming gold mosaic. I slotted my memory pin into the cochlear implant behind my left ear, leaving my finger on the small cold steel circle long enough for it to record my print, accept the pin, and secure it in place. Three ascending tones sounded inside my head as the implant acknowledged successful receipt.

I walked from the elevator out into a long, wide, red-carpeted corridor that ran past the high-roller rooms. Between frosted glass screens I glimpsed glittering chandeliers as big as small cars, and red-faced men with loosened collars and fat cigars. On the other side of the corridor loomed fine paintings on the wood-panelled wall; someone told me once, breathlessly, that two of them were Renoirs. I didn't care much either way, but I suppose there was an appeal to having something of true beauty to counter the empty gaudiness of this place. A member of staff recognised me, nodding as I walked by. He wore a trim blue and black uniform, which seemed at once somehow futuristic and authoritarian.

The end of the corridor opened out into an expansive poker room, the air thick with cigarette smoke and exhortations in Cantonese and Mandarin as players willed this card or that to fall. The hotel refused to make it a non-smoking room, thus ensuring it remained the most popular in town. As I made my way through the tables someone whispered *gweilo* to the person next to them. My neural implant translated it as 'foreigner', but it was a term that really depended on who was saying it, and how. It meant 'ghost man', or sometimes 'devil man', in Cantonese. At best they were calling me an outsider. At worst, a white devil.

I sat down with half a million yuan in chips. The regulars round the table nodded at me from behind the screen of smoke, and gave me the smiles they put on for the mark at the table. Half wore face masks, but still I could see the shine in their eyes as I was seated. I didn't go there to win, so the condescending camaraderie never bothered me. I sat down to feel the rush of the big bluff, the burn on my lungs as I worked though pack after pack of Double Happiness, and the heat in my chest as I downed thousand-yuan glasses of single malt whisky. That's the service I paid for, and that's the one that was provided.

The night went the way I wanted.

At some point I opened my brown envelope from Mister Long and started playing through that, too. A young guy sat down late into the night, Macau local, big ears. He was talented, but too arrogant to appreciate the most basic premise of cash game poker: keep your customers happy. He insulted me in Cantonese for a bad bluff I made and I responded by breaking his nose with the back of my hand. He lay on the stained red and gold carpet, struggling to breathe though a mouth full of blood, while the regulars at the table patiently explained to the floorman how it was the young man's fault. Soon the boy was dragged away between two heavy-set security guards and I was free to lose the rest of my money to good-humoured, respectful, and convivial company.

When I staggered outside a new dawn was staining the thin edge of the horizon purple. The wet heat of the early morning hit me as I stood swaying on the curb. The doormen knew me, knew I needed help into a cab, even knew my home address, I guess. That's where I ended up anyway, sprawled on the couch, Blundstones still on my feet.

I dreamed:

I dipped the fresh-baked bread into the beer and chilli sauce of the clams. I bit into it and closed my eyes, savouring the taste: delicious. Delivered straight from A Lorcha, the food was expensive, but someone in my line of work ain't saving for retirement, as a rule. I sat in my apartment at the Venetian, looking out at the view across the outer harbour, through the light rain, at the mammoth, bulging casinos draped in neon. Bulging as though they were fit to burst, having gorged themselves on the dreams of their inhabitants. A bottle of twenty-one-year-old Glenfiddich stood open next to me, the tai screen on the far wall showed the cage fight, live, from the City of Dreams. The announcers exclaimed in the background as the white fighter kicked the brown-skinned fighter in the head and I worked on my buzz.

My on-retina display read:

21:43

22°C inside / 42°C outside

Venetian Hotel, Cotai Strip

The meal was soon finished and I sat back, satisfied. I tapped out a cigarette from the pack and searched my pockets for the lighter.

"Yes, I fucked him – so?"

I started and turned, cigarette unlit, and there she was, Jian, standing near the kitchenette I hadn't cooked in since moving into the hotel. Her arms crossed, hair pulled back, no trace of her ready smile.

I stood, cigarette dangling from my lips and asked, quietly: "You what?"

Her face remained impassive. "It was the office party and I'd had too much to drink. He was insistent and I hadn't seen you in two weeks and it happened."

I took a step forwards and found myself in the little place we used to live in on the Rua da Gamboa. The gloomy but cosy apartment with its dark wood floors, and weird wallpaper of faded red with black silhouettes of belly dancers. The sight of the room brought back memories long forgotten, filling my nostrils with the scent of the incense that Jian used to burn of an evening.

I said, louder: "You fucking what?"

"Don't try your tough guy routine on me," she said, uncrossing her arms.

I screamed: "YOU FUCKING WHAT?"

She took a step back. The flat indifference on her face was gone, replaced instead with fear, sparking behind her eyes. "Don't touch me, Endel."

I advanced on her, fists clenched.

5

I awoke with a start to an ache in my chest and the cloying taste of incense in my mouth. Ragged daylight pierced my hangover. I remembered my name and, after a pause, where I was.

I fumbled a finger against my cochlear implant. "Make it dark."

A voice, flat and uninflected, responded from inside my head: *Did you want the kitchen to prepare dark coffee, Mister Ebbinghaus?*

"I said make the *room* fucking dark."

A pause. *Right away, sir.*

The implant turned the windows down to the deepest gloom, but it didn't help. I'd never been good at sleep and I'm terrible at it when I'm pissed off. So I tossed and turned on the couch to no avail for another hour, throat dry and neck sore from sleeping at an unhealthy angle. Eventually I swore, loudly, into the empty apartment and stumbled over to the kitchenette on unsteady feet, and ordered a coffee from the machine, black. I put a slug of whisky in it and stood over at the windows, increasing the opacity enough so I could look out over the wet Macau morning. The distant, muted sounds of traffic, and wind, and rain seeped faintly into the room. Beyond the levees, a storm-tossed, darkling sea.

A lone white gull hovered above the distant waters, and a flash of memory came to me, of Australia: waking to birdsong. Though less a song, and more a cacophony of demented avian fauna. The screech of the cockatoo, the warble-gobble of the magpie, the rhythmic raucous laugh of the kookaburra. Here you'd be hard-pressed to see even one. Bird flu wiped out most of them in Macau twenty-five years back, plus three per cent of the human population. They reckoned the new breed of genetically modified birds were immune and safe, but many saw them as a bad omen. And bad omens did not sit well with a city of superstitious gamblers, not one bit.

I burned through a half-dozen cigarettes and two more coffee-and-Scotches like that, at the windows. Then down to the gym, where I punished myself with an hour on the treadmill and thirty minutes on the heavy bag. Then a long hot shower, head bent under the powerful spray, trying to wash away the stink of sweat and incense.

The rest of the day was spent lying on the couch, watching kickboxing on the big screen, taking it easy with a few quiet beers. Late that afternoon a chime sounded in my ear, waking me from a doze. A reminder appeared, on-retina: School. I got up, washed my face in the sink, and headed down to the garage.

I waited on the glimmer bike under the cemetery wall. Class seemed to be running late, twenty minutes past seven and still no sign. As time dragged on I began to crave a cigarette. When it dragged on some more I started to feel claustrophobic in the helmet. Sitting there as sweat trickled down my brow, waiting for the rain to come, hands shaking from the heat or exhaustion or alcohol withdrawal, finding it harder and harder to breathe. I tried taking deep breaths, but every time I sucked in the closed air of the helmet it tasted like I was inhaling more of my own sweat and fear. Another few minutes and I couldn't stand it anymore, getting off the bike, unsteady. I yanked the helmet up, gasping, and leaned forwards with hands on knees, chest heaving. I let the helmet fall to the sidewalk.

The beating in my chest slowed. I wiped the sweat from my face and glanced over at the school. Still no kids. I slipped on a pair of mirrored sunglasses and eased out a pack of smokes from inside my leather jacket.

I had the lighter's flame an inch from the end when a voice, close and soft, said: "Endel?"

I started and turned. Jian stood there, not two metres away, uncertain smile on her face. Jian, wearing faded jeans and a simple green blouse and her effortless grace. As beautiful as ever, no make-up, that single small mole below her left eye on otherwise flawless skin.

"Oh," I mumbled through my cigarette. "Hi."

She tilted her head to one side, eyebrow raised. "Laconic as ever, Endel. What you doing here?"

"Um…" I took off my sunglasses, wincing at the light. I felt my face going red. "Just having a smoke."

"You look terrible."

"Cheers."

She let a smile touch her eyes. "And you smell worse: like gym socks soaked in bourbon."

I couldn't help but smile at that.

She looked at my glimmer bike, then over at the school, where straggling gangs of red-and-white uniformed kids were now emerging from the front doors. "I've seen that bike sitting over here in the shadows before."

I said nothing, just returned the lighter to my pocket, the cigarette back to the pack.

She looked me in the eye. "Has it been you all this time, Endel? I thought it was some freak stalking the kids."

I cleared my throat, but still, my voice came out thick. "I—I just wanted to see Kylie."

She nodded slowly and something in her stance changed. Her eyes gleamed. "You know you can just call me. You can see them anytime."

"Jian," I said, the word coming out like surrender. "I'm a violent man. You know this."

Her eyebrows drew together for a moment. "Kylie misses you, Weici misses you." She took a deep breath. "I miss you."

When she said *Weici* something plucked at my mind. "Weici? Is that your new girl?"

She tilted her head slightly. "What do you mean?"

I stared at her. I was missing something. A phantom memory, passing, just beyond the edge of my waking mind. Like I'd walked into a room for a specific purpose and now I stood in the middle of it, not knowing what the hell I was doing there. I said back: "What do *you* mean?"

She looked me up and down again, and the expression on her face was the one I always dreamed in my dreams: disgusted and shocked and sad all at once. "What have you done to yourself, Endel?"

The sense of my missing something expanded and I shook my head, like I was trying to jar the elusive thought loose. I took a step backwards, knocking the helmet with my foot. It skittered on the polycrete, spinning in a slow circle while Jian and I stared at each other.

She blinked, real long, leaving her eyelids closed for two eternal seconds, and when she opened them again her face had softened. She reached out. "Endel, she's…"

But static filled my ears, white noise eating into the edge of my senses. All I could think of was Jian, lying on the brown wood floor of our apartment, her brow split and bleeding, and I grabbed the helmet from the ground and jammed it on my head while I said sorry over and again.

I jumped on the bike and gunned it. Jian grabbed the elbow of my jacket and was yelling something, screaming it, but I think the wind caught it.

I spun the wheels.

6

I drove straight to the Scarlet Street bar down on the waterfront. I told the barman – who went by the name of Paddy the Mex – to leave the bottle; he did without a word and returned to cleaning highball glasses with a white cloth. Paddy was a skinny Cantonese speaker from Hong Kong. No-one had a clue how he got his nickname.

I watched the fight on the screen over the bar and worked my way through the bottle slow. My drunk wanted to come on in a rush, but I didn't want that, not yet. I wanted to remember Jian, standing there as dusk approached, smiling as though the betrayal and brutality of four years ago had never happened. I had my memory pin play back the time sequence at the school. I closed my eyes and watched my point-of-view of an hour before, a perfect three-dimensional recording made by the nanos attached to my optic nerves and encoded onto my memory pin. I scrolled through the school at dusk, through pulling the helmet from my head, through the conversation with Jian until the moment she smiled that small smile at me. I told my implant to freeze the image.

I eased myself back in the bar stool, eyes closed, and stared. She was exactly how I remembered her. The slightest hint of new lines under her eyes as she smiled that smile, but that was it – like the movement of time had left her behind. I sighed. Jian: the free-spirited, down-to-earth merchant's daughter from Shanghai. I still remembered – without any artificial assistance – how she looked when we first met in the bar at the City of Dreams. She stood next to me in her faded jeans and calf-high boots and ordered a lager. I asked her if she was here for the fight. She told me she was here to dance, and with a twinkle in her eye as she looked me up and down, asked me if I was going to join her. I transferred my ticket to the nearest barfly and gave her my arm.

So beautiful and smart and so damn *good,* and as I looked at her I just couldn't understand why this woman, with the world at her feet, would have anything to do with an immigrant street thug. But it happened. She called me her Australian cowboy and I called her my Chinese princess and we didn't care what anyone thought about us.

That I remembered. I couldn't remember if we were happy or not, but somewhere deep down I felt that we were. I couldn't remember how long that happiness lasted, and when I tried to bring up our history on-retina, all I found was yelling and angry silences. The former from her, the latter from me. Just the same fights over and over, variations on the theme of my lifestyle or her career.

When I opened my eyes the picture of Jian remained, hovering about three feet away, visible to my eyes and my eyes only. I left it on-retina. In the end I'd probably forget everything else, but this one brief memory of her, this I wanted to keep.

I burned through a pack of Double Happiness, made small talk with Paddy the Mex, and used the grog to bring back some life to the deadness inside my chest.

At one point my on-retina display flashed with a news alert that my implant had decided I'd be interested in. I closed my eyes and watched a story about what looked like a gangland killing.

The victim seemed familiar: a small guy with a full head of brown hair that probably wasn't real. The wilfully stupid ticker tape at the bottom of my vision read: *Found Dead with Bullet Hole in Forehead, Forced Entry into Apartment, Police Suspect Foul Play*, glowing in red holotype. I felt this gnawing sense of déjà vu as I looked at the picture of the man – a nanotech designer at Baosteel, said the report.

I shook my head. I got these bouts of déjà vu all the time. I'd meet someone whose face was strikingly familiar, but when I'd nod and say hi they'd introduce themselves with some name I'd never heard before. Some days I'd get this feeling that I was the butt of some joke that the rest of the world was in on. Other times – usually when I was drinking – I'd get all metaphysical and wonder whether part of the human mind could know the future, that we'd glimpsed it in our dreams. That maybe we'd lived it all before, the eternal return, like that guy said. Then I'd blearily fear, for a few seconds anyway, that I had some sort of precognitive talent, like in those science-fiction books Jian used to read.

In the end, though, I'd just smile at myself. The most likely explanation was that I'd seen something similar before, and my booze-marinated mind simply found it hard to tell the difference anymore.

This was the series of thoughts I went through while I watched the report about the dead white guy. I shook my head, switched off the feed and smiled at myself while I poured another whisky.

I drank until the edges faded and the evening blurred into the Great Drinking Session, until it became the dream-state of drunk, where sitting on the chair at that bar at that time could have been any joint in this town, at any time. Where so many years and so many days could simply be interchanged with one another, where the drunk was the same and bled into all the others. My life was divided into three states: the sleep-state, the sober-state, and drunk, and drunk had been the dominant one for so long I wondered if that was my reality, and the dreams and the daylight were the illusion.

After, well, I'm not sure how long, I turned off the on-retina of Jian. The static image stayed warm and kind, but as the night wore on it made me feel sick. I didn't want her to watch me anymore with those too-forgiving eyes. Look into eyes like that long enough and I might just forget the truth of my nature.

It was time, then, to do what I was good at.

The place was hopping. Loud music, shouted conversation, the air a cloud of body heat. Life swirling around me as I drank, a dark island in a sea of human connection.

Someone bumped my back.

I took a slug of my drink.

They knocked me again, harder this time.

I turned. Tall Chinese guy, big white teeth, shiny silk paisley shirt. Woman with him, teeth just as white. "You right mate?" I asked.

He looked down at me. "[Are you talking to me, *foreigner*?]"

"Seems that way."

"[We got a problem?]"

"Boy, I hope so."

The woman narrowed her eyes and looked up at the man. His smile faded for a moment and then came back strong and mirthless. He opened his mouth, looking for another line, but nothing came out. Guys not used to fighting were like that: unable to multitask, once the adrenaline hit.

I looked him over, and then the woman. To her I said: "How much is he?"

"[What?]" she asked.

I jerked a thumb at the guy. "How much?"

"[For what?]"

"He's a male hooker, right?"

She looked confused.

I indicated his shirt.

"[Watch your mouth,]" said the man, puffing out his chest.

"Bold fashion choice," I said. "Just woke up in this and thought: gigolo. That's the look I want."

"[Shut up, you drunken slob,]" he hissed. "[You can barely sit straight on that stool.]"

"True. Not to worry though, mate – I throw up on that and no-one will notice."

The woman smiled, briefly, then tried to press her mouth into a straight line.

The man reddened and balled his fists. I waited. The music blared. Customers shouted orders at the bartender. And the paisley shirt guy – well, he lashed out. My head jolted to one side, pain flashed, then ebbed just as quick. I turned back to face him, and then it happened, the creeping realisation clear on his face. He said: "Oh."

"Thank you," I said.

I grabbed his arm, twisted it, and chopped down with my other hand. His elbow snapped, he screamed. The woman screamed. I breathed that great sigh of exultation, felt the fire in my eyes and in my teeth and in my chest.

I let the man drop to the stained floor, writhing, while around me the crowd parted. They moved away and in that space an image came, unbidden. Jian, arm outstretched as I turned and hopped on the glimmer bike. Yelling something, desperation in her voice—

I clenched my teeth and whirled, leaping over the bar and snatching a bottle from the hand of Paddy. His eyes wide as I opened my mouth and poured it in, didn't care what it was, the fire burning in my chest and I had to smother it all, kill it all.

People were yelling. Someone was grabbing me.

And, well, it all went downhill after that.

Paddy the Mex and two of the bouncers tried to restrain me, but I'd gone blood simple, splitting open faces and breaking the ribcages of anyone within arm's length. I got hit across the back with a pool cue and when I turned to face the man who did it, he just threw the broken stick away and ran. I was roaring, wanting more. But no-one would give it to me. No-one would let me bridge the lack. The club cleared and I was alone, save the noise. The noise, falling on my mind like a summer storm, would not quit, just wouldn't.

Wangaratta Nguyen arrived about the same time as the cops. I was sitting at one of the unbroken tables by that point, trying and failing to pull a cigarette from the pack with bloodied fingers. Everything after that was a blur.

I could have played back the evening from my memory pin, see what I did. But it had been a long time since I'd looked back on a drunk. The self-loathing of the alcoholic is sufficient without constant fucking replay.

So I guess – but don't know for sure – that Wangaratta paid off Paddy the Mex and the cops, same as always. I do remember one final thing, though – Wangaratta dumping me face down into the back seat of his car and saying: "This can't go on, Endgame. Even you have limits."

"I know," I said, "I know. I can't stop." But he didn't hear me. He was in the front driving me home by then and my face was pressed into the leather seat, muffling my words.

I dreamed:

"Yes, we slept together – so what?"

I started and turned and there she was, Jian, standing with arms crossed, hair pulled back, no trace of her ready smile.

I stood, cigarette dangling from my lips and replied, quietly: "You what?"

Her face remained impassive. "It was the office party and I'd had too much to drink. He was insistent and I hadn't seen you in two weeks and it happened. It was just, it was just..." She hesitated, putting a hand against her forehead.

We were in our little place on the Rua da Gamboa. The apartment was gloomy, but cosy, with its dark wood floors, and weird wallpaper of faded red with gold silhouettes of belly dancers. My nostrils filled with the scent of the sandalwood incense Jian used to burn.

The scent faded and I said, louder: "You fucking what?"

"Don't give me your tough guy routine."

I stepped forwards and shouted: "What did you fucking do, Jian!?"

She took a step back. Fear sparked behind her eyes. "Don't threaten me, Endel."

I advanced on her, fists clenched.

7

A few days later – or maybe it was a month, it's hard to be sure –
I was sitting with Wangaratta and his woman, Fourhands Ha,
at my local, MacSweeny's, the Irish pub at the Venetian. A faux
Irish pub in a hotel built on land reclaimed from the sea, a hotel
modelled on a long-demolished casino in Vegas, which in turn
was inspired by a city in Europe now underwater. An illusion built
upon a dream built upon faded memory. Maybe that's why I came
back here, time after time.

Normally I could forget everything. The drink and the drugs
from Mister Long and the epidemic of memory loss that the world
is now heir to meant I was usually living on the thin edge of the
present. But the last few days, I'd kept going back to Jian's face,
to how she looked while she was talking to me. I re-watched it
more than once, to be sure, to remind myself. She wasn't angry,
wasn't scared, not at first anyway. And when she was yelling as
I rode away on the glimmer bike – the audio was muffled – she
said... something. Something that hovered always on the edge
of my consciousness, deep behind my forehead, refusing to
reveal its secret.

I ached every time I thought of her yelling. Something wasn't
right and I needed to talk, to understand what was happening.

Wangaratta and Ha were the only two people I socialised with anymore. They invited me over to their apartment from time to time for dinner; we'd drink rice whisky and play classic video games on a wall-screen, laughing and yelling as we drove little cars around a psychedelic track and shot each other with turtle shells.

Fourhands was part of the entertainment at the Grand Lisboa. Six nights a week, plus a matinee on Saturday, she juggled flashing blades and bricks and flowerpots and flaming torches while acrobats flung themselves around the stage. Stunning displays of fine motor skill, ignored completely by the Pai Gow players down on the huge gaming floor. Ha kept her hair short so it wouldn't get caught in the implements she was juggling, and was way too smart for such a shitty job. She swore a lot. I liked her.

They sat opposite in the deep green seats of the booth, drinking pints of beers at a dark faux-wood table that was as pristinely clean as the rest of the pub. I turned the large glass of beer in my hands and said: "Something isn't right, guys. My memories, they— they're all getting mixed up. It's getting so I don't know what's real and what's a dream anymore."

Ha looked at Wangaratta, then back at me. She usually did most of the talking. Unlike Wangaratta, she was born and raised in Vietnam, but still, she spoke English close to perfect. She said: "This has been troubling you for a while now, Endel."

"Yeah."

"I thought you were going to see someone about it."

"I was thinking about it, yeah."

"Last time we were here you said you were going to."

"Last time?"

She raised an eyebrow. "You fucking drunk. You stop sucking down a quart of whisky over breakfast and you'll find your memory problems magically disappear."

"What do you mean last time?"

"Three weeks ago. You don't remember?"

I shook my head. "This is what I'm talking about." I emptied my glass, wiped the back of my hand across my mouth, and said: "You ever worry what they do to your memory pin when they take it, Wangaratta?"

He shrugged. "Not really."

"Of course we think about it," said Ha. "But we compare our memory timelines sometimes, and they always look fine."

"Do they?"

She sipped her beer. "Yeah."

"You ever give them your pin, Ha?"

She frowned at the question. "No. Of course not."

"Not that you remember."

"They'd have no reason to ask, and I'd have no reason to say yes."

"They would if they needed you to provide an alibi for Wangaratta. Ensure you two had synchronised memories, in case the police wanted to look at a particular timestamp. Something like that would sound reasonable. Something maybe you'd say yes to."

"But they haven't..." She stopped herself. "I see. Yeah, I see what you mean."

I said: "I need to go to someone, find out which of my memories have been falsified. Find out about..." My beer was empty. I signalled to the barman; he nodded back.

"About what, Endel?" asked Ha. Something in her eye told me she already knew my answer.

"I want to know what happened with Jian and me. Where it all went wrong."

She shook her head. "I'll tell you what I told you last time we sat here: those are bad memories, Endel. You don't want to go raking them over."

"I can't stop. Something—something inevitable is happening in my head."

"That so?" She leaned back in her seat. "The only inevitability I see is the whisky-fuelled rocket ship of self-destruction you're riding high into the sky. The inevitability of gravity."

I raised my eyebrows at her. "Gravity, and *opinions*. This one from the puppy juggler lecturing me on lifestyle choices."

A small smile touched the corners of her mouth. "Yeah. Life's three great certainties: gravity, opinions, and you stumbling over to our apartment for Sunday lunch, smelling like stale beer and three days' worth of ball sweat."

We all laughed at that.

"You sure you're not Australian?" I asked. "You talk like one."

"I'm fluent in crude, if that's what you're asking."

We smiled and drank our beers.

As our glasses were slowly drained, and our smiles faded, Ha put her eyes on me and said: "Jian was a friend of mine. I miss her too. But look at the life you lead. You can't have kids in this world." She reached over, squeezed Wangaratta's hand. "David and I have talked about it. If we ever manage to have children." She lowered her voice. "If we ever have kids we're going to get out of this place, Endel. This city, it just swallows you up in its black, bottomless maw and nothing remains."

I'd forgotten David was his real name, so was confused about who she was talking about for a second. But what she said was right, about this town, it rang true.

We exchanged small talk after that, neither of us wanting to revisit old wounds, until Wangaratta and Ha excused themselves for dinner. After they left I drank pints of beer and ate crisp soy chicken wings with a hot sauce dip. The clientele flowed through the place, tourists for the most part, mainland Chinese and the occasional wealthy European. I'd look over the Euros with mild curiosity before returning to my thoughts. They were a dying breed now. Another waking dream in Macau.

I sighed. I had to be sure, about Jian. Had to see the one person utterly verboten to a guy like me.

8

The Omissioner was younger than I expected, maybe thirty-five. Swarthy, southern European perhaps, she wore a sleek blue *qipao* and her black curly hair down. The name *Om. Aletheia Milas* glowed in soft green holotype across a black-backed plaque on her brown wood desk. A curved dark-wood ashtray sat in the centre of the table, gleaming in the low light. Real wood, most likely, given her lucrative profession. Large tai screens hung near two of the four walls, their black frames empty.

The walls themselves were full of prints, rows upon rows in black and white. Simple icons: a clenched fist, black on white; large, full lips, white on black; a four-leaf clover with a cross through it; a revolver; the letter S; black Buddha on a white background; white elephant on black; black belly-dancer on white; a playing card, the ace of spades; the circle-and-cross gender symbol for woman; an open palm; a top hat; uppercase letter C with a small c inside; an optical illusion of a man walking up and up an infinite staircase; and on and on and on, filling the walls from floor to ceiling. The only variation to the rows of prints were the tai screens, and behind the Omissioner, a long hologram of a landscape: bucolic, green, a soft wind blowing within the picture, pushing low white clouds across the scene and silently rustling the leaves.

She leaned back in her black ergonomic chair and intertwined her fingers.

I stopped for a moment, considering the woman.

"Expecting someone Chinese?" she asked, apparently knowing my mind.

"I mean…" I said, then shrugged the *yeah*.

"Greek civilisation is also known for its expertise on memory."

"It is?"

The woman shook her head to herself, eyes closed momentarily to damp her irritation.

I shook off a feeling of déjà vu and said: "Anyway. Omissioner."

"Please. Aletheia."

"I'm Endel. Ebbinghaus."

She looked at me for a couple of moments, one thick black eyebrow raised in vague amusement at a joke I didn't get. Then the eyebrow stood at ease and she said, "Endel Ebbinghaus – that's a Dutch name, isn't it?"

"No."

"Mexican?"

"Mexican?" I narrowed my eyes. I was definitely missing a joke here.

"German?"

I nodded slowly. "I'm Australian, but yeah, it's German."

She indicated the seat opposite her. I took it.

When I began to speak she held up her hand and said: "Let me guess. You're having recurring dreams, but you're not sure anymore if they are dreams or memories. You're starting to worry that perhaps your cochlear implant has downloaded a memory virus. You re-watch episodes from your life to remember your past, but they seem unreal, like you're watching someone else's life. Sometimes you find yourself in bars or restaurants, and you don't know how you got there; or standing on the street, confused, unsure of what day it is or where you are going. Everything feels like déjà vu, like you did the exact same thing an hour, or day, or month before." She tilted her head. "You've got a green glass vial in your jacket pocket. In the vial is a liquid you've been dripping into your alcohol. You do this regularly, at the behest of your employer who you refuse to name, in a job you refuse to talk about." She raised her eyebrow at me. "Right?"

I shifted in my seat. "What the fuck?"

"You told me, Endel."

I shifted again, jaw tightening. "Bullshit. What is going on here?"

The Omissioner reached into her desk drawer, pulling out an elegant jade cigarette case. She popped it open, slid out a slender white cigarette and glanced up at me. "I'm not a mind reader, Mister Ebbinghaus. I simply have a good memory." She lit her cigarette with a lighter that matched the case and inhaled, closing her eyes for a moment. She blew the smoke out through her nose, slowly, and repeated: "Just a good memory. But the way the world is now, a good memory can be mistaken for magic."

Her smoking made me want to, so I lit a Double Happiness. The tension abated in my jaw as I took a deep drag. "I'm going to need something more concrete than your word, Omissioner."

"And you'll get something far better than my word, but first I'm going to have to ask for your memory pin," she said, and held out her hand.

"Why?"

"Because you'll want me to analyse it."

I paused, then said: "Bullshit. If I've been here before, as you say, then you've already run a scan."

She tapped her lighter on the table, looking me over. "You're right. Nonetheless, I need you to give it to me as a precaution. I'm just going to leave it here, in plain sight. I think you understand why."

Yeah, I understood. I pressed my finger to the cool steel of my implant, and mumbled the command phrase. The head of the pin popped out a few millimetres; I extracted it with my fingernails.

Aletheia indicated the tai screen to my right with her eyes. "Now watch," she said, then spoke towards the screen: "Give me a visual of my last meeting with Endel Ebbinghaus. Play from the beginning."

The empty space between the frame flickered gold for a moment, then a three-dimensional image resolved itself, shot from a high angle in the Omissioner's office. I watched myself enter the room:

The Omissioner leaned back in a black ergonomic chair, her fingers intertwined. The angle of the nanocam emphasised the curve of her breast under the green silk qipao.

I watched myself say: "Omissioner?"

She nodded. "Yes. Call me Aletheia."

"I'm Endel. Ebbinghaus."

She raised a single thick black eyebrow and said: "Endel Ebbinghaus – that's a Dutch name, isn't it?"

"No."

"Mexican?"

"Mexican?" My eyes narrowed. "No."

She smiled. "I'm kidding. It's German, of course."

I nodded slowly. "Yes, it's German."

She indicated the seat opposite her. I took it.

"Stop." The image froze and Aletheia looked at me. "Look familiar?"

"That's a recording of the conversation we just had. I don't understand."

"No," she said, shaking her head. "Look again, at what I am wearing."

Her elegant, neck-to-calf *qipao* was blue silk with silver trim, shimmering in the low light. I glanced back at the image, now frozen and hovering. In there, her dress was green. "Some kind of trick," I said.

"This is a recording from three weeks ago. You came in here, Mister Ebbinghaus, and you did tell me everything."

I blew a heavy cloud of cigarette smoke. Something in the ceiling was noiselessly sucking the idle serpents of smoke from the room, keeping the air clear and fresh. "Everything?"

"Well, not everything. But I ran a diagnostic of the memory pin scan I made when you were here last, as you paid me to do. It showed me glimpses of a number of rather unsavoury incidents that may or may not have been real. You told me some of the rest. You had to, in order to give me some identification tags for my search of your memory line."

"I wouldn't do that."

"Legally, our session is confidential." She drew on her cigarette, exhaled a languorous cloud of smoke, and said: "But of course, you're not one to concern yourself with legalities. I can bring up the recording of our conversation now, if you want, for you to verify."

"No." I shook my head. A new tension rose in the back of my mind. This woman was a problem. She'd been into my head, now maybe I was going to let her in twice. A lot of things in there shouldn't be seeing the light of day. "No. Tell me again. I want to know what is happening to me. I need to know what is real."

Omissioner Aletheia Milas sighed. "I spend a lot of time repeating myself in this job."

"And I spend a lot of time breaking people's kneecaps. Every occupation has its unpleasant necessities."

She looked me over at that, trying to maintain her professional patina. She'd fooled me at first, but now I could see her fear: the stiffness across her shoulders, the way she blinked too often, like some instinctual trigger in her mind was trying to unsee the situation I'd placed her in.

Aletheia smoothed the dress over her legs with one hand, shifting in her seat. "The facts of life: organic memory has declined precipitously for ninety per cent of the population. Natural memory is now merely a few scattered remnants, mainly what we call *reminiscence bumps* from youth or childhood – seminal experiences we tend to remember, no matter how weak the memory function. However, in general, the natural formation of long-term memory is slowly becoming extinct." She pointed her cigarette at me. "I take it you've heard the theories as to why?"

"I read somewhere it was genetic engineering polluting the food chain."

"That's the dumbest of them, but yes, it's one." My jaw clenched.

She continued: "Another is that a virus has spread through the nanotech contained in our cochlear implants and optic nerves, one of the consequences of which is an impairment of our memory function. That one's quite popular, but wrong.

"In my opinion, the right one is this: freewave addiction has altered our brains. The human brain is a powerful, yet malleable creation. Our neural pathways are infinitely adaptable; they change as the world around us changes: in response to trauma, language, environment, and when we introduce new technologies to everyday life.

"The biggest technological revolution in the last thirty years was the cochlear-glyph implant. It gives us the freewave, sent right into our skulls, every waking minute of the day. Ironically, this has huge implications for the part of our mind that hasn't really changed in millennia: our Neanderthal brain. This old part of our brain is geared, as a basic survival instinct, to hunt for new information. Where once it hunted for food, looked for shelter, or changes in the weather, now it hunts on the freewave. It gives us – the user – a dopamine hit with each new snippet of useless information, with each new connection on social media, with each alert coming through our on-retina displays. Nearly the entire population are, literally, drug addicts, albeit to a natural drug.

"This has rewired our neural pathways. We need ten minutes to encode memories. Just ten minutes, bouncing around somewhere at the edge of our conscious mind, until they are stored. The problem is that the human brain can't hold a single thought for ten minutes anymore, we can barely hold them for one. So the collapse in memory occurs at the most basic level: encoding. We have poor memories, not because we have trouble storing or retrieving our experiences, but because they were never absorbed into memory in the first place."

I'd let her speak it out, but she hadn't come to any particular point I could see. "I don't care about any of this. Memory pins have solved all these problems."

"Ah yes. The memory pin," she said, shaking her head. She stubbed out her cigarette butt, then lit another, her gaze pausing for a moment on the frozen picture of us up on the tai screen. "Most see the memory pins as our salvation. The artificial recording and replication that gives each and every one of us photographic recall. I see it differently." She picked up my pin from the table. "This is the final nail in memory's coffin. Memory pins ensure that the areas of the brain needed to form memories are no longer needed. Unused, they atrophy. The historical decline in memory, whatever the cause, was gradual. Decade after decade the slope of recall and attention fell ever so gently downwards. Then the memory pins were introduced, and it dropped precipitously."

"You still haven't made your point, Omissioner."

"Yes, you said that last time."

"I was right then, as well."

She turned my pin in the light. "The point is this: anyone who gets hold of this can do whatever they want with your mind. They can implant any memory they like."

I feigned nonchalance with a shrug. "It's part of the job."

"*Idiot.*" She hissed through her teeth. "This isn't just a piece of technology, a feed recording to manipulate so you can fool the police when they subpoena it." She tapped on the spot behind her ear, at the empty space where her cochlear implant should be. I was surprised – it had been a long time since I'd met someone unplugged. She continued: "This is your soul. This is everything you are, your experience of the world, your fears and phobias, your friendships and failings, your mistakes and triumphs. Everyone you've ever loved, everything you've ever cared about, every fibre of your character is memory. This is the sum total of your being, everything, save the thin edge of the present."

Her fear was now gone, replaced with clear distaste. "And people like you just give it away."

I was silent, letting the information settle. She was right and I knew she was. Every time I handed over the pin, I knew it. But deep down the alcoholic knows the booze is killing them, as well. They're just too cowardly to finish it quick. I handed over that pin because I yearned for that erasure, to hide my dark heart, even from myself.

I said: "The pin only stores three years at a time. So at least I know that if I do manage to remember something from before then, that it will be real?"

"No."

"No?"

"Normally false memories and memory wipes are reserved for trauma victims, as a way to help them get on with their lives. Done this way, all the alterations to memory are legal, transparent and on record. But I've dealt with men and women in your profession before, and for you it isn't so simple. When they give you a false memory, first you watch it late at night, right?"

I nodded.

"They do this so you understand the shape of your new memory. Then it is programmed to encode during REM sleep, by inserting certain images and phrases when you dream. It's more effective this way, because today the sleeping mind has a longer attention span than the waking. So if they do this, Mister Ebbinghaus, who is to say they don't insert episodes into your dreams from when you were a child or a young man? Trojan memories slipped in elsewhere on the pin?"

"But…" I shook my head. "Childhood? I would know. By the *weight* of the memory, I would know what is real and what is imagined."

"No," she said. "It's virtually impossible to tell an imagined memory from a real one. Fake memories may trouble you, you may even choose to reject some of them, but scientifically there is no way we can differentiate. The research on this is clear. Not without independent verification. Not without hearing an eyewitness account of the memory, or watching a third person's memory feed."

"So even you can't tell the difference?"

"Unless there are obvious production flaws. No."

"And I can't? In my own head?" It felt like the ground was opening beneath me, to reveal the abyss.

The Omissioner sighed. "Look. Those reminiscence bumps I mentioned? They often have combined mnemonic elements that are impossible to fake. The memory of a smell, for example, during a particular event. No-one can know that. Only you. But…"

I waited. "But?"

She tapped her lighter on the table, like she was thinking me over. "Let me tell you a story. You know Richard Ho, I take it?

"You mean the guy who owns half the casinos in Macau? Yeah, I know him."

She nodded. "When he was young – barely a toddler – his nanny took him for a walk down at the waterfront in a stroller. The nanny was European, of course, French I believe. She'd take him out very early, often before five in the morning, as he was a terrible sleeper. Anyway, this one day, two young men – she said they were Vietnamese – tried to kidnap him. One knocked her over, the other grabbed the stroller. She screamed and she fought, nearly scratching the eyes out of one of them. They ran, the child was unharmed.

"Richard Ho remembered every single detail of the attack. Decades later, the memory was crystal clear to him: what the nanny was wearing, what the men said to her, the blood on her fingernails, how she wept and held him in her arms in the purple dawn."

Aletheia took a drag on her cigarette, elbow resting on the arm of her chair. "There was just one problem with the story: it was all a lie. The nanny came forward years later, when Ho was an adult, and returned the reward – a platinum necklace – the family had given her in thanks. She admitted to him that her story was a complete fabrication. She confessed that she was desperate for money. Her son had been sick and she wanted to pay for the nanomed treatments that would cure him. But she said she couldn't bring herself to sell the necklace, such was her guilt. She said she saw him on a c-cast, retelling the story, and she couldn't bear it any longer.

"So here was a complete fabrication, which Ho remembered as a diamond-hard reality. He remembered it so vividly because he'd been told the story by his parents many times as he grew up. He believed it because memory is highly susceptible to suggestion. Think about that, Mister Ebbinghaus. This was all before memory pins, yet one poorly educated immigrant woman from France could forge a perfect false memory in a child from one of the richest families in Asia. If memory is susceptible to a verbal suggestion, imagine what a high resolution, stereo sound, on-retina feed can do."

I shifted in my seat.

"Imagine, Mister Ebbinghaus, what happens when you double down with memory drugs." She held out her hand. "You want to give me that glass vial you're carrying?"

I patted my pockets until I found the one I'd put it in and handed it over. The vial gleamed green in her hand.

She said: "This is called Neothebaine. We Omissioners call it memorybane. It's a sophisticated version of what was known as laudanum, about two hundred years ago. In essence, aside from being an addictive narcotic, it produces short-term amnesia. It dissolves even the residual fragments of the natural memory – colours, sounds, a turn of phrase you may have heard. This way, there is no doubt in your own mind about whether an implanted memory is real. It's a way of tricking your mind, to help the new memories embed. All they need to do – the people giving you the new timeline – is seed your false memories with some things that really did occur. Make it more plausible. That way, in combination with the memorybane, you won't reject your memories, either consciously or unconsciously."

Fear was spreading in my chest. Fear at the depths of my illusions, about what I'd done, who I had killed, who I really was. Maybe I'd murdered no-one. Maybe a hundred innocents had died by my hand. There was no way of knowing.

I thought about Mister Long, staring right through me with those dead eyes. Oh, I had killed for that motherfucker. Guilty, innocent, right or wrong, he'd bid it done. And I—I would do as tasked, for I was a violent man. That was no illusion.

Then I thought of Jian, the way she looked at the cemetery, the pain that caused me. I held my chin up. "Except in here," I said, finger to my heart. "I'll know in here, somehow, that something isn't right."

She sighed and said, "Yes, for a time, Mister Ebbinghaus. We call that emotional resonance. But even that fades. Another year, maybe two, and you'll be exactly who they want you to be. You'll become as you are programmed, merely an instrument to the will of another. You'll become what we call a recall drone."

I sat in silence after that, smoking, trying and failing to understand how far the implications reached.

"So there's no way of knowing how deep this runs?" I asked, finally.

10

"It runs deep, Endel." The Omissioner leaned forward. "Let me ask you this: when you do recall your memories on-retina, what is your emotional response?"

"What?"

"The problem with all these false memories is that they drain you of authentic emotions. Artificial memories only have an aural and visual component. There's no emotion attached to them, because they never happened. You feel empty, detached, alienated, yes?"

I shrugged agreement.

"And you certainly smell like you've got a problem with alcohol."

I stared at her.

She tried to ignore the glare, and continued: "These are common symptoms of pervasive memory tampering. You turn to drugs, not for the high as such, but so you can *feel* again. Drones like you have high substance abuse rates."

"But the Richard Ho story – you're saying it wouldn't matter if I had a good memory? That it would be fucking me over the same way as my—as my employer is fucking me over?"

"No," she said, and her eyes lit up as she spoke. "I'm saying natural memory is beautiful. I'm saying that, at its best, it improves your understanding of the world. It accretes with a new layer of meaning every time you remember something. Nanotrace scans show that every time you recall a memory, it is a *new* memory, forging a new neural pathway. Integrated with all the unique experiences you've lived since, more complex, more alive. Natural memories are multidimensional, charged with emotion that can never be faked or replicated by a machine. It means that over time, memories sing with the experience of our lives, our interaction with the world."

I wasn't so concerned with singing. More with whether I was a mass murderer. "So what can I do?" I asked.

"There's no real way to correct the damage, or even to tell what the damage is. Unless..." She paused, furrowing her brow.

"Unless?"

"Unless we consider the more resilient types of memory, which you may still retain. Haptic memory, which is, in essence, remembering by touch. This instinct persists. Specific objects may help link you to your past, when you hold them in your hand. Olfactory memory is another, sometimes a smell will spark a series of remembrances." She focussed on me. "The wife you keep mentioning."

"Yes?"

"Jian? When you are with her, the ways she smells, the way she holds you – this could, perhaps, bring back some—"

My face went hard. "I don't want her dragged into this."

"But Endel, this might—"

"This cannot involve my family," I said, each word jagged, emphasised.

The Omissioner held up a hand, her fingers slightly curled. "Okay." She thought, and after a time, she said: "You'll forget all of this. I'm not going to send you the feed of this meeting, it's too dangerous. For both of us. Instead, you'll take one last drop of memorybane right now, and I'll give you a different recollection, of a bar near here called The Third Man. Go there after this, have a drink. That will seed the false memory enough so that in a day or two, it'll feel like the real one."

"Go to a bar. Drink. That I can do."

Her eyes narrowed. "I'm also going to download a program into your pin – it will encode during your next sleep cycle. This will imprint the following advice: stop taking Neothebaine. Stop giving your memory pin to others. Ease back on the drinking and start thinking about a change of career. Now, a day or two from now, you won't remember why you need to do these things, but you'll know it is the right thing to do."

I nodded to myself. "You didn't download the program last time I was here?"

She intertwined her fingers. "Last time I made a mistake. I tried a program meant to evoke reminiscence bumps from your past, as a way of providing certainty for you on aspects of your history, and thereby of your character. You've been having flashbacks?"

"A couple."

"Consistent?"

"Kinda. No. They keep shifting."

She shook her head. "As I suspected. Unfortunately, the memory manipulation you've been subjected to is far more pervasive than I feared, and I think it is causing interference even on your most deeply encoded episodic memories. This new program is really about limiting the damage."

Frustrated, I rubbed my forehead. "Will it work?"

"I don't know, Mister Ebbinghaus, I really don't. I can plant the desire for travel, for escape. Maybe nudge you into leaving, if that is what you want?"

"Yeah," I said. I exhaled a long breath. "Yeah, that's what I want."

She was watching me intently. "Why you doing this?" I asked.

Aletheia shrugged "You're paying me good money."

"No." I waved away her answer with the end of my cigarette. "That's not it. There's more here."

"You're going to remember if I tell you."

"I'm not going to remember *anything* you've told me, but you gave me this long fucking speech, anyway. So?"

She set her slim jaw and said: "I'm doing this because memory is sacred, Mister Ebbinghaus. Memory is civilisation. My job is to defend that civilisation. The people you work for are trying to tear it all down. Tear away our humanity for nothing more than the sake of a lucrative business deal. Without memory we are animals, creatures that respond only to the base instinct of the moment."

We sat in silence after that and finished our cigarettes. I stubbed mine out in the wooden ashtray and looked her in the eye. "You need to get out of town, Omissioner."

"What do you mean?"

"I mean you need to leave town, for your own safety."

"Is this a threat?"

"No. A warning. They must know I've been here. If they can fry my mind so completely, then they can put in a memory of you being a police informant against the cartel I work for. Or, say, of you threatening to kill me while I try to eat my dinner. Anything. Make it easy for me to come back here and put a bullet through your brainpan, paint that hologram behind you with blood and brain matter."

I pulled a gun from inside my jacket, large calibre, polished wood and dull gunmetal. Naked fear sparked behind her eyes. "People never leave this town," I said, "even though it's the most logical response. You mess with the wrong crowd here, you're dead. This place is unforgiving and completely, utterly, indifferent – it just swallows you up into its black, bottomless maw, and not a shred of your identity remains. Someone else will move into this flash office. Your family will receive trauma counselling. The type, *you know*, that'll help the memories of you fade real quick. Everybody knows how it works here, and yet everyone believes this somehow does not apply to them. So here you are, sitting in your expensive office, trying to disbelieve this gun in my hand. My identity may be imagined, my thoughts someone else's, but this," I turned the gun sideways, "this is real."

She'd let her cigarette burn down to the filter, and was staring at me eyes wide open, waiting on what I'd do next. I stood, slipped the gun back in my shoulder holster.

"And if I don't come, someone else will. Another recall drone. Get out of town, Omissioner. Leave this mirage from a dead sea, and find somewhere real to live your life."

11

The police found me at home that evening, ducking into my suite between leaving the Third Man and moving on to McSorley's. Two of them knocked on my door as soon as I walked in. They must have been watching my place. One of them flashed a sergeant's badge and demanded to know where I was on such-and-such a night. When I asked them why, they said that some guy I'd never heard of, went by the name of Fred Bartlett, had been found with a bullet in his forehead. Police drone footage showed someone matching my description leaving his apartment block around the time of the murder. I told them I was nowhere near the place.

The hard-eyed sergeant barked at me in Mandarin: "[Got any witnesses?]"

I smiled and said: "How many do you want?"

They didn't like that answer at all, and promptly cuffed me and marched me down to the station. My lawyer – or Mister Long's lawyer, to be precise – was already there by the time we arrived. The lawyer was a big, rotund man with a big, rotund smile that was inversely proportional to the frowns on the faces of the police when they saw him tapping his white-topped patent leather shoes on the grimy tiles of the cop shop foyer.

I was in and out in two hours. All they could find when they pulled up the relevant timestamp on my memory line was point-of-view vision of me eating fresh baked clams in my suite at the Venetian, watching the fight.

As we were parting on the pavement outside the station, the smile dropped from the lawyer's face. "Mister Long wants to see you."

"When?"

"Tomorrow, first thing."

I shrugged, noncommittal.

He gave me a hard look. "Be there."

Later that night I sat up at the kitchen bench eating room-service Singapore noodles and drinking rice whisky. I thought over the day, such as I could, looking into the bottom of my glass. Whatever I was, was slowly fading away. Maybe that didn't matter. Maybe it was like Ha said, that it was wrong to bring family into a world as violent as this. There were worse things I could do than simply fade away.

I didn't want to dream about Jian anymore. It was just the same thing, over and over. The images churning and churning through my mind, sending me mad with exhaustion, soaked in self-loathing.

I took a sleeping pill with three fingers of Maker's Mark before I collapsed into bed.

But still, I dreamed:

"We, we slept together."

I started and turned and there she was, Jian, shoulders slumped in resignation, no trace of her ready smile.

I stood, cigarette hanging from my lips and replied, quietly: "You what?"

Her face remained impassive. "It was the office party and I'd had too much to drink. He was insistent and I hadn't seen you in two weeks and it happened. It was just, it was just..." She hesitated, putting a hand against her forehead.

I was in our little place on the Rua da Gamboa. The apartment was gloomy, with stained dark wood floors and weird wallpaper of faded red with black silhouettes of elephants. My nostrils filled with the scent of the sandalwood incense that Jian used to burn.

I said, louder: "You fucking what?"

"Don't give me your tough guy routine."

I stepped forwards. "What did you fucking do, Jian?!"

She took a step back. Fear sparked behind her eyes. "Don't threaten me, Endel."

I advanced on her, fists clenched.

Her back pressed against the red wall and I raised my hand. Her eyes widened.

Then everything became a blur and Jian was screaming and Kylie was lying on the ground with blood on her face.

I was bent down over her and Jian was yelling: "What did you do, Endel? What did you do?!"

My hands shook as I tried to pick up Kylie. She lay there with eyes open, her breathing shallow, in shock at the sudden blow to the head.

"Get out," screamed Jian and she was now close behind, yanking at my collar, trying to pull me up and push me out. I let her, stumbling towards the apartment door.

As I stepped outside Jian yelled after me: "She's your daughter, Endel – she's your daughter!"

I woke up, sweating, to the smell of sandalwood. I remembered my name and, after a few moments, where I was. I asked for the time, my implant put it up on-retina: 4:07am. I tossed and turned for a while before giving up on sleep, lying in bed instead and smoking cigarettes. I watched the smoke drift and pool near the ceiling.

I got the urge to run. Not just down on the treadmill either. I put on sneakers and tracksuit pants and caught the lift down. Walked through the expansive, golden-hued lobby, past the drunks and the degenerates and the Filipino service staff and their fixed, permanent smiles, and out into a sultry pre-dawn.

The streets were lit bright against the darkness. I took the sidewalk that ran across the bridge, over the outer bay, from the Strip back into Macau. The air was hot and thick and my shirt soon stuck to the sweat on my back. After a time I stopped, breathing heavy, and wiped my brow. I found myself on the Macau waterfront. I hadn't realised this was my destination. A man with a black top hat, black face mask, and silver-handled cane walked unsteadily past, but other than him it was deserted in the humid pre-dawn.

As I stood there, a memory popped into my head, unbidden. Of the casino tycoon Richard Ho as a child, with his nanny, walking past the spot where I stood. I shook it from my mind and walked along the water, out to a small man-made island connected to the shore by a thin polycrete causeway. In the centre of the island was a gold statue, maybe twenty metres high, of what looked like a female Buddha in a long dress.

I stood and watched as the thin, purple edge of dawn rose on the horizon. I licked the sweat off my top lip and put my hands on my hips, wondering what the hell I was doing there. Out of nowhere, pain flared behind my eyes and I staggered, hands to temples. Gritting my teeth, I eased myself down, sitting with some relief on the low barrier that surrounded the little island.

The memory of Jian, again, *yelling as I rode away on the bike, surfaced from some dark place;*

then shooting a man twice in the belly with explosive-tipped rounds and leaving him to die in an anonymous dark alley;

then messy drunk, at some expensive, shining bar while a high-class hooker looked at me with contempt as I realised I'd pissed myself;

angry, beating a man with a fire extinguisher in a dank apartment stairwell;

laughing, as I rode past a small Sichuan restaurant on my glimmer bike, spraying the storefront with bullets from a compact machine gun;

in shock, hands shaking, standing over Kylie, staring at the blood on her face.

I threw up into the ocean. One long, hard, puke that took everything inside my stomach and projected it into the water. I wiped my mouth, the taste of bile and incense in my throat.

Then the rain started. Heavy drops came down, flailing against the sea, my back, the polycrete of the walkway. Warm rain that gave no relief from the heat: water that ran down the skin as hot as sweat, not cleaning, but saturated with the recycled moisture of a hundred dead waterways and the sweat of a thousand drunken tourists.

My tears mixed in with the rain, unseen, my broken lament unheard under the crash of water on water. I stayed that way, bent over the dead sea, for I'm not sure how long.

The rain slowed.

I stood. I knew what I had to do. A moment of perfect clarity: leave town, never look back. It was the only way to keep Jian safe, the only way. I also knew, without one shred of doubt, that if I went to meet Mister Long this morning, they'd kill me.

I had to run.

12

I took what casino chips I could find around the suite and cashed them out. I packed my duffel bag and looked around. Nothing here meant much to me. I couldn't remember anyway what belonged to the hotel and what was mine. I paid one of the bellboys to have my glimmer bike waiting out back, then stood at the window and smoked two cigarettes, watching the grey morning wash over Macau and turn the glittering, neon dream of the casinos into the dull steel and smudged glass of day's unadorned reality. Giant white turbines stood on the distant ocean horizon, turning slowly. I shouldered my bag, holstered my gun, and left.

I found the cheapest hotel I could and reached out to some contacts. The earliest I could get out of Macau was the next day, via a smuggler's hold in a fishing vessel. I waited, not daring to leave the room, and put an automated message on my cochlear implant, telling any callers I was asleep. My alcoholism would buy me a few hours of credibility for that excuse.

Messages pinged on-retina all day. Pretty much all were associates of Mister Long. I dozed on and off, between pings, exhausted, but couldn't find solid sleep.

Near midnight I received an on-retina alert from Wangaratta. It said: We have to talk. Saint Michael's. 2am tonight.

I sat up in bed. The message was as succinct as I usually got from Wangaratta. Bit vague, but the location spoke to the details: Saint Michael's was the cemetery I waited next to, when I watched Jian pick up Kylie after school. He had something to tell me about her. That was the only explanation. I had to go.

I cleaned and loaded my pistol. My hands shook as I did so. I hadn't drunk all day and my body didn't like that one bit. I lit a cigarette and went out into the fetid, waiting night.

13

The only light inside the cemetery came from distant casinos, their gargantuan bulks rising up over the line of the stone wall that surrounded the grounds, bathing the interior in a thin neon backwash. A bent old man had let me in, nodding as I approached the gate and locking it after me. That was the last I saw of him.

Down a slender concrete path past a small, two-storey chapel. It was a Christian place, Catholic I think, the epitaphs on the graves in Portuguese and English and Cantonese. Some of the graves were simple, but many had large, weathered statues of angels or crosses; others the surprisingly subtle fusion of a Buddhist pagoda topped with Christian icons. The place was built into the slope of a hill, high on my left and low on my right, as I walked the path.

The nanos in my optic nerves responded to the low light, giving me partial night vision – everything became a mix of deep green and washed-out colour. I continued until I saw the heavy figure of Wangaratta standing further along, eyes shaded by the rim of his porkpie hat. I smiled and walked up to him, holding out my fist for him to bump it. He looked down at it like I'd offered him a dead rat. Up close he smelled of bourbon and his eyes were bloodshot. Uncharacteristic. Wangaratta generally went easy on the booze, especially if he was working.

I said: "You look like shit, mate."

He was tense, his fists clenching and unclenching. He said nothing, just stared at me.

I squinted at him. "Mate? What's going on?"

"Wangaratta needs to ask you something."

I turned quick in the direction of the new voice. Standing in the shadows between tall white headstones was Chrome Linh Phu. She was wearing slim, mirrored sunglasses and a bomber jacket. Her jacket, like the leather one I was wearing, probably had spideriron weave in the lining. Good for stopping most kinds of bullets and blades. I had no idea why she was wearing the glasses.

"Why did you come?" Wangaratta asked, his voice a strained whisper.

I looked back at him. "Of course I was going to come."

"I told you he would," said Chrome, from the side.

Wangaratta ignored her. "Why'd you do it?"

"Do what?"

"Ha," he said, voice breaking.

I glanced over at Linh, then back at Wangaratta. "What happened? What happened to Ha?"

"You killed her," said Linh. She took a step forwards; in each hand appeared the long, double-edged chrome daggers she'd earned her name with.

I took a step back, facing her, hand moving to the gun holstered under my arm, when movement flashed at the corner of my eye. My head snapped to one side and I staggered away, tripping over the edge of the path and sprawling over a stone grave. Everything a groggy blur for a few moments and when my mind returned, I was flat on my back on the stone, one arm up to ward the next blow. Wangaratta stood over me. My jaw ached and motes of light danced at the end of my vision. He had a good right.

"Why'd you do it, Endgame?" he asked, quiet, determined.

I planted my hands on the grave and started to push myself up, but stopped when he drew the gun on me. I lay back, hands in open-palmed surrender, and rested my head against the tombstone. The gun barrel was dull grey in the washed-out green of the night. Sure, I'd looked down the barrel of plenty of guns. But not one pointed by my best mate. Grief, unbelief, distorted his features. Quiet settled on the graveyard, complete, an oasis from the sound and fury of a hundred casinos and a million desperate punters yelling against odds immutable.

I hesitated. Spoke slow, careful. "Wangaratta. David. Mate. *I don't know what you are talking about.*"

His face twisted. "Don't you call me that," he yelled. It was the first time I'd heard him raise his voice. "Only she ever called me *that*."

He raised his boot and stamped down on my gut with the 'that'. I doubled forwards, hands around my stomach, barely able to groan through the pain. He followed with an overhead strike, hitting my forehead with the handle of the gun. My head cracked backwards against the tombstone. I fumbled for my gun, but suddenly Wangaratta's huge hands were around my throat, squeezing down, choking. I grabbed each of his wrists but he was strong, too strong, wrists like iron bars.

He screamed: "You fucking killed her. You raped her and killed her, you fucking animal. Die DIE DIE DIE DIE DIE!"

He rammed my head back against the gravestone with each yell of *die*. My vision faded, hands slipping ineffectually as I tried to pry his wrists free.

With what strength I had left I brought my knee up between his legs, the air went out of him and I kicked up a second time. Wangaratta grunted and I tore his hands from my throat, rolling with him off the stone grave.

I staggered to my feet, gasping for air, bracing myself against the statue of an angel, my legs shaking. Wangaratta was scrambling for something on the ground.

I groaned. "No."

He found his gun and rose to his feet.

"It's a false memory." I tried to yell, but my voice came out bruised, husky. "No – Ha was my friend. No!"

Wangaratta raised his pistol.

I shot him in the head.

As the boom echoed round the graveyard I spun, groggily, and aimed at the spot where Chrome Linh had been standing. She was gone.

"I'm relieved, Endgame. I thought Wangaratta was going to finish the job before I'd had any fun." Her voice bounced around the graveyard, coming from all directions.

I turned slowly, gun level. "You fucking cur. You killed Ha."

"Are you sure? It could have been you, Endgame." Just her voice, still no sight of her.

I paused, and then said: "No." I kept turning, watching for a flash of movement. "I wouldn't have done that."

"Really? Your best friend is dead, by your hand. You shot him without hesitation, as with so many others. You attacked your wife and children. You're a violent man."

"You're a liar," I rasped. "No false memory would have made me kill Ha. It needs to be seeded with the truth."

"Now you sound like your friend, the Omissioner."

"Who?" I asked.

She laughed, short and sharp. "Poor, confused little man." Her voice seemed closer now and I turned again. But all I could see were the white stone statues on the graves and the blinking, distant lights of the casinos.

"But you're mostly right about Ha. One of the boys bled

her out and put a new memory on her pin. Of you, *Endgame*. Wangaratta was most distraught after he watched it."

I swore and fired into the darkness. The shot boomed and echoed and she laughed again, light and dancing. It was the first time I'd ever heard her genuinely *happy*. It was an ugly sound.

I took a deep breath. Concentrate, I needed to concentrate. While her voice seemed to come from all around, my hearing, like my eyesight, was enhanced. The more she talked the closer I'd get to pinpointing her. She was downslope and behind me, I was sure of it.

I heard the softest of footfalls, not three metres away, and I fired again. This time there was a reply. A white light bloomed to my right and on instinct I turned towards it.

And went blind.

Searing, incandescent, burning deep into the back of my skull. I stumbled backwards, knowing instantly that she had me. An optics flare: a simple weapon, designed to burn out the nanos attached to the optic nerves. It was the jujitsu of street-fighting weapons – the better the optical enhancement, the more effective the flare burst. Mine were top-of-the-line. I gasped and shoved the crook of my elbow over my eyes on instinct, snapping off three quick shots.

Something stung the back of my pistol hand and my right leg, above the knee. I staggered, warmth on my hand, dripping from my fingertips. Blood.

I'd been cut, and deep.

Nano-sharpened blades parted skin and bone with the ease of a glimmer bike slicing through twin lanes of automated cars: a glittering flash, gone before you knew it was there.

I gritted my teeth and said: "I'm going to tear your fucking arms out of their sockets."

She laughed again and still I couldn't pinpoint her voice. It came from all around. "You're blind and bleeding. You're too big, too slow, and I've been thinking about this a long time. I am going to enjoy this, Endgame. I am going to do you slowly."

I had a basic nanomed combat implant; I could feel it kicking in, releasing endorphins to dull the pain in my skull from where Wangaratta had bashed it against stone. My adrenaline control had opened up, stimulating my reflexes and senses, sharpening my hearing. A cloud of clottocyte nanos would be in my bloodstream now, closing and coagulating wounds.

Still, that didn't add up to a whole lot when I didn't have any eyes. And Linh would have the same sort of implants, likely even better.

Steps fell softly behind me, I swung an elbow, meeting only air, and something stung my cheek. I fired a shot, masonry exploded, and after that, Linh's laughter. And so it went, soft rapid footfalls, me flailing an arm or leg or firing a lone shot, another slash on thigh or face or hand. Again and again, tripping over graves and swinging punches until my chest heaved and my arms ached from holding up my heavy pistol. The clottocyte swarm running though my bloodstream could only stop so much bleeding and I could feel it, running down my neck, my legs.

Her voice, smooth and close by, said: "What are you fighting for, Endgame?"

I said nothing. If she wanted to talk, I was going to catch my breath.

"You don't even know who you are, who your family is, or who you work for. I bet you don't even remember your own birthday. So why are you fighting for a life you can't remember?"

Again, I said nothing. The darkness of my vision started pixelating with spots of light. It was recovering. Slowly. I needed more time.

She said: "You think you work for a drug dealer. But the truth is Mister Long works for Chinalco. He's head of industrial espionage here in Macau."

I found myself wanting to listen. What she said somehow had the shape of the truth. "Why are you telling me this?"

"I told you I was going to do you slowly, and I meant it. When you bleed out here on one of these graves, you're going to be glad when the darkness comes. You're going to want the big sleep, after you've heard the truth, I *promise*." She said the last word with a hiss.

My shoulder brushed against something hard. I leaned against it – some sort of large tomb. A quick check with my fingers told me it was high, higher than my head anyway, and I was at an iron doorway. The entrance to the underworld. I leaned against it, satisfied there was one direction at least she couldn't come at me from.

She spoke again, her voice closer now. "How long since you separated from your wife?"

I pushed my back, firm against the door. "Four years."

Laughter, again. "It's been one, Endgame. Ever wonder why your family didn't seem to age? That your eldest daughter didn't move on to high school? It's been a year, Endgame, but Mister Long has given you memories enough for four."

I shook my head, trying to shake the implications away. "No."

"Yes." She was insistent, closer. "Another question: how many daughters do you have?"

"Touch my family and—"

"And you'll what, exactly? Your threats don't have much currency tonight, Endgame. Now, I asked you a question, and I think you're going to want to know the answer. How many daughters do you have?"

A thought, unwanted, was pushing at the back of my mind. "Leave them be, Chrome. They don't know what I do, what Mister Long does. They—"

"I don't care. I don't care because I don't need to. I'll enjoy the moment, with you, and after this, I'll go to your old apartment and enjoy the moments I have with your wife and children. Then I'll never think on it again. I won't even know that I've done it. Now tell me: how many daughters do you have?"

"Fuck you."

"How many?"

Again, the pressure in my mind. "One," I said, spitting the word out. "I've got one daughter. Who's never hurt anyone or anything in her life."

She said with contempt: "You've got two, Endgame. Weici is yours, as well. Chinalco chipped away at your memory until she was just a phantom. We took away your daughter without you even knowing. Another year and Jian and Kylie will be gone, too. You could have saved them, Endgame. All you had to do was forget them. But you couldn't even get that right, could you? You had to go see that Omissioner bitch, with her tongue that dives about like a prawn."

"No," I said, but it was too late. Something detached itself from the mists of my mind and fell with a clunk. The memory of Jian, as I drove the bike away from the school, it cleared.

I jumped on the bike and gunned it. Jian grabbed the elbow of my jacket and was yelling something, screaming it. I heard her:

"She's your daughter too, Endel. Your daughter!"

That's why she was disgusted with me. I didn't know my own fucking child.

Linh spoke: "How can your family matter when you can't even hold them in your mind?"

"No," I repeated, gun and hands against my face, though trying to hold my head up under the weight of new memory.

"Yes, Endgame, yes. Maybe it is even worse than that. Maybe they aren't even your family. Maybe they are just three innocents, drafted in by Chinalco and given false memories of you as their father and husband. I've seen them do it to others. *Leverage*, they call it."

"No."

"And maybe you aren't even Endel Ebbinghaus. Ever wonder about that? You could be anyone. Your only evidence is memory, and that's all gone."

I took my hands away from my face, still staring down at the ground. My vision had pretty much cleared, just some white static at the corners of my eyes. I was standing on white marble shot through with black veins, the entrance to the tomb at my back. Bloody footprints stained the stone.

I could see, but that didn't seem to matter somehow.

"That's not true." My voice was clear. "They are my family."

"It doesn't matter if it is true or not," she said, something insistent in her tone. "It doesn't matter if you are who you think you are. That's not the point. The point is this: our world – yours and mine – is perfect. Without memory there is no morality, no constraints, nothing but the perfection of the moment. Nothing we do matters, Endgame, so therefore we are able to do *anything*."

I raised my head, my purpose now clear. She had given me, unintentionally, power. She had given me the one thing I'd sought above all else: clarity.

I could see her now. Chrome stood about five metres away, next to a large headstone. I had her dead to rights. In a blur I had the gun on Linh, her eyes lighting up with panic as I pulled the trigger.

It responded with an empty click. I swore.

Her eyes went from shocked to amused. A small grin played at the corners of her mouth.

I didn't care. I threw the gun away and limped towards her, fists raised. "The fuck you talking about, Linh? Taking night classes in high-school philosophy now?"

She bared her teeth.

I continued: "You're not free of morality because you can't remember what you do, Chrome. You're free of morality because you're a low-grade whore with a fetish for thrill kills."

She cursed in Vietnamese and came at me, stepping outside my clumsy front kick and flowing into an overhand strike aimed at the base of my throat. I'd figured that'd be her move, and also figured to use an immutable characteristic of her chrome daggers against her: their perfection. I held up my hand and the point of the blade passed clean through it, all the way to the slim hilt, until the bottom of her fist was pressed against my palm. I didn't even feel it. My hand spasmed and closed around hers. The sneer dropped from her lips and she tried to tear her hand free, but my fingers had snapped shut like a steel trap. She swept low with her other blade, I turned and it glanced off my armoured jacket.

I twisted my crucified hand savagely, Linh stumbled and I swung my free fist overhead, roaring, striking her shoulder. Her arm came out of its socket with an audible pop.

She screamed.

My butchered palm was slick with blood; she slipped from my grasp, staggering. I followed through with a right hook with enough power to take her head clean off, but even in the haze of pain and shock, she managed to duck, the blow glancing the top of her head. Still, it was enough to knock her down and send her other blade skittering across marble, into the darkness.

She got to her feet quickly, clutching at her mangled shoulder with her good arm, a trickle of blood running down the centre of her brow. She looked at me with shock and hatred, raw. I held up my chin and grinned, a mad, red avatar of violence, and slid the blade out slowly from my left hand. A lot of blood came with it.

I walked towards her, bloodied knife in hand, and said: "Normally at this point I'd let you have a cigarette, maybe a last drink. But for you I'm going to make an exception. For you I'm going to cut your fucking heart out of your chest while you're still alive."

She didn't give my proposition much thought. She ran. One arm bouncing, like a puppeteer had cut the string for that limb, she disappeared into the darkness.

I didn't try to chase her. I stood until I was sure she was gone, then sank to one knee and splayed the fingers of my good hand against the blood-splattered marble, dropping the blade. My arm shook. My whole body was shaking.

I smiled. I was used to having my bluffs called. Nice to get one through for a change.

A warning popped up on-retina.

Warning: Blood Loss Significant. Body will be placed in an induced coma while your nanomeds heal major damage. The nearest hospital will be notified of your location and an ambulance despatched.

"No," I said. "Keep me conscious."

Warning: Continued consciousness will result in death. Combat medical system is not rated for this level of physical trauma.

I spat a clot of blood onto the marble. "Then let me die. Keep me conscious."

The system didn't answer, just left a flashing warning at the corner of my vision. A red hand, palm open in the sign to stop, winking on and off.

I limped out onto the path and walked past Wangaratta's body. The top of his head was blown off, dead eyes watching the flow of the Milky Way as it moved across the night sky. I didn't stop. I just swore revenge for him and Ha, eyes gleaming as I staggered towards the cemetery gates, jaw set as I left the body of my best friend on the soil of an indifferent city, dead by my hand.

I slumped against the glimmer bike, leaving a bloody handprint on the shimmering fuel cell casing. I straddled the seat, placed a single shaking finger against my implant. "Automatic drive. Take me to my old apartment on Rua da Gamboa."

I prayed the bike had the street number in its memory. I sure as hell didn't.

The implant whispered: *Yes, Mister Ebbinghaus.*

I leaned forwards, good hand gripping the handle. "As fast as you can."

The engine hummed and the glimmer bike moved onto the road. I turned my head to one side and leaned my torso against the handles. The lights of the city whipped by, faster and faster. The neon of the bars, the bright lights of the casinos, the headlights of sleek limousines and yellow taxicabs, blurring past, all merging into each other. The world faded and somewhere I heard and saw an on-retina message bleeping at me. But I couldn't read the words or hear the sounds.

Then, the darkness.

14

I was being rocked. Consciousness trickled back in real slow, but the fact of being gently rocked seemed to somehow stretch right back, back into the darkness of the void.

Someone was gripping my hand. A voice, familiar, said: "Endel? Can you hear me, Endel?"

I opened my eyes to a blazing white light. I put my other hand over my face, trying to blot it out.

A hand pressed against my forehead and the voice, the voice of Jian, followed. "It's okay, we're going to be okay."

I couldn't see. The lights overhead too bright, nausea making my stomach churn. "Kylie. And—" My mind reached for what it had always known. Always should know. "The girls. Where are the girls?"

More hands touching me then, little hands on my chest, a small palm on my cheek. A voice, also small. "We're here, Daddy. Where did you go? Are you okay? You're all sticky. This boat smells. Can we get some ice cream when we—"

"Hush now, Kylie, Daddy's tired," said her voice, strained, and her hand patted my chest. "We're all here, Endel. Now rest."

I bit down on my lip, the joy and the pain washing over me. I rested.

15

Jian and I sat together in the high-rise apartment overlooking Hong Kong. Modern, sleek, minimalist, belonging to a friend of Jian's, she said, out of town on business. No-one could trace us here. I'd purchased a wave scrambler just in case, sitting now on the smooth white bench behind us. Bought another pistol as well, costing me – together with the scrambler – nearly all the hard currency I had left. With the change I got a new set of clothes and boots, and a pack of cigarettes. Until we got out of town we couldn't use our credit electronically. Too easy to trace.

My nanomed implant had healed all the knife wounds. Jian told me she counted more than twenty. I was weak, probably still had a low blood count, but, other than the bandage around my left hand, the only real signs of the damage were thin red lines on my arms, legs, and face.

Jian told me that I'd banged down the door of the apartment, yelling to get the kids out. Soaked in blood, delirious, I'd babbled that Ha and Wangaratta were dead, then somehow managed to give her the name of my contact on the fishing boat. I'd collapsed after that, staining the wood floors dark with my blood. I was out for pretty much twenty-four hours. But Jian did it. She just took my word and got us all out.

The kids were on the carpet in front of the tai screen now, watching some show about a talking pig. I looked over at them, smiling despite myself.

Then the smile disappeared, and I turned back to Jian.

"I'm going to have to leave you again."

She furrowed her brow. "No. Why?"

"I am a violent man. I'm a danger to you. To the kids."

"You are not a violent man, Endel."

"All the things that I've done, Jian, you wouldn't believe. Evil things."

"Yeah," she said. "You told me some of those things, Endel, in your delirium on the boat." Pain crossed her face at the memory. "But I know," she continued, reaching out and gripping my hand. "I *know* you. You're a hard man, but not a violent one. You came from a tough neighbourhood, but that doesn't make you a killer. You liked a drink, but you were never an alcoholic."

I sighed through my nose. "Even if that were true, I'm not sure if it matters. I don't know who I am anymore. I don't feel real."

"I'm not surprised. You're a caricature. The way you live your life, drinking and gambling, living in a casino. You're someone else's idea of a tough man from the wrong side of town. A rich person's wet dream about the life of the street thug."

I looked down at her hand, her delicate fingers resting gently against my scarred knuckles.

"I don't know what I'm programmed with," I said. "I don't know if I can trust myself, Jian."

"Endel."

"It's true. I could be made to do anything."

"Anything?" she asked. "Hmm. Does *all* programming have to be bad?"

I glanced up at her. "What do you mean?"

"I got a little money put away. Maybe I could purchase some

of this *reprogramming* I keep hearing about." A smile twinkled in her eyes. "You know, so you'd put the seat down after you use the toilet, be able to make a tasty risotto, maybe wax your hairy barbarian butt."

I smiled, despite myself. "Jian."

"I mean, it is pretty hairy, Endel."

We both grinned.

I looked at her. "How do I know you're real?"

She tilted her head slightly. "What?"

"You're too good to be true. You're like someone's idea of a faithful wife."

Her smile disappeared. "That's not true either, Endel."

We were silent for a few moments, looking out through the windows over the city. I pulled a cigarette from the pack, remembered the kids, and put it back. I shifted in my seat, a soft white cushion in a moulded burnished-bronze frame, running my fingers over the arm rest. Two Cs, little one inside the big one, were engraved on the arm.

I took in a deep breath. "Jian, did I…"

"Did you?"

"Did I ever hurt you? Was I violent?"

She shook her head, sadness on her face. "No. You never laid a hand on me."

I breathed out a long breath. It felt like I was expelling a cloud of poison from my soul. "So it was all a lie – you cheating on me, me hurting you and the kids. All just a fucking lie."

She sighed and there was a small smile on her face. But there was no humour or warmth in it anymore, just sadness. "Life isn't so simple, Endel."

Jian hesitated, then put her finger against her cochlear implant and whispered under her breath. She held out her hand to me, her memory pin between thumb and forefinger. "You need to know what happened. Use my memories." She grabbed my palm and put the pin in it.

I weighed it in my hand and said: "This is called transactional memory."

"What?"

"Transactional memory. We can form a dyadic system, that's how I can recover from all this. I can encode with our joint memories."

"Where the hell did that jargon come from?"

I shook my head. "I have no idea. It just—it just popped into my mind."

Jian still looked sad, resigned. "Watch the memory of our last fight. Then decide if you really want to pay the price of this transaction."

I nodded slowly. I removed my pin and slipped in hers. An unfamiliar static of memories – Jian's memories – descended on me. I asked the pin to mute them, for the moment, then closed my eyes and ran the memory trace to that last night we had.

"We… we slept together."

I saw the view from Jian's perspective. I saw myself rise from the lounge, an unlit cigarette dangling from my lips. I looked younger, stronger.

I also looked confused when I said, quietly: *"You what?"*

Jian couldn't bring herself to look at me, it seemed, and the centre of the vision switched to my feet. At the top of her peripheral vision, though, I could still see my face. Jian spoke, her voice breaking with emotion. "You'd started gambling and drinking more and more, God, sometimes you wouldn't even know what day it was. And it was the office party and I'd had too much to drink. This colleague was— He was insistent and I hadn't seen you in two weeks and it happened. It was… I was disgusted with myself afterwards. God, Endel, I'm so sorry." The vision went blank; I figured she'd put her hands over her eyes. *She sobbed.*

After a few long seconds the sobbing slowed and she looked back up at me. Our apartment on the Rua da Gamboa looked comfortable – stained dark wood floors and weird wallpaper of faded red, marked with gold silhouettes of belly dancers. Large windows bathed the room in a warm light and there was a stick of incense burning on the kitchen table, behind my left shoulder.

The confusion fell from my face, replaced by disbelief. I said, louder: "You fucking what?"

Jian put up her hand, she whispered: "Not too loud. The kids."

I stepped forwards, ugly with rage. "You. Did. Fucking. What?"

She took a step back. Her voice quavered as she said: "Don't threaten me, Endel."

I advanced on her, fists clenched, and threw the punch, a heavy crunching sound followed. Her vision spun for a moment before it focussed on me again. I was standing next to a large, gaping hole in the faded red wallpaper, the wood-and-plasterboard wall underneath. I pointed a bloodied fist at her. "Fuck you."

I spun and stormed out of the room. A thud and a muffled cry followed; Jian ran over to the door I'd just walked through. And there, on the other side, was Kylie sprawled on the ground with blood on her face. I was bent down over her. "Sorry honey," I said, "Oh Kylie, I didn't see you."

Jian yelled: "What did you do, Endel? What did you do!?"

I watched myself, my hands shaking, as I tried to pick up Kylie. She laid there with eyes open, her breathing shallow, in shock at the sudden blow to the head. I looked up at Jian, eyes gleaming: "She was on the other side of the door. I didn't—"

"Get out," screamed Jian and she grabbed Kylie, pulling her from my arms. I let her, turning and stumbling to the apartment door.

The door slammed and Jian looked down at Kylie, vision blurred with tears—

I stopped the recording, opened my eyes. Jian looked at me with tears in hers. We sat like that for a few minutes while I bit down on the anger in my stomach and her eyes blurred distant. Part of me, I guessed, had known about it for a year, but the conscious part was just finding out. I clenched my jaw. Either way, there was reason enough to be angry with Jian and to hate myself.

"Sorry," she said, wringing her hands.

I stood, rubbing my mouth with the back of my hand. I couldn't look at her. I walked away but the only other space in this apartment had my girls in it. They lay on their bellies, watching the show and Weici, seeing me, turned on her side and smiled.

Memories, deeply buried, stung. The love of a child is like no other. All they want is your presence, your attention, your arms to hold them. They think you are perfect, which is of course the hardest lie. But they think it anyway and it makes you want to deserve that love.

God, and I nearly threw it away. I nearly lost it all, in a fugue of drugs and deletions. A black mass, filling up all I ever was. I didn't know this little girl, but God I knew that smile.

I circled back to Jian.

"I haven't fucked it up, have I?" she asked.

I shook my head. "No, no, no." I said, my voice catching. "It's just one moment in time that has grown to represent… everything. But it's gone now. It's not who we are. Is it?"

She took my hand. "No. No, it isn't. I am sorry, Endel. Oh God I am. It was a clusterfuck. We just needed a break, for the sake of the kids, for our own sake. But you— That's the last I saw of you. You just disappeared. Your number changed. I heard you were living in a casino, but Ha refused to tell me which one. She and I never spoke much after that. And now she's…" Her voice broke and so did the dam of her tears, twin lines running down her cheeks.

I held her and she let me, putting her face against my shoulder. I looked over her head at the girls, but they ignored us, heads pointed the other way, at cartoon pigs jumping in muddy puddles.

After a time, I drew back and said: "We've got a lot to catch up on. But not now. Now we have to get out of Hong Kong. Get far away from that cesspit, Macau. The things I know, buried somewhere in my head – they're dangerous. They'll try to take me back."

She nodded, relieved maybe to set her mind on something other than our past. "I'll talk to some friends, back in Shanghai. See what I can organise." She paused, and then said: "So you're coming?"

"Yes. No." I sighed. "I don't know, Jian. Maybe for now, but—" I tapped my cochlear implant, "—I've got a lot of things to relive."

Jian stood. "We had a lot of good years. You'll see." She put her hand on my shoulder, looking down at me, her eyes gleaming. "You were a good father, too. Your daughters need you back. Come back to them, Endel. Come back to me." She smiled, then turned and left the room.

I watched her leave. After everything, she still moved with that effortless grace. I figured that was a good place to start. I closed my eyes and sent a trace back to the night Jian and I met.

I remembered.

PART TWO
Memory Town

"But then again I wonder if what we feel in our hearts today isn't like these raindrops still falling on us from the soaked leaves above, even though the sky itself long stopped raining. I'm wondering if without our memories, there's nothing for it but for our love to fade and die."

– Kazuo Ishiguro, *The Buried Giant*

16

Your name is Endel Ebbinghaus.

It's Wednesday, 3 September, 2101. You're in Shanwei,
Southern China. You have two daughters: their names
are Kylie and Weici. Your wife's name is Jian. You and
your family are fleeing Macau. You are trying to get
to Shanghai.

Your former boss and Macau drug lord, Mister Long,
has been wiping your memory of your identity, including
knowledge of your family. He had your close friends Ha
and Wangaratta killed.

Now he is coming after you.

I groaned and rolled over in bed. I read the on-retina message
twice, trying to get my mind around it. As my brain ground into
a half-life, I fumbled at the side table, found my cigarettes, and
tapped one out. I blew clouds of smoke at the ceiling for half a
cigarette before deciding to sit up. The hotel room could have been
a mid-range franchise hotel anywhere in the world: brown carpets
patterned with off-white circles, tan lampshades, mirror facing the
bed. A foldout bed to my right, its linen piled up.

The crack of light coming through the window was too bright

to allow a glimpse outside. There wasn't much to see anyway. Half the city was submerged, flooded after dykes built by corrupt contractors burst, concrete brutalist apartment blocks hovering over the city, empty shells staring down with darkened eyes. The other half was closed coal-fired power stations and rusting automobile plants and plastic doll factories and other relics of the fossil fuel age. Rich as it was, the Chinese government deemed Shanwei too polluted to rebuild, too ruined to rescue.

Our hotel was one of the few remaining in town and the manager was desperate enough for guests that he accepted cash. As such, it was perfect.

The door to the bathroom was open, revealing a narrow space of scratched, mostly clean tile and a stand-up shower. It was empty.

My family were gone.

"Jian," I said into the empty room, as though the word was a spell that would snap me out of this dream, and I'd wake up, next to my wife and children. It did snap me out, I suppose, insofar as the echo of my voice filled the space where my family should have been.

When I reached for my gun on the bedside table I saw the note. Flashing in green, on the flexiscreen: Getting breakfast. Back soon.

The tension abated from my chest. I leaned back against the wall and smoked another cigarette. My mind drifted back to me, and I savoured its presence along with the nicotine. I'd felt better since I'd absorbed a lot of Jian's memories. I'd downloaded a simple exo-memory assistant program off the freewave while we were back in Hong Kong. We weren't allowed even basic exo-mas when we worked in Macau, just a compromised version supplied by the Syndicate. The first few days after we'd fled, I had the program pick out the major events in Jian's memories that included me, and had it deliver them at night, in my dreams.

The transactional memories were working, building up a sense of what Jian and I had together. What we had was pretty damn good, actually.

Jian's recollections even managed to fire some of my own atrophied neurons. Recovering slivers of my life I'd thought I forgotten, dredging them up from whatever dark crevasse they'd been stuffed into. I'd had to put in an older memory pin – the one I'd been using had long been tainted with a mnemonic poison of Mister Long's making, turning my heart against itself.

The old one was full, with three years of memories. I'd kept it against my better instincts, sewn into the lining of my leather jacket. It wasn't a smart standover man who kept detailed visual recordings of his crimes. Sure, the worst of them would be wiped, the ones the police took an interest in, anyway. But a lot of that life would remain: my contacts in the underworld, my haunts and misdemeanours.

I'd had to wipe one year from the pin – I chose the oldest memories – to make room for new ones. All exo-mas were programmed to leak historic memories into dreams, as a way of retaining and building on a sense of the self. So every now and again I woke up thinking I was a few years younger, imagining I was still in Macau, living in a small but nice place in the best part of town, the apartment I had with Jian and Kylie – then a loud and precocious three-year-old.

But it got weirder. The memories I absorbed from Jian, before I returned her pin, would sometimes, just for a moment, make me think I was Jian. Caught up in her recollections of a meeting at work, or a sick child, or sometimes, the husband who'd abandoned her.

So on balance, sure, things were getting better, but it still was far from good. I'd wake up with the family in another nondescript hotel room, and sometimes I'd have forgotten my daughter's names and what we were doing there. I'd call them "honey" and "sweetie" for fifteen minutes while I stared out the window, drinking coffee, waiting for my past self to catch up. I started dictating reminders to be played on-retina when I woke up. That helped.

So did staying clean. Hard as the desire to drink came on, it wasn't hard enough to allow myself to stink of vomit and bourbon in front of my daughters, or to smash up a hotel room as some sort of sacrifice to the demon rage that welled up inside after I'd had too many. My hands shook sometimes, and the headaches were bad as my body longed for the drink, but I managed.

Thirty minutes later I was standing at the window watching the carpark below, white T-shirt and jeans, black shoulder holster and pistol. I was sipping a bitter double espresso and thinking about my next cigarette when the door flew open. I turned, hand on gun, my coffee cup bouncing on the floor.

The girls tumbled in, squealing, Jian followed, unhurried. I quickly slid the gun back in the holster, before they noticed. Weici and Kylie located me and charged, clinging to my legs and laughing at me for spilling coffee on the ground. *Silly Daddy.*

Jian handed me a bag and told me to eat.

"Sick just thinking about it," I said.

"Endel," she said, a one-word admonition. "The hollow-eyed, pasty-skinned, jittering junkie in need of a fix look may pass inspection with the girls, but it doesn't with me."

"What's a junkie?" asked Weici, eyes wide at her mother.

"A man who lives inside a trash can," replied Kylie, with the iron certitude only an eight-year-old can provide to a younger sibling.

"That's true," said Jian, the corner of her mouth smiling. "And who doesn't eat his breakfast."

"Are you a junkie, Daddy?" asked Weici.

I grizzled and took the bag from Jian. "I guess not." The bag had two baozi with red bean filling, if the smell was any indication. I sat down on an off-white faux-leather chair near the window and forced myself to bite down on one. The taste was far better than expected, given the drab, run-down neighbourhood of cracked bitumen and mosquito-enriched puddles.

Jian watched, eyebrow raised, until I took another bite. My stomach twisted, halfway between nausea and hunger, but held it down. A small nod from me told Jian it was good; she changed her focus to the girls, directing them to collect their toys for another move. I hadn't eaten much and hadn't wanted to since leaving Macau. Coming clean from the booze always did that. All I could think about was the drink I wasn't having and the cigarette in my hand.

I took another bite. But today, somehow, this breakfast was hitting the spot. Shit, maybe I was on the improve. I'd always wondered what that would be like.

"I'm sick of moving," said Kylie, accentuating *sick* with a foot-stomp.

"*Kylie*," warned Jian.

"Sick sick sick sick," *stomp stomp stomp stomp.*

Kylie's face was red, pigtails bouncing, while she made a slow circle. I couldn't remember if she was always the strong-willed one, but she was gunning for the role right then.

Weici packed her bag, oblivious. She liked adventures, she kept telling us all.

"Kylie," said Jian, with ice enough for her daughter to stop.

Kylie's bottom lip immediately began to quaver. She'd been showing the sort of pent-up emotion and confusion that an eight-year-old torn from her home in the dead of night had every right to show.

I shoved my arms straight out, hands floppy, and groaned.

Kylie tilted her head to one side and said: "*Huh*?"

I lurched forwards a step. Weici squealed and started bouncing up and down on the bed near her suitcase. Kylie smiled and said *huh* again.

I lurched and groaned again and Kylie hopped up on the bed, her and Weici clutching each other as they jumped up and down, squealing with big grins. "A zombie!" said Kylie.

"A zombie!" repeated Weici.

When I reached the bed Kylie hit me with a pillow. *Whump.* I grabbed them both as I fell, zombie death-groaning, while the two beat at me with tiny fists, still squealing.

After the giggling died down, the two managed to wiggle their way on to my chest. I said: "I'm sorry we have to keep moving from place to place, girls. I promise it won't be for much longer."

"Why did we have to leave?" asked Kylie, and Weici echoed her immediately.

I sighed. "There are—there are bad people in Macau."

"Did you poop in their toy box and not tell anyone and someone else got blamed and now you're scared to go back to their place?"

Everyone looked at Weici, silent for a few moments. "Um," I said. "That's quite specific, honey."

Jian laughed. "Something like that, Weici. Something just like that." She stopped laughing and feigned seriousness. "Now you two, *pack your bags.*"

The girls sighed and took to packing. Jian guided me by the elbow back over to the window.

"We're getting low on money," she whispered.

"I blame you."

She raised an eyebrow. "And how do you figure that, cowboy?"

"Well, if you'd acted like a real gangster's moll, we'd have more bling than you can poke a stick at."

"A real moll would have dumped your sorry arse and upgraded a long time back."

I ran a hand over my high forehead, through my thinning hair. "A dashing young buck like me, how could you leave?"

Jian stepped in close, glimpsed back to make sure the girls were preoccupied with packing, slid her hand down my jeans, and grabbed me. "There's only one thing you've consistently impressed me with, cowboy." She squeezed gentle and continued: "Now when are we going to consummate this storybook reunion of ours?"

I felt heat on my cheeks and, well, on that spot her hand was wrapped around. "The girls," I stuttered, grinning like an idiot.

She withdrew her hand, unimpressed, and walked over to where Kylie and Weici had stopped packing and were now dancing on the bed.

"Girls," said Jian. "I've got a surprise for you."

They both stopped jumping immediately. "*Shi mama*?" Kylie asked in Mandarin.

"Next hotel, we're going to get you your own separate Kylie-Weici room that will have a giant special jumping bed. How does that sound?"

The girls jumped up and down squealing, Jian looked back at me and winked. I kept grinning.

17

A rusted recycling truck, grunting biodiesel, made its way ponderously down the main road. I looked up at the noise, but the speed of the truck and the way it was being driven raised no alarm bells.

I didn't have the money for a high-tech disguise, so I'd gone analogue. Black baseball cap imprinted with the Queen of Spades, a short rough beard, wraparound sunglasses. It'd been cloudy and raining for the entire drive east, making it hard for satellites, and we'd travelled through the worst parts of the worst towns, where many of the locals would be invested in jamming technology against drones. There was the chance of Mister Long getting access to on-retina feeds, locating us through the eyes of some civilian going about their everyday business. But those were expensive to hack, highly illegal to do so, and sifting through all the data took a lot of computational power. I'd allowed myself some cautious optimism.

We were in the carpark, downhill from the recycling truck. I was putting what luggage we had into the boot while Jian wrestled the girls into the back seat. There was a breeze up and the morning heat was bearable. Fucken miracle. Soaking wet or stinking hot: I'd rarely seen southern China do anything else.

But this morning was different, and it'd been a long time since I'd simply stood and let the breeze wash over me. So I let it. I wore jeans, cowboy boots, and my battered leather jacket with its spideriron weave. Up behind the slow-moving truck the skyline consisted of half-built skyscrapers and their abandoned cranes. Sentinels, black against the rose-coloured morning sky, keeping the long watch over the fading memories of this place. As China's population declined, so ghost cities like this became more common. Opposite the carpark was a small sidewalk café, cheap brown plasteel tables topped with white tea urns and glasses of rice whisky. Old and grizzled and dead-eyed Chinese men sat circled around their drinks, watching me and the family, as curious as they should be about travellers who had chosen this withered branch of Chinese civilisation to traverse.

The other direction, the direction the truck was headed, was the remaining inhabited part of town. Solar panels glinted here and there between improvised wiring running above and through the tenements. Two-and-three-storey buildings with dirty white façades, the sag of neglect heavy on their shoulders.

It was because I took that moment to breathe, eyes resting on the horizon, that I saw the three cars as soon as they surged over the crest of the hill. Clearly not from around here: latest-model Yunque ultras, black tinted windows, sleek, aggressive. Driving close, nose-to-tail. There wasn't much between us and the cars. On the far side of the road a line of mainly boarded-up shops, save the sidewalk bar, on this side muddy earth and patches of dying grass, until the turnoff to the hotel.

"Jian."

She looked at me over the roof of the car. "Don't snap, Endel, I'm—"

"*Drive.*"

She looked at where I was looking, then back at me. "Who—"

I pulled my gun from its holster. "The back exit out of the hotel," I said, my words sharp and controlled. "You take the girls and you drive and you do not stop."

The girls were watching me, wide-eyed, through the back windscreen.

"I will *not* leave without you."

"Do. Not. Stop." I looked to her, briefly, our eyes locked and with hers she pleaded. I answered by running towards the oncoming cars.

Jian swore. But a few seconds later I heard the door slam behind me, and the engine start.

I took cover behind shoulder-height signage at the entrance to the carpark. The brick base of the sign was ten feet long, atop it was a holo-projector showing the Chinese ideograms 玉山酒店, 'Jade Mountain Hotel', in glowing red holotype, rotating slowly in the air. There was a glitch in the projection, the 山 flickering in and out of view.

The hydrogen whine of Jian's vehicle receded, replaced by the squeal of rubber on road as the black sedans hammered down the hill towards the hotel. My hands shook as the adrenaline hit, then quickly steadied as my internal combat regulator kicked in. My vision sharpened and narrowed on the cars, as did my hearing. I felt excited, yet somehow sanguine at the same time. Combat nanos or no, I did like a fight.

The first two vehicles sped down the road. The third took a more direct approach; it turned off the bitumen and pointed its nose right at me, gouging up clots of damp earth as it hammered through the rough field.

As I centred the windshield of the third car in my sights, its wheels slipped out from under it on the muddy ground, and it slid sideways. Fifty metres away, I fired at the exposed flank. The *boom boom boom* of my pistol sounded like a shotgun blast. One shot embedded itself in the siding, two in the windows. The windows were bulletproof, apparently, but not big-calibre bulletproof – the driver's and rear windows bloomed with cracks.

I had my aim in now, emptying the rest of the twenty rounds into the front and rear. Bodies bucked, pink mist sprayed inside the vehicle, and I turned my attention to the other cars as I ejected the spent magazine.

A man hung out the side of the second car, firing a machine gun. It chewed the ground in front of me and exploded a couple of bricks as I stepped back under cover. The firing was erratic, the gunman too eager.

I took three quick steps and popped out the other side of the signage, firing. I hit armoured panelling, cracked a window, and blew out the front right tyre of the first vehicle. It veered left, throwing up mud on my side of the road before overcorrecting, swerving back across the asphalt and slamming through the tables of the café, then continuing straight on through the wall of an empty shop.

My mind took a snapshot of the car as it hit the café. Most of the patrons had fled, save an old man with a long, thin tuft of a beard and a second man, middle-aged, trying to pull the first away from the firefight. The car hit the table, shattering a teapot, spraying shimmering liquid into the air, and snapping the two men over its bonnet. They were carried with it into the guts of the shop next door.

The last car, belatedly figuring out the best way to approach its target, skidded to a halt and disgorged five gunners. They immediately took cover behind it, spraying machine and pistol fire. Bricks exploded around me, their thin red dust filling the air.

I had to move.

Breathe.

I had thirteen bullets in the magazine, give or take.

Breathe.

Five gangsters of middling competency, heavily armed, protected by an armoured car. A couple of guys in the crashed car who might be able to drag themselves out and fire an angry shot.

A brick exploded near my head. I gritted my teeth and shook the dust from my hair.

Breathe.

Jian had a two-minute start. Not long enough.

Breathe.

Two weeks since I'd had a drink, more than a year since I slept with my wife, forever since we'd had one fucking day as a normal family.

Breathe.

Something tickled my cheek and I swiped at it, my hand came away bloody. There was a pause in the fusillade, replaced by silence. Just the low drone of the recycling truck in the distance, idling, stopped halfway down the slope, unwilling to shuffle on into the middle of a firefight.

Yeah. That'd do it.

I burst from cover, running low, emptying the rest of my bullets at the car. A gangster with a long dark coat and pistol in each hand had left cover, was halfway to my position, maybe hoping I'd bought it during their spree. She fell, screaming, bullet in her knee, and the rest of my shots were enough to force the others to duck down behind the car.

I ate up the distance between myself and the truck in long, powerful strides. The gangsters clued in when I was about halfway across the open space. But their firing was wild, whizzing above my head, spraying the earth ahead of me. I dived behind the truck, rolled, and rose slowly, back against the cabin, chest heaving. I banged on the driver's side window with my fist. "Open up and get the fuck out."

Silence from the driver. Bullets from the gangsters.

The metal of the truck was as thick as I'd judged, and nothing came through. The *bratatat* of submachine gun and *fizz-whine* of ricocheting bullets filled my ears as I banged on the window again, angry.

My last blow shattered the safety glass and I yelled: "Out now, driver!"

"[Fuck your mother!]"

I smiled. The balls on this guy. I holstered my pistol, grabbed the door frame with both hands, and heaved. Rusted metal moaned, then screamed, as I opened up my shoulders, pulling angry.

The door tore from its hinges and I hurled it a dozen yards away. A little Chinese man with a blue Mao cap and eyes popping lay across the seats. He barely had time to swear at me again before I threw him as far as the door, one handed.

I hopped into the cab, ground the stick into gear, and stamped on the accelerator. Nothing happened. For a few seconds anyway, and then the truck lurched and started to trundle leisurely down the hill.

"Shit."

I ducked sideways as a spray of bullets came through the windshield of the large, slow moving, easy-to-hit target.

"Shit."

Still flat on the seats, I crammed the gearstick into third. There was a long scream of protest from the gearbox. Third gear clearly wasn't a place it had visited for some time. Safety glass bounced off the dashboard, then me, as the truck rumbled down the hill.

"Shit," I swore, this time in pain, and jerked back my hand. I held it against my chest on instinct for a moment before checking it. A bullet had torn open the outside of my palm, blood flowed down my wrist.

Just a scratch.

As the seconds dripped by, the truck waddled on, and bullets ripped apart the back of the cabin, I figured my gambit way dumber on second glance. But then gravity and an old motor built to last by the Chinese kicked in. The truck gained speed. I dared a one-eyed glimpse over the dashboard, adjusting the wheel so the rusting rolling crate was aimed down the centre of the road, directly at the sleek Yunque that shared the same space fifty metres on.

I popped my head back down as the muzzle flash and *bratatat* persisted. I told my c-glyph to give me the image. It popped up in the corner of my eye on-retina: four shooters, two behind the car, one on either side. Fedoras and knee-length black jackets, machine guns, facial expressions set to kill.

My combat system enhanced reflexes, spatial judgement, and reaction time. With the freeze frame on-retina, I could hold the truck on its current course, centre road, without having to look over the dashboard again.

I stuffed the accelerator as far into the floor as it would go and held the wheel steady. The truck groaned long and throaty, and something in the engine popped, but still the truck accelerated. At the last I sprung back up in the seat, copped another flash image of four gangsters looking kinda surprised, and jumped.

I hit the soft earth and rolled as iron struck reinforced carbon fibre with a loud *thud-snap-snap*. On my feet, moving; a gangster trying to pick himself up from the ground, his compact machine gun close by. I took a one-two-three step and kicked his upper arm; it snapped audibly and the man tumbled along the ground, howling.

I picked up his machine gun – a dark blue-metal Chinese-made Type-107 – and turned to where the car once stood. Another gangster was on one knee, blood trickling down his forehead, looking at me in a split-second of shock. He gave me enough time to put a long burst of lead into his chest and face.

I turned again at the *snick* of a gun being cocked. The female gangster I'd shot in the knee was lying on her side twenty metres away, pistol pointed at me, her face pale. She fired as I did. I grunted, spraying bullets in the air as I took a round in the shoulder. It took me a second to get my aim back on the woman, but it didn't matter.

She was now lying on her back, giving the long stare to an empty sky.

I walked back over to the gangster with the broken arm and kicked him in the face. He stopped trying to get his pistol out of the holster on his hip, and lay still on the ground instead. I looked around, the 107 raised.

The recycling truck had flattened the front of the car and driven it another hundred yards up the road, joined together by the force of the impact. At that point it had slanted off the bitumen and bogged itself down in the moist earth. Two red smears on the road indicated how quick the other two triggermen had been in getting out from behind cover.

I winced and worked my shoulder. The bullet hadn't punched through the jacket. Would just leave a nice fat bruise.

I walked over to where the first car had crashed through the sidewalk café. Shattered chairs, tables, and teapots littered the trail the car had made through two walls. Standing out in the light, looking into the dim interior of the shattered store, it took my eyes a moment to adjust. Shapes moved inside the car and I fired, my ears ringing, emptying the rest of the magazine through the back window.

The shooting stopped, but my finger stayed tight around the trigger and I found myself at the end of a long, hard scream. The motherfuckers.

I breathed, lowered the gun.

Silence, now, after the roar of battle, save my heart thumping in my ears.

I searched the bodies of the dead, taking spare magazines and a second Type-107. Then I walked back and grabbed the last live one by the hair, dragging him past the car that had come at me over the mud. The interior of that vehicle was painted in blood, the four men inside split open by explosive tipped shells. I moved on, the man I was dragging feebly batting at my hand with his.

I was in the hotel carpark deciding which car to steal when Jian drove in. I dropped the groaning gangster to the asphalt. Jian hopped from the car and walked over to me, her face set. When I tried to speak she slapped me. Not a word about the smoking cars, bodies strewn over the battlefield, or the bleeding thug at my feet. Just a sharp slap and she said: "Shut up. I'm not playing the loyal absent wife while you play the self-sacrificing husband. Get in the damn car."

I opened my mouth to reply—

"Daddy," said Kylie, hanging out the window and staring at the car crash back up the slope, thin trail of smoke trailing up from the wreckage. "The truck smashed into the car."

I moved to block their view of the carnage. "I know, honey," I said, fake-smiling. "Daddy was driving."

Kylie's mouth popped open. "You're a terrible driver."

Weici pushed wiggled out the window, right next to her sister. "Who's that man with you? Is he a junkie?"

"He's a… friend."

"Why is he groaning like that? Did he eat too many pancakes for breakfast and then a block of butter as well because no-one was watching?"

"Back in the car *now*," said Jian with enough force that dark clouds descended over the girls' faces as they got back in their seats.

I glanced around. A small crowd of patrons had gathered inside the glass doors of the hotel lobby, watching. The police in this town would be corrupt, slow, and largely uninterested in crime, but even they would have to show up to a fourteen-person massacre. More problematic, in front of me stood an angry Shanghai princess who was not in the habit of taking no for an answer.

"Back the car up to me so the girls don't see," I said. "We're taking this guy with us."

18

I popped the boot in the underground carpark of a motel. We'd rented a room for an hour. The place was a rotting polycrete eyesore thirty kilometres out of town. Stained rust red from the elements, half the windows missing, a nameless, all-but-abandoned rats' nest surviving on the patronage of the occasional prostitute or drifter. An automated receptionist had a slot for cash or a thumbprint for credit. God knows if the rooms were ever cleaned. I told Jian to lock and chain the door, gave her a pistol, and had her link me through her c-glyph. I had her visual in a small box in the left field of my vision on-retina.

The gloom of the carpark stunk of decay and wild animal.

The gangster screamed as I turned him over, his broken arm trapped underneath him. I waited while his breathing steadied and he focussed on me. The light from the boot revealed a young guy, mid-twenties. Slicked-back hair that was now sticking up all over the place, his front teeth missing from where my boot kissed him, and an unusually large mouth. He had those features somewhere between South and Southeast Asian that told me he was probably Burmese.

I slapped him a little to get his attention.

The first thing he tried was bravado. "You're dead, Endgame," he slurred, in reasonable English, "dead." He tried to smile after he said it, but the effect was spoiled by his bloodied, gap-toothed mouth.

I showed him a short, sharp blade with a serrated edge I'd found strapped to his ankle. "Listen: there's a door. And you're going through that door, whether you want to or not. The only choice is whether you walk, or you crawl."

He didn't compute. "Door?"

"Yeah mate. A door marked: 'everything I want to fucken know.' See, you're going through it, one way or the other. That's the only choice you get to make. But you will talk, boy. The most logical thing is to talk easy, preserve your physical integrity. Look for a moment when I'm distracted, then try to overpower me." He tried to say something, but I pressed the blade against his lips, "*Shhhhhhhh*. Or you could bank on my mercy in exchange for your compliance. I've been feeling strange of late; it's possible I could find a way to let you go. But here's your problem – gangsters always think the immutable laws of torture don't apply to them: that somehow, they will remain silent even after their eyeballs have been removed, or testicles hung around their throat, tied with a length of their own sinew. So here you lie, alone, trying to disbelieve the knife that's about to enter your eye socket." I moved the point of the blade so it was a centimetre from his eye. "So tell me: walk, or crawl?"

His eyes said *walk*, but his mouth said: "Crawl."

I grabbed his head to hold him steady. He grunted: "You're dead. Chrome is coming. She bleed you, Endgame. *She bleed you*."

I pushed his head to one side and he choked with pain as his busted arm twisted underneath. I tapped the steel of the c-glyph with the point of the blade. "I guess you're transmitting our conversation back to Mister Long?" Yeah. That was it. I leaned in close and whispered: "Hi there, Long, you painted fucking cadaver. I know what you're wondering, as you sit there on your chaise longue, painting your nails: *how the hell can a man without a past yearn for revenge?* It's hard to imagine what that man is angry about, as his grievances fade, as the memories of the close friends murdered, by you, become shadows flickering on the cave wall. So let me take a moment to explain: there's this great, yawning chasm I got inside me, Long. I can feel it. All I know is that you put it there, and the only thing I can do to ease the pain is to stuff that emptiness with bodies. Your foot soldiers, then your lieutenants, every single one, into my abyss. I'm going to tear it all down and fill myself with the rubble. Then, only at the last, then I will kill you. I will see you burn."

I turned my attention back to the gangster, slapping him before tapping the c-glyph again. "Put your finger here and give it your print, say your password, and pop the control and memory pins." His eyes were wild with fear, but he kept his mouth closed and shook his head. A bunch of gangsters were behind his eyes, watching. Keeping face in front of some thugs hundreds of kilometres away was apparently more important than the threat of dismemberment, right here. Like I said, the logic of the pre-tortured is never great. "Boy," I said, and I said it soft. "I'm the hardest man Mister Long ever had. I've been here before and these things go but one way. I'm telling you: you ain't going to last an hour. So—" I turned the blade in my hand, "—walk, or crawl."

He surprised me.

"*Crawl.*"

19

"Not answering?" asked Jian as she let me in the room.

"I'm not asking."

A little crease formed between her eyes. "Why?"

"You."

The crease remained. "Babe. What are you talking about?"

"Something's changed. Since Hong Kong."

"What's changed?"

I rubbed my forehead. "If I'm working from instinct, everything is fine. But for something pre-meditated, like—like having to use *persuasion*, you're there with me. Standing there inside my head, with that disapproving look on your face."

She paused, eyes distant, then said: "The memories. My memories."

"Yeah. I took too many. Overcompensated. Sometimes I think I am you. Which isn't so bad, I suppose. Until I have to get real uncivilised."

Jian crossed her arms. "This man wants to kill you, me, and our children?"

"Me mainly, but yeah. All of us."

"And he knows how they managed to track us here?"

"Don't know. Yeah. Probably."

She fixed me with a stare that made me stop thinking about anything else. "That motherfucker wanted to kill my daughters. You have my permission to go in there and *ask* him anything you want. You got that, Endel?"

I nodded. "Yeah. I got it."

20

I wiped the blood off my hands and sat down on a pile of bricks out the side of the motel, watching the Milky Way as it flowed across the sky. I lit a Double Happiness, and as I sucked down my second favourite drug, the shaking in my hands abated. I spent two more cigarettes like that, under the vast indifference of the universe, and made my plans.

21

Jian was playing with the girls on the floor when I entered. Weici squealed *Daddy* and ran over, hugging my leg. Kylie stayed intently focussed on the puzzle spread over the floor. Jian looked at me, asking the question. I picked Weici up. "I'm bugged."

"Bugged? But we checked."

I shrugged. "With a scanner, borrowed from your friend in a mid-sized company, normally used for corporate espionage. I'd been worried it'd miss the high-end stuff."

Jian helped Kylie slot a puzzle piece in place. Weici started wiggling; I popped her onto the bed. She started running in circles on the covers, big smile on her face.

Jian said: "Nanotrace?"

"No. Synthetic toenail."

"Is he telling the truth?"

"I got his memory pin. I can cross-reference with his visual feed if it hasn't been tampered with, I guess. But yeah." I smiled hollow, thinking about what was left of the man. "He's telling the truth."

"Which one?"

"Which what?"

"Which toenail?"

"He doesn't know."

"So…" she winced.

"Yeah," I replied. "I'll have to pull them all out."

"Jesus, Endel."

"Yeah."

She paused. "So…"

"Not now."

Crease. "Why?"

I sat down on the bed, made a play at grabbing for Weici as she trundled past, she laughed and fell onto the pillows.

Jian waited. Then said, with a warning tone: "Endel?"

"It's me they really want. All you are to them is collateral damage."

"Endel."

I glanced down at my foot then back at her. "I got the means here, to lead them away. Keep you safe."

"*Endel.*" There was anger enough in her tone for Kylie to look up and for Weici to stop her falling-over game.

"Keep the girls safe, too."

"No. *No.* Not again."

The girls were looking from me to their mother.

"The only way, Jian."

"Don't talk to me like your mind is made up. *Don't talk to me* like I don't have a part in this decision."

"The decision was made when those three cars came over the hill."

Jian stood up, her mouth set. "No."

Weici, more sensitive to these things, started crying. Quiet, tears running down her cheeks. "Kylie," said Jian, firm. "Take care of your sister."

Jian went out the front and waited on the polycrete walkway. I followed, closing the door behind. She was wearing denim jeans and an old leather jacket, but she moved elegant, oblivious to the cloying wet heat. We looked at each other instead of talking, and that was a pleasant change. Her eyes were red from the sleepless nights, but she was as beautiful as ever, a living, vibrant non-sequitur in the dissolution of this fading motel, this drowned land. I ran my fingers over her cheek, the mole under her left eye. She smiled, real small, as I touched her.

Then I remembered what that hand had just done, and pulled it away.

"The only way, Endel?" she asked.

"You know this, Jian. This way you and the girls will be safe. The only way."

"Then how does this end, cowboy?" She reached up, fingering the collar of my leather jacket. "That scumbag you worked for, who killed good friends of ours and turned you against your family – he doesn't sound like the quitting type."

"He's not. He's the other type."

"Then how does this end?"

I shook my head. "I don't know yet. I'm making this up as I go along. The first step is leading them away. After that…"

Jian waited for me to finish the thought. When I didn't, she said: "I don't want to wait another year, Endel. Not knowing if you're dead or alive, lying to the girls about where you are." Her eyes glistened. "I don't want to live that way."

I told the truth: "Nor do I. I want a life with you. I'm sick of living in the gutter of these false memories. I just want my family."

"Promise you'll come back," she said. "Promise you won't let these people hurt you again."

And then I lied: "I promise. Give me two months, to sort this. Then I'll be back, and we can get on with the rest of our lives."

Jian wasn't one for making demands, nor was she prone to wishful thinking. But she was a human being. She was tired and scared, and in need of comforting lies. I was tired and scared as well, and I needed to tell them.

She put her head against my chest and we stayed like that for a minute. The low rumble of thunder rolled in over the half-sunken city, dogs howled in distant streets.

Jian slapped me on the arse, drawing back my attention. "I haven't been laid in over a year. We better make it quick."

"I haven't either," I said, smiling. "So *quick*, I can do." Then I added: "But the girls."

She raised an eyebrow. "The shower?"

"Hot water?"

"Yeah, I checked."

"Here? A miracle."

Jian grabbed my hand. "It was meant to be." She pulled me after her, though the door.

22

Your name is Endel Ebbinghaus. It's Sunday, 7 September, 2101. You're in Chongzuo. You're travelling to Vietnam to draw your pursuers away from your family. You're not going to remind yourself of your family's names or final destination. Better not knowing.

One of your toenails is synthetic, a tracker put there by your enemies in Macau. The people following you will kill you if they catch you.

Before you cross the Vietnamese border, you will remove the bug.

I sat in the carpark of the station, watching the glittering train as it swept by high on the track. The red double-C of Chinalco embossed large on its side. I was sitting in a beat-up Nissan Tomorrow. Cracked dashboard, faded red faux-leather seats, the persistent smell of stale body odour, and a plastic gold Buddha hanging on the rear-view mirror. The car was so old it didn't have auto-drive, didn't go faster than eighty, and had a solar battery that lasted only a couple of hours after the sun went down.

The woman who sold it to me – overalls, grease-smeared,

needlessly rude – said she'd added a biodiesel tank and *take it or leave it, motherfucking gweilo.*

I took it.

It had the virtue of being untraceable. No freewave link, GPS removed and sold. Borderline illegal, without all that, but the cops in this part of the world weren't looking to enforce the traffic code. The car was a straight swap for the second Type-107 machine gun I'd taken. The first lay across my lap. Blue metallic sheen, each side of the short barrel engraved in flowing, copper script. My translator informed me that it was Burmese language. One side said: *There's only two ways: go crazy, or go extraordinary!*

I didn't mind that.

The other side said: *Actions are new, consequences are old.* I didn't like that one so much. I had enough to worry about without adding karma to the mix. I lit a cigarette, cracked the window, blew the smoke out. My hand shook. I needed a drink. My chest hurt. I needed something else more.

Jian, Kylie, and Weici weren't on the train. They were still in the car headed to… the memory was fading now, but yeah, it was somewhere in Shanghai. I'd instructed my c-glyph to delete all discussions of Jian's destination. If they got me, at least the directions wouldn't be there in my pin in crisp, clear detail. And if I managed to hold it in my real memory, I'd never give it up. Never.

I thought about the young Burmese bloke.

I took a drag on my smoke. My hand still shook.

The tracker was still in one of my toenails, so they'd know I was here. They'd also know the glimmer train left around the same time. Eight-hundred kilometres an hour, all the way to Beijing. From there, with the right ticket, you could get a train anywhere. Ulaanbaatar, Moscow, Warsaw, Frankfurt, all the way to Paris. From here you could go to Yangon, or Bangkok, or Kuala Lumpur.

The New Silk Road, unfurling its grasp over Southeast Asia, North Asia, Europe, even North Africa. The trains always ran on time, they said, in the Chinese Century.

I looked at the palm of my hand, the spot where Chrome's blade had gone clean through. It itched, the white scar, over an inch long. Staring back at me, a slitted white eye. I closed my fist. New scars all over now. Thighs, backs of my hands and forearms; two long scars criss-crossed, over my right cheek, and a third that went up my forehead at an angle and into my hairline. No hair grew where that scar went, so it was visible right up into my scalp.

Large drops of rain fell, marking their destination with splashes half a hand wide on the windscreen. Just a few at first, like the drummer in a jazz band tuning his kit. Then many, then a blur on the windscreen and in the eardrums as the storm came. I couldn't see the train tracks anymore, could barely see the other cars in the park – just smudged outlines sinking underwater.

My hands still shook and I'd had enough of that weakness, of all of them, piling one on top of the other, just fucking done with it so I hammered the dashboard to make the shaking stop. The lip over the instrument display snapped off under the third or fourth blow and I glimpsed myself in the rear-view mirror so shattered that as well, then elbowed the driver's side window, safety glass blossoming with cracks.

My rage was hidden within the storm. Drowned out by the storm. Irrelevant to the storm.

Hand throbbing, I tried to breathe. I couldn't, chest heaving, throat tight, the air in the car too close, too thick. I opened the door, spilling out to the rain and the asphalt. It rained hard, but I barely felt it, gasping for breath as the last things that mattered drove away along the back roads to Shanghai. I wiped the water from my eyes and for the first time noticed the neon signs of the stores lining the station carpark.

I stared at one of the signs. I'd promised Jian I'd keep away from the booze. I smiled, bitter. I'd said I'd be back, too; I'd said I'd take care of everything. I'd said a whole lot of bullshit that we both wanted to hear, and desperately wanted to believe.

I flipped my collar and walked through the grey rain, towards the flickering neon lights.

23

I threw the bloody pliers and half-empty bottle of cheap rice whisky onto the passenger seat. I stowed the 107 in the boot, in the space where the spare tyre normally went, and covered it over with thin carpet. My pistol was in my shoulder holster, under my jacket. I locked the car, though with the driver's side window a mess of cracks it wasn't going to take a master criminal to get inside. It was late afternoon, but still hot out, the air thick with humidity.

I hobbled across the parking lot towards the bar. A red sign engraved in thick black plasteel above the door said: *The Mildred Pierce*. A sign in English meant that mainly immigrant workers drank there: Filipinos, Sri Lankans, Australians, maybe some dregs from Europe. Looked less of a dive than the average immigrant bar, though – the green exterior fresh-painted, the large windows all intact, the sign only slightly faded.

I winced as I took the two steps up to the door and pushed through. The room was clean, with dark faux-wood everything, though well-lit by the large windows. It smelled of cigarettes and fresh beer. A middle-aged Chinese bloke with a shaved head, thick at the stomach and neck, stood behind the bar, wiping down an already gleaming bar top. Music was playing, though not too loud:

some guy with an English accent wailing against a hard, heavy beat and hyperkinetic guitar.

The barman came over when I sat at the bar. I said: "Maker's Mark, Australian beer, soy chicken wings with hot sauce. You got all that?"

He answered by giving me an Australian beer, a Maker's Mark, and ten minutes later, a sizzling bowl of soy chicken wings.

I raised an eyebrow when the wings came. They looked edible. I nodded at the barman. He ignored me and went back to wiping the bar.

I decided it was my kinda joint.

A slender Thai guy two seats down was holding a gin and cigarette in one hand. He showed a lot of teeth, and said in his own language: "[Saw you walk in. What happened to your feet?]"

"I kicked the shit out of someone who asked too many questions."

The Thai guy kept smiling and moved to one of the booths out of my eyesight.

The soy chicken wings were crisp and tasty. I ordered a second bowl and worked through my bourbon and beers. The tai screen above the bar was showing some regional MMA matches. I wasn't happy, as such, but I was comfortable. The drink felt fine and the place felt right. Like an old haunt. The bar started to fill up around dusk and was packed an hour after that. A couple of women sat down next to me: an Eastern European and a Filipino, tight tops, shining hair, exaggerated laughter. I guess they were pretty, but it'd been a long time since I'd thought about that kind of thing.

I found myself looking at the Filipino woman's nails. Each set of five fingernails was intricately decorated with a royal flush, hearts on one hand, diamonds on the other. I wondered at the sort of woman who would spend so much time on such gaudy little accoutrements. All day on those things, just to linger in dingy bars all evening trying to attract men who would never even notice.

The woman caught me staring at her. She stared back.

I went back to watching the tai screen. They returned to their conversation. I clenched my jaw at the strange sentiments I was feeling; when they didn't go away I ordered another bourbon and beer.

Pretty soon the women got that attention. It was from a big guy, bigger than me even. His accent was mashed-up British, the way he moved suggested an endoskeleton, maybe even Chinese built; the pair of bronze knuckledusters hanging from his belt produced by some tough guy fantasy. The cashed-up thug wasn't taking no for an answer from the two women, though that was the only answer they were giving him. I was more concerned with catching the bartender's eye, when memories flashed of all the times some gorilla had tried to pick me up at a bar. Breathing all over my neck, placing an iron-hard grip around my slender upper arm and leaving it there, insisting on buying me a drink.

"You heard her, arsehole, back off." I found myself talking and on my feet, two things I hadn't been planning on doing that evening.

The British guy squared his shoulders and turned to me. Half a head taller than I, unshaven, breath like an open grave. "These bitches are mine, ya fackin cunt."

I slapped him. It sounded like a two-by-four hitting a side of beef. His eyes made circles and he took a step back with the blow. Everyone in the place was watching now. The barman helpfully turned the sound on the tai screen down.

I said: "I *hate* that word."

I had enough time to realise Jian's memories were driving me before he came back swinging.

My mobility wasn't so good, what with my feet and all, but he was more power than art. While he was fast and smooth and clearly jacked up on top-of-the-line hardware and software, he didn't have anything else bar those things.

I blocked or ducked most of what he threw, though as I backed away and we circled I felt blood trickle from my nose. Didn't matter. Six seconds of him swinging and I had his number. He came in with a big overhand right, like I knew he would; I ducked and counter-punched, two left jabs into his ribs, a right uppercut to his jaw. His head snapped back and he staggered a little.

I waited for him to refocus on me. It took a while.

I said: "Really? All dressed up in three-hundred pounds of juiced muscle, and you don't even know how to dance?"

He swore at me, but his eyes were already showing defeat.

I pointed at his waist with my chin. "Put 'em on."

He stared blankly, not understanding what I was saying.

"Your knuckledusters, mate. Put 'em on."

His fingers went to the big brass knuckles at his waist. His eyes said he didn't believe.

I backed up a couple of steps, give him space to get his weapons out.

"Actually," said a voice, off to my left. "Do as the scarred man says. Put them on."

When I fought it was with tunnel vision, so I never saw much else of what was going on. I glanced quickly around the room. A circle of patrons had formed. The man speaking was at the front of the crowd, a Filipino smiling a big smile.

The big guy looked over at the boss man as well, then back at me. His pride was hurt enough for him to forget how outmatched he was. He put on the knuckles. Fat letters jutted out of each: 'JONNY' on his right hand and 'BRASS' on his left.

I laughed, genuine. "You poor bastard. I am going to enjoy this."

He came hard. His pride helped him remember a bit of technique.

It wasn't enough. I got him off balance with a trip he wasn't expecting then slipped in behind as he tried to right himself. I threw the hardest punches I could, right-handed, big wind-up: kidney, kidney, ribs. The first two he yelled in pain, the third an audible *crack*. I spun him around and gave him a left-cross, his eyes rolled up in his head and he fell back into the circle of patrons. They parted like he was diseased, and he hit the floor.

I looked around to see if anyone else wanted a little, as well. None did. Silent, save the commentators on the televised MMA match, exclaiming quietly in the background.

I went back to the bar.

The European woman was looking at me, eyes wide. Her Filipina friend was less impressed. She said with an American accent: "Thanks and all that. We're just here for a drink, buddy."

I said: "Love your nails," and turned to face the room, bourbon in hand. Everyone was moving back to their seats now, save six guys, including the Filipino.

They walked over to me.

I pulled my gun.

The Filipino was out front. He was smiling a smile that was three-quarters genuine, his hand up in the air signalling *take it easy, take it easy*. In his other hand he held my cap, Queen of Spades shining under the lights. It'd been knocked off in the fight. Those with him kept their hands away from their weapons.

The Filipino man passed me my hat, I took it. He stood a couple of metres away. He had thick eyebrows and a thick stomach, heavy gold rings on his knuckles. He nodded his head upwards in greeting and said: "I didn't think a man who drives a Nissan Tomorrow could punch so hard."

His people laughed a little. I sipped my bourbon and slipped my gun back in its holster.

"Where you from?" he asked.

"Couple of places."

"Macau?"

I looked at him, sharp. He smiled back, eyes flicking over my left shoulder, at the barman, at my gun, back to me. Moving moving, his eyes never stayed still, perpetual motion within the orbits. I had this strange feeling of déjà vu.

"Macau is a tough town," he continued, using the silence I'd given him. "Ever work security?"

"Nah," I said.

"Ha." He stuck a thumb over his shoulder, in the direction of the big man bleeding on the floor. "Really?"

"Yeah," I replied, face blank. "Just as an enforcer, hitman, bootlegger, armed robber, torturer, arsonist, wheelman, racketeer, and recall-drone."

He nodded, flickering eyes straying to the women at the bar. "And feminist."

I smiled a little and finished my bourbon.

"The name's Happy Jhun. What's yours?"

I hesitated.

He seemed to take that as an answer, nodding and smiling. "Looking for work?"

"Is it all going to be as easy as this?"

Jhun lost his smile for a moment. "No. No, for me the work is not like this. For me the work is real."

"I'll need an advance." I nodded over my shoulder, at the bald barman. "Lest Chuckles here takes umbrage at my not having a yuan on me for the bill."

Jhun nodded at the barman, who seemed satisfied by the gesture. Jhun passed me a gold hipflask. "So it is settled, then."

I took a shot. It was a smooth, expensive rum. I decided I liked this guy. I said: "Yeah."

Jhun turned to the group. "This man here. Actually, let's call him Three Scars." He smiled a little. "Three Scars Mildred. After the place we found him."

"Pierce."

Jhun turned to me, feigning surprise. "Huh?"

"Three Scars Pierce is fine."

"I thought you were a feminist."

"That's just a hobby. My profession is breaking the legs of people who piss me off."

Jhun kept smiling and turned back to his people, eyes flicking. "Three Scars Pierce is my third-in-command now." He pointed at a hard-eyed Chinese woman with a bionic right arm of stripped-down black titanium. "Jackson Street Amy is the new number two."

She glanced at me then nodded at Jhun.

I pointed at the British guy on the ground, who'd started moaning himself conscious. "That was your number two?"

"He was," said Jhun. "Actually, you do me favour. I always suspect this one only tough for the easy fights, you know? Come."

I joined Jhun and his crew at their tables.

They were mostly small-time tough guys. None of them held themselves right, none of them were ready to fight. Not in the right way, anyway. All were working on steel teeth or basketball-sized shoulders or ostentatious weaponry.

One guy even had a battleaxe. I thought it was some sort of joke at first, but the edges of the double-blade had a nano-sharpened sparkle, and the wild-eyed, heavily bearded American lugging it around didn't come across as the joking type. He called himself The Axe and liked to talk about axes and hitting people with axes.

Of the crew only two looked serious. The first was Jackson Street Amy. She had a well-maintained machine gun sitting next to her on the seat. She didn't speak much, but when she did it was Mandarin with a Taiwanese accent. A mercenary, I supposed, wandering the Earth after the destruction of her homeland. Everyone called her Jackson. She sat there expressionless most of the night, but when the barbarian with the axe spilled a drink on her feet, she gave him a look that made him mumble apologies under his breath and change seats.

The second was a Mongolian. He was only as wide as the side of a barn and as talkative as a brick. He looked like a sumo wrestler and moved like a ballerina. Under all that flesh he'd be packing some serious implants. His eyes were glinting slits between fat eyelids; he didn't seem to much like anyone at the table. He liked eating and drinking though, and as the night wore on the vodka loosened his tongue enough to do some throat singing. A strange, ethereal noise a human shouldn't be able to make, a noise that came from everywhere and nowhere at once. His name was Sukhbaatar. Everyone called him Sukhie.

Of the rest there was a large Japanese guy called Big Tuna, and a distracted ice-nine addict from Vietnam called Billie, who talked a lot or not at all. She wore a large, silver six-shooter on her thigh and sported two of the most bloodshot eyes I'd ever seen. Last was Abbadabba, a Nigerian with scarified tissue on his cheeks and hands big enough to choke a horse.

As the night wore on I found myself with a belly full of good food, and enough whiskey in me not to feel my feet anymore. They'd pulled up couple of tables to a booth and the crew were enjoying themselves, drinking hard and telling war stories. I was in the booth with Jhun.

He leaned in close, ever-moving eyes stuck on my face. "Why you running?"

"Who says I'm running?"

"You take my offer very quick, Mister Pierce. Didn't ask me where we were going, where the work is, nothing like this."

"In my experience the work is all the same, everywhere. We're sitting in a bar in the last town before the Vietnam border, so I know where you're going. Running services for the Chinese occupiers on R and R." I lit a cigarette, blew the smoke upwards. "What's your crew do? Drugs?"

The Filipino shook his head, eyes now back to his people, the room. "Casino security."

I nodded.

"I see you like this."

"Yeah," I replied. "I don't mind a game of cards."

"There will be much time for cards." Jhun pursed his lips. "This town we're going to. Actually…" He trailed off, replacing the end of the sentence with a chug from his drink.

"Actually?"

"Actually, it is not like other casino towns, tourist towns, not like them."

"What's it like then?"

The evening had long gone and now we were on the other side of midnight, drinking through to dawn. It was dark in the bar, smoke-filled, so the thing that stood out about Jhun was his eyes, shining along with the glass he held in his hand. "Strange. Like living in a memory, not like this—" he indicated the room around us with his eyes, "—this place is real. Back where we go, is not so real." He looked at me then. "More dangerous than the real world. Stay with your crew. Sleep in the casino, nowhere else."

"What happens if I don't?"

"Maybe you end up in someone else's dream, Mister Pierce."

He wouldn't give me anymore after that, and I didn't push him too hard on it. Macau was the toughest town in all Asia. If I could handle that, I could handle some tourist trap in northern Vietnam for Chinese soldiers and superannuated Europeans looking to squander the last hard currency of that dead civilisation.

Jhun's eyes were on me again. He grabbed my forearm. "Actually, Pierce, it doesn't matter how tough you think you are. Doesn't matter how hard the place you're from. Stick with your crew. Don't mix with anyone outside it. Sleep in the casino. Got me?"

He was a sharp man, Jhun. He was right that I was too eager to accept his offer; but it hadn't escaped my attention that he was pretty eager to make it. I couldn't quite see that angle, I couldn't see why he wanted someone he didn't know as his third-in-command. That needed to be thought on.

I shrugged his hand from my arm and said nothing. He smiled and returned his roaming gaze to the room.

24

Your name is Endel Ebbinghaus. You are travelling under the alias 'Three Scars' Pierce.

It's Tuesday, 27 September, 2101. 1100 hours.

You're in Xuan Tang Resort, North Vietnam. You work casino security for a man called Happy Jhun.

You had a barman send your toenails to Inner Mongolia.

This is your sixth day on the job.

I groaned and rolled over in bed. I read the on-retina message twice, trying to get my mind around it. As my eyes flicked over the message I fumbled at the side table, knocked an empty glass onto the carpet, then found my cigarettes. I tapped one out.

Also on-retina a little icon flashed, of a lock. There was something encrypted, in my exo-memory. Something that couldn't be read if my feed was hacked or my memory pin removed. Only a request, matching my voice print, while the pin was in the cochlear implant, would decode the message. I had a feeling I didn't want to read what was in there right then, and smoked my cigarette instead.

I blew clouds of smoke at the ceiling for a time before trying to sit up. My head spun and I groaned again, but I managed the journey.

I was in a plush hotel room. The bed alone was larger than most of the rooms I'd stayed in over that past couple of weeks. Most of the wall opposite comprised of a state-of-the-art tai screen. The closed curtains were deep blue and expensive looking; one door opened to a marble-clad bathroom while the other opened to a large living area with an automated kitchenette, a wet bar, and a sectional couch my girls would have spent all day running back and forth over.

The thought of Weici and Kylie made my chest hurt, cut through my morning fugue.

I replaced the thought with talk, fingertipping my neural implant. "What's the name of this hotel again?"

"The Golden Dragon," my c-glyph whispered, direct into my ear.

"Add that to my reminder when I wake up."

"Yes, Mister Pierce."

"Do I have to be somewhere?"

"For what purpose, Mister Pierce?"

"For work."

"You have no specific starting time. Rather, you are considered on-call at all times. When not directly engaged in work prescribed by Happy Jhun, you are expected to spend your time in the casino. While in the casino, you are to be alert for suspicious activity, and are to report the presence of the casino's competitors in Xuan Tang." The c-glyph had an accent-less voice with all the personality of a metronome. Listening to it wasn't helping me wake up.

"Well," I said. "I've decided to watch for suspicious activity here in my living room. Have the kitchens send me up two double espressos and some fried eggs on toast."

"Right away, Mister Pierce."

I was standing at the window finishing my second espresso when someone knocked at the door. I was on the thirty-fourth floor of fifty. The Chinese were superstitious about the number four – and gamblers are the most superstitious creatures of all – so floors with a four were stuffed with foreigners with different sets of superstitions. I was up higher than anything else the town had to offer. The sun was out, reminding anyone who cared to look how drab a tourist trap looks in the light of day. The raw wash of daylight bleaching out the promise of sex and vitality that seemed so assured the evening before.

Now I was waking up the feeling came back to me: something being not quite right. Askew. I couldn't shake it since I'd arrived. There were a lot of military police in town. Of the score or so I'd seen, most wore gold watches and rings, and stood idle while fat tourists and Chinese military officers walked by.

None of that was strange. What was strange is that I hadn't seen them shaking anyone down, in the bars, the brothels, the casino, patrons doing all types of illegal right in front of them. When I asked Jhun if they were getting kickbacks for leaving tourists be, Jhun stopped smiling and said that this is the kind of place where you didn't ask those sorts of questions.

Jhun's reaction was strange. Police being on the take wasn't a big deal; it was the price of doing business in a town like this. So his response didn't fit, and nor did anything in the rest of the joint. I never saw a place in town more than a quarter-full, and I never found a business where the staff didn't treat what few customers they had like shit. Like the MPs, they had no hustle. The booze they served was cheap, the food ordinary, the prices either too cheap or too expensive.

The previous afternoon I'd gone out for breakfast at a café near the casino. The place was deserted, even of employees. When I went behind the counter to make myself some coffee, the surly Chinese manager appeared from nowhere and told me to piss off. I slapped the sneer off his mouth, of course, but that didn't make me feel much better. As I walked out of the place I just couldn't shake the disquiet that had settled on me ever since coming to town.

The only spot with good staff and good service was the casino. The only place where the bars were busy, everything worked, and all the staff hot-footed it. Three floors of table games, two floors of bars, one floor for the massage parlours: always jumping. A lot of security – solid men and women in blue suits emblazoned with the hotel's curling dragon insignia – keeping order.

I wasn't with regular security. My job was apparently to go with Happy to meetings in other parts of town and eyeball the muscle from the other crews: the red-light district, the bars, and the military police.

Hadn't had to sink fist into flesh since I'd arrived. That bothered me, too.

So the knock at the door came and I picked up my gun, more out of habit than concern. "Yeah?"

"It's The Axe," said a man with a deep, American voice.

I whispered to my c-glyph: "Verify voice print."

A pause and then: *Verified. Voice pattern matches The Axe.*

I unlocked and unchained the door. The Axe nodded at me and entered. Faded denim jacket with fur collar, cowboy hat, and steel-pointed boots. He had his ridiculous axe strapped to his back and was carrying a pump-action shotgun in one hand, resting it on his shoulder. His thick beard had been tied off with a blue band, just below his chin. After some initial aggravation towards me, The Axe had decided he was going to be my protégé. There were whispers among the casino crew that I was a big-time enforcer for a big-time gangster in a big-time town. That impressed him. There was also the matter of The Axe apparently idolising Jonny Brass, right up until the point I'd broken the man's jaw.

The Axe nodded at my empty breakfast tray and untouched glass of brandy as though that contained some essential lesson, and said he had to take a leak.

When he came out he jabbed a thumb over his shoulder and said: "What happened to your mirror?"

"Huh."

"Broke."

"Oh," I said, after a long pause. "We all gotta punch a mirror every now and again. Gangster therapy. Now, what's up?"

The Axe collected his thoughts. "Ah. Meeting."

"The Four again?"

"No. Just Three-Iron. He's complaining about all the business the Golden Dragon is taking away from them."

"They stop serving watered-down drinks from dead-eyed waitresses, might help a little."

"Yeah," The Axe said, smiling. "And you're a gangster who knows his drinks, right Scars?"

I strapped on my gun holster, face blank.

He said: "Drink hard, fight hard, *fuck* hard – that's my motto."

I put on my black cap and ran my hand through my short beard, brushing out the crumbs.

The Axe stopped smiling and pretended to find the view interesting while he waited. I grabbed my leather jacket. As I shrugged it on I asked: "How much time do we have?"

"A little, man. Was going to suggest some drinks down at the mezzanine bar first."

"I got a better idea."

He looked interested. "Yeah?"

"Exo-memory upgrade."

He looked a lot less interested. "Oh."

"Any Omissioners in town? Must be – the average age of tourist here is sixty."

"Yeah man," he said. "I know a guy. But, man…"

"But what?"

"You really want to remember the shit you get up to?"

I shrugged. "There's a first time for everything."

25

The town's setup was simple: a main road, along which sat the bars, restaurants, cafés, and a couple of hotels. At the head of the street, at a T-intersection, was the Golden Dragon, perched like a vulture gazing down over everything. Though in this case it didn't have to do any work: the carcasses came to it. Each street back from the main got seedier, all the way to the last, Dazhalan Lane, which served as the red-light district. Up behind it all, set on a picturesque green ridge, were the luxury long-term apartments. I never saw many lights on in those; never saw many vehicles crawling over the high roads, back there.

Behind that, lush jungle for three or four kilometres. Then razor wire, electric fences, and more razor wire, circumscribing the entire town. A ring cleared of jungle, scorched earth, two hundred metres wide on the other side of the wire. A free-fire zone that anything – animal, vegetable, or mineral – entering would result in a fusillade of nano-hardened projectiles to puncture and pierce and shatter. There were seismic sensors in the ground to make sure nothing burrowed underneath and air defence systems to stop anything flying over the top. Drones were the particular concern, captured by the Viet Minh and repurposed to hunt for Chinese targets. Repurposed was the usual explanation anyway; a number of Chinese news channels ran outraged opinion feeds noting that the drones appeared to have components made in the Former United States.

All just a precaution, this far north. This area had been *pacified*, according to the Chinese government. Perfectly safe for tourists, they said, certainly safer than the crime-ridden, destitute European cities; safer than the burning protest fires that punctuated South America, beacons of social upheaval in that roiling continent. The Chinese did have a point, come to think of it.

Halfway down the main drag, one street back, was the memory business. The only English in a mess of Chinese ideography was a red neon sign over the door that said: *Memento*. Inside was a stereotype of a stereotype. Frosted glass doors inscribed with a large double happiness symbol opening into a gloomy, incense-marinated wood-panelled room. The panelling was etched with long, thin dragons with large, insane eyes; red lanterns hung from the ceiling; discordant cymbals played somewhere off-camera. The Axe waited while I was led down a dark corridor to a treatment room very similar to the reception room, albeit with added gold statues of Buddhas and Maos and other historical figures philosophically opposed to gold statues and material accumulation.

An ancient Chinese man watched me enter in silence. He wore a red and black silk robe, his hands hidden in the sleeve of the arm opposite, and a Mandarin hat. A lined old face, wisp of a grey beard hanging to his chin, quiet intelligence shining out from between tight eyelids. If you went on the freewave and asked for a picture of a Chinese Omissioner, this guy would come back as the number one stock image.

Like everything else in Xuan Tang, the place and the man felt askew. I couldn't help but shake the feeling that the business was a joke at the tourist's expense, and wonder if the Omissioner was laughing on the other side of that impenetrable mask of weathered, lined skin and studied intelligence. I asked for the exo-ma upgrade, he uttered some ancient wisdom in Mandarin with an accent so strange that I couldn't quite figure the region.

For all that, the Omissioner knew his stuff. He laid me down on the Kandel-Yu machine. Looked kinda like a dentist's chair with a green neon halo, one that he pulled carefully down over my head. Then the old bloke downloaded the exo-ma program with no headaches, no memory static, no confusion. I was in and out in an hour.

26

The meet between the casino and bar crews was in a place called Ray Quan, a poorly lit café two streets behind Memento. Happy Jhun and the head of the bar crew, Jacky 'Three-Iron' Pham, were sitting at a table alone in one of the darker corners of the joint. Pham liked expensive pin-striped suits and never took his white homburg off his head. He smoked long, thin cigarettes that he'd light with an ornate platinum lighter featuring a bas-relief golden bear on the side. What some mistook for laziness in Three-Iron was actually an economy of motion: no word, gesture, or glance was surplus to requirements.

The rest of us sat towards the front, facing each other. The Bar Crew were all Southern Chinese, Yunnan Province in the main. They were rumoured to have military links and I'd have been surprised if it were otherwise. There were five of them here, in various poses of feigned nonchalance at the tables, watching us. They all wore red bandanas. Gangsters often liked to play dress-up. My new exo-ma placed the names of the gangsters on-retina, the glowing script floated above the heads of the men opposite: 'Two Points'; Dong 'Flat Nose' Wang; Kang 'Red Belly' Zhou; 'Wooden Rabbit'; and Quan 'Cloudy' Tseng.

It was refreshing to be able to remember names, places,

conversations again. With the exo-ma loaded, I could ask my cochlear implant to give me all these types of details of the men in the room with me. It could tell me what other people had said about them as well, rumours about where they liked to drink, or brothel they liked to frequent. I could have glimpsed one of these guys out of the corner of my eye on the street a week before, never registering it consciously, and yet have that data on the c-glyph waiting to be accessed. The exo-ma could take all these pieces of information and add them all together, making a rough profile of the individual. And that was just a basic feature.

Two Points was slurping down a bowl of pho, Red Belly was eating a tempeh sandwich with a knife and fork. The rest were smoking cigarettes, orange points in the gloom.

There were only three of us against their five, which I didn't like so well. Billie was our third. Like most of her countrywomen she didn't much like the Chinese, so she was uncharacteristically alert, hand twitching, throwing glares full of venom. I had The Axe sit three tables away, shotgun across his lap. Give the bar crew two different targets, different angles if things got messy.

Jhun and Three-Iron were getting animated, the former occasionally raising his voice. They were speaking in Mandarin; I caught pieces of it in translation—

"[…I can keep them for as long as I please…]" and "[…lower it if you…]" and "[…only so much longer…]"

—until Three-Iron let his eyes drift over the room before telling Jhun to be quiet.

I had a notion.

The guy eating the sandwich, Red Belly, was making a lot of noise: *chomp chomp chomp*, then *smack smack smack* with his lips. Short hair, black tank-top, large tattoos of naked women and skulls on his shoulders.

"You," I said, pointing to the sloppy eater. Red Belly glanced up, irritated, from under his brow. "You a dog?" I asked, loud in the still of the room.

His face reddened.

"The disgusting noise you make, eating that sandwich. Sounds like a dog eating its own vomit."

Everyone was surprised by that, including Axe and Billie. The Bar crew looked at each other, then to the sandwich eater. Red Belly paused for a moment, mid-chew, then resumed: *smack smack smack*, staring me in the face.

I stood, gripping the edge of the hard plasteel chair I was sitting on. It was heavy enough. I hurled it overhanded.

The sandwich guy had time to look surprised before the chair hit him. Something crunched and he fell and stayed down. I had my pistol on the rest before they'd even moved.

One of the gangsters – Flat Nose – reached for his gun. I said: "*Ah-ahh*." He stopped reaching.

Billie had her pistol out. The Axe fumbled with his shotgun for a long ten seconds before he finally pointed it in the right direction.

"[What is this?]", said Three-Iron, still sitting, still placid, looking over at Jhun.

Jhun was looking at me, not smiling, when two garishly clad Chinese tourists chose that moment to enter. They stood stock-still in the dusk and heat of the café, a couple with loud shirts and conical bamboo hats of the type Vietnamese farmers wore, sold on every corner here. The tourists were middle aged, with good skin and white teeth. They held hands.

The door closed with a slow creak behind them.

"Um," one said, looking at everything but trying not to look at anything in the room. "[We're just here for cocktails,]" and then, as thought that weren't enough information. "[Daiquiris.]"

His faced reddened as he spoke and his partner rolled her eyes at him.

144

"They water the drinks at this dump," I said. "Try the casino. The mango daiquiris are excellent."

They bobbed their heads up and down in enthusiastic thanks as they backed out. The door creaked shut and silence returned to the room, save the thug on the floor groaning.

"[Let's kill them,]" said Billie, eyes alight. "[Kill these Chinese dogs and take over the bar district.]"

Three-Iron was still looking at Happy Jhun. He blew out a languorous cloud of smoke and said: "[Get your people under control.]"

Jhun's eyes flicked around the room, *flick flick flick*, to me, to Billie, to the red lampshades, to the broken chair on the floor, then back to me. He smiled. "Billie, now put down the gun. Actually, this is simple misunderstanding." His eyes flickered on me for more than a moment. "Is that not right, Mister Pierce?"

"That's right." I agreed. "I mistook Three-Iron's people for a real crew. But I realise my mistake now. They're just a bunch of fucking amateurs who couldn't hold a piece of ground or protect their boss, in a real town."

Three-Iron's eyes finally drifted from Jhun, coming to rest on me.

"So why we giving a superannuated slug like you a break here, Three-Iron?" I asked. His men were frozen, but their faces burned with seven shades of rage. Red Belly was on one knee, blood coating the lower half of his face from a broken nose.

They waited on their boss.

Something stilled about Three-Iron. Light reflected off the immaculate white of his homburg, his eyes in shadow. "[When I was last in a bar in Shanghai, a man spilled his drink on my shoes and did not apologise. Instead he insulted my suit and laughed in my face. I had slivers of bamboo hammered under his fingernails and into his feet. If you are careful and experienced, the bamboo will begin to grow from the wounds. We had him in a tiger chair for three weeks while the bamboo grew. Each day he begged and apologised. By then it was all too late.]"

If the room had been quiet before, it was dead silent after that. Jhun's eyes flicked between me and the red bandanas.

"He had a point," I said. "With that suit you look like the wannabe boss of a two-pig village in buttfuck Mongolia."

Three-Iron's eyes widened. Jhun held his hands up. "Actually, I think our negotiations are over for this day." He backed away from Three-Iron, hands where they could be seen. The Axe started to follow him out, then paused as Billie and I stayed, our weapons still drawn.

"Come on, man," whispered The Axe.

Billie's eyes flicked over to mine. I made a thin line with my mouth and let the barrel of my gun rise until it pointed at the corner of the roof.

Billie looked disappointed, but walked out all the same. I backed out last, Three-Iron's eyes shining as he watched me leave.

We got in the car. Jhun turned to me. He wasn't smiling; his eyes were locked on mine. "Mister Pierce. Why are you trying to fuck me?"

I lit a cigarette.

"Actually, not just me. You want to fuck everyone. A war, I think, you want to start."

"You'd know it," I said around my cigarette, "if I went to war."

"Another tough-guy line. You're full of them, I see. Now: why you try to start a war?"

The Axe and Billie were sitting opposite on a black leather bench-set, watching us.

"I said it all in the café, Jhun: they're weak. Lazy. Unprepared. We could take them, easily. We should take them."

Billie nodded. Jhun looked at me for another moment, then

146

smiled. He settled back in his seat, eyes ranging. "It doesn't work like that here, Mister Pierce."

It was my turn to look at him. "Then how does it work?"

He glanced at Billie and Axe, then back out the window. The sun was high overhead, the streets deserted. "Actually, we find it better to cooperate. More profitable."

When I said nothing, Jhun filled the silence. "Why do you care how business is done? Since when does a hard man care about where his money comes from?"

The Axe and Billie looked to me for an answer. I gave them none.

Jhun sighed. "Now I will have to make this right. Now Three-Iron has leverage. This is a thing I do not like."

I looked out through tinted glass at the crisp, new neon signs along the gleaming façade of the main street. At the bars with new furnishings, used occasionally by the hired thuglings of the four factions, and rarely by actual customers. Bars fitted out with new cleansteel pipes that leaked, with top-of-the-line cooling systems that failed during the hottest hours; that served expensive drinks in dirty glasses.

I looked out over a mirage and considered my next steps.

27

I was at the main bar at the Golden Dragon working on another drink. It'd been quiet since I'd messed with the bar crew, and I didn't like that. The casino had been mostly quiet, as well.

Some Chinese officers had got in a fight over how one had sung 'My Way' at the karaoke joint up on the fourth floor. The fight spread to officers representing different army groups, and the regular casino security was overwhelmed. The opportunity to crack the heads of some officers was a rare one and I had some fun. Not as much as Billie, though, who set about them with a force rod on full charge. In all the time I'd know her before she died, I only saw her laugh once, and that was while she was plunging a blue-crackling rod into the groin of a screaming Chinese colonel.

That was the most exciting thing to happen in a week. So I sat up at the bar on the mezzanine, dissatisfied, watching the soccer-field-sized gambling floor below. It was busy as usual, patrons spewing their chips over tables of Sic Bo and blackjack. Swarms of Chinese tourists from the mainland, smatterings of Chinese military officers – Xuan Tang was an *officer-only* R and R retreat – and a handful of Europeans sweating over the turn of the card at the blackjack tables. Up on the stage alongside the casino floor were a trio of shapely white women swinging burlesque around golden poles. Like any casino filled with real gamblers, no-one looked up at them.

"What the fuck am I doing here?" I mumbled, to myself.

A lock icon flashed on-retina, at the corner of my vision. Some secret, hidden, that right then I couldn't remember. I sighed. "Oh. Right. Better not be fucken stupid."

I was turned on my bar stool looking out, elbow on the bar top, trying to decide between drinking at the bar or drinking at a poker game when a thin Chinese gentleman sat down next to me. Steel-rimmed glasses, a grey flat cap he took off as he sat down, wearing an old but good-quality grey suit. His face was too kindly to be in a casino.

He nodded at me, expectant. I ignored him. He cleared his throat, changed his mind about talking, changed it again and said in perfect English: "Quite a view from up here."

I drank.

He cleared his throat again and said: "Have you been staying here long? At the casino I mean, not the bar." He tried to smile.

I was intending to ignore him until he left me alone, but he reminded me a little of Jian's father. I'd never met the man, but the spark of her memory in me did. So I said: "Couple of weeks."

"Longer than most."

"Is that so?"

"I'm forgetting myself." He held out his hand. "Professor Samuel Kam Ching. Pleased to meet you."

I hesitated and then shook it. "Three Scars Pierce. Don't know if I've ever met a professor before, not one who felt the need to work it into an introduction, anyway."

He smiled briefly and pushed the frames of his glasses back up his nose. "Nerves, I suppose. You've a rather raw edge to you, Mister Pierce, and thus I feel the urge to give more information than I would otherwise. Though having noted that, a man who introduces himself as 'Three Scars' ought not to give too much mind to something as humdrum as 'Professor'."

I smiled at that and finished my drink. I signalled *two* to the barman.

"I've been here a few days now," he said.

"Sure. This town's a real peach."

"Whiskey sour?" he asked when the drinks arrived.

"You want to drink with me or not?"

The professor shrugged with his eyebrows and took an experimental sip. He nodded and raised his glass to me.

I said: "Yeah. The best sour in town."

"To be honest, I'm here looking for a friend."

"Not that sort of town, unless you're talking about fucking. And if you've come to me looking for that, all you'll find is a swan-dive off that mezzanine."

"No," he said reddening at the thought. He hesitated, lips parted for a moment. "A true friend, a good friend from the University of Hong Kong. He'd been reading up all about the buzz, the *hullabaloo* about this place, and decided he was going to holiday here. He's a widower now, you see, gone these past five years, and he wanted to spread his wings a little, as they say."

"The only buzz you're going to get from this place is the one you're holding in your hand."

He nodded, but not at what I had said. I finished my drink.

"Tell me, Mister Pierce, does anything seem strange here, to you?"

Finally, I turned to face him. He flinched a little. "There a particular reason you decided to talk to me, Professor?"

His mouth tried a couple of different positions while he pushed his glasses back up his nose. "Desperation, I suppose. I've been to the police, you see, and they say they are not babysitters, that the tourists here come and go as they please, and they don't keep tabs on that sort of thing."

"You're desperate," I said, "but that's not all of it."

The professor drank his whiskey sour. Either the booze or nervousness was making him go red. "I saw you the other night. Beat up those men that were causing trouble. Three of them, at the poker tables, all big. You – ah – you went through them like they weren't even there."

I made a dismissive motion with my hand. "And?"

"And I'd like to hire you to help me find my friend. And furthermore—" He paused, cleared his throat. "Ensure nothing happens to me."

"I've already got a job."

"No doubt." He indicated the bustling bar with his glass. "A man of your talents in a place like this – no doubt at all. Tell me, Mister Pierce, is there a clause against freelancing in your current employment contract?"

I leaned back against the bar, considering, while I lit a cigarette. "No."

"Well then…" He gave me this look of *hope*. The kind of look that always stank of weakness, the kind that made me want to reach over and slap the man.

"Don't give me half a story, Professor. My aim tonight is to sit in this chair and drink until security has to help me find my room. I got plenty of time to listen."

His face broke into relief and gratitude, and I had to grip glass and tighten teeth to restrain myself.

The Professor pushed his glasses back up his nose and then started. "My friend's name is Henry Yun, also a *professor*." Small smile. "We've known each other for thirty years now, Henry and I. He was a lost soul, in many ways, after his wife died. Sunken, as though some of the life had gone from him; distant, as though he was already halfway out of this world and heading towards the next. Then he started talking about what the press was saying about

151

Xuân Tăng, as a place to get away and reinvigorate, to be free of
the gloom and the rains of Hong Kong."

I held up a hand. "That's the second time you said that. What
press?"

The professor looked surprised. "You haven't heard?" I gestured
for him to continue. He said: "Well, it's become quite popular on
social feeds, especially with a more mature, well-heeled demographic.
So Henry went and it seemed, at first, like it was exactly what he
needed. He acquired a new Vietnamese girlfriend, got himself a
nano-cleanse – he looked twenty years younger. He seemed to
spend a lot of time around the pool with a drink in one hand and
his attractive young lady friend in the other. He even had videos
up on his Ego feed, one dancing very badly at some nightclub here,
another direct-to-camera saying he was having the time of his life.
And, you know, he *looked* to be having the time of his life."

"The problem?" I asked, in between a drag on my cigarette and
an exhalation of smoke.

"The problem is I didn't believe a word of it. While I could
hesitantly accept he'd find himself a younger woman, I certainly
don't believe he'd be so brazen about it. I can believe he needed
this," he waved a glass at the room, "to break out of the cloistered
world of the academy and do something wild. But I couldn't believe
he'd go the route of every other stereotypical older, wealthier
Chinese male. He is one of the most ethical men I have ever met,
and whatever the poison he needed to get out of his system, and
whatever sensations he sought – if merely to remind him he was
alive – I just don't believe the way it was presented on the freewave.
Everything seemed slightly awry. We talked regularly via c-feed
and had lengthy discussions via email – he was old-fashioned that
way – but at some point our conversations seemed to switch to
something pro-forma. Like he was going through the motions."

"You married, Professor?"

"I… what?" he asked, his concentration broken.

"You married?"

His default smile disappeared. "I'm not some lonely, doddering old man, Mister Pierce. I'm the current chair of the Faculty of Architecture at one of the world's most prestigious universities."

"One thing has nothing to do with the other, mate. Big brain or not, everyone gets lonely."

The professor took a slug from his drink. Whatever annoyance he had now passed as he looked down into the glass. He put it down on the bar and resumed the identity of the kindly mentor he'd chosen to inhabit some decade past. "When I asked you if you've noticed anything strange here, you didn't answer me."

I tapped my cigarette on a nearby ashtray. "Keep talking."

"This town, it looks like the brochures, on the surface anyway. But it's dead inside. There are hardly any locals and no local culture—"

"That's what military occupation is, Professor."

"Yes," he said, nodding. "But it's more than that. There's no depth to the human interactions. When I speak to people – the police or a proprietor – they look right through me, as though I barely exist, or some sort of apparition. I've gone to all the places that Henry posted on his Ego feed, the discos and the bars, the cafés, that shooting range out at the edge of town – they all look the same, but they *aren't* the same place. There's no life in them, just staff staring into space and customers sitting around, dully surprised, like they are waiting for something to happen. You know those old movies, those westerns, where they're walking down the dusty main street through a small town, but you the viewer knows none of the buildings are real? They're just wooden façades erected on a film set in the Former United States somewhere. That's how I feel walking down these streets, like I've entered the idea of a town."

"Right." I said, non-committal. "And you can't find him."

"No."

"Why don't you think I'm in on it?"

"What?"

"What you think is going on but you're too scared to say, because all the hyper-educated fear the word, is conspiracy. Something isn't quite right with this entire town, and you reckon, somehow, it's all related to your missing friend. Now that sounds to me like a conspiracy." I took a drag on my smoke. "The problem with conspiracies, Professor, is that everyone is in on it. Especially the bloke who's working security for the biggest place in town. So tell me, why don't you think I'm in on it?"

He fixed his eyes on mine. "Because you're not, are you?"

I shrugged. "I'm expensive."

"I wouldn't want you to come cheap."

I ran a hand through my thinning hairline. "Stay in the hotel. I'll have a look around. I reckon your friend will turn up any day now, at the end of some bender that got out of hand. But I'm still going to charge you full price until he does."

The professor held up his drink. "It's a deal, then."

I clinked his glass and drank up.

28

I was eating a bowl of pho at The Stranger on Main Street when a bomb blew out the front windows. It was just me, the waitress, and an unfortunate female Scandinavian retiree hunched over a flexiscreen. The Stranger also happened to be the place Henry Yun had been the night before, according to his Ego feed. The Professor had sent me images of Henry dancing in a circle with his girlfriend and a bunch of Chinese tourists. He appeared to be having a whale of a time.

When I showed the waitress a picture of Henry she said she couldn't remember seeing him. He was distinctive enough, a thin guy with a large head and an infectious smile. When I asked her if she'd been here the night before she couldn't remember that, either.

So I was at the bar finishing my pho when the blast hit: a bright light, percussive shockwave, and then darkness.

When I came to, my medical system was flashing on-retina:

Mild Concussion.

Lacerations to the back and right shoulder.

Shrapnel above right hip.

Pain relief has been applied, clottocyte response has staunched bleeding.

I was on the other side of the bar. Whether from the force of the blast or quick reflexes I wasn't sure. The waitress was lying next to me, half her face bloody. She was breathing. It took me a moment to realise I couldn't hear anything other than a long, persistent ringing in my ears.

I touched a finger to my implant. "I can't hear anything."

"I'm not detecting any problems with your ear drums, Mister Pierce."

I wiped the dust from my face. Combat programs weren't perfect, but if it couldn't detect a problem, then the damage probably wasn't serious. I pulled my pistol and looked over the top. The front wall of the bar had been shattered, the large windows gone, save a couple of recalcitrant shards hanging from bent frames. The tables lining the front splintered, and the Scandinavian, who'd been at one of the window seats, had been reduced to little more than a red smear across the floor, ending in an unidentifiable side of meat near the counter. Her flexiscreen was lying a few feet away, still functioning. She'd been looking at her Ego feed.

It took a moment for my eyes to see through the bright white heat of the sun to the street outside. There was a crater three metres across in the main road and enough spare parts littered around to suggest a car bomb. Two more vehicles nearby were burning wrecks. I couldn't see anybody, save the blackened husks in the cars.

I made my way from behind the counter, gun steady, ringing in my ears constant. I slipped in behind a brick pile where the front wall used to be, and peered up and down the street. There weren't many vehicles and the ones that were there had stopped. Thirty metres away a woman stared at her bloodied arms with mouth open, her dress torn to strips. If she was wailing I couldn't hear her.

I saw no profit in venturing out further.

Instead I settled back among the bricks and glass and twisted steel, and lit a cigarette. The ringing in my ears abated. Smoke and the raw heat of the day drifted in through the front window.

A line of sweat ran down my cheek as I propped the cigarette in my mouth and checked the magazine of my pistol. It was peaceful there, in the rubble. No cars or voices. Nothing, save an alarm in the distance and, closer, the crackle of flames. I put my gun down and felt around the small of my back for the shrapnel. With a grunt I removed a three-inch splinter of metal. I got an on-retina message saying the damage wasn't too bad, but, hey – have a lie down and don't do any heavy lifting. I flicked the splinter away and finished my cigarette.

After a time there were sirens, then sometime after that the shouts of angry men. I emerged from the rubble and walked in the direction of the noise. Past the blackened crater and the smouldering cars, the fractured façades of the cafés and bars, past a shredded corpse on the sidewalk.

The air smelled of smoke and, strangely, almonds.

Military jeeps and an armoured personal carrier were parked fifty metres down the street; others were coming from the other direction to seal the road. A score of white-helmeted Chinese military police were swarming around the vehicles, yelling and waving guns in the air. The white-with-green-striped military cars looked familiar; I turned back towards the crater. The two blackened vehicles near the epicentre of the explosion were the same model.

It was the first time I'd seen MPs either swarming or agitated. Normally there were four of them, and they were sitting, top two buttons undone and helmets placed nearby. Watching the main street with a drink in hand, or inside the casino watching a Sic Bo table at close range. Jhun had said they were a special company formed specifically for Xuan Tang, and left it at that.

The local Vietnamese police were at the site as well. Thinner, uniforms rumpled, six or seven gathered underneath the shade of a storefront across the street, marking the commotion with lidded eyes. They wore green, red-banded caps, carried unloaded revolvers and white batons, smoked an endless supply of cheap cigarettes, and stayed away from everyone else's business. Their presence was much like mine: curious observer.

As I neared, I saw what the MPs were yelling about. In their midst were three Vietnamese, two men and one woman, dressed liked they worked in a nearby café. The MPs were yelling "who did this" and "you did this" and "you fucking dogs". The three staff were too busy taking kicks from hardened boots to address the accusations.

A black car with small fluttering flags on the front corners pulled up, the yelling stopped. It was the ride of the military police chief, a taciturn woman who went by the name of Broken-Tooth Koi. Koi had unblemished skin, small rounded lips, and always wore white gloves. Koi was young and beautiful, and the people that knew her would never think of her as either *young* or *beautiful*.

She eased herself from the back of the car and walked over to the commotion, gaze as flat and smooth as an ice rink, and shot one of the Vietnamese detainees in the head. I stopped ten metres away, shocked. Even the MPs managed a little surprise, especially the two with the spray of blood and brain matter on their uniforms.

Broken-Tooth Koi pointed the pistol at the next Vietnamese, the woman. The MPs near her let her arms go and backed away. "[Tell me who did this. You have five seconds,]" Koi said, calm, matter-of-fact.

I believed her.

"[Five.]"

I swallowed my disgust and made to move on past, up towards the Golden Dragon Casino at the top of the hill. Find an air-conditioned space not liable to get filled with shrapnel.

"[Four.]"

The thin Vietnamese woman looked at the barrel pointed at her face, outwardly calm. She didn't seem to be considering the demand; she simply seemed to be waiting. I took another step and something jabbed at me from the corner of my thoughts.

"[Three.]"

I took another step and the world was silent, waiting for the trigger to be pulled. The phantom there in the corner of my mind, it expanded—

"[Two.]"

—as did the pain. The prick of conscience, foreign to my own.

"Stop!"

I was on the footpath, no more than two metres from Koi and the Vietnamese woman. The gun wavered in Koi's hand as she turned to look at me. Her men turned as well.

"You're Chinese," I said. "We don't behave like this."

Koi smiled, surprised, the blue-metal caps on the top row of her teeth glinting in the sun. I found myself tired and not a little irritated at having my wife's memories hijack my actions. At the start I liked it. I liked the flashes of memory that involved my daughters, vignettes of them as babies or toddlers. I liked that I had memories of myself that extended beyond breaking someone's legs with an axe-handle or blowing up a rival gang leader with a booby-trapped cigarette lighter.

But I didn't much like moments like this. When Jian's ideals ran up against the grim reality of a world where the rain fell on the just and unjust alike.

The military police were all around; I felt their dark intent pressing in on me. I took a step away so my back was near the shuttered door of a shopfront. Jian's thoughts, her memories, the primal matter of human identity, were retreating now as my adrenaline rose.

Koi's eyes unfocussed for a few moments before tracking back on me. "[Three Scars Pierce. You're with the casino.]" Her eyes ranged over me. "[I see a lot more than three scars. I also see a third-in-command with far less sense than he should.]"

The Vietnamese service staff kept their eyes down.

I cleared my throat. "Executing people on Main Street doesn't seem too smart to me, either. This is a holiday resort, not some deserted paddy field where you people can do as you wish."

The men around had hands on weapons, shoulders tense, waiting on the signal from Koi.

Koi lowered her gun to her side. She took three steps, calm and measured, and stood face to face with me. Her dead gaze now curious as she looked up into my eyes. But that only lasted a few moments. "[Yes. Happy Jhun was right not to tell you. A basic model thug.]"

She turned her back on me, raising her pistol again as she stepped towards the Vietnamese woman, and shot her in the head. Those were the woman's last moments: standing on the baking asphalt, treated as an outcast in her own country, hands clasped together in front of a white smock she wore as she served officers of an occupying army who either saw her as someone they could fuck, or not at all. Her head kicked back and she dropped to the baking hot pavement, cheap plastic shoes shining under the white sun.

Broken-Tooth Koi looked back at me, teeth glittering as she smiled.

Yeah, that'll do it.

One of the MPs had let himself stand too close to me as his eyes drifted to Koi. Two very stupid mistakes. I grabbed him by the shirt collar and groin, heaved him above my head, and threw him into the thickest clot of white helmets. The next guy didn't have time to pull his pistol out before I shattered his jaw. As I pulled my fist back to punch the next man, I noticed the brass knuckles gleaming with blood. I didn't recall slipping them on.

I waded towards Koi swinging, breaking arms and heads.

Koi's expression didn't change as she watched me fight my way towards her. If anything, her smile widened. My vision blurred with rage and sweat and I heard myself yelling; I could see only one thing: blue-capped teeth, shining in the noonday sun.

Two white-helmets managed to get close and hit me with their force rods, discharging a full load of the dancing blue electric charge into my ribcage. It stopped my forward momentum and I staggered, teeth gritted, but didn't fall. My not-falling shocked them. I knocked one over with a left hook, the other backed away.

I gasped for breath, heart ready to burst, sides throbbing.

There were two rings around me. One of fallen military police, a second of them standing two metres back, force rods crackling. That no-one else had tried to draw a gun and shoot me suggested that Koi had given them a command, through their implants, to take me alive.

She stood at the edge of the ring of men, casting her eyes over the carnage. At least eight of her police were unconscious or clutching at broken limbs. A dislodged white helmet sat at her feet, three drops of crimson slowly making their way down the dome.

Broken-Tooth Koi held something metallic in her hand pointed at me. It looked like a grey box with a wide, circular opening at the front.

"[Now I see why Jhun likes you so much,]" she said, and shot me.

29

We were silent for a few moments, looking out through the windows over the city. I pulled a cigarette from the pack, lit it, savoured the sting of the smoke on my lungs. I shifted in my seat, a soft white cushion in a moulded burnished-bronze frame, running my fingers over the armrest. Two Cs, little one inside the big one, were engraved on the arm.

I exhaled a cloud of smoke and said: "Jian, did I…"

"Did you?"

"Did I ever hurt you – was I violent?"

She shook her head, blue mohawk glinting in the light, sadness on her face. "No. You never had the will to do what was necessary."

I breathed out a long breath. "So it was all a lie – me cheating on Jian, me hurting her and the kids. All just a fucking lie."

She looked down at me with incurious eyes. "Life isn't so simple, Endgame."

Your name is Endel Ebbinghaus. You are travelling under the pseudonym Three Scars Pierce.

It's Sunday, 2 October, 2101. 0726 hours.

You're in Xuan Tang Resort, North Vietnam. You work casino security for a man called Happy Jhun. This is your eleventh day on the job.

You have been hired by a man called Professor Samuel Kam Ching to find his friend, Henry Yun. Like you, the professor thinks something isn't right about this town. Sometimes it feels like everyone else knows the secret, except you.

I groaned and rolled onto my side. I read the message twice, trying to get my head around it, past the dregs of some dream circling the drain of my subconscious. Next to the names of the two professors were their pictures. Professor Ching looked familiar.

A small icon of a lock flashed on-retina as well. There was something encrypted, in my exo-memory. I had a feeling I didn't want to read what was in there right then, and reached for my cigarettes on the side table. I found only air. After a few seconds I realised I wasn't lying on a soft mattress in a luxury hotel, but on a hard plank of wood, and my finely appointed room was a grey polycrete cell, water dripping from the ceiling. The space smelled of wet dog and toilet.

"[Sleep well?]"

I jolted upright on my bed plank. When the room stopped spinning, I managed to focus on the person sitting on another plank in the opposite wall, no more than two metres away. He was a thin Vietnamese man, one foot up on the wood, back against the wall, arm resting on his knee. Young, hollow-cheeked, stained green singlet, intelligent eyes under unusually large eyebrows.

There were bars to my right, windowless wall with a rusted steel toilet to my left.

"Got a cigarette?" I grunted.

He smiled with one corner of his mouth. "[I was about to ask you the same thing,]" he said, in Vietnamese.

I leaned back against the wall, wincing as I did so. My hands and feet had little feeling in them, save for some distant tingling at the extremities. The muscles I could feel ached like buggery.

"Where am I?"

"[I'll give you one guess.]" His hand – the one resting on his knee – moved a little each time he spoke. Like he was conducting his half of the conversation.

I winced again as I tried shifting to a comfortable position. "This doesn't feel like a hangover."

He gave me the one-corner smile again. "[Not drunk, my friend. Broken-Tooth Koi shot you with a nerve siren after you beat up a dozen of her men. The whole block is talking about it. They'd all shake your hand, if they could.]"

That explained the pain. Nerve sirens were normally wall-mounted, static defence systems. They were expensive and relatively rare, an area-of-effect weapon not known for its accuracy. The memory returned of the military police near me screaming as Broken-Tooth pulled the trigger, blood gushing from their noses. They collapsed as I screamed, every nerve on fire, eyes blurred with tears. I fell to one knee and tried to pull my pistol from its holster. My fingers spasmed and I dropped it. Then I vomited.

The last thing I recalled was looking up and seeing her teeth, shining in the sun.

"It stinks in here," I said.

"[You pissed yourself.]" He shrugged. "[Don't worry about it. People have done a lot worse in this cell.]"

I leaned forwards and sniffed. I was pretty ripe. "Fucking nerve sirens." I flexed my fists, trying to get the feeling back in them. "What's your name?"

"Kien. [I know yours.]"

"That so?"

"[Yes.]"

"So what you in for, Kien?"

"[Being Vietnamese in a time of war.]"

"Sounds serious."

"[Yes. Quite serious.]"

"Many of you down here?"

"[Yes. They rounded us up last night after the attack.]"

The memory of the burning cars drifted into my forebrain, I nodded. "I saw it. Your people hit their mark: at least two cars, maybe eight military police."

If Kien had any reaction to that news, he didn't show it. He just flicked his hand as he said: "[Who says they are my people?]"

I said nothing, and went back to making and unmaking fists.

"[Why'd you help?]" he asked, after a minute.

I looked up from my hands. "Help what?"

His eyes were fixed on mine. "[The three Vietnamese they captured.]"

I paused, the incident seeping back to me. "Blame my wife."

His eyes narrowed. "[What?]"

"Nothing," I said. "I don't know. Your war is none of my business."

Kien gave me no reaction to that. It was quiet in the prison; cool, as well. I figured we were underground. There was the occasional groan from down the corridor, but otherwise silence, save the drip of water on polycrete.

After a few minutes Kien asked: "[Would you like to hear a story?]"

"No."

"[No?]"

"I want to lean against this wall and not think and wait until I can feel my toes again."

"[You will find this story interesting.]"

"Why would you reckon that?"

"[Intuition.]"

I grunted. Kind of grunt that says *I don't care* and *shut up*, elegantly, in a single exasperated sound.

"[Something isn't right with this town, is it?]"

I looked at him, sharp.

"[You feel it too, don't you?]"

I hesitated. "Again: why would you think that?"

"[Because *we all do*. Everyone here either thinks it, or denies it. The occupiers you hospitalised? They're the sort to deny it. Mercenaries like you are too, normally. But most mercenaries don't end up here.]" His conductor's hand indicated the cell with a *voila*.

I made to tell him I wasn't no fucking merc. But then I thought about it and decided I had the harder side of the argument. I sighed and motioned for him to talk.

Kien talked. "[I'm from this town. I was born here, lived here my whole life. But the strange thing is I just can't seem to remember much from my youth.]"

I settled back against the wall.

"[But I do remember one incident distinctly. I remember hunting frogs in the rice paddies, late at night, with my uncle. I remember him being like a giant, with a beard so thick it was the envy of all the men in the village. He would give a bag of the frogs he caught to my mother, once a week. He with a battery torch and me following close behind, only seven years old, hypnotised by the beam as it bobbed back and forth, back and forth over rice and water.]"

"[The paddies were tiered up the hillside. Up and down the rolling hills, rising until they intersected with an almost vertical jungle. During one of these excursions, when the moon was full, I saw a large frog splash from the water up onto one of the raised dirt paths between the fields. On its forehead it had a yellow diamond. I swear it was a diamond. I chased it, down the path, across more water, always just out of reach, almost like it was leading me on.

I don't know how much time passed, following that frog. But when clouds swept over the moon the frog disappeared into the water and I looked around and realised I was lost. My uncle was nowhere, nor was any house, or any landmark I recognised.]

"[I wandered for hours, crying, hungry, scared. I should have been able to find the way home easily, but the moon was gone and the yellow diamond frog had led me so far away.]

"[The next morning I awoke underneath a stand of trees. Mud dried on my arms, dead frog clutched in my hand. I didn't remember catching it, and the yellow diamond was gone. In the early dawn I saw, straight away, where I had wandered to, and made my way home. My parents and grandparents scolded and hugged me in turn when I arrived. My father stony-faced – though in his eyes I could see his relief – and my mother clutching me to her chest, like she'd never let me go ever again.]

"[She sat me at the kitchen table and made me a large meal. I was famished, being a young boy and not having eaten since lunch the day before. She put the frogs' legs on the cutting board, so fresh they twitched as my mother seasoned them. When she served me the legs for breakfast I threw up on the floor and cried.]

"[I heard my father and uncle arguing outside. My mother never made frogs again and my uncle stopped bringing them over. Two months later my mother left us. Some years later I found out she'd gone to Hà Nội to live with my uncle.]"

He stopped and waited, watching me.

"Yeah," I said, clearing my throat. "Real poignant, mate. Not that strange, though."

He corner-smiled at my indifference. "[No,]" he agreed. "[Not strange. Just a vivid, sad little tale from my youth. It explains, you see, why I no longer have any real connection with my family, why I hate Hà Nội, some other things.]"

I thought about smoking. He kept speaking.

"[What's strange is that a man I used to work with – he left Xuân Tăng a month back – told me a story once about his upbringing. We were drinking, reminiscing about the way things were before the Chinese arrived, like always, like everyone. He told me this story about catching frogs with his uncle, about getting lost after chasing one with a diamond on its forehead, and finally about his mother leaving his father for his uncle.]"

I thought I'd misheard him. "What?"

Kien leaned forward, both feet on the floor, and lowered his voice. "[I mean, Mister Three Scars, that his vivid memory of his youth matched my own, almost exactly. I mean, since then, I've found another two Vietnamese locals who remember variations on the same incident. The diamond-headed frog a constant in both their stories.]"

"The fuck?"

"[Yes,]" he nodded. "[My reaction, also]."

We were silent for a few moments until I said: "Why you telling me this?"

Kien smiled, mirthlessly. "[You have a trustworthy face.]"

"I have a fucking smashed-up face."

"Hmm." Kien thought it over for a spell. When he spoke I wasn't sure if it was his first thought, or his third. "[Like I said: you are an insider who yet doubts this reality.]"

I wasn't going to get much more than that, so I said: "I don't suppose you handed in your memory pin when you got your job."

Kien sat back and assumed the same position he'd worn when I woke up, head resting against the wall, one foot up, forearm on his knee. His hand twitched. "[I have no recollection of that, Mister Three Scars, but yes, I wondered the same thing. I do know that many here were unplugged. Too poor to afford connection. Lucky then, that every employer here offers a neural implant and memory pin as a condition of service.]"

My hand went to my pocket for a cigarette on instinct. It came away disappointed. "It makes no sense, go to all that trouble."

"[And not even bother to provide unique histories? Yes. You're coming to this quick, Mister Three Scars, coming to it like a man who's known the dreams of others.]"

I waited.

"[Though from another perspective,]" he continued, "[unique histories, for this particular town, are not easy, either. To have the pattern of the truth, memories have to be well researched. It's an investment of time. The villagers here are poor, they don't have lives that exist on the freewave, they cannot be scrutinised and measured by computers, can't have pasts woven out of the virtual threads of their existence. To create a history for each villager requires research by an actual human being. So maybe they didn't have time. But I don't think that this is the case.]"

Kien's hand became more animated as he spoke, the only outward sign of emotion. "[What I think, Mister Three Scars, is they don't see us as equals. I don't think they comprehend us as individuals that live out full lives in four dimensions. What I think is that they see us the same way as every occupying force has seen the occupied in every century in every continent on Earth: less than human. One life is much the same as another.]"

I nodded. It was true. "But why?" I asked.

"[Yes,]" he said, eyes alight. "[Why? Why all the trouble? Why do the few locals left think that the casino and the bars and whorehouses are all so good for this town? Why do they all think the service is great, that all the tourists tip big and then leave this place happy? Why do they believe exactly what the freewave believes – that this is a party town where the more mature tourist may indulge their desires, eat fine cuisine, experience idle days and wild nights, all while being treated like VIPs, waited on hand and foot by smiling, young, beautiful people.]"

"And why don't you think the same thing?"

"[Simple.]" He placed two fingers on the middle of his forehead. "[Because I'm dreaming, Mister Three Scars, as are you. That is the only possible explanation. Because isn't reality what the majority remembers? Isn't reality what the collective believes it to be? This is a dream.]"

I sighed through my nose. "Nah mate. If this were a dream I'd be in a bar with a cool beer in my hand, not sitting here in a pair of jeans stiff with my own piss."

Kien nodded distractedly, uninterested in my levity, and started to reply when he was cut off.

"Pierce," said a voice, crisp and clear. Broken-Tooth Koi looked down at me through the bars, much like a leopard might consider a piglet in a sty. I wasn't quite sure how she'd managed to walk up unheard. "[Happy Jhun is here.]"

"About time," I said, groaning as I stood.

Koi let me out, then closed the cell door. "[My contact details.]" She held out a green card.

I raised an eyebrow. "Give me a moment here." I waited as the jabbing pain in my feet subsided. "Lot of white hats in this town already, Koi. Not sure why you need another."

"[Competent men are hard to find,]" she said.

"You're police. Chinese military. Pretty sure they don't have openings for Australians."

"[Let's call you an independent contractor.]"

I shrugged. "I already got a crew."

"[You like to gamble, I hear. I don't. I only take sure bets. Of all the crews in Xuân Tăng, only one is military. And the military is the biggest crew you'll ever know.]"

"I thought we were all friends here."

She gave me that predator's look again, but kept her hand extended. I took the card. I saw a glint of blue metal in her mouth as I did so.

Footsteps in the corridor and soon we were joined by Happy Jhun and The Axe. Jhun smiled at me, flicking his eyes over Koi and Kien and the walls. The Axe nodded at me and couldn't quite bring himself to look at Broken-Tooth.

Jhun said: "Making friends again, Pierce?"

"Koi gave me her business card. So I guess that's a yes."

Happy Jhun glanced sharply at Koi; The Axe furrowed his brow. Koi said nothing. Jhun handed me my pack of Double Happiness and steel lighter, my pistol, brass knuckles, belt, and a fifth of brandy I'd forgotten about. I stowed it all, pulled a cigarette from the pack with my lips, and lit it. My lungs sighed with the recognition my addiction gave to its drug.

I'd started to leave when I had what you'd call a moment of clarity.

I walked back down the corridor, gave the pack to Kien through the bars, and lit one for him. He nodded and put the Double Happiness in his top pocket.

"Casino's always looking for good workers," I said. "Look me up when you get out."

He glanced at the others waiting nearby, then back at me. "[I will, Mister Three Scars, I will.]"

As I walked from the cell, Kien said: "[Enjoy your comfortable bed tonight, and dream well.]"

30

They found Billie later that evening six bullets heavier. I went out to the red-light district to pick up the body with Happy Jhun, Abbadabba, Sukhie, and four of the regular security guys from the hotel. There were no military police there when we arrived, just a handful of the girls from the Parlour Crew. A skinny Vietnamese from the local police loitered nearby, but he was likely there as a curious patron, lured by the commotion.

Ilona 'The Island' Lysenko was the boss of the red-light district, a Ukrainian migrant with the empty stare of the sex-slaver. She was wearing a black-with-silver-trim corset that looked to have a spideriron weave. Black leather pants, silver rings on every finger, a green-spiked punk haircut. Her lips looked a little too large to be real.

The Island wasn't armed as far as I could see, but those around her made up for it. Three women and one androgynous male holding shotguns or AK-47s. They were dressed for work: tight shiny pants, gold-sequined bras, red eye shadow and lipstick, eyes bright with drugs. Unlike their boss, they were nervous, knuckles white, heads on a swivel.

The Island said: "It wasn't us, Jhun." She waited long enough to see him nod before adding: "You have the right to the body and all the *residuals*. I want it gone in ten minutes." She spoke in heavily accented English that would have been sexy if not delivered by a porcelain-skinned madam with a reputation for whipping her whores with a coat hanger if they failed to earn.

When Jhun nodded again she turned and led her girls from the alley. The cop went with them.

Billie lay on her stomach in the dark brick alleyway, silver six-shooter still holstered. All the shots were in her back. Our crew stood guard, guns drawn, while Jhun and I ran torches over her body, making sure we didn't miss anything obvious before we moved her. Her cheek was pressed against bricks slick with water. One eye visible, open, shining in my torchlight. Her lips were parted, like she was about to kiss someone.

It was only when Happy asked me if I was okay that I realised I was staring. I grunted and went through her pockets. I got her wallet, a battered soft pack of Double Happiness and a plastic lighter, a small silver Buddha with hands over his eyes, some loose bullets for her gun, and a piece of paper inside a plastic cover. The wallet had her ID and two thousand three hundred yuan in cash. It was only after I moved the body I saw the baggie. Her chest had been pressed against a crushed metal can, and the baggie wedged underneath that. Distinct golden crystals of pure ice-seven. I held it up to the light of a torch so Jhun could see it. He nodded. He didn't smile once the whole time we were there.

We drove back to the casino, The Axe and I facing Jhun and Sukhie. Billie was wrapped in plastic in the boot. Sukhie was eating boiled peanuts with one hand. I was crunching on the ice that had gone with my glass of whisky.

Jhun still wasn't smiling when he said: "This was the Bar Crew."

No-one said anything. We just looked at him.

Jhun looked back at me. "Retribution from Three-Iron, for your insults."

The others looked at me, as well. I said: "Maybe."

The Filipino shook his head. "No. No maybe. Actually, it is about respect, Pierce."

I didn't like that sentence much. Jian's memories weren't too fond of it either. "*Fuck* respect," I said. "Gangsters and their fucking respect. Seems to me to be a lot of delicate flowers in the criminal class. Vain little people overwrought by the smallest perceived slight." I leaned forwards. "Let me tell you how to really insult someone. We get ourselves a rocket-propelled grenade loaded with a hexogene mix and put it through the front door of Ray Quan. The rest of us go down to the pool hall his men hang out in, a half-dozen Type-107s loaded with armour-piercing rounds between us, and put a thousand shots into the building. Then we take anyone left alive, put out their eyes, and run them out in the jungle for the Viet Minh to feed on.

"Then you want to know what you'll get in this pissant town? *Respect.* A big fucking truckload of it: respect enough that your people are never going to have to worry about a bullet in the back, even when wandering down the dirtiest back alley in town, looking for their junkie fix. So you're right, in a way, Jhun: this is about respect. If you had a little more of it, Billie wouldn't be wrapped in plastic in the back of this car."

The Axe's eyes popped wide as I spoke and Sukhie shifted forwards, a snarl on his lips. Happy Jhun stayed the big Mongolian with a hand on his arm.

I'd shifted position to meet Sukhie; when he eased back slowly into his seat, I did the same.

Jhun said, still calm: "Actually, there is another thing much worse that this desire for respect. This other thing is stupidity. Even when things go so well, even when we have the money, even as we live this gangster life we always dreamed of: the fine clothes, and the women, and the high-stakes gamble, and the cuisine, and the hotel room bigger than the whole house we lived in when we were young. We must be stupid. We must *will to violence*. This black urge of destruction." His eyes did not flicker as he pointed a forefinger at my face. "You have this black urge, more than the worst. You have this stupidity, ruining the good things we have here." Jhun took a deep breath. He smiled. "Any more of this stupid, Mister Pierce, and I will put out your eyes, take your tongue, and feed you to the jungle."

31

The Professor was late. I sat in the mezzanine bar, where we'd first met. I was in a small, maroon-coloured booth at the back, and near the railing, so I could keep an eye on the casino below and people entering the bar. It was three in the morning and the place was packed. The gambler's din rose from below: the clacking of chips, the spinning of balls and wheels and dice, the yells of the lucky and unlucky alike. They were crammed shoulder to shoulder up in the bar, some hanging over the railing to watch the people below, booths filled with old men and young women and highballs and smoke. I downed my whisky and caught the waitress's eye. She nodded and two minutes later brought me a crystal glass with another.

As I took it from her, I said: "That Hong Kong professor. Steel-rimmed glasses, smiles too much. Comes in here regular. You seen him?"

She furrowed her brow. "[The fat-headed one with the Filipino girlfriend?]"

"No. The naïve one with principles."

"[Oh, him.]" Her eyes unfocussed as she looked at something on-retina. "[No. Not for three days.]"

I thanked her and drank. There'd been no progress finding Henry Yun. He'd made a couple more Ego posts that showed him living the high life. One was a blurred, neon-strobed picture inside a nightclub on the main street; the second was at The Prince, an expensive Italian restaurant on the second-to-top floor of the casino. The photo caption at the restaurant said *The high life with the low lives* and showed Henry raising a glass to the person taking the photo. There was a young Vietnamese woman at the table wearing a black cocktail dress and red lipstick, her dark hair up, and a third person, a middle-aged European in an expensive suit. The Euro was in profile to the camera, shoving a triangle of medium-rare steak into his mouth. The back of his head was flat and he had a nose shaped like a baked potato. The woman was the sort who, after meeting her only once, you'd throw a stranger off the back of a train for, if she asked you to.

A few days back, when I'd showed him the photos, the professor hadn't recognised the two strangers. There was no record of a reservation at the restaurant, though security footage showed the trio entering and exiting together. The uppity Italian maître d' said he couldn't remember, and had no feed record of the party of three. That seemed strange, but I believed him.

I lit a cigarette, sighed out a cloud of smoke. Now both professors had gone walkabout. Both of them were wrapped up in this somehow, this – whatever it was – happening in Xuan Tang. Small pieces of a bigger picture I couldn't even see the shape of yet.

The Axe entered the bar, smiled when he caught sight of me, and walked over. He'd stopped wearing his ridiculous battleaxe around the casino – Happy said it scared the customers – and instead had taken to wearing a long grey, brass-buttoned trench coat. Hidden, hanging underneath one armpit, was a pistol-grip shotgun, under the other a gleaming hatchet, handle downwards, in a bespoke axe holster he'd had made specific.

As he sat down, the waitress appeared. Axe said: "What he's drinking, and a bowl of ramen noodles."

I took a drag on my Double Happiness and said: "Any sign of our man?"

The Axe shook his shaggy head. "I tossed his room. Nothing. His suitcases, some real books, a half-drunk bottle of red wine, old man slippers, the smell of aftershave."

I shook my head. "Like there's a fucking black hole in this resort somewhere."

The waitress brought a steaming bowl of noodles and a glass of whisky, smiled at the big man, and left.

The Axe plucked up his chopsticks and started slurping down his ramen. I watched the casino floor, the punters with their heads bent over green felt tables, monomaniac attention on the fall of a dice, the turn of a card.

Axe stopped stuffing his cakehole and asked: "You check his Ego feed, man?"

"What?"

"You know – Professor Samuel's Ego feed. That should tell you what he's up to."

"I don't have access to his account."

The Axe raised a bushy brow at me and held his glass between thumb and fingers, overhanded, as he inhaled his booze. "Dude. You don't have an Ego feed?"

"I'm a gangster. The fuck I'm going to put up videos of? 'Hey everybody, check out this guy squealing as I pull his molars out with pliers – *thug life, yo!*'"

The Axe placed his empty glass on the table. "Dude. Everybody has an Ego page. *Especially* the gangsters. Look." He unclipped his flexiscreen from his wrist and unfurled it, whispered his password. The screen sprung to life and he turned it around so I could see it.

EGO: for the glory of you, shone in gold-glowing letters, before fading to reveal a picture of The Axe, chin raised high, wearing mirrored sunglasses, standing astride a one-metre-high block of yuan. He was bare-chested, making some weird signs with the fingers of one hand, holding a gold-leafed bottle of champagne in the other. His chest was a mess of dragon tattoos, and he was wearing leather pants. His hair was in a top knot.

The name of the Ego page was: Ryan 'White Eagle' Lee.

I looked at Axe, eyebrow raised. "Seriously?"

Axe went a little red. "It's just an Ego page, man. A way to connect with people."

"You're an *actual* gangster, Axe." I looked back down at the picture. "What are you trying to dress up as here? A male stripper?"

"Well, man, I—"

"Are you standing over the money you've been collecting in your G-string?"

"Dude."

"'White Eagle' – is that the pet name for your dick?"

The Axe laughed.

I tapped the flexiscreen. "Seriously Axe, do you want the police to find you?"

He shook his head, on surer ground now. "It's been altered. You can't see my eyes, the name is fake, the tattoos changed, the shape of my face too, slightly, so recognition programs don't work."

"Oh. So why you doing it?"

"Like I said, man, it's a way to connect with people."

"But it isn't you."

He shrugged his heavy shoulders. "Most of the people I'm connecting with aren't real either. They're just, you know, alter-egos, man."

"So how do you connect with people if nobody is real?"

"Really, dude? Welcome to the modern world."

I shook my head. The waitress came past to ask us if we wanted anything else. I shook my head. She smiled at The Axe again, and when he ignored her in favour of the noodles, she sighed and left.

"So what does your Ego feed have to do with the Professor?"

The Axe looked at me to see if I was joking. When he decided I wasn't, he pressed a few buttons on the flexiscreen. "I'll send a friend request," he said. And leaned back in his chair. His screen pinged almost straight away. "That was quick," said The Axe, and tapped the screen. The page switched to Professor Samuel Kam Ching. There was a picture of him in front of a blackboard, hair neat, smiling uncertainly into the camera.

"Doesn't use it much," said The Axe. He pressed his finger on a picture. "Though that went up only last night."

The picture enlarged. It was of Professor Samuel standing next a skinny man in a bar. It took me a moment to register that the second man was the one we'd be looking for – Henry Yun. They were smiling, holding cocktails. The caption said: *Old friends, reunited.*

"Bullshit," I said.

"That's the Blue Cockatoo bar, right here in the casino."

"*Bullshit.*"

The Axe shrugged again and leaned back in his chair. "You can get lost in this place, man, even the guys with big brains. That's what it's designed for. Losing yourself in a place that never judges, just, you know, indulges. Lot of people don't want to be found anymore, man."

I drank my drink, smoked my cigarette. The Axe was right, but wrong on the professor.

I'd come around on The Axe. Behind the ridiculous gangster front, I'd thought there was just another thug that craved violence, craved the attention he never got as some beaten-down child in the abandoned tenements of San Francisco. But I was wrong. Axe had something going on there, under the shaggy beard. Pale blue eyes that watched, quiet, everything in the room, in the faces of the people around him.

So I made a mistake, and asked: "You got any actual people you connect with?"

Axe looked at me strange, picked up his glass, but didn't drink from it. I winced at myself for asking, and was about to tell him not to worry when he began speaking.

"I used to work in Japan," he said, putting his glass back down on the table. "Everyone's old there, man, especially the gangsters. They have to draft in young muscle from overseas. There was this time, after this bloody week of burning down warehouses and cutting off toes, where we went to this shrine in the centre of Tokyo, the Meiji Shrine. A king or an emperor or someone was buried there. I think our boss was feeling, you know, the need to atone or something, for all the bodies piled up behind us in Shinjuku. Anyway, this shrine, people would go there and write their wishes down on this thin card. This fake wood or something. Then like a priest or whatever would bless it and you'd hang it on this circular wall. It looked like a scam to me – you had to give the guy money in order to write the prayer – but my bosses took it all serious and solemn. So they're off praying or washing or whatever and I'm just standing there looking at this big circular prayer wheel – I don't know what you call it – where you can hang these little plaques. This wasn't just Japanese people, you know, it's like all these languages, man, tourists from all over the world. But you know, Scars, they all said the same thing: help me pass my exam, or keep my family happy, or please let my kids be healthy, over and over man. Like a mantra, all these disconnected people from all these different cultures, yet they come to this holy place, this secluded wood in the middle of this metropolis, and they all want just the same thing. I don't know what it was, dude, but I was crying, cheeks all fucking wet. Had to walk away, so no-one saw me."

His eyes were shining. I said, "And you? What did you pray for?"

The Axe shook his head. "That's the thing, Scars. I never worried about an exam, or a family, or some kids. The fuck I pray for those things, know those things, with this life I lead? None of that applies to me, not that I can remember anyway. A family? I couldn't bring them into this and if I did, I'd wipe it all from my mind. Protect them. What sort of person brings a family into this? We exist outside the world that all these other people live, separate from it. That's what all those prayers were saying: people like me, like you, we're not human. Not the way these other people are. We've left that all behind. We're warriors, and the only mantra a warrior needs is in their code. You, me, Jackson Street Amy, Sukhie, the real warriors in the crew, that's all we can have. We kill and we hurt people, but never the innocent; we break the law, but only the law of a corrupt system, man; we die and when we do, it is in an unmarked grave."

It was the most I'd ever heard him say in one piece, and he'd said it better than I'd thought him able. He waited for me to reply, but I just nodded and gripped my glass tight as I brought it to my lips. I thought about Jian and felt a weight bearing down on me, just below the heart.

32

The Axe left soon after his speech, said he had an errand to run.

The lock, on-retina, corner of my vision, sat waiting patiently. Get used to that, easy enough, walking around with a HUD. Everyone did. Got to a point where you didn't notice it, lest you needed it. But something told me I needed it now. Wanted to look, now.

I left the bar and returned to my room, flopped down on my couch.

I put a finger against my c-glyph and said: "Open the encrypted item."

The metronome voice of the c-glyph answered: "How many scars on your left foot, Mister Pierce?"

I couldn't remember passwords, and keeping them in a special 'password' file in my cochlear implant was self-defeating, so the next best thing was a voice print and a piece of information only someone in the same room as my body would know. Imperfect, but the best I could do.

I pulled off my boot, and winced. My toes were not a pretty sight, sans toenails. "Top of the foot?" I asked. "Seems to be two big scars, one little one. Every toe is a mess."

The flashing lock opened.

Soft green-glowing words appeared:

Happy Jhun works for Mister Long. He runs the concession of Xuan Tang, granted by the Chinese military. Everything is allowed. Drugs, prostitution, the works. So long as the Chinese officers who use the resort are kept safe and happy, anything is permissible.

All the different factions in the town take their cut, and pass the rest up to Long. The current peace between the crews is based on the division of the profits. Two things are likely: first, that the cut Mister Long takes from Happy Jhun, The Island, Broken-Toothed Koi and Three-Iron is more than they'd like. Second, there is bad blood between the crews on how the tourist market is divided. The Island runs the whores, Koi runs the drugs, Three-Iron runs the alcohol and cafés, Happy Jhun runs the casino. Everyone is looking over their shoulder, thinking the other bastard is getting too much.

There's something else, as well, that they're all in on. Behind it all, something bigger, and darker. But you haven't figured it, yet.

But you do know this: Mister Long killed your close friends Wangaratta and Ha. He tried to kill you, twice, and is looking for you now. He will never stop until you are dead. He will kill your wife and children if he has to, just to make an example. The only short-term solution is to stay away from them, never switch on the freewave, and never make contact with them under any circumstances. The only long-term solution is to destroy Mister Long's empire from the ground up, and then him.

Happy Jhun knows your real identity. He has known since he first met you. You don't know why he has kept it hidden from Long, but this is going to change very soon.

I'd read the encrypted message a few times now. Added little bits over the past two weeks. I always got a surprise when I opened it; there was always a sentence or an implication I'd forgotten. Without the mnemonic package I'd bought from the Omissioner, and with a little time, I'd forget the whole thing.

Except for Happy Jhun. I recognised him from the first moment I saw him. Took me a while to figure exactly where, but it came to me. I'd seen him in Macau, and more than once. I'd watched over meetings between Jhun and Mister Long up in his suite in the Grand Lisboa. Enough neurons of an old memory print lingered to give me a photoflash of Jhun, smiling and drinking rum, and Mister Long, holding a slow-smoking cigarette between elegant, pale fingers.

That came to me four days in. Jhun could have had me killed ten times over in that space. Why he'd let me live, why he'd kept my identity secret from the others, any reasoning behind it was lost in the fading scroll of my life.

I had a feeling Happy Jhun would be less inclined to mercy real soon.

The last line of the message read: Today, you start a war. You'll need to do six things:

I read over the list, nodding.

I finished my drink and took out Broken-Tooth Koi's card. It was two-by-one inches of flexiscreen contained within a slender black plasteel frame. The only thing on the card was a number. The chief benefit of the Baosteel Business Card was that it created an encrypted link between two people that the bottom-dwellers on the freewave – the Russian government hackers and the anarchic American nihilists and the corporate anti-privacy crusaders and the rest of the darknet scum – had yet to break.

I pressed my thumb against the surface of the Card; it began to pulse, the green numbers growing in brightness. After ten seconds Broken-Tooth Koi's face appeared.

"Mister Pierce," she said, without a trace of emotion.

"Got a hot tip, Commander."

She waited.

"I think the red-light district may be involved in the drug trade. Found a bag of ice-seven on Billie."

"[Billie could have got that anywhere,]" she said.

"They'd gone over her body carefully. This baggie—" I held up the golden crystals, "—was wedged underneath her, hidden by some garbage. Ever wonder why they called us, kept you out of the loop completely?"

"[I wonder about everything, Mister Pierce,]" she said, with about as much expression as a cleansteel wall. "[Like why you are calling to give me this information. You are not a snake.]"

I nodded slowly. "I guess that's true. But I can tell which way the wind is blowing. In the great race of life, you should always bet on self-interest, Chief."

Koi paused, pressing her lips together, moistening them. I felt like she didn't believe a bloody thing I was saying, but any good police chief always made you feel like that. "[As I said: those drugs could have come from anywhere.]"

I punched a button on the edge of the small screen. "Here's the chemical composition and purity of the sample. I suspect it doesn't match your supply. I reckon it didn't come from anywhere, I reckon it came from one place and one place only."

Her eyes flicked over the numbers. "[Thank you for the tip, Mister Pierce.]" She switched off the screen.

I let out a long breath after she cut the link, like I'd been holding it.

Step one.

33

I left my room and made my way down to the kitchen of the buffet on the second floor. Kien was working there now, scrubbing dishes, on my recommendation to the shift manager. I nodded at him as I walked past. He blinked an acknowledgment and went back to his work.

Step two.

34

"My friend, did you really think I'd let you come?" asked Jhun, smiling. He was sitting on a dark leather couch, glass of rum in one hand and pistachios in the other. He was cracking them between tough fingers and letting the shells fall onto the richly patterned purple wool rug. Happy's digs were a three-room suite a few floors above mine: bedroom, lounge room, an entertainment area with a full bar, stocked pantry, and view of the whole town. Where there weren't expensive rugs there was expensive hardwood floor, where there weren't floor-to-ceiling windows there were unexceptional and expensive abstract paintings. In the corner, a grand piano Happy used only as a shelf to keep two small pistols, some wads of yuan, a deck of cards with the king of hearts on top, and a crumpled fedora on its closed lid.

The room smelled of cigarettes and the fresh flowers the maids brought in every morning.

I sat opposite Jhun on a matching leather couch, drinking whisky soda and eating the soy chicken wings he'd had the kitchens bring up. The only other person in the room was The Axe, who'd insisted on going to the meeting with me. He was sitting up at the bar with his eyes closed, out of earshot, watching something on-retina. Probably old Japanese cinema again.

I sipped my drink. "You could be walking into a trap."

"I'm not, my friend. All our problems are behind us."

I grunted. Billie was forty-eight hours dead. "At least take Sukhie, and Jackson, and six others. Walking in weak may invite a new set of problems."

Jhun popped a pistachio in his mouth, eyes flicking to the view of the town, to The Axe, to one of the shitty paintings, and back to me. "Sukhie and Jackson, yes, I will bring them. Don't confuse a liking for peace with being stupid, Mister Pierce."

"I don't think you're stupid." I pulled a package out of my pocket and handed it over. "And I think you're right about promoting peace."

Happy leaned forwards and took it, resting it on his lap. It was a small silver box. "And what is this here?" he asked, smiling.

I indicated for him to open it. He did, pulling the lid off. He paused, smile wavering, and reached in. Happy held a glimmering platinum lighter. Three lines of rust-red iron were etched on one side.

"A peace offering," I said.

Jhun turned it over in his hand, flicked the lid open. A small, intense green flame purred as he did so. He flicked it shut again and placed it back in the box. He smiled at me. "This gift, actually, it is very fine."

"The glimmer particles act as a back-up power source. Adaptable to any device."

Happy's drink had been placed on the small table near his feet, he reached forwards and picked it up, taking a sip on the way back. "What is this, Pierce, what is this you are doing?"

I finished my drink, put down the glass, and stood. "Being smart, like you suggested. We got a good thing going here, Jhun, and only a fool would try to tear that all down over a dead Vietnamese smackhead."

Jhun nodded at what I said, but his eyes didn't. They danced over me, up and down, like he wasn't quite sure what he was looking at. I tapped The Axe on the shoulder, he followed me out.

Step three.

3 5

I pulled the rocket launcher and two RPGs from the heavy black duffel bag. The grenades had a hexogene core surrounded by a layer of primed C-6. I linked the targeting system in the launcher to my c-glyph, a green-glowing grid overlaying on-retina before slowly fading. I wiped the sweat from my forehead and loaded an RPG into the launcher with a satisfying *snick*, before slowly rising to one knee, settling the weapon on my shoulder. I was on the roof of a dealership that rented out shiny motor scooters to tourists. Opposite and three stores down was the 888 Pool Hall.

What I was doing would have been impossible in Macau. Any reputable gangster hangout there would have a perimeter of sensors set up to detect high-yield explosive of any size out to a hundred metres, right down to the few grams contained in a bullet. Or they'd have a small EM field in operation protecting key parts of the facility. Or both.

But all Three-Iron's boys had at the 888 was one guy, feet up on the chair in front of him, dozing next to the entrance under the shade of a wide awning. A fan whirring nearby played with the napkin on the table, held in place by a steel spoon.

"Fucken amateurs," I said, and fired the rocket.

I ducked back behind the parapet of the roof just as the RPG punched a neat hole through the tinted plate-glass window, right above the *H* in *POOL HALL*. I closed my eyes; an incandescent white blast seared though the backs of my eyelids, highlighting red veins. Then the shockwave hit.

I clamped my hands over my ears and roared as the world around me roared. The blast flipped me once, onto my back. Then the wind died down, concussive echoes rolling out over the town. I groaned and shook my head, dislodging a fine coating of white dust. I coughed out some more and rose to my knees, looking over the polycrete parapet. The pool hall was gone, replaced by rubble and flame. I'd gone for a relatively small amount of high explosive, but it had been enough to flatten the cocktail bar on one side and the strip joint on the other. A car parked near the entrance was now propped up on its side, folded in the middle, windows gone. Sirens had yet to wail.

I put the spare RPG and rocket launcher back in the duffel bag, zipped it up, and threw the strap over my shoulder. I headed for the ladder on the side of the building.

Step four.

36

Dusk. The car was driving me back up to the casino when my pocket started to vibrate. It was The Axe. I'd bought a couple of pairs of Business Cards, given one of the pairs to him. He was pale, eyes dilated, streaks of blood on his face.

"Axe. Constipated again?"

He ignored that and said: "I knew you were making a move."

"Did you?"

He nodded. "Yeah. Three-Iron is gone."

"What happened?"

"Well…" he seemed unsure of what I meant. "Well, you killed him, Scars."

I didn't react. "Just tell me what happened."

The Axe looked around. He was in a dimly lit corridor, probably in the bowels of the casino. He rubbed the back of his hand against his face, smearing the blood. "We met in Ray Quan Café. Three-Iron and Happy up the back, rest of us at the front like last time, eyeing each other off. Happy gave him the lighter. Three-Iron didn't say anything, just tested it and nodded. Happy smiled big, and everyone seemed to relax. Then it happened, I was—" Axe shook his head, like he was still coming to terms. "I was looking right at Three-Iron when he lit his cigarette. This white light, this perfect circle, just ate Three-Iron's arm up to the elbow and melted his fucking face off, man." The Axe's eyes widened a little, his breathing picked up again.

"Then what happened?"

"Then Three-Iron's clothes burst into flame and the shooting started."

"Who started it?"

"Happy. He pulled a pistol out of each pocket and started laying down fire, gat in each hand. I mean, I just watched the replay on-retina then, everything happened so fast at the time. But, anyway – Happy's fucking jacket was smouldering from the heat, man, his face red like it was sunburned, and he doesn't even blink. Just *pow pow pow*, you know."

I nodded.

"I mean, the way it went down, I thought Happy was in on it."

"He wasn't in on it."

"Well, I know that now."

"How's that?"

"Because he put a fucking price on your head. There's ten guys out on the street right now, looking for you."

I was silent for a few moments. "Oh. He's playing it that way."

The Axe shook his head. "How the fuck else could he play it?"

"Something else happened, Axe, what was it?"

The Axe took a deep breath. "Jackson Street Amy is dead, man."

I said: "Dammit," and was a little surprised that I meant it.

The Axe was shaking his head. "Yeah. Just bad luck. She'd opened up with her assault rifle, taking out three guys with a long burst. Only one managed to get his gun out and he was just firing into the ground, dead I think, reflex or whatever. She took a ricochet in the temple."

"So that's why you're pissed at me."

His eyes were fixed down the line at me. "You put me into a firefight, man, no heads up. Let me just walk into it. I don't know what the fuck game you're playing, man."

I instructed the car to pull over. The Golden Dragon was two klicks up the road. Military police cars, lights flashing, barrelled past in the other direction.

"Okay," I said. "This is what I'm doing, mate. First: I've taken out the rest of Three-Iron's crew. The 888 is rubble. So now the other three crews are going to think Happy has made a move, no matter how much he tries to blame a rogue member of his gang. The delicate balance is upset. Island Lysenko and Broken-Tooth Koi will be preparing to make a move against Happy, clip his wings a little, make sure he doesn't claim too big a share of what's left of the market. A negotiating tactic counted in the bodies of dead foot soldiers. But, you see, there's this complicating factor: the military police are, right now, in the red-light district. Looking for the drug factory that made the ice-seven Billie had on her when she was shot. Broken-Tooth Koi's the kind of person who ain't going to stop until she finds it and burns it to the ground."

"Shit, dude. It's going to be war."

I tapped a cigarette out of my soft pack of Double Happiness and lit it. Around the cigarette I said: "Yeah." The streets looked deserted. Just a European guy banging on the glass door of a café with a *Closed* sign hanging there, and back a few blocks, a pyre of black smoke rising from the spot the 888 used to be. "That's not all," I continued, "*I gave Koi the tip*. So it looks like Happy is running an angle, trying to create bad blood between the red-light district and the cops. And there *will* be bad blood between them, real bad. So I figure Happy Jhun needs every man at the barricades right now. I figure there's enough in our crew angry that we never responded to Billie getting hit, and that taking out Three-Iron feels right."

The Axe looked around again, leaned against the wall. He looked tired, beard stringy with sweat. "I don't know, man, Happy hasn't smiled since the shootout. Some of the men really liked Jackson. They never liked you much either, an outsider and all, blasting right past them. Suddenly best friends with Jhun, acting like you're above the rules all the rest of them have to follow. They'd probably kill you even if Happy changed his mind."

"Try to."

"What?"

"Try to kill me."

"Yeah, Pierce. Sure."

"You haven't asked."

"What?"

"Why I did it."

"It's in your nature, man. Mine too. In the end, all a warrior wants is war."

Some tourists parked their scooters right in front of the car. Man and woman, early forties, Chinese, taking hesitant tourist steps across the sidewalk, under a flashing red neon sign, and into a bar.

"They'll come after you, Axe. They all know you run with me. Deny everything; deny breathing, if they ask you if you did any in my presence. They put me in metal bracelets and tell you to end it? You get that fucking big axe of yours out, and end it."

The Axe was tired, but the look he gave me wasn't. "I don't rat, I don't turn, I don't walk away. Not for anything, man. Not for money, not for a woman, not for my life."

"You're making me blush," I said.

"Shut the fuck up, Pierce, and get out of Dodge."

I cut the connection and stepped out of the car into a suffocating North Vietnamese evening. Where the weight of the heat and the water in the air bears down on you, and all you can think of is running a cool bottle of beer over your forehead inside an air-conditioned room. I was wearing denim jeans and leather jacket, my boots, and the cap. My pistol holstered under my armpit. I slung the duffel bag over my shoulder and ordered the car to drive to police headquarters and wait for me there. It drove away. Sweat trickled down my neck.

I crushed the Business Card in my fist and threw it into the gutter. Then I got on one of the scooters the Chinese tourists had left behind. I used my knife to pry open the control panel on the handlebars and cut out the little black box that held the GPS and drive information. I threw that away, crossed a couple of wires and the bike hummed, its hydrogen cell engine awoken.

I didn't think as I did all this. It all just happened on instinct. Muscle memory deeper than anything a higher brain function could forget or mis-remember or lie to itself about. Subterranean, buried in my hands, in the feel of a blade as I directed it with my forefinger, in the satisfaction of the components coming apart in my palms.

I drove off as the sun dipped under the horizon, as the lights of the façades along the main road lit up and the casino on the hill shone with its bright lies. Insects flickered in my headlight as I turned away from the casino and down darkened streets.

I slowed the scooter as I hit Vietnam-town. An old woman, back bent, carried a thick bamboo pole across her shoulders, counter-balanced baskets at either end laden with vegetables. She wore a conical hat, eyes focussed on the ground as she concentrated on each step, oblivious to me and the swarms of Chinese scooters swarming around her. The air was rich with the smell of faux meat cooked on skewers at roadside barbeques, and with the raised voices of the local Vietnamese as they haggled and argued and talked about food. I eased back until I moved at walking pace, weaving in and out of the bikes, and the sellers of sweetbreads and helium-filled balloons and shoe repairs; past a bicycle with speakers mounted on a handlebar basket laden with fruit, blaring out the phrase *fresh mango, fresh pomelo*, over and over in Vietnamese. Heading into evening, yet young families had their children out on the sidewalk, playing or tottering or staring at the street life. A small slice of the country as it used to be, once a heated, vibrant, defiant culture pulsating across every dust-filled laneway and paddy field and gleaming glassteel business district, now reduced to a curiosity. A minority that tourists came to ogle at as a kind of side-show spectacle to the main attractions: the bars and massage parlours and poolside cocktails; a minority in their own country.

After I passed through the Vietnam quarter I increased speed, slipping through back alleys. My freewave still switched off, bike locater removed, lights out: a ghost, virtual and physical, as I sought darker shadows still to reside within.

37

I flopped back with a groan on the plastic-covered couch. I was up in one of the long-term apartments overlooking the valley. There wasn't a security system, not that I could detect anyway, so I busted a ground-floor window with my elbow. The block I chose had a dozen two-storey apartments, all of which looked empty. A couple places down the end of the street, in a separate section, had lights on, but that was all I could see on the long avenue. I'd gone up and back on foot in the darkness, and for the most part all I found were the sounds of the jungle behind, and the wash of the Milky Way as it ran across the sky. No lights, no cars, just plastic-covered furniture visible through rear windows. Most looked incomplete internally – bathrooms without fittings, wires hanging out of the walls. Completed, they would be luxurious.

I zipped open the heavy duffel bag sitting next to me on the couch and took out the Type-107 and a bottle of Maker's Mark. I laid the semi-automatic across my lap, one hand resting on the hard blue metal, and took a swig of the bourbon with the other. The metal was cool against my fingertips as I ran them over the engraving on the side. *Actions are new, consequences are old.* I sighed. Karma was coming for me, one way or the other. Deeds, though long forgotten, demanded recompense. This was immutable. All I could try to do was deal mine out, first. My family was safe now, and if I believed that I had to do everything I could to take down Long while I could. Because taking him down would keep them safe, forever.

I lit a Double Happiness and waited for the show to start. The plastic on the couch squeaked as I shifted and turned my attention to the wide windows overlooking the valley of Xuan Tang. At first glance things looked normal, even peaceful out there. The blanket of orange lights across the large town, the red and green neon strip of the main drag, the bright lights of the casino on the hill, on my right and level with the apartments, a few kilometres away.

On the surface, all seemed well. Underneath, it seethed. The firefights today were merely a clearing of the throat.

Later that evening, one-third through the Maker's Mark, the eruption. Across the valley, an explosion shook the windows and painted the sky three shades of amber. I jumped, knocking the 107 from my lap. Then I smiled. Smoke billowed and smaller chain-reaction explosions followed, some so bright they hurt to look at, right about where you'd find the headquarters of the military police. Headquarters largely unguarded as Broken-Tooth Koi launched a series of raids right across the red-light district, looking for the lab Island Lysenko had set up to make ice-seven. Headquarters filled with military-grade small arms, anti-riot gear, high explosives, and armoured vehicles. All briefly vulnerable to coordinated attack from a highly motivated enemy.

I'd guessed there was a small group of Viet Minh, not much more than twenty. From what I'd seen over the past two-and-a-half weeks, most of the local Vietnamese were memory-wiped into a sleepwalking collaboration. In a dream state, where the war was something that merely pricked from time to time at the back of the consciousness, a lost country reduced to the same sensation as a misplaced set of keys. Kien, wide awake, seemed to me the sort of man that might change all that. Die trying, anyway. I told him which night the HQ would be largely empty of white hats; he'd just nodded and gone back to the dishes.

Now three inches of the horizon was on fire. Fire that lit up the undersides of the storm clouds as they rolled in, and dulled the lights everywhere else.

Step five.

38

When I awoke it was to a splitting headache and pictures of two girls, superimposed on-retina. I groaned and rolled over, grunting as I hit the floor. After a few seconds I realised something was sticking into my back, I rose to my arse, wincing, and pushed away the two-thirds-empty bottle of Maker's Mark I'd fallen onto. I was mildly surprised it had anything left in it at all. Was a time I could go through that and more, easy. But of late I'd had this hesitation every time I put a drink to my lips. Faint, distant itch, that grew worse and worse the deeper I'd try to get into my cups.

I patted my pockets until I found my cigarettes, then lit one up.

The girls on-retina – Weici and Kylie, that's who they were – were full colour and vibrant against the washed-out real world behind them. The pre-dawn, leached of colours. A smattering of lights down in the town, and – it took me a minute or two to find it – smoke rising from the ruins of the police headquarters. Smoke idled from my cigarette as well as I refocussed on the girls, smiling up at me from the dark wood floor of our small apartment on the Rua da Gamboa. Sunlight bathed the room with its warmth and the two sisters smiled with identical, yet somehow different, white-toothed smiles: mischievous from one, wide-eyed and wondrous from the other.

I sighed out a cloud of smoke and turned the photos off. Returned to the grey world, my pale feet sticking out, pointed towards the *demimonde*. This place where nothing was as it seemed to be, where all was in shadow, where I couldn't even see the edges of all the lies.

My mouth tasted like some small creature had first crapped, and then died in it. I spat and it didn't help one bit. So I sat back and listened to the sound of my blood pounding in my head in the stillness of the room, thinking about a long, cool glass of water and whether any of the taps in the apartment were working.

Silence, complete, not even a bird trilled. My hand paused mid-air, on its way to delivering a cigarette to my lips. Not even a bird, though the apartments were nestled into the jungle.

My hand was on the blue-metal machine gun when I heard the footstep. I craned my neck to look back, behind the couch, towards the front door. The silver doorknob turned.

I raised myself to one knee, 107 to my shoulder, and fired a burst, *bratatat*, through the door. Still loaded with armour-piercing rounds, they punched easy through the faux wood. Someone screamed. One second of silence as I tried to figure through the fog of my hangover where the exits were, then fire was returned.

The *bratatat* of submachine gun and *boom boom boom* of large calibre pistol and shotgun sounded. All the windows in the rear shattered, orange blooms from the barrels of guns lighting up the grey outside, wood and marble splinters flying, something punched my bicep and I rolled and rolled and flattened myself against the floor. Adrenaline kicking, fog clearing, implants pushing the booze out of my bloodstream and putting extra oxygen in it.

I took stock.

The apartment was on a hill, its front a storey above ground, all glass, looking out at the town. The rear met with the rise of the slope to be at ground level. In this room a single door and a few

windows across the kitchen and living area. I was wearing my jeans
and leather jacket: the latter was good, it had a spideriron weave.
The bullet I'd taken in the arm would leave a large bruise, tingling
in the fingertips, but that was it. I had the 107 with a thirty-round
clip in my hands, pistol still in my shoulder holster. I wasn't wearing
boots and didn't have time to look for them. I'd rolled to a point near
the far wall, couch obscuring my view of the rest of the apartment.
My senses were fully engaged now, but the colours hadn't changed.
It was still grey and shadow. Heavy clouds overhead, perhaps.
Good for me.

I whispered: "Details of assailants, verbal."

"At least seven, Mister Pierce," replied my neural implant. "All
located to the rear of the building. Three armed with semi-automatic
weapons. They are ten to thirty metres away."

"How many ways out of this apartment?"

Footsteps again outside, the *clack-clack* of a shotgun loading.

"I don't have schematics for the long-stay apartments.
Searching your retina feed I note, when you first entered, that
you glimpsed a plasteel door at the end of the corridor to your
right. The distance to the door is twenty metres, which means it
is at the outer edge of the apartment. It likely leads to fire stairs
between apartments."

I raised myself to one knee again. A shadowed face peeked
through a shattered window over the tap-less kitchen sink, I
fired, the head snapped back, and I raked the rear wall with fire
as I stood and ran. Running to my right, leaping the couch, I was
nearly at the corridor when the next fusillade replied. The windows
all along the front shattered this time, my ears ringing, plascrete
exploding in fist-sized clumps from the walls around me, the door
was down the end of the corridor and I ran for it roaring with
battle, the air filled with dust and hot metal, something punched
my side and I staggered, shoulder brushing the wall, stumbling,

but I righted myself and roared again as I hit the door with my other shoulder.

The door snapped open, lock shattering, and I tumbled into a darkened stairwell.

The metronome voice in my ear whispered: "Correction: at least thirteen assailants, Mister Pierce, located to the front and rear of the building. Seven armed with semi-automatic weapons, from ten to thirty metres away. There is also a machine gun located one hundred metres away, on the road, likely mounted on a vehicle."

I breathed out, wincing as I did so. Whatever had hit me had either broken a rib or pierced the skin, or both. Didn't have time to check. Stairs down, stairs up, similar door to the one I'd just burst through opposite. I stood, kicked the next door in. It creased down the middle, snapping the lock under the blow, but also reminded me I wasn't wearing boots. I limped into the next apartment, turning to the sound of voices behind me, back in the direction I'd just come from.

I fired a long burst, the rest of my bullets, back into the first apartment. Again someone cried out, the 107 said *click click click* and was done. I threw the gun strap over my shoulder and pulled my pistol, jamming the bent door closed behind me, moving moving running as the next storm descended.

Something hit me again as the fresh apartment sang with exploding glass and the reports of a thousand bullets, my teeth locked together as I dove through an open door into an empty bedroom. Whole chunks of masonry fell from all directions, one landing on my left hand.

"Correction: at least twenty-two assailants, at least fifteen armed with semi-automatics, to the front and rear of the building, and in the apartment you just left. A fifty-calibre machine gun almost certainly mounted on a vehicle, and I believe a sniper has taken up position on the ridge behind, two to three-hundred metres away."

I patted my pockets with a bloodied left hand. "Any of them got cigarettes? I've dropped mine somewhere."

"Witty repartee is not part of my programming, Mister Pierce. Although this is available through an upgraded subscription. If you wish to—"

"Okay okay. Jesus. Seriously." I shook my head. "Do something useful and tell me my injuries."

"You have been shot in the left buttock, and part of your left ear is missing. Neither wound is life-threatening, at this point."

I grunted and rolled onto my side, pistol raised towards the door. My butt did hurt, now the implant had pointed it out. But so did everything else: dull ache in my back and shoulders where shots had been absorbed by my jacket, throbbing feet where I'd been stepping on marble splinters and glass; my body recognised them all first, and second pulled the curtain slowly across the pain as the endorphins kicked in.

Dark in the room, quiet, after the roar of gunfire. Something else flashed through the window and distantly I was aware of the lightning.

Glass tinkled, followed by footsteps, a shadow in the doorway, and I popped low through the door and fired.

The bloom lit up the surprise on the woman's face as the bullet hit her under the chinstrap of her helmet. An MP. A squad-mate tumbled past her as she fell back, I fired low into his unprotected thighs. He screamed as I rose, his shotgun falling from his hands, and I took two long strides and caught him before he hit the ground, dragging him against me, chest to chest, using him as a shield, I fired again into those piling in through the fire exit behind him. My pistol was deafening in the confines of the corridor, *BOOM BOOM BOOM BOOM*, a short, four-part orange strobe lighting up the bodies of the four others who had barged into the apartment. They fell or jumped sideways, the last tripped back through the fire exit. The smoke hanging in the air stung my throat as I turned and flung the arms of the MP over my shoulders, heaving him along on my back like a meat-cape.

As I dragged him towards the next fire exit, gunfire lit up the apartments again. If they knew I had their man, they didn't seem to care too deep. I sped up, staggering under the weight and the noise, something stung my face. I felt the man on my back spasm multiple times, crying softly, before not crying at all, his body limp as I dragged it across the last few metres.

"Correction: thirty-one assailants."

"Will you learn to fucken count if I upgrade the subscription?"

I kicked in another door, screaming, pretty sure this time I'd broken my foot, and collapsed into the next stairwell. The body of the soldier landed next to me with a wet slap. I tried not to look at it too hard, turned, and threw up volubly on the stairs. Enhanced though my liver was, even it couldn't process the better part of a bottle of Maker's Mark in two minutes.

I looked up, head spinning. I hated going up. But I was leaving small pieces of myself behind in each apartment I crashed through, and couldn't see much currency in leaving any more.

I hauled myself to my feet, holding the wall briefly for balance. I checked the clip – four bullets left in my pistol – and limped up the stairs, drizzling them with blood that I hoped was mostly someone else's. I was gasping for breath by the time I hit the ladder, to a trapdoor above. Yells somewhere beneath me, I holstered my pistol and climbed, punching through the thin metal cover at the top.

I flinched as water drummed my face. I paused for a moment, looking up into the darkness, before throwing myself into another storm. I rolled once and lay on my back on the tiled roof, soaked through almost instantly by the downpour. Thunder rumbled, lending its timbre to the orchestra of small arms fire blazing around the apartments.

My chest heaved as I pulled my gun out again and looked around. Nothing, bar wet tile drumming with rain and the edges of the sloping roof barely visible in the darkness of the storm and pre-dawn. The nanos attached to my optic nerves reacted quickly, giving me adequate vision in the low light. Washed out, deep in shadow, but enough to see where the roof ended.

Someone fired a bunch of bullets up the ladder, shattering tiles around the exit. I swore, head still resting against the roof, and closed my eyes for a moment. Wondered briefly why I was fighting so hard. Being dead simplified things. Made it easier for Jian and the girls, in the long run anyway. Being dead gave Long and Broken-Tooth Koi and all the others what they wanted, brought an end to this little subplot in someone else's something bigger.

My eyes popped open. Mister Long. That's right: revenge. That was a thing that still needed doing. The thing in itself. My heart thumped in my chest. *Fuck yeah.*

I pushed myself up, took a step, collapsed with a cry, and slid down the angled roof briefly.

"Want to turn up the pain relievers? I think my foot is broken."

"Your foot is broken, and your endorphin release is at maximum capacity. You have a second bullet in the upper thigh, and there are at least forty military police around this location."

I gritted my teeth as I got to my feet again. "You got anything useful to say, better make it now."

"I suggest you run, Mister Pierce. Immediately."

I ran, slid, staggered over the rooftop of the apartment complex. They were all connected, the line of twelve, and I had about three apartments left before a three-storey drop. I got about halfway and slipped, my feet slick with the blood and wet, and landed on the apex of the roof with a grunt. My pistol popped from my hand and slid with tantalising slowness all the way down to the edge before disappearing from sight. I watched it, chest heaving.

The thing about being augmented – hardened bones, titanium joints, all that stuff – is you get heavy. I was pushing one-hundred-and-fifty kilograms. My enhancements were dated, even when I got them. Deliberately so: you see, the older model Baosteel joints could never be bettered for power, only for weight when next-generation alloys and nanomaterials arrived. Slow and heavy as I was, I had all this extra weight to use to my advantage. A battering ram in hand-to-hand combat, gravity assisted elbows and knees. What I gave away in speed I made up for with raw, brute strength.

That all changed when it came to falling. Weighing half again what you would naturally became a hindrance. Guys like me were wary of heights, because nothing wrecks a state-of-the-art endoskeleton like a ten-metre drop. For guys like me, gravity was a bitch.

I ran towards the edge, the tiles around my feet dancing as bullets traced different paths towards me. There seemed to be a lot of firing, way more than forty soldiers. Closer to a hundred, down to my left and right, firing all over the place, all directions. But these thoughts were distant, vague. Something my martial training pondered remotely while I bounded the last four steps along the ridge of the roof and leapt.

Into darkness.

I hit a branch on the way down, snapping it off completely. I spun forwards, the long wet grass rushing up to greet me. There was a second or two of consciousness, of muffled small arms fire and the welcome embrace of the hard wet earth.

39

I was staring at the floor. An old Chinese man looked up at me from a square below, maybe three feet away, and said: "The mad cunt awakens. Afternoon, mate."

My mouth was dry, lips cracked. I tried to ask: *Where?* But the sound came out as a vague croak.

A wrinkled hand appeared below me holding a paper cup and a straw, positioning it so I could grab it with my lips. I did so, sucking down the water. As I drank I realised I was suspended above the floor in a bed or something similar. The old Chinese guy in the window below looked vaguely familiar.

I couldn't touch my implant, nor could I see my hand or apparently move it. So I said: "Implant. Facial recognition."

The Chinese man's face grinned again. Belatedly I realised it was his reflection in a mirror, placed on the floor. "Sorry mate, I turned that off. In answer to your question, I'm the Omissioner you saw a couple of weeks back, to get your exo-ma program."

I licked my cracked lips. The fog was still on my thoughts and somewhere something itched. My foot maybe. "But…"

"But suddenly I have an Australian accent, that's the first thing. Mate, when I'm talking to the hoi polloi I carry on like a pork chop. Mysteries of the East: robes and incense and those bloody cymbals going clang clang clang, all that *oriental* bullshit people mistake for culture. You see, I *am* an Omissioner. The Chinese have the best that go by that name, and deep down, people don't think that it is just because China has the premier scientific civilisation. Oh no, deep down they think it's a kind of cultural voodoo."

"But…"

"But I'm Aussie, as we established, yes. Don't want to stun you with this revelation: but there's profit in the prejudice of others."

"But…"

"I switched off your exo-ma, because I've been doing what an Omissioner does, and sifting through the train crash you call a cerebral cortex."

I paused. "Motherfucker."

The old Chinese face in the mirror crinkled in delight. "Friend, you don't know the half of it."

I tried to move. A leg, a fist, a little fucking toe. Nothing. My body was dead, save a tingling in my lips. "What have you done to me?"

"Ah settle down, settle down," he said. His face was animated, the opposite of the joyless mask he'd had on when we first met. "Just patching you up. You've broken two ribs, a foot, both ankles and a wrist. 'Tis but a scratch. Your mug got messed up – looks like it's been smacked around with an iron-studded ugly stick. And that was *before* you fell face-first off a three-storey building." The old bastard was really enjoying himself. "Couple of bullets in yer arse," he continued. "I prefer a slap in that region, myself, but I suppose you're more hardcore."

"Are you for real?"

"Mate," he said, face suddenly mock-serious. "I am the *realest* thing in this entire dung-heap of a town."

"Good," I said, voice hoarse. "'Cos if you were a dream, I wouldn't be able to appreciate the feel of your bones as I snap them with my bare hands."

He laughed at that. "Don't get angry, young fella," he said, apparently delighted by my threat. "We're all friends here. Your appetite for destruction is on the large side, and you're as cunning as a dunny rat. We like both of these qualities."

"We?"

"Kien and his mob. They're the ones that brought you in. How else do you think you got here? Certainly not your looks, or your charm, or" – his nose wrinkled – "your attention to personal grooming."

"What do you want from me?"

"Right now? All I want you to do is listen."

His face disappeared. I heard him shuffle away, then silence. The itch on my foot was becoming unbearable. A noise came that sounded like metal on metal; the old man hissed under his breath, followed by a kind of sucking sound. The itching in my foot stopped, replaced by the sound of wind chimes.

"Hear that, mate?" the old man asked.

"The chimes? Yeah."

"Good good."

"How about this?"

This time it was a piano, tinkling. Like a performer in a lounge bar, playing idly while patrons ignored him and flapped their lips. It also became clear that I wasn't really hearing it, as such. It was more the feeling I had when my c-glyph was talking to me, the sensation of a voice being right inside my head.

"Yeah. Tell him to lay down a blues track."

A chuckle. "And this?"

I flinched as the sound of an electric guitar blared. Right into the core of my brain, a teeth-rattling wail in ascending scale. It felt like the metal components in my body were resonating with the sound, that my lips were transformed into the soundwaves themselves.

I clenched my eyes shut and yelled: "TURN. IT. DOWN."

The noise cut out. I heard footsteps as the Omissioner walked over, and was surprised at that; surprised I could hear anything. I blinked the water out of my eyes.

The old man's face, grinning, appeared back in the mirror. "Beauty," he said. "Now, back to sleep, sweet prince: you're gonna need your rest."

Darkness descended.

4 0

I was sitting in a cluttered living room opposite a batshit-crazy Aussie and a Vietnamese insurgent leader. My ankles ached, so I rested my feet on the thin carpet gingerly. Both were encased in a stiff, clear resin, as was my wrist. A pair of old wooden crutches leaned against my seat.

Kien was dressed in what looked like black pyjamas but was more likely his running-around blowing-up-stuff gear. A spideriron vest poked up near his neck under his uniform, and an AK-47 with a large capacity banana-magazine lay across his lap. He was smoking a cigarette slowly, like he was savouring it. Otherwise he said nothing, watching me carefully from under a thick pair of eyebrows.

The Omissioner hadn't deigned to put on pants for our meeting. He was wearing white undies and a black T-shirt that said *AC/ DC – Back in Black* in dramatic lettering on the front. I had no idea what the garment was referring to. I hadn't noticed it earlier, but the Omissioner had a shock of thick white hair sticking out in all directions. He grinned as though everything in the room was deeply amusing, creasing his face with a plenitude of lines.

It was a dark room, no windows, lit by a couple of red-shaded lanterns and, on a work bench against the wall to my left, the blue light of a Bunsen burner. The space smelled like cigarettes, old man, and the mouth-watering scent of the fried soy chicken the Omissioner had placed on the small table alongside me. Next to the chicken was a small tub of hot sauce, a packet of Double Happiness and a tall glass of water.

"I take it you've been in my memory stream," I said, waving a hand at the food.

The old man cackled, Kien said nothing.

"Not quite right, though, you're missing a cold glass of beer."

The old man shook his head vigorously, pursing his lips. "You're in recovery, body and mind, old mate. Best ease off on the demon drink."

"Just get us a fucking beer."

The Omissioner made an 'O' with his mouth, then leaned over and popped open the cleansteel cooling unit sitting on the ground next to his seat. It was near-buried under a clutter of real books, takeaway food boxes, and a large pair of silver headphones. The old man took a tall can of Huda from the fridge and pitched it over. I fumbled it, swearing as I opened the tab and it sprayed foam into my face. The Omissioner thought that was hilarious.

I sipped the foam off the beer, put it down on the table, and replaced it in my lap with the bowl of chicken. My stomach lurched with something between joy and surprise as I swallowed my first mouthful.

"I'm starving," I said, around a mouthful of soy.

"Yeah, unsurprising," said the Omissioner, "It took three days to complete the upgrades." He waved his beer can towards my feet. "Nanos are nearly done fixing your bones. You'll be raring to go by this afternoon."

I paused mid-chew. "What upgrades?"

The Omissioner's eyes popped, excited, and was about to tell me when Kien cut him off:

"[What are you doing?]" the black-clad Vietnamese asked me, quietly.

"What?"

"[What are you doing? What is your plan?]"

I resumed chewing. They watched, waiting, while I washed it down with some beer.

I said: "I'm shaking things up."

Kien raised his eyebrows, wanting more. The Omissioner just smiled and nodded, like he knew exactly what I was talking about.

"Chaos," I said to Kien around the next mouthful. "I couldn't see the shape of what was happening here. I didn't have the time or the memory to investigate, deduce, shine a light into dark corners, all that shit. I needed a shortcut. Chaos has a habit of shaking things loose. Chaos smashes the structures men build around hidden places, and by the time the dust clears, you see what lies underneath."

I wiped my hand on my pants and lit a cigarette. Inhaled, watched the smoke rise from the orange tip, before putting eyes back on Kien. "So I decided to start a war. I figured, if I set my enemies against each other, this thing they're part of here will be revealed. All the trouble they went to, something big, some big lie spread over this town like a blanket, seems like the knowing of it would help me get revenge on my real enemy, back in Macau. Long. I know that old dragon is tied up in all of this."

I indicated both of them with the end of my smoke. "It's worked. Because here you are about to give me the grand reveal. So: talk."

Kien and the Omissioner looked at each other. The old man nodded, Kien hesitated.

"I got to take a piss anyway," I said. "You two sort out your speeches."

The Omissioner smiled and sprung up from his seat, opening a faded wooden side door and pointing down a narrow corridor. I got up, grabbed the crutches, and hobbled slowly through it, found the toilet at the far end of the corridor, and relieved myself. There were no windows, just a naked bulb shining overhead. On the wall at eye level something had been written in black paint in neat flowing script.

Remembrance

When the loud day, for men who sow and reap
Grows still, and on the silence of the town
The insubstantial veils of night and sleep,
The meed of the day's labour, settle down,
Then for me in the stillness of the night
The wasting, watchful hours drag on their course,
And in the idle darkness comes the bite
Of all the burning serpents of remorse;
Dreams seethe; and fretful infelicities
Are swarming in my over-burdened soul,
And Memory before my wakeful eyes
With noiseless hand unwinds her lengthy scroll.
Then, as with loathing I peruse the years,
I tremble, and I curse my natal day,
Wail bitterly, and bitterly shed tears,
But cannot wash the woeful script away.

Aleksandr Pushkin

I zipped myself up and read the poem a second time.

When I returned to the living room and sat myself down, I asked: "Well?"

Kien said: "[We used the attack on the military police compound to disable the defensive grid. The automated weaponry on the perimeter was out for six hours before they managed to turn it back on remotely. We moved hundreds of Việt Minh through the breach. We've taken everything, the whole town, except the casino.]"

"Five hundred klicks behind enemy lines. Suicide, you stay much longer."

"[As you say, friend. Chaos has a habit of shaking things loose,]" said Kien, eyes flashing.

I smiled.

"[When the dust has cleared, the whole world will know two things.]"

I waited.

"[The first is to show the occupiers are not safe, anywhere. Can be struck at, anywhere, in this country. The second is the story you know: of the frog with a diamond on its forehead.]"

Kien glanced at the Omissioner, and then returned his gaze to me, cynical eyes in a young face. "[We need your help.]" It was clear he disliked saying those words.

"Yeah?"

"[Yes.]"

I drank some beer. "Like I said when we first met, I don't care about your war."

Kien nodded, but not at what I said. "[Yes. I understand this, Mister Three Scars. There is something in it for you.]"

"Hmm. What would that be?"

"[Revenge.]"

The Omissioner was smiling absently, staring into space. I had the feeling he'd lost track of the discussion. I took a drag on my smoke. "Well, you're speaking my language now, Kien. But what I'd like to hear is a specific."

"[Specifically, Mister Three Scars, it is something that would gut Mister Long's business model. Something that would break him completely.]"

"If it's true, that's a *something* I can work with." I put my beer down. "What's in it for you?"

Kien looked over at the old man. "[Uncle?]"

The Omissioner's eyes had fallen closed. His breathing heavy with sleep. Kien's question roused him from his daydream.

The old man sat up. "What? Huh?"

"[Uncle. The casino.]"

The old man sipped his tinnie; it seemed to help him focus. He looked at me. "Right, yeah, of course. Mister Pierce, the grand reveal: Mister Long isn't a drug kingpin. He's a memory tsar."

The Omissioner paused like he was waiting for my applause. I smoked and waited.

"Bah! You tough guys make a tough crowd. So right, ah, yeah, conspiracies: Mister Long works for Chinalco, which aside from glimmer trains, hydrogen batteries, and throw pillows, is the biggest producer of memory pins in the world. Mister Long is in charge of 'special operations', which is another way of saying he's the boss of doing very bad things. Corporate espionage, assassination, and, oh yeah: producing memory pins that sabotage natural memory. What they're doing, young fella, is giving everybody Alzheimer's." The Omissioner waited again for my response.

I leaned forwards in my chair. "What the fuck?"

He beamed with pleasure, apparently, at my taking interest. "The pins release a nanotech virus. Very subtle, almost impossible to detect, that blocks the synthesis of a particular protein your brain produces in the hours after learning, in order to remember things. Several months after exposure, the victim develops complete dependency on their memory pin. Among other things, this means a lot of money – a shit-tonne of it – to the makers of said pins."

"The fuck?"

"Tip of the iceberg, mate. You see, if you're smart, you can start making subtle changes to the pins themselves, and to the exo-memory assistant programs that drive them. Maybe those programs suggest that you buy certain products, or have positive feeling towards certain companies, maybe even whole countries. Think about it: what if you always had favourable memories about a geographical neighbour? Maybe recalled them having a legitimate historical claim to your land? What if you believed your culture was closer to that of the invaders, rather than those of your countrymen down South? Make wars like this a whole lot less messy, ay?"

"This is—this is—but how can they get away with it?"

"They can't. Not yet. I mean, not the memory control anyway. The steady erosion of natural memory is a game they've been quietly playing for many years now. The wholesale *infiltration* of memory across a population is far more complicated. First, it'd take a far more powerful pin. Second, they'll need to test the concept in a controlled environment."

"Controlled environment?" I asked. "You mean Xuan Tang."

The old man's eyes shone. "Ahhh. Sharper than you look. Yeah mate: Xuan Tang. You wouldn't believe some of the garbage I found inside Kien's head. Crude at the moment, unrefined. But effective enough. Smooth off those edges and soon enough, the world will be imagining the right things – the right brand of cigarettes to buy, the right clothes to wear, and the right kind of geopolitics to support."

I clenched and unclenched my fists. I wanted to snap bones. To that end, I asked: "So what do you need me for?"

He sighed, smile gone for a few moments. "Like I said at the beginning – you got an appetite for destruction. You're *motivated*. This thing we need is vital, and if you can't get it, I don't reckon anyone can. We need *evidence* to take them down, mate: my theories are not enough. We need you to break into their lab, download the code they've been using, and bring it back. Once we have all that, Long, his bosses, the whole Syndicate will be finished."

"It's more than that," I said.

"Huh?"

"Something as big as this, it's more than Long."

"Yeah," the old man nodded. "Yeah, it is."

"It's Chinalco."

"Hmm."

"Half the Politburo."

"Not quite that many. But, yeah."

"It's the most powerful people in the world wanting me dead. Sort of people that make Mister Long look about as threatening as a Thai massage."

"Yeah. Yeah, that's right. So?"

"So my family is dead twice over, I go and do this."

"I dunno, mate. You go and do this, they'll have a lot more to worry about than something as trivial as your estranged wife."

"There is nothing trivial about my family."

The Omissioner's eyes shone. "Indeed. But I am quite serious, young fella. In the aftermath there will be a maelstrom, political and economic. In that moment you'll find yourself with time: time enough to get your dearly beloved far, far away."

I ran a hand through my thinning hairline. The scar on the palm of my hand itched. "What upgrades did you give me?"

"We'll get to that," he said, and put a hand on Kien's arm. "You got business, Kien. Don't worry about our mate here. Come the moment, cometh the man."

Kien glanced at me, unconvinced, but nodded, slung his gun over his shoulder, and walked out.

41

The Omissioner was silent after Kien left, still for a few moments. "*Toska*," he said, eventually.

"What?"

"An old Russian word, it means *spiritual anguish without cause; longing with nothing to long for.*"

"I don't care about your Russian crap, you old fart."

He laughed at that and said: "Ah, shit. I know it's a cliché and all, but you gangsters don't all need to be philistines."

"And you Omissioners don't always need to be a bunch of condescending cunts."

He laughed again, harder this time. When the old man had done being jolly, he settled his attention back on me. "We need to talk."

"About?"

"Who the hell you are."

I indicated for him to continue.

"You got some knuckledusters with Jonny Brass stamped on them. Everyone here calls you Three Scars Pierce. No prize for originality on either count. Pretty obvious, given everything, you ain't either of those blokes. So I dug a little deeper into your memory stream, and came to the conclusion that you are most likely Endel 'Endgame' Ebbinghaus."

I made a not-committal noise. "Most likely?"

The Omissioner's eyes were unfocussed as he looked at the beer in his hand, and said: "Well, you have one life as a street-level enforcer for a drug cartel in Macau. This is your natural memory we're talking about here. And yet some things don't chime quite right." His eyes shifted from the beer to me. "I guess you've had your fair share of wipes and false memories?"

I grunted affirmation.

"Then before that, you were a married man with kids. And yet, still kind of a thug, really. More complex, I guess, in a clichéd way crooks often are – love the wife, dote on the kids, all that bullshit. But still, at your core, a glorified crook."

"Cheers."

"And then there is the third one—"

"The third one is my wife."

"Hmm?"

"My wife, I downloaded her memories. Too many, I think. They've been—They've been changing the way I act sometimes, making me do things I otherwise wouldn't."

The Omissioner dismissed that with a gesture. "Oh that? I cleaned all that up."

"What do you mean?"

"I mean I cleaned all those memories out."

I crushed the beer can in my hand. "The fuck?"

"Settle down, young fella," said the old man. "No need to get your knickers in a knot. I mean: I filtered out the mnemonic static you absorbed. The important moments between you and her – and those cute little girls of yours – they all remain."

I stared at him until he made a disapproving *ahhhh* in the back of his throat. He said: "I'm not a butcher, mate. I took the oath. I fix minds: I don't fuck them." The old man sighed. "I get it: a man in your condition, you wanna hold on to every last scrap. I only wiped the events that weren't about you. The things that were just about your missus as an individual, the steady grind of a life that all of us lead. They say that the way we spend our days – especially the bloody boring ones – is the way we spend our lives. Her days aren't yours. The memories of others, even if it is the woman you love, they will drive you mad in the end."

I smoked for a while. "So, what's the third?"

"Dunno. It…" the old man trailed off.

"It what?"

"It – whatever *it* is – is buried deep, Ebbinghaus. A memory print, a pattern of them, different from all the rest. You've been deleted and copied over so many times, I'm surprised you can still function at all. Oh, that reminds me." He reached into his pocket and drew out a white plastic pill container. "You will need to start taking these." He threw them over. He had a good arm, for an old bloke.

I turned the container over in my hand. It was unmarked. "What are they for?"

"Depression and Alzheimer's."

I felt my jaw clench, heat on my cheeks. "Are you fucking kidding me you mad old cunt? Sitting there scratching yourself, getting pissed, talking about revolution, staring off into space. Now you pass me a bottle of fucking happy pills?" I'd let the pills drop to the floor and was clutching the arms of the chair, leaning forwards.

"Maaate." He held up a finger. "Please. Depression is connected to memory loss." He raised an eyebrow. "Are you saying you aren't a storm cloud? That you aren't walking around brooding over your lot in life, looking to punch jaws?"

"You've given me plenty reason to punch yours, old man."

"Listen: you're lucky you are walking around at all. I don't understand how you can be, with all that they've done to you. You should be in a feed-coma, staring at the moving pictures inside

224

your head, drooling onto white sheets. The person you were – that third pattern, buried deep down there – must have been someone *extraordinary*." He pointed at the pills near my feet. "They will help stabilise your condition. Stimulate the productive neurons in the hippocampus, activate some dead dopamine receptors, kick-start the grey matter up top. Just *don't* treat them like booze. Three a day. No less, no more."

"Why?"

"Well." He scratched his neck. "Schizophrenia."

"Fucken hell."

"Yeah. Too right."

I unclenched my jaw, took a fresh cigarette out of the soft pack with my lips, and lit it. I said, through a cloud of smoke: "I don't know what your angle is here, old man, but I don't believe you. My capabilities haven't been reduced. Even with my memory the way it is, I know it."

The Omissioner leaned forwards to put his can of beer down, causing his thick mane of hair to shake. Back upright, he asked: "Can I tell you a story?"

"Fucken hell. Every cunt I come across wants to tell me one."

The Omissioner made a thinking noise at my reaction. *Hmm.* "And maybe you just want to tell your own? Know your own?"

I clenched my jaw.

"I get it, mate. I do. My job, after all. But you see, this story is about you."

I unclenched my jaw. I listened.

"Starts with a puzzle. A task. Two triangles, one slight smaller than the other, one inside the other. The object is to trace a line between the two triangles, but you can't look at it directly. You're only allowed to look at the image reflected in a mirror. It's bloody hard to get it right, at first. The strange thing is, you present this problem to someone with total amnesia, they still get better at tracing every time they do it. They have no memory whatever of trying to, even once before, yet after a while they can do this difficult problem with ease. You see: this is why you're so good at killing people. In fact, you'll probably get better and better at it, despite everything. Not premeditated – nothing that involves planning. But in a life-threatening situation, your muscle memory and your instincts make you a stone-cold killer, based on a long history of violence you simply cannot remember.

"You need to take these pills, young man. You need to keep using the top-notch exo-ma program I put in your cochlear implant. And you need to never have another wipe or false memory implanted again. You're close to the edge, mate, so close. You're nearly in that place – a place where all you'll be doing is tracing the triangle. Eat. Kill. Sleep. Repeat. No room for growth, no chance to evolve. You'll be the Escher Man. Stuck inside the painting, walking in an endless loop. An infinite journey to nowhere. To the beginning, again and again and again. Unable to love, to change, to be. That's you, that's where you're headed, anyway. The Escher Man."

"Right," I said. "Who the fuck's Escher?"

The Omissioner leaned back in his chair. "Like I said: a philistine."

I flexed my fist, trying to stop the palm itching. Trying to stop me thinking, too, of what the old man was saying. I breathed. "This shit doesn't matter. What matters is me getting out of here. Apparently I've got a global conspiracy to expose."

"Don't you want to know about your upgrade?"

"Oh right, yeah. Sure. The upgrade."

The Omissioner popped up, went over to the Bunsen burner, and plucked a long needle I hadn't noticed, whose point was sitting in the flame. The tip glowed red. He walked over to me, picking up the big silver headphones on the way.

"Let me run the test first," he said, and popped the headphones on. He held the pin out towards me and said, loudly: "Stick this into your hand."

I looked from the pin to him. "The fuck?"

"Your hand," he yelled. "Stick the bugger in."

I sat, brow furrowed, not understanding. The Omissioner gave me a raised-brow eyeroll, his hand flashed out. I jumped to my feet, mouth open in preparation to scream, clutching at the back of my hand where the Omissioner had plunged the needle into it.

Instead, I heard music. The wail of a guitar riff, followed by the clash of cymbals and the heavy beat of a bass drum. No white-hot pain, just some old-fashioned rock and roll. I looked from the pin to the Omissioner, bobbing his head up and down to the music. Music that came from inside my head, like the voice of a cochlear implant.

The Omissioner mouthed the words, head banging up, as the voice in my head started singing something about getting a motor cleaned.

I plucked the needle from my hand and let it drop to the floor. The music quietened. The Omissioner popped off his headphones, faced creased with disappointment. "Come on, *mate* – it's Accadacca."

"It's what?"

The old man made a pained expression. "The best band of the twentieth century."

"Huh?"

"AC/DC. Our country's *greatest cultural export*."

I stuttered. "The—the—what the fuck's a hundred-year-old band doing in my head?"

The Omissioner beamed at that, creases changing direction. "Ah, so it's working? You beauty."

The music had gone now, replaced by a throbbing sting on the back of my hand. I said: "Remember how we talked about punching jaws."

The Omissioner patted me on the chest with both hands, cackling, pushing me to sit. I remained standing. He shrugged and returned to his seat. After making me wait too long he said: "I rewired your brain."

I waited.

"Ahhh. You're a cranky bastard." He sighed. "Synaesthesia."

"You mean like, smelling colours."

"Yeah," he said, delighted at my answer. "Just like that, mate. Your neurons, the wiring for your different senses, are pretty much all the same. I simply switched a couple around – sense of touch with your sense of sound, with an added splash of rock and roll."

I flexed my hand, still stinging where the needle had stuck it.

He answered my question. "For severe pain only. Once it meets a certain threshold, touch is replaced by my favourite song of all time – 'You Shook Me All Night Long' – from the best band of all time." He tapped his black T-shirt as he said the last bit. "Now you can't be distracted by pain as you complete your mission, and can't be tortured if they capture you. There's a lot riding on this, Ebbinghaus. We need every edge we can find."

I decided to sit down and smoke. "Every motherfucker I meet acts like I'm giving them an open invitation to crack open my head. Tell me how to think and how to feel."

His smile faded. "The mess inside your head? Seems to me like you were the one giving out that invitation."

I finished my cigarette. "Yeah, well. I feel like breaking something. When do we start?"

42

The percussive blast of mortar shells rattled the cleansteel elevator as the technician swiped his access card and thumbed the button for subbasement three. I stood in the corner, 107 machine gun trained on him. Blood trickled from his busted mouth, fear leaked from his stance.

The cameras and weight sensors in the elevator had been sabotaged, but there hadn't been time to override the thumb and voice prints required to get down. So I'd snuck into the casino through a rear entrance past midnight, under the cover of a concentrated attack by the Viet Minh on the front of the building. Xuan Tang was chaotic. Cars and businesses burned throughout the night, the sky stitched with the kinetic poetry of tracer fire. Helicopters circled somewhere above, the *dubadubadubaduba* of the rotor blades the bass rhythm for the music of war: the roar of artillery, the screams of the dying, and the whispered orders of black-clad insurgents.

The elevator door pinged open. As the tech turned towards me I clubbed him in the temple with the butt of the 107. The man's head snapped sideways and he fell, half-in half-out of the elevator as I emerged, gun level.

I stopped, eyes widening. Inside was a football-field sized room, bright white lights above, pale blue-lit machinery below. Curved, cleansteel girders and railings, a conveyor-belt down one side of the room seemingly made of glass, the hum of machinery, not a speck of dust anywhere.

Behind me the elevator said: *clear the doors, clear the doors, clear the doors...*

Two men stood about twenty metres away, looking at me the way I was looking at the room. One of the men was old, large grey eyebrows, European; the other young, short dark hair, Chinese. Both wore clear plastic gloves and facemasks. I reacted first, firing a triple burst into the chest of the younger tech. He staggered, blood spreading on a white jacket, and fell sideways, his head striking the floor with the sound of a coconut dropped onto plascrete.

"Don't move," I screamed at the live one, "don't open your *fucking mouth.*" I walked forwards, eyes flicking from side to side, 107 trained on the older tech. Six feet away I pulled a small black pistol from the back of my jeans and pointed it at his head. "Who else is here?"

"Um," his mouth popped open, and didn't seem to know what to do after that. "Ahhh."

I pulled the trigger. A blue arc of light discharged into the man's face. He bucked, threw his head backwards, blue electricity dancing around his left ear, and crumpled onto the floor.

A mnemonic print on-retina read:

First: find head technician and disable his neural
implant

It faded and was replaced by:

Second: have technician show you the Merzenich Drive
and interface

I glanced down. The old man was curled into the foetal position, hands shaking, his mask fallen off. He coughed a little.

I said: "Motion detector, on-retina." A growing green circle, spreading outwards from my position, appeared. I waited for three waves to blip. It picked up nothing.

I kneeled and slapped the guy. "Where is everyone?"

His eyes were wild in their sockets, ranging all over the room until I slapped him again, harder. He managed to focus on me.

"Ladislaw – where are the others?"

He coughed as he said: "Gone. Evacuated."

I nodded. That's the intelligence Kien had given me. The crew of twenty departed, save a corrupt Omissioner named Ladislaw Tauc and his assistant. The man's face, name, and title hovered in another corner on-retina. My visuals were pretty cluttered today.

"Take me to the Merzenich Drive, dickhead," I said, shoving the barrel of the blue-gleaming 107 under his chin.

I yanked him to his feet. He started moving back along the gleaming metal floor, I nudged him with the gun to speed up, and adjusted the straps of my backpack. Our feet echoed on the smooth surface, machines hummed, the motion detector let off a soft pinging sound inside my head.

We stopped where the floor gave way to a hole two feet across. Coming out of the hole was a slim metal tube a handspan wide, ending in a mess of black cables that crawled along the underside of the white ceiling like vines. At eye level, halfway up the tube, were a series of glassteel panels glowing with an inner red light.

"The Merzenich Drive," he said, with an open palm.

A new prompt appeared:

`Third: insert tetrapin and wait 10 seconds before removing`

I pulled a soft pack of Double Happiness from the inside pocket of my leather jacket, tapped one out, and pried the steel lighter out of the top pocket of my jeans.

"This is a quantum computer," said the old European. "A delicate, complex piece of machinery. One doesn't smoke around it." All this came out with a sneer, like he was talking to a Neanderthal trying to make sense of a pocket watch.

I punched him, thirty per cent power, in the stomach. Tauc folded and collapsed, making the deflating-balloon sound of someone trying and failing to breathe. I lit the cigarette and blew smoke at him.

I took a transparent glass tube from my other jacket pocket, popped the top, and withdrew the red metal tetrapin. I stuck in into the slot on the side of the quantum computer.

Ladislaw Tauc started breathing again and slowly got to his feet. He didn't disguise his disgust as he looked at me. Calm old bastard. The average civilian would go to water in the face of a dead colleague, shock to the head, and a mild beating. This old guy was equal parts composed and contemptuous.

"Cigarette?" I asked.

He gritted his teeth and said nothing.

I kept my eyes on him as I un-slotted the tetrapin, put it back in the glass tube, and returned it to my pocket.

The final prompt appeared:

`Fourth: break something`

I smiled at that.

Ladislaw Tauc watched me smoke. His eyes glittered with a venom I quite enjoyed; his large mouth set in a thin line. Tauc had the thin, stooped shoulders that no-one but an academic would have any use for. He smelled like used furniture.

"Let me ask you something, old man."

His mouth quavered a little, like he wanted to insult me, but he kept it shut and waited.

"People had a habit here of disappearing, but not disappearing. You know anything about that?"

Tauc's gaze flicked to the left, then back at me. He pressed that thin line of his mouth tighter.

I looked where he had. Only thing worth seeing in the cleansteel-and-blue landscape was an unobtrusive door in the wall. It seemed to be the only door in the whole floor, save the one I entered by, and a couple at the far end leading into glass-front offices.

"Oh," I said. "Answer's in there, is it?"

His lip curled so I stuck the barrel under his chin again. "You realise I don't need you anymore, right? You realise I'm a killer, stone cold, and putting a hole in your brainpan means about as much to me as scratching an itch? I'm not even going to remember you tomorrow, old man, and the way this world is, nobody else is either."

Tauc licked his lips, and I could tell he heard the truth of it. He said: "I realise. If I show you what's behind that door, how it works, what's *really* been happening here in Xuân Tăng, will you let me live?"

"Sure," I said, around the cigarette in my mouth. "Won't harm a hair on your head."

"Your word," he said, like a man used to faking gravitas. "As a *warrior*: your warrior's honour."

I clenched my jaw. "Too smart for your own good, Omissioner: sure. Sure, I won't kill you. Now show me the fucking room before I change my mind."

Tauc walked me over, punched a password into a flat control panel on the side of the door, and pressed his thumb against it. Something clicked inside the wall and the door opened. A short corridor, the same routine at the next door, and inside. We stood in a circular room, five metres across, steel mesh floor, walls like we were inside a sphere. Green metallic wiring jammed into the join between the top and bottom halves of the sphere, circling the room, told me the curved surface doubled as a holo-unit.

"Before we get started," I said. "Why'd you do it?"

He raised a bushy eyebrow. "Why what?"

"Betray your profession. Turn the population into docile cattle."

Tauc snorted. "Oh dear, really?"

"Yeah, really."

He took a moment, thinking, and then decided to say it all:

"Have you *seen* the world we live in? The population are *already* docile cattle. They credulously believe in the most venal of demagogues. They prefer the transparent lies of game simulations over the hard truth of reality. They are known better by the giant corporations than they know themselves. They have no free will: they buy what they are told to buy, watch what they are directed to watch, hate who they are trained to hate. Any innovation I conjure through the science of memory will not change one jot the supine and pathetic stupidity of the common person. It will be merely a refinement, of all that has gone on before."

I clenched my jaw. "I asked a question, you old fuck. *Why this*?"

He drew in breath, like he was preparing to give a speech he'd said a dozen times before. "We insist, particularly Westerners like you and I, that there is some sharply delineated 'self'. Some essence which we believe is sacrosanct. Though neuroscience rejected the notion more than two-hundred-and-fifty years ago of a soul residing in the pineal gland," he placed his forefinger at the base of his skull, "most of us insist on thinking that there is a unique being, here, in our brains, pulling the levers. Why should the 'I' be so sharply and primitively defined? We never assumed that the self extended to a book, or a movie, or a diary, all these analogue technologies that were indispensable in their time. Yet each of these things were forms of exo-memory. Each of these ancient devices showed that our memories are bound up in more than just the neurons in our brain. The memory pin merely represents the final point of a transformation that has been underway for centuries. Memory – the true place where the human condition, the soul, the essence of who we are lies – has always extended beyond our minds.

234

Memory, in its natural condition, is a highly fallible, flawed tool. I am perfecting the human condition. What I am doing in here is enhancing a flawed creation, and raising it up from the darkness and the lies of human recollection. This is *evolution*." His eyes shone as he said it all, like he really believed it.

"Oh," I said. "So you're one of those."

"And what would that be?"

"A cunt."

Tauc opened his mouth to retort; I placed the barrel of the 107 in it. His eyes went wide.

"Seems to me," I said, "that the bigger the brain, the more thorough the rationale for evil. Don't you people take an oath?"

I withdrew the barrel and he swallowed, as though trying to get the taste out of his mouth. "Who says this is not a way to protect the integrity of memory?"

"All the non-cunt people."

He looked at me, eyes flat. "It's not going to matter soon, what you people think. It's just not going to matter anymore."

I opened my mouth to ask him why when my pocket vibrated. I took out the business card in it.

`Kien: the attack has been repelled. The Chinese have sent in a division. Get out now.`

I looked back at Tauc. "I'm wasting my time anyway with a sick fuck like you. Now," I nodded sideways at the wall, "Turn this thing on."

Tauc wiped his mouth. He muttered a few words into the air; the spherical wall faded, replaced by glowing screens showing images in three dimensions, covering the entire surface. Each was the moving picture of a person, by day or night, at rest or partying, usually always smiling and with a drink in their hands. Hundreds of screens, all seeming to blend into the other, switching every few seconds at random to show another person in another scenario.

"The fuck is this?"

The Omissioner cleared his throat, hesitating.

"Shit. No lecture? No mad scientist speech? This must be truly messed up. Now, I asked you a question: the fuck is this?"

Tauc licked his lips. "This wasn't my idea—"

"You don't answer my question, one more time, and the not-killing-you deal is off. Speak."

"This," he said, chin up, looking around at the screens, "is a simulation. Happy Jhun, Koi and the others felt something should be done with all the spare computational power of the quantum computer. At the start we were just manipulating the memories of the local Vietnamese, on orders from Macau. But my assistant – the one *you* murdered – had the idea. We feed in all the data from the guests. Everything they've ever put out onto the freewave, everything they've ever revealed about themselves in a search or a purchase or through conversation or point-of-view entertainment. All this gives us a close-to-perfect simulacrum. A virtual being that acts exactly as the real one would on the freewave." He started getting the shiny-eyed look again. "Given most of our lives are lived out virtually, one almost wonders if we have not created the first ecosystem populated by artificial intelligence. Crude, yes, but enough to pass as real to all the friends and family who look upon these virtual lives and *believe* them to be real."

"Professor Samuel Kam Ching. He inside this monster?"

Tauc shrugged and said the professor's name out loud. One of the screens glowed brighter than the others and expanded, taking up the space of four profiles. It was the professor, steel-framed glasses shining in the light, sitting on a lounge with a glass of red wine in one hand, smiling a modest, uncertain smile. But still, he looked happy. Behind him and to the left, arms crossed, leaning against the wall was his good friend, Henry Yun.

"And where's the real professor?"

Tauc's thin smile wavered. "What?"

I nodded again at the screen. "The real professor – where is he?"

The old man shook his head slightly. "Could you really be this stupid?"

"The real stupid here," I said, struggling to resist the urge to break the man's neck, "is the skinny old cunt insulting an angry man holding a gun."

The card vibrated again. I glanced at it.

Kien: we're withdrawing from Xuân Tăng. The town has been retaken. Get to the jungle beyond the perimeter within thirty minutes, and we'll find you.

I slapped Tauc twice, his head snapping left and right. Then I grabbed him by the collar and made him look me in the eye.

"Dead," he said, the iron of his arrogance finally dented. There was fear in his eyes, blood on his lips. "If your friend is in that computer, he's dead. They killed them, drained their bank accounts, sold off their assets. But they made it so it looked like they were still alive. That was the genius of it, updating their social network feeds, using voice samples to simulate conversations, send the occasional e-mail if it fit the profile. Well-heeled old men and women, especially widowers, having a late-life crisis – you'd be surprised how easily people believed it, family and friends believed it. It wasn't me." His voice rose in pitch. "It wasn't my idea. They all were in on it. The police, the local government and military, all the businesses, all the bosses, everyone in this town was *in on it*. The money was bigger than the cut they got from Macau for the memory pins. A lot bigger. They kept it all to themselves. There's a church outside of town, a Catholic church." His attention wandered, eyes caught in the distance. "Everything, *everything* that happened here was a dream. Think about that. Isn't that something remarkable? I think it might be something quite extraordinary."

I looked at the picture of the professor. "Conversations?"

"Huh?" Tauc was finding it hard to focus.

"What do you mean, '*conversations*'?"

"Well, you can talk to the simulation."

I don't know why, but I felt this need. Some strange compulsion to talk with Professor Ching. No time, none at all, but still I said: "Put him on."

It took Tauc another slap to get him to understand what I was asking; when he did, he put me through.

The image up on the wall changed to that of the professor, in his hotel room in the Golden Dragon. Book open on his lap, glass of red in hand.

"Professor."

He looked up in surprise. "Hello?"

"Professor Ching. It's Mister Pierce."

He closed his book. "I see. Where are you, sir?"

I winced. "Um, let's just say I'm speaking through internal comms."

His expression went from surprised to quizzical. "Ah. Mister Pierce, yes, what can I do for you?"

"I hear you found Mister Yun."

"Ah, yes. I had forgotten I'd told you about that. Yes, together again." He seemed somewhat distant as he spoke. I figured our meetings had only registered on the cameras of the casino, and nowhere else, so the system had almost no information to go on, about our relationship. This professor didn't really know me.

I cut to it.

"Professor, you're dead."

"I beg your pardon?"

"They killed you for your money. You're living inside a simulation."

"Is that so?"

He took it well. Bemused, more than anything, edges of his mouth tweaking into a smile. He was dead and I was right, but still: I felt kinda stupid under that gaze.

"Ah, forget it. I'm talking to a ghost."

"Evidently."

I'd turned to Tauc to tell him to cut the connection when the professor said, with some hesitation: "Mister Pierce."

"Yeah?"

"Do you have any evidence?"

"Evidence?"

"That I am living in a simulation."

I was running out of time, and didn't have much inclination to discuss philosophy with a character in someone else's movie. But something itched at my conscience. Yeah, that fucken useless thing. "I dunno, mate. Ever feel like you're just going through the motions?"

"Don't we all?"

"Nah. I mean, deep down." I motioned at the room around me. "Dunno how this thing works. Takes your online life and replicates your character out of that, or something. Seems to me, though, if that were true, you wouldn't have much of an inner life."

The professor's smile faded. His put a finger to his bottom lip, rubbed it slowly.

"I'm not sure," I continued, "but I figure even the most powerful supercomputer doesn't know what the taste of wine is like in your mouth. In mine."

The professor put down his glass.

"Look mate, I got to go. You do too. Sorry."

"If it is true that I have been killed," said the professor, "you taking the time to tell me so is passing strange."

"Yeah. Yeah it is."

"But I want you to know, Mister Pierce, I appreciate you doing so."

I grunted.

"I've often wondered if I'm the dreamer or the dream. Yet, when I did, I always came to the conclusion that this rumination serves no purpose. Dreamer or dream, there are still worlds to live within. Dreamer or dream, free will is either an illusion, or is real. One is much the same as the other. You see what I am saying, Mister Pierce?"

"Not really, mate. All I know is that I'm alive and you're dead, your body lying in a mass grave near a church. All I know is, that where you are, revenge means nothing. Here it means everything."

The professor opened his mouth to reply. I cut the connection.

Out the main floor, I pushed Tauc towards the Merzenich Drive. "Where're the other exits."

"Exits? There's only one."

I said *bullshit* and struck him across the forehead with the stock of the 107. He staggered and fell on his butt. As I unshouldered my backpack he said, blood trickling down his forehead: "Beat me all you want. There's still only one exit." He pointed a crooked finger at the elevator. "And that's it."

I looked around the factory. I couldn't see a lie in the man's face, nor could I see a second exit. I looked up at the roof near the Merzenich Drive, where the black cables twisted out of the ceiling.

Yeah. Yeah, that was it.

I kneeled and carefully withdrew the contents of the bag. Four bricks of hexogene splice-linked to a Caretaker system.

Tauc looked at the explosives then back at me. His voice was tight. "What *exactly* are you planning on doing?"

"Could you really be this stupid?" I asked, backhanding him before he had a chance to answer.

I ran back to the elevators with one of the bricks. I said: "Endel Ebbinghaus. Number one, wait until the doors open at one of the floors above. If there are people with guns waiting, explode."

A small strip of flexiscreen on the underside of the brick lit up with the words: Yes, Mr Ebbinghaus.

I stuck the brick to the inside of the elevator, near the control panel, out of sight to those opening the door, and pulled the unconscious tech clear. As expected, the doors closed immediately. I ran back to the Merzenich Drive. Just as I got there a muffled explosion sounded from somewhere above. The elevator doors shook and bent slightly, warping the smooth, gleaming metal. Dust drifted down from the ceiling.

Tauc was dazed, still sitting, blood on his face. He looked pale and weak. I grabbed another brick of hexogene, hooked a boot into something no doubt delicate on the Merzenich interface, and hauled myself up. I set the brick in the cables and said: "Endel Ebbinghaus. Number two: wait until I'm behind cover, then detonate."

Yes, Mr Ebbinghaus.

I grabbed the other two bricks and jogged back towards the rear of the room. Tauc, realising what was happening, groaned to his feet and staggered after me. I hunkered down behind a large piece of machinery at the end. The roof blew.

I closed my eyes against the white afterimage of the blast, and then the ear-splitting *boom*. The room shook, the glass façades of the offices at the end of the room shattered, a wave of silica collapsing to the ground. Tauc lay on his side screaming, hands over ears. I checked the magazine in my 107. When the roar stilled, I stood to see the damage.

Above, a hole fifteen metres across in the roof. Below, rubble, and no trace of the quantum computer. The air drifted with dust, a small fire crackled somewhere. A silver car – a Tesla Europa – had fallen from the carpark above, front end in the rubble, rear fender caught on the edge of the hole.

I nodded. "Nice."

Tauc stood next to me, looking at the damage. He mumbled: "My God. You savage. What have you done?"

I grabbed him by the collar, half inclined to punch him again. But he was already as beat as he was gonna get. Bloodied, face covered in dust, eyes watering. I let the collar go and the beaten dog slipped to the ground.

I held up the bricks: "Endel Ebbinghaus. Numbers three and four. After I climb up the Tesla and am out of sight, wait one minute, then detonate."

Yes, Mr Ebbinghaus.

Yes, Mr Ebbinghaus.

I stuck one to the large piece of machinery near Tauc – I figured it was the pin-printer – then jogged over to the entrance of the nightmare room, and planted the other high on the wall. I hesitated. A memory came, brief, of the old man, Professor Samuel, looking at me. Uncertain smile, hope in his eyes. The scars on my face itched.

I shook my head and ran towards the car, jumped onto the bonnet, and pulled myself up. It creaked under my weight, dust fell from the corners of the hole, but it held. As I hauled myself into the darkness of the carpark above, I heard a voice from below. "Wait!" Omissioner Tauc scrabbled onto the bonnet, made it to the windscreen, and slid back down again. His voice, thin and pleading, drifted after me, begging me to stop as I turned and ran towards a neon green exit sign in the distance. The carpark was expansive and mostly empty, as the two levels above it would be.

I slammed through the exit door and into a bright white stairwell. The only way was up. I took the stairs three at a time, past the second sub-basement and halfway to the first when the hexogene went. I gripped the railing as the rumbling, like that of a minor earthquake, shook the stairwell. Plaster fell from the walls, something metallic rattled under my feet, but that was the anti-climactic extent of it.

I made it to ground level and stood, chest heaving. I could continue up, I could go through an alarmed exit to the outside, or I could push through a door opposite the exit, that led out into the main casino floor. I listened at the exterior door.

As my ears dialled up I could hear voices, talking in Chinese. Clipped, interspersed by rough laughter. Maybe military. I turned the motion detector back on. Six signatures, maybe seven. Maybe I could burst through, gun them down. Maybe. Then the alarm would sound and I'd have a minute before the rest arrived. Up, there was only more up. A good idea if cornering myself or taking a long dive were my intention.

On the other side of the casino floor were the gleaming kitchens. On the other side of the kitchens, the loading bay. In the bay, heavy-duty delivery trucks that would probably still start to my thumbprint. Probably.

I opened the casino door a crack. Less than two metres away were the thick red curtains that surrounded the main gambling floor. The sounds of K-pop and the clatter of clay chips seeped through. I eased in.

There was a guard's station back here somewhere. I walked along the circumference, hidden by the curtain, until I found it. A recessed area with a sink, coffee and tea machine, some cheap plasteel chairs. Two uniforms hung on the wall, but both were far too small. I took one of the blue security caps emblazoned with the logo of the Golden Dragon, and stretched it down over my head. The curtain ended at this point. The only way across the floor to the kitchens was to walk it.

I took stock of my weapons. I had the 107, with close to a full clip of thirty rounds, plus three more clips in the harness under my leather jacket. I had the disrupter pistol, which was pretty much only good for blowing out neural implants at a range of less than six feet. My knuckledusters were jammed into the pocket of my jeans.

The explosives were all gone. I lit a cigarette, smoking it as I took off my jacket, hooked the strap of the 107 over my shoulder, retracted the stock and fitted the gleaming blue weapon under my arm. I put the jacket back on and finished the Double Happiness.

I sighed out my last cloud of smoke, flicked away the butt and stepped out into the room.

43

You'd hardly know a war was going on.

It was still half-full inside. Bleary-eyed gamblers hunched over gaming tables. Sweating on the roll of the dice or the fall of a tile. White burlesque dancers up on the stage, shaking hips and shoulders provocatively to catchy music; no-one watched them. A floorman at each group of tables, watching the gamblers; four security staff, that I could see, watched the gamblers as well, walking slowly between the green-felt hardwood tables.

I hunched my shoulders, kept my head down, and walked across the room.

I was ten metres from the kitchen doors when Abbadabba and Big Tuna walked through them. The large Nigerian and larger Japanese stopped and blinked at me. Abbadabba wore a red leather jacket, his black head gleaming under the lights; Tuna wore a knee-length, shiny white coat and white-framed sunglasses.

I hoped for a moment of hesitation, even as I swivelled the 107 out from under my jacket, some recognition of our status as former crewmates. All I saw was the glint of professionalism and the shifting of hands to weapons. A triple burst hit Abbadabba high in the chest as he yanked at the pistol in his shoulder-holster, he half-turned and staggered; Big Tuna pulled a silver, pistol-gripped shotgun from under his coat and fired at the same moment I did.

I dived, ear stinging, behind a thick column coated in tiny mirrors. The stinging disappeared quickly, replaced by the start of a rock song inside my head, a guitar wailing. Not too loud, but distinct, in the background. I got to one knee and unclipped the gun strap, placing the 107 at my shoulder while patrons around me screamed and ran.

The music played:

Baamp!

bah-da-dup bah du-bah!

bah-da-du ba bah baum

I breathed out slow; two tables over a Chinese man trying to place a Pai Gow bet yelled at the dealer as he left the table. I popped around the other side of the pillar.

Nothing. Keeping low, I crab-walked, trying to flank the position Big Tuna had dived behind.

Three things seemed to happen all at once:

wood splinters from the gaming table exploding next to my face—

me flinching—

and an ear-splitting boom.

I spun to see a security guard lining up his shotgun for a second shot; I pumped the 107's trigger, the guard spasmed and fell. Footsteps, a voice singing to an insistent drumbeat, the *boom* of shotgun fire as I dived from one table to another.

I swivelled and fired as a security guard rounded a table, he folded, dropping his shotgun, as the triple-burst hit his groin, I swivelled again at the swish of clothes and the 107 was smashed from my grasp. Big Tuna, still in motion, levelled his shotgun at my head. I grabbed the barrel and pushed up as he fired again *BOOM*, this time into the ceiling.

My ears rang, the music played, I yanked Big Tuna forwards into my elbow. His white sunglasses shattered.

A cacophony of *bratatat* and *BOOM,* I staggered forwards as something struck my back. Chips on the tables around me danced as bullets rained down, I took three steps and forward-rolled, picking up the 107 from the carpet as I did so, and rose firing up at the mezzanine. Close to ten security personnel and military police were lined up, like a firing squad, at the glass-fronted railing overlooking the gambling floor, shooting down at me; at my return fire the glass boomed inwards, kneecaps were punctured, a helmet blown clean off.

The 107 clicked empty.

I ran towards the kitchens, swapping in a fresh magazine.

The firing started again, from above and behind, I jumped over Abbadabba's dead body as the music got louder and louder.

I hit the kitchen door at full speed with my shoulder; it snapped clean off its hinges and I flipped over the steel-topped kitchen bench beyond, while the guitar solo wailed:

Beuwwwwww!

Dede-ne-now ne-now

I stood and Broken-Tooth Koi was standing at the other end, machine-gun toting MP on either side of her. She smiled metallic and pointed something at me; it looked like a grey box with a wide, circular opening at the front.

The music roared inside my head:

BA-NA-NA-NEH NA-NEH NA-NEH NAH-NEH!

I smiled, head bopping to the music, and fired back. A split-second image of Koi's eyes going wide, then the nerve siren shattered and her white gloves were painted red. She bent over, the perfect skin of her face creased with shock, while I shot the men on either side of her in their heads.

Still bent over, Koi staggered, dripping blood, out the doors to the loading bay.

I followed.

The music played.

I found myself limping. Glancing down, I was surprised to see my leg bloodied from the right knee down. It wouldn't matter. It wouldn't matter so long as I could keep moving, get to that truck and drive out of all this, into the shadows of an impenetrable jungle.

The music abated, though only slightly. I stepped out into the sultry Vietnamese night.

Two trucks were parked in an otherwise empty bay. Koi was gone, trail of blood leading along the plascrete into the darkness.

The song ended.

I'd taken three steps, even smiled, when I glimpsed the flash of metal.

On instinct my fingers went to the side of my neck, quickly finding the thing lodged there. I yanked it out and stared at it under the naked white bulbs of the loading bay. A silver needle, three inches long, coated with the thin sheen of my blood. My fingers spasmed, the needle fell from my grasp. The 107 clattered against the plascrete.

Chrome Linh Phu walked from the shadows at the side of the bay. Black singlet, her bare arms populated with tattoos of slim, coiled blue dragons that undulated as she walked. Purple eye shadow and matching lipstick, head shaved save a short black mohawk. In her hand glimmered an electric blue needle pistol. She smiled at me and that felt a lot worse than staring down the barrel of a gun.

"Y—y—y—y—" I stammered, fighting unresponsive lips and tongue. An unwinnable fight: the neurotoxin coursing through my system was shutting down all muscle control.

"Endgame," she said. "It's been too long."

44

Sukhie, the huge Mongolian, pushed me down into the chair. Handcuffed, hands in front. My jeans cut off from the right knee down, leg wrapped in an old-fashioned bandage. Back aching, blood stains on my shirt, and a scattering of shotgun pellet holes in my left forearm, dried up now and healing.

Opposite, Happy Jhun was slumped in his dark leather couch, glass of brown liquor in his hand. Bags under his eyes, sheen of sweat on his forehead. He wouldn't look me in the face. Standing near the wall behind him, next to the piano, was Broken-Tooth Koi, right arm in a sling. She wasn't much for smiling, either. Beside her a large military policeman holding a machine gun with a drum magazine, his shining hair neatly parted right down the middle. The Axe was over to my left, sitting at the bar, a shotgun resting across his lap. The big American nodded, so very slightly, as he looked me in the eye. Sukhie took up position near the window to my right, arms crossed, frowning at me. He wasn't armed that I could see, though he wasn't the sort of man that needed to be.

Chrome Linh Phu stood at the front and centre of them all, hands on hips, looking down at me with the slightest curl of a smile at one corner of her mouth. Her long daggers in holsters under each arm, needle pistol at her belt, victory in her eyes.

"Endgame Ebbinghaus: a one-man wrecking crew." She paused as she shook her head. "Do you ever wonder how one, solitary individual could take down an entire chapter of the Macau Syndicate, demolish a secret memory-pin factory, and turn one of the most popular resorts in Vietnam to a pile of smouldering rubble?"

The question wasn't directed at me.

Jhun shrugged and drank.

"[He had help from the Việt Minh,]" Koi hissed, eyes like wet steel.

"No," said Phu, keeping her back to Koi, "He *enlisted* the Việt Minh to his fight. Quite a remarkable thing, for a simple foot soldier in a criminal gang, don't you think, Jhun?"

Happy looked up at her back from his empty glass. "Actually, this foot soldier is the one you ran away from in the cemetery, is it not?"

Anger passed over Linh's face. But it was brief. Still she kept her back to them.

"Strange," Linh said, "Happy Jhun, that you never reported Endel's presence to Macau."

Jhun returned to looking at the glass in his hand.

"Had you done that, we might not have lost one of the most lucrative sources of income for the Syndicate. Believe me, Jhun; after Mister Long has finished with Endgame, you're the very next person he'll be speaking with." Jhun didn't react to that, just turned the glass in his hands. The Axe shifted in his seat.

"Now," Linh said to me, "you've been unusually quiet, Endgame. Got anything to say?"

"Yeah. Got a cigarette?"

"No."

"I could really use a cigarette."

"I said no."

"Then you better shoot me, you mewling sociopath. I'd rather take a bullet than have to listen to you wax stupid for the rest of the night."

Linh laughed, and took her time doing so. "Ah, there he is. The man I've been longing to see." I blinked at that, such a strange thing to say. She kept speaking: "Ah no, I'm not going to kneel you down and put a bullet in your brainpan at Mister Long's behest. Please, he's not some peasant Chinese soldier, he's the most powerful man in Macau. What he has planned for you, Endgame, is exquisite."

Chrome did a slow turn, taking in all the others in the room. Koi glowered, but said nothing, the others averted their eyes. Linh finished the turn and stepped over to me. She took a knee and rested the inside of her forearm on my uninjured leg. Daring, just daring me. I shook my head at the balls on this woman. She smelled strangely good up close, like some sort of flower whose name I couldn't quite remember. Linh ran a finger down my forearm, lingering on the wounds made by the shotgun pellets.

"Before all that," she said, eyes meeting mine, "I have to get the bottom of the mess these incompetent dogs allowed to happen in one of the most tightly controlled spaces of our domain. Before I ship you off to Macau, Endgame, you, me, and everyone here, are going to have a little talk."

She stood up again, and retook her position, giving them all her back again.

"Anyone lies, and they're dead. I think you should all be dead already, but Mister Long, in his wisdom, has opted for finding the truth of things first. Now, Endgame: speak."

"My jacket is hanging on the bar stool over there." I said, nodding in that direction. "Give me my smokes from that, and I'll tell you everything."

Linh hesitated, before nodding at The Axe. He found my soft pack in an inside pocket and brought it over. I pulled one out, distracted for a moment by a dried bloodstain on the back of my hand. It looked like the king of hearts.

I put the cigarette in my mouth and The Axe lit it. He blocked Linh's view as he did so, and asked the question with his eyes. I shook my head *no*, he returned to the bar.

I took a long drag, savouring the bite of the smoke on my lungs, exhaled a slow, thick cloud of smoke, and told her the story.

"This is what happened, Chrome. Downstairs, under the rubble, is a quantum computer. I guess the virus you've embedded in your memory pins takes a lot of computational power."

"Ah," she said.

"Yeah. *Ah*," I replied. "I discovered that one. Doesn't worry you too much, I suppose. Building a world of amoral, brain-dead feed-zombies susceptible to suggestion by thugs and tyrants would be right down your alley. Widen that social circle of yours."

Her smile didn't reach her eyes. "You know, Endgame. Mister Long wouldn't mind at all if I cut your balls off before I returned you. Long as you're alive, he isn't so particular on the quality of it." She paused, considering. "I wondered about that tetrapin I found in your pocket. I guess you were planning to blackmail us with the information."

I took another drag on the cigarette, using two hands because of the cuffs. Sukhie was three metres away. About the right distance for a forward roll, followed by an elbow to the throat.

"The problem is," I continued, "that Mister Long spared no expense. The quantum computer had far more power than required. So someone here had a good idea – an inspired one, really. Feed all the personal data of a tourist into the computer and create an online simulation. Problem was, once the crews saw how easy it was to kill the tourists and dispose of their assets, they realised they were sitting on a gold mine. So they made the oldest mistake, the same mistake every stupid fucking gangster makes, and got greedy. They started to fight among themselves over the shares each crew got from knocking off superannuated Chinese. Jhun wanted everyone to slow down, partly because he didn't want to get caught, but also because the Golden Dragon was well run and profitable on its own. The others wanted things to go down faster, because their businesses were a joke and they wanted to smash, grab, and get away before anyone was the wiser. Situation like that, plenty of spots for me to find to place the wedge, break it all apart."

Linh's eyes narrowed. The man with the hair perfectly parted down the middle shifted on his feet, glancing at Koi.

"Jhun," I said, speaking past Chrome. "One thing I didn't quite get: this all seems like an awful lot of murder for a guy like you."

"Actually, it is," Jhun replied, voice clear. "At first I thought: fuck them. It was these wealthy Chinese. These people who own all the land, all the business in the Philippines, who buy our politicians. These people, I thought, are just more greedy Chinese, like the ones who fished out our oceans because theirs are all empty. Like the ones who traffic our women, because they don't have enough of their own. So fuck them, this is my thought." Jhun rubbed his forehead. "But it worked too well, this nightmare machine. It could copy almost any tourist who came here, and if we killed them, it could liquidate all their assets. Very clean, Endel, very easy. So we became like them. You're right, old friend: we became greedy. This place now, all that's left are the ghosts." Then he said to Linh: "Endel did not do this thing. We cursed ourselves."

Sukhie unwound his arms. Koi's teeth glinted as she glared at Jhun. I figured one more blast to burst the damn. "The four bosses you placed here to run Xuan Tang decided to rob Mister Long," I said. "Now, Chrome, they're going to have to kill you. Because that's the only way for them to get out of this alive – buy themselves just enough time to clear out, disappear under a rock in some anonymous city somewhere in Southeast Asia."

Happy Jhun said: "*Paalam*, Endel, my old friend," and reached under each arm, pulling out his twin pistols.

All hell broke loose.

Shots rang out as—

Koi barked a command as—

The Axe roared and—

I dived and rolled at Sukhie, rising sharply, elbow aimed at his throat. It was a good plan. Toughest gangster in the world can't fight back too hard with their breathing tubes crushed.

But he tucked his chin in. Still, I struck it with full force, followed with another elbow to the same spot, and front-kicked him in the stomach.

He hit the glass behind him. The window shook, but held. Normally when I hit someone in the jaw as hard as I can, that jaw breaks. The only effect on Sukhie was a couple drops of blood at the corner of his mouth, and a mad gleam in his eyes. The huge Mongolian bellowed and charged, flashing strikes with open palms. As I tried to block the blows he rammed me with his chest and shoulders, driving me back into the wall behind, smashing the wind from my lungs as the wall behind me cracked, and the music started again.

The guitar, wailing.

Baamp!

bah-da-dup bah du-bah!

bah-da-du ba bah baum

I was getting tired of this song.

Sukhie's elbow was up in my throat, trying to choke me out. Handcuffed, arms down, I couldn't get a good strike in. The music got louder, my vision started to fade, I kneed him in the stomach. He smiled at me.

The lead singer screamed. *Yeah yeah yeah!*

As I blacked out I caught a snapshot view of the room behind

Sukhie's shoulder: Jhun, black pistol in each hand, pinned to the couch by a chrome-handled dagger, his shirt stained red. He stared at the floor to one side, unmoving. Koi and her gunner slumped against the far wall, eyes open and staring the way Jhun was staring: at nothing, at eternity. The Axe on elbows and knees, one hand gripping the stump of his wrist, blood pumping out. He was crawling towards his severed hand, six feet away on the carpet.

Finally, Chrome Linh Phu, sitting on a bar stool, one leg swinging idly. Watching Sukie and me fight, her eyebrow raised. That was the last image I saw as I blacked out: Linh, watching me choke to death, a mixture of curiosity and mild disappointment on her face.

The music woke me up.

Sukhie was lying on my bad leg. He raised himself slowly with his hands and shook his head, dislodging a layer of dust.

A chunk of broken plascrete lay on my chest. Sukhie got his bearings and fixed his small black eyes on me just as I heaved the rubble off my chest with both hands and smashed it over his head. He grunted and fell sideways; I staggered to my feet with that damn song ringing in my ears.

The wall in between lounge and bedroom had collapsed.

Sukhie got to his feet, face a mask of blood.

"Stop!" I yelled, straining to hear myself over the music. "Mister Long is your enemy now, him and that bitch in the next room. You beat me here, the next thing you'll feel is her blade at your throat."

I don't think he heard me. Sukhie was listening to something in his own head. The demon song of rage. He yelled something in Mongolian and charged. I twisted, tripping him as I grabbed a double handful of the back of his shirt, and flung him in the direction he was already headed. His arms flailed as he careened towards the window, two-hundred kilograms of fat, muscle, and reinforced bone, headfirst into the plate glass. The glass bloomed frost-like with cracks, shattering with a volume that momentarily drowned out the music, and Sukhie was gone. Replaced by the vista of a smouldering town and a squall of warm wind.

I ran back into the lounge room, staggering as I put pressure on my injured leg. I dropped down next to The Axe, yanking the belt off my jeans as I did so. Facedown on the carpet, I wrapped the belt around the stump of his wrist, and pulled him over.

The Axe stared at the ceiling. His beard was matted with blood.

Linh laughed softly, directly behind me. My music played underneath it all.

I roared as I tore the hand axe from the holster inside my dead friend's jacket, spinning, blade flashing, and Linh cried out, rolling with the blow. She got to her feet as I got to mine, blood trickling from high on her forehead.

The leather handle creaked as I grasped it two-handed, as though trying to crush it, bearing down on the weapon with all of my hate. I said: "I'm going to cut your hands off and feed them to you."

Linh had her blades in her hands, gleaming with blood, but she backed away.

I stepped forwards. I didn't care anymore. To get within range of this woman's blades was to commit to bleeding out here on this plush purple carpet. But I *didn't care*. At that moment all I wanted was the peace to be found in crushing my enemy's windpipe with my bare hands. Just one more body to stuff into the abyss, before I followed.

Linh took another step back. She'd been around monsters like me long enough to see what was written, down there.

She said: "Your daughters."

I gripped the handle even tighter, if that were possible, but stopped moving. "*What?*"

"Your daughters. Mister Long has your daughters."

45

I sat in the lounge chair opposite Jhun's body, smoking a cigarette, looking down at The Axe.

Mister Long was there, projected on-retina, sitting a metre behind the dead American. Linh sat on one of the bar stools, cleaning her needle pistol. She'd unlocked my handcuffs. She knew me well enough to know they weren't needed anymore.

Long wore a pressed red silk shirt with a stiff mandarin collar. He sat on a comfortable leather lounge, one leg crossed over the other, gentlemanly. Between his middle and ring finger he held a cigarette, the filter smudged with his lipstick. He looked out at me from behind the mask of a face made young with the miracle of modern nanotechnology. Behind the young face, old eyes that shone with the ancient animus of the dragon.

He looked me over, not much bothering to hide his contempt. I wore a white T-shirt stained with grime and sweat; my leather jacket was shredded in the spots where I'd been shot, exposing the dull shimmer of spideriron underneath. My face crusted with dried blood. I took a swig from the bottle of expensive whisky I'd found in Jhun's bar. The scars on my face and forehead itched.

Long waved his cigarette at my clothes. "[Charming. You always dress perfectly for your role, Mr Ebbinghaus.]"

"Yeah, well, I've killed fifty of your men in three days. That's the look I'm going for."

"[They are all replaceable.]"

"No," I said, looking at Jhun. The Axe. "No, they are not."

Long took an unhurried drag on his cigarette, eyes watching me over the top of his hand. Smoke curled from his lips. He said: "[You are playing chess, Mister Ebbinghaus, I am playing Go. You indulge in crudities, bound by an eight-by-eight mind. I am limited by possibilities as numerous as there are atoms in the universe. You attack, attack, kill, capture the pieces on the board, until finally the king capitulates. But there is no king in Go. Nor is there the mindless and relentless killing. The capture of stones is a trivial aside, peripheral to the careful taking of territory, the strategic move and countermove, feint, and reply. I have colonised your mind, Mister Ebbinghaus, I have your family; there is no place you can move to that I do not already occupy. You sacrificed everything to get to the king. But here I am, just a stone. Incidental to a larger strategy you cannot possibly comprehend.]"

Weariness was falling across me like snow. I said: "Fuck me. Can't cunts like you ever just get to the point without a stupid fucken analogy? What do you want?"

He pressed his lips together. Linh, out of Long's line of sight, smiled briefly and shook her head.

"[Three things,]" said Long, barely above a whisper. "[First: kill you. Second: humiliate you. Third: enslave you]."

"How—"

"[No questions,]" he said. Not insistent, not hard, just dead and final and all I could do was quiet. "[You either accept that this is going to happen, or your wife and two, adorable, little daughters will die. You have ten seconds to make your decision. One—]"

"I'll do it."

A flicker of surprise on Long's face as he opened his mouth to say *two*.

"Just let me say goodbye to my wife," I continued. "Let me see that she is still alive."

Long took his time blinking. He waved his cigarette. A second image appeared.

Jian stood in what looked like a modern apartment. Her usual warmth was gone; she looked defeated, hunched in on herself, smaller somehow. Someone said something off-screen and she looked up, seeing me for the first time. She started to smile, but the smile faded as she saw my condition. "Oh, babe. What have they done to you?"

"Nothing. They can't touch me."

Jian wore no make-up, a single small mole below her left eye on otherwise flawless skin. It certainly looked like Jian. Though I'd been seeing a lot of ghosts lately.

"Where are you?" she asked.

"Tell me about the first time we met."

She glanced to her left, off screen.

"Don't worry about these people. They don't even exist. Just you and me."

Jian nodded, *yeah*. She half-smiled as she began speaking. "In the bar at the City of Dreams. I was ordering a beer when this Australian swaggered up to me in cowboy boots and a denim jacket. Like some tanned peasant fresh off a horse. But when he spoke to me, when you spoke to me, Endel, there was something gentle down under the chainsaw accent, and something vibrant behind those blue eyes." Her smile widened. "Though, you know, when we went dancing afterwards, you did dance like a peasant."

"Hey," I said, my smile mirroring hers.

"I bought you a jacket to replace that ridiculous denim thing you always wore. Though it doesn't look like you've been taking care of it." Her smile faded. "Or yourself, for that matter."

"Never was much good at that."

"No. No you weren't."

"Are the girls okay?"

"Not really. But if you are asking if they've been hurt, then no, they haven't been hurt."

I cleared my throat. Over at the bar, Linh looked angry for no obvious reason. Long looked bored, eyes glazed as he smoked his cigarette. I said: "Tell the girls I love them."

"They know, Endel."

"Tell them anyway."

Jian bit her bottom lip. It glistened as she said: "Don't, Endel."

"There are no choices here, babe."

"Fight. *Fight.*"

"All I know how to do." I sighed, and in it was the weariness, in every fibre and every bone. "But I'm all punched out. The only choice I have now is between me, or you and the girls."

She shook her head, water in her eyes.

"So this is goodbye."

"No, Endel." Her voice cracked.

"Start again. Promise you'll start all over again."

"*No.*"

"You will. You'll be a great mother. You are a great mother. With or without me."

Her smooth skin creased with pain. Tears welled. "I can't do—"

The connection blinked out. "[Excuse me, Mister Ebbinghaus, but I have a weak stomach. All those saccharine platitudes are making me ill.]"

"*Motherfucker.*"

Long took a drag on his cigarette, old eyes watching. "Hmm. [Curious, how the ultra-violent can be so prone to such intense – if formulaic – sentiment. So strange.]"

"Don't you touch them." I jabbed a forefinger at his image. "We have a deal."

"[Yes. We have a deal.]" His delivery was detached, deadpan, like he was confirming a dinner order.

I felt the scream, buried there under my heart, wanting to tear itself from my body. "Swear you won't hurt my wife and children. Swear you'll let them live their lives."

"[Oh yes, I swear. Of course.]"

"Swear it on your mother's soul." With monsters like Long you sometimes wondered if they even had mothers, but it was worth a shot.

The shot worked. Something shifted in that mask, and the cold malignancy of his gaze wavered, if only for a moment. He wet his lips. "[I swear, Mister Ebbinghaus. Now, I have wasted too much time on this cascading failure. Goodbye, Mister Ebbinghaus. Miz Phu has a bullet for you. Use it, or I'll flay the skin from your daughters myself.]"

The image blinked out and it was just Chrome and me again. The wind gusted through space where the window had once stood in the next room, rain pattered on the glass and carpet.

Linh looked me over with an expression I didn't recognise. "You were a good man. You only became weak after you met Jian. Love made you a bitch."

"The fuck you know?"

Disappointment. That was the look. It passed quickly. She opened her hand, in it glimmered a memory pin. "The bullet."

I flinched inwardly. A stranger's pin. A suicide trip. Not deft manipulation, but a brutal ripping away. A mind like mine, so frayed, so attenuated, couldn't ride against that.

"Who will I be?" I asked.

"Does it matter?"

"No." I took a drag on my cigarette. "No. I guess not."

After a pause I asked: "Do you know who I used to be?"

"Yeah."

"Then tell it. Give me that before I go."

She ran a hand over the shaved section of her head, next to the mohawk. As she did so I glimpsed a wound on her bicep. A red gash, like a bullet would make. Jhun had made a mark, at least, before he'd taken a dagger to the heart.

"What would be the point, Endgame? Memory is pain. Memory is weakness. Memory is the chain that binds us."

I drank from the bottle, sucking air through my teeth as the fire of the booze hit my chest. "Are you even human anymore?"

"Yeah," she said. "A stripped-down version, Faster, more efficient, less encumbered by trivia."

"Trivia?" I took a drag on my cigarette. "Like morality, love, free will?"

She laughed, long and genuine. "We're fucking gangsters," she said, "not first-year philosophy students. Morality? From the man who just murdered fifty. Fuck that hypocrite's game. Free will? There's no such thing, just the streets, Endgame. All of it: the streets. The language of the streets isn't fucking Confucius, it is violence. It is the music that flows from the barrel of a gun. It is the syntax of shattered kneecaps. The wails of the desperate secretly wishing to ride the Styx. I am merely an instrument of that language, like the calligrapher's pen."

I furrowed my brow at the phrase. "Why did you—"

"But I'll tell you who you are, Endgame. A last request before your execution."

She reached behind the bar, grabbing herself a green, white-labelled bottle of saké and a small glass. I hadn't seen Chrome drink before, nor laugh. I guess she figured revealing some of herself didn't matter so much, now we were at the end.

Linh poured herself a shot and downed it, all in one smooth

motion. She savoured the taste, rolling it over in her mouth, eyes closed. Then she poured herself another and let it sit in her hand while she told her story.

"Jian walked straight into a safe house in Shanghai. It was a trap we'd worked into her memory during a regular check-up with an Omissioner. An insurance policy if you ever ran. There was no way you were ever leaving Macau. But you knew that somehow, didn't you, Endgame?"

I lit another cigarette. "I know you were threatening to kill her. The kids. There in the graveyard. That I know."

"I don't kill children," she said, sharply. "In the graveyard I was trying to *motivate* you."

I narrowed my gaze. "Huh?"

She waved away my confusion. "Quiet. Listen." She continued: "Happy Jhun and you knew each other. When you split up from your wife to draw your pursuers away, you went straight to a part of the world where you'd knew he'd be. Was it the Mildred Pierce?" I said nothing, but she caught something in my face and continued: "Yeah. Well, Happy owned that pub. You'd probably met him there a few times. Some echo of memory brought you there, searching out safe ground. But that's the thing. Long has fucked with your mind so thoroughly, every path in it leads back to him. He has surveillance and informants, sure. But his most reliable informant is *you*. You will always betray yourself to him, Endel. Always.

"So: you were close, you and Happy. Two poor immigrants who'd worked their way together up through the ranks of the Syndicate. You were thick as thieves, you two, discussing your plans, making your plays. You were a boss, Endgame, not a foot soldier. That's the reason you could come here to Xuân Tăng and make it a bloody playground for your revenge. You were one of the smartest, toughest bosses in the Macau Syndicate." She looked me over. "You're a shadow of that man now. Now you're dumb, and here, trying to fight a losing battle."

"Feel like I've been fighting that battle my whole life," I said, thinking. As she spoke, something sparked in my memory and an old, faded thought resurfaced. A tattered photo of Mister Long's suite in the Grand Lisboa, of me sitting with Jhun and Mister Long. The scent of smoke from Mister Long's cigarette, held between elegant fingers; the vividness of Jhun's smile, his darting eyes while he talked business; lights of the city below; no sounds in the picture, but I knew we were talking business. All bosses, equals, discussing our next moves. Something strange grew in my breast then. Pain, but yet an old pain. Ancient grief, for someone I used to know, from someone I used to be.

"Happy was protecting you," said Linh. "When you turned up, out of the blue like that. He knew you were on the run, he must have known. Long had sent messages to all the bosses, telling them to look for you."

Linh drank her saké, again with eyes closed. When she opened them, she was looking down at Jhun's body. "An unhealthy occupation, being your friend."

I sat there in my exhaustion, my music playing in the centre of my head, softly. Sukhie must have caused some internal injury when he put me through the wall.

Rage flickered inside, at this woman, the blood of so much of me on her hands. But there was something else there, as well. A weight on me such that I couldn't even raise words against her. This burden, pressing down, much more than the exhaustion of waging a war. Wangaratta, Ha, Happy Jhun, The Axe, every member of my crew, all those bodies weighed heavy on me.

"God. You're too smart to be a street thug, Endel. We used to run Macau."

I looked up at her. "We?"

Linh poured herself another drink, ignoring the question. She held the glass again, filled to the brim, as she spoke. "But you met *that woman,* and you changed. Didn't want to do what needed to be done. Didn't want to be a boss anymore."

My scars itched. Or maybe it was my memories. There was an image there, on the tip of my brain, which I couldn't quite grasp. "So—so what happened?"

Linh sighed, a pissed-off one. "You made a deal with Long to ease you out of the organisation. Cash yourself out. Wipe all the memories of our activities. Start a new life."

"Then—But—"

"But you trusted Mister Long to do it. *Idiot.* Happy had moved to Vietnam, so you couldn't ask him. Long didn't let you go, how could he? He kept you close, made sure you weren't compromised. Maybe he found you useful as a triggerman, as well, taking out the competition. Whatever it was, that painted cadaver is a fucking monster and you were a fool for thinking he'd do as you asked."

I exhaled a cloud of smoke. "No. That's not right. I wouldn't have trusted him. Not with that much."

"You wanted to know who you are. I'm telling you."

"For someone claiming to be so stripped-down, you seem to have a whole lot of trivia on me on file."

She drank her saké.

I said: "About seventy-five per cent of what you said seems about right, maybe has the shape of the truth."

"Seventy-five per cent is pretty good for a man who's been walking around with zero for two years."

I raised an eyebrow, *true,* and buried my face in the whisky bottle. I'd gone through three-quarters already and was starting to feel it. No itch to hold me back now, no desperate hopes. Mind and focus drifting, music in my head, rain in the next room. Chrome seemed in no rush. She looked over my head, out the window to the town beyond, purple lips glistening with the saké.

I smoked a cigarette, decided it was time. "How we doing this?"

It took her a moment to refocus, get what I was saying. "Our Omissioner here seems to have gone missing. We'll have to take you back to Macau to do it."

"No. I just want to get it done."

"How?"

"There's another Omissioner in town here. A Chinese guy, real good."

Linh made to protest, I cut her off. "I don't want to wait until Macau and whatever butcher you've dredged up there. I want to break those chains of memory, like you say, and be done with it. So let's get it done."

She held her glass up at what I said, and downed it. "Okay, Endgame," she said, soft. "Time for you to come home."

46

Not even my dreams could hide the footsteps. You get bound up tight for long enough in this life, and no motherfucker can sneak up on you. Maybe I'd been in youth detention, watching the eyes and the hands of every inmate passing by. Maybe I'd been shifted from home to home, a foster kid, and so learned it then. Maybe.

Lot of maybes, because those parts of my life weren't there anymore, for me to ponder. More it came from my joining the dots. Different places I remember living. Flashbacks of faces, different faces, hovering above, twisted in anger or something worse. The way I spoke, the accent and the words I used. They are of a specific class in Australia, and of a specific place. It wasn't so smart, to try to figure these things, better leave those black dogs sleeping. Problem was the mind had this yearning, a primal urge to seek answers to the mystery of the self. The more these things were kept hidden, the rougher the hunger to find the truth.

So I dreamed of another man's life, dreamed these snippets that I could never truly know were real. Dreamed these dreams, fully in this floating world, and yet still I heard the footsteps coming. Even as the tendrils grasped at me, clung to the corners of my eyes and my mind, I reached down under the mattress, to the metal shelf made to hold my gun.

"Attack!" said a high-pitched voice.

I let the pistol go as the two bodies hit me. Two small bodies, one on my chest and the other below the navel. The air expelled from my lungs, my back rising a couple of inches from the mattress. The girls giggled.

I groaned, rugged, like a roused bear, and rose from the waist, toppling Kylie off onto the bed. "Girls."

"Mummy said we could," said Kylie.

Weici hit me with a pillow. *Whump.*

"She did?"

"Mummy told us to jump on Daddy."

Weici hit me again. *Whump.*

"Okay honey, stop that."

"I'm going to yoga." I looked up and Jian was in the doorway, arms crossed, smiling, look on her face daring me to issue a complaint. Her hair was back, she wore her sleeveless grey sweatshirt, sunglasses on her head. The morning light glowed on the side of her face, and ah, man, this woman—

Whump.

"Great," I said.

"And then maybe brunch with friends."

"What?"

"I'm celebrating."

Whump.

I must have looked confused because she said: "My birthday."

"Oh right, yeah," I replied.

Jian, still smiling, said: "Oh. Right. Yeah." And left.

The smell of coffee wafted into the room. A pot, ready to go, as compensation for her nicking off all morning.

Whump.

I roared and picked up Weici, she screamed with delight. Then Kylie as well and they both squealed. I threw them onto the bed and tickled them both, their squeals getting wilder and wilder, limbs thrashing, sheets and pillows kicked off the bed, until I couldn't stop laughing and slumped back down next to them. They clambered back onto me and rested their head and hands against my chest, temporarily stilled. The primal need of the child to touch the parent, feel the safety of that embrace. I rested my hands on them and felt the ache in my legs and my back, tensed up even while I slept. I breathed, tried to let that tension go.

I asked the girls if they had school and they said *no silly, it's the weekend*. Great, I said. So we played 'zombie' until a plate got knocked off a table and broken. Then we played 'tea with zombie', and Weici put a pink unicorn hat on my head and pink scarf around my neck, while I moaned and drank air tea from a tiny plastic cup. This went on, with the game mechanics and zombie commands getting more and more complicated, until I said:

"Stop being so arbitrary, Weici."

"I like being arbitrary!"

I laughed. "Do you know what arbitrary means?"

"Um," she pondered. "That I make all the rules."

"Ah," I said. "Well, yes, kinda."

"Then I'm very arbitrary!"

I ran a hand through my hair. "Ha. Um, how about you girls watch the blue dog show?"

"Yay!" they chorused, and ran over to the beanbags, flopping down and commanding the apartment to put their program on.

I sighed and poured myself a cup of now-cold coffee. Reheated it, and drank of the acrid addictive beautiful brew. *Fuck yeah*. A cigarette would have made it perfect, but instead I sat down on one of the high kitchen stools.

And swore.

A face had appeared, just outside the kitchen window. Tight narrow green side path, where Jian grew her tomatoes and her chili.

I could have sworn some old bastard was there, peering in. The cup made a *clunk* on the tabletop as I put it down. I stood, moved to the window, looked left and right. Nothing.

I checked the apartment security data, on-retina, but there was no record of anyone on the property.

I ran a hand through my hair, doubting myself, looking back out the window. The tai screen murmured in the next room. I breathed in the faint smell of oranges, courtesy of the small green kumquat tree in the near corner.

"Daddy?"

"Huh?" I looked down and Kylie was suddenly there, looking up at me. "Did you get Mummy a present?"

"Um. Sure honey."

"*Daddy.*"

"What does that tone mean?"

She narrowed her eyes. "Remember last time, Daddy?"

I sighed. "Well, everyone keeps reminding me. So yes, I remember last time, which helped me to remember this time."

She raised a perfect little eyebrow, just like her mother did. "Well?"

I reached up to one of the high cupboards. One that Jian hates to use, as it requires her getting on tippy-toes and awkwardly extracting whatever she is looking for with fingertips. I pulled down a white box. By the time I'd retrieved it, Weici was there as well, big round eyes fixed on the container, unblinking.

I placed it on the kitchen bench and opened the lid. "Ta-dah!"

"Chocolate," breathed Weici.

"And more chocolate," said Kylie, pointing.

"Little marshmallows," said Weici, reaching out.

"Chocolate drizzle," said Kylie.

"Ah." I tapped Weici's wrist with a finger. "No touching."

"*Please.*"

"No."

"Just one little—"

"Weici," I said, voice low, absurdly low, exaggerated.

It was a towering thing, narrow and high. At some point food becomes so wanky, so performative, it isn't really food anymore, but a piece of art to look at and admire. Like those tiny dishes rich dickheads gaze upon at Michelin-starred restaurants. The cake wasn't quite at that point, but it was out of my comfort zone.

Still, it had everything the girls – all three – liked, according to the little card that had been set in front of it, as it sat behind curved glass in the store. 'Triple Chocolate Cake': *dark chocolate, salted caramel, chocolate chips, chocolate fudge frosting.* So I bought the tottering extravagant bloody thing, and the looks on the faces of the girls told me I had chosen correctly.

"We should put it on the dining table," said Kylie. "It looks nice there."

"True," I said.

"I'll take it," said Weici.

"You're too little," said Kylie.

"I am not." Weici grabbed the edge of the box.

"Careful, honey," I said.

Tippy-toes, hand on either side, she slid the box towards her. Kylie reached out and grabbed the open white cardboard lid. "I'm doing it."

Weici yanked, Kylie resisted, and I saw it all coming, a rough, "NO," rising in my throat but too late, Kylie's fingers slipping, Weici staggering back, the box tipping forwards, and the various forces of gravity, two competitive sisters, and Murphy's Law came into play.

Plop.

Weici's bottom lip jutted out a country mile, quivering.

Kylie screamed: "Weici!"

Weici exploded. Tears. Wails. Snot.

"I'm s—s—s—sorry, D—D—D—"

The jagged frustration over the dead cake quickly pushed aside, I hugged my daughter. Weici's shoulders shook.

"Oh honey," I said, smiling. "Don't worry."

I drew Kylie in with my other arm, and she, taking my lead said: "Don't worry, Weici, don't worry."

The sobs receded and Weici drew away from my chest, my shirt now blodged with snot and tears.

She said: "It's ruined."

I sighed. "Yeah."

"But it was chocolate."

"Hmm." I looked down at the cake. "You know, that top bit there hasn't touched the floor."

"Oh," said Weici, clutching her hands together.

"Oh," said Kylie.

"Get me a fork, Weici."

Her face brightened, and she did so. I speared a piece of the moist chocolate underside, which had now become the top of the cake.

"But we're not allowed," said Weici. "Are we?"

"Let me test it first. Hmm." I rolled the cake around in my mouth. "That's bloody fantastic."

"Me too," said Kylie

"Me too!" said Weici.

"Well," I said. "Get three paper plates."

The girls scrambled.

47

"What on earth are you doing?"

Jian was standing in the doorway, gym bag over her shoulder, eyes wide. The three of us were sitting in a circle, cross-legged, around a mound of shattered birthday cake, plates held up near our chests, forks in hand.

"Happy birthday, honey," I said.

"Happy birthday, Mummy!" squealed the girls. Weici held her fork aloft in the air, chunk of tasty dark cake on it.

"Is this how Australians eat cake?" she said, eyebrow strategically raised. "Looks about right."

"There was an accident," I explained.

I fished a candle and lighter out of my pocket, placed the candle on the highest point of the broken delicious mess, and lit it.

"No, Endel," she said, and her facial expression said: *No. Endel.*

"It's yummy!" said Weici.

"It's gross, girls."

"But our bits hadn't touched the floor. Daddy said."

"There's a six-inch rule," said Jian.

"Huh?"

"It can't be within six inches of the floor," said Jian, authoritatively, "Otherwise, scientifically: it's gross."

I pointed to the top of the cake pile. "That's more than six inches."

She raised her eyebrows. "So you keep trying to claim."

I made a *what the hell* expression and opened my palms.

She smiled, wicked, then sighed. "Is this the sum total of my birthday presents? Floor cake?"

"Top of the cupboard, bedroom," I said. "Behind the sleeping bag."

Jian dropped her gym bag on the seat. "Good."

She walked out, sashaying.

"Come on, girls," I said. "Finish what you have, and I'll get rid of the rest. It is kinda gross."

"But, Daddy…" said Kylie.

"I'll buy another one, okay?"

"The same?"

"Sure, exactly the same – now go watch your show."

They did and I cleaned the cake up, dumping the remains in the compost. The tomatoes would enjoy it, at least. I was wiping down the tiles with a sponge when my mind registered the absence. Of sound. The tai screen was off, the beanbags empty.

"Girls?"

I dropped the sponge on the kitchen bench and walked into the lounge room.

"Girls?"

Probably hiding.

I went into the bedroom to ask Jian. Her back was turned. There was something about her shoulders.

"Have you seen the girls?"

She turned. I grunted and jumped back.

"I love it," she said, holding up a silver necklace. But it wasn't Jian. *It* was an abomination. Her face was gone, replaced by that of an old man with a wispy beard. Everything else the same. Her body, her yoga clothes, even her hair. "You shouldn't have, Endel," said the thing, fastening it around her throat.

"What the fuck?"

"What's wrong, honey?"

The uncanny horror of it made me want to stave it in. I fumbled around next to the dresser behind me, glancing down and locating the metal baseball bat I kept there.

"Where the fuck are—"

It was gone. Glanced away for a nanosecond and the sick hybrid was gone. The end of the bat made a *clonk* on the wood floor. "The fuck?"

A breeze blew. Inside a room with a closed door and yet a breeze blew, and particles of the cupboard caught in the wind and it started to disintegrate, as did the floor nearby and then the side table and *what the fuck is happening here—*

48

Jian called. I grasped the doorframe to steady myself, and walked back through, without a rhythm.

"The bear awakes," said Jian, soft smile. She was standing behind the kitchen bench, steaming cup of coffee in her hand.

"Ah."

"Well?" she asked.

"Jian?"

"You are terrible in the mornings, Endel."

I looked down at my body. I was in my sleeping shorts. A dream, I guess it was—

"Your daughter wants you."

"Huh?"

Jian indicated the girls' room with a tilt of her head.

I looked back. My bedroom was still there, the bed was still there, sheets ruffled. *Just dreaming.*

I went to the girls' bedroom, assurance coming back to me, *just a dream, you're awake now.* Kylie was sitting on the edge of her bed. Just one bed, not a bunk. I blinked at the thought. *Why would she have a bunk?*

Kylie, red-and-white uniform. So cute and lonely and scared sitting there and something twisted, just a little, in my chest. I took a knee in front of her. She was so small in the expanse of her bed, tiny against the aura of her fears.

"What's wrong, honey?"

She looked down at her hands, clenched in her lap. She shook her head, *nothing*.

"First day of school," said Jian, from behind. "She's worried the other kids won't like her."

"That's not true," I said, scandalised. "They'll love you."

Kylie shrugged.

"The teachers will be nice."

"*They won't*," whispered Kylie.

"And if they're not nice," I said, with a light voice, "I'll burn down the school."

"Daddy!" said Kylie, looking at me now.

"That's not helpful, Endel," Jian said, from behind.

"I'll run in and grab my baby girl," I said, as I picked up Kylie and put her under one arm. She said: "*Wheeeeeeeeee*."

I started running around the room. "And kick over all the tables."

"*Wheeeeeeeee*."

"And throw you into the flying escape car!" I threw her onto her bed and she laughed.

I twirled, yelling about the school, and the old man was there again, in Jian's body. Again. I stopped. "The fuck?"

There was less of her this time, more of him, his shock of white hair sticking out in all directions. "Do you like my new style?" he asked, touching the sides of his wild hair.

He saw the expression on my face, and dropped his hands. "Just joking. It's a nervous habit. One that involves too little wit and too much emotional, ah, obtuseness."

I clenched my fist and imagined snapping the old man's spine with it. But then I remembered the beautiful scared little girl at my side, and breathed. She was back in the position I'd first seen her. Sitting on the edge of her bed, looking down at her hands.

"Kylie?"

I touched her knee. "Honey?"

She looked up and her face was gone.

I yelled. *Her face was gone.*

I leaped backwards, arms reaching out, trying to find something solid, something fixed, to stop my world spinning.

"Daddy," she said again, and her voice was muffled, her blank featureless empty face still pointed at me.

I couldn't take it and so whirled to find that old cunt. "What have you done?"

He wasn't scared. But any bonhomie he'd had was drained, and he was really looking at me now, eyes clear and fixed. I stepped towards him and he backed away. Not with fear, no, more like resignation. "You came to me, mate."

Kylie had stopped making noises behind me. Somehow I knew she was gone. Knew it but didn't want to turn and confirm. Redoubled my gaze on the old fuck in front of me. He moved into the next room, I stalked him. He was just an old man now, no hints of Jian.

"The fuck you talking about?" I asked him.

The man took a long breath, rubbing his mouth. "This is your subconscious, fighting. It happens, sometimes."

"Fighting what?" I asked the question even though I knew the answer. Somehow, knew, there, at the tip on my mind. The old man indicated the lounge-room tai screen behind him, and on it was an image of me walking hand-in-hand with Kylie in her school uniform. I knew it was today, the first day of school.

It flicked to Jian and me. A Lorcha restaurant. Smiling at each other, drinks in hand, moving in slow motion. Anniversary. Flicked to: picking Jian up in my arms, stopping traffic, forcing a random person to take us to hospital when she had fallen from her bike and broken her arm. Flicked to: the City of Dreams, her approaching me, knowing smile on her face.

The old man was gone again. Of course he fucken was, into thin air and I was left looking back at the screen, the images flicking faster and faster. "No," I said.

The screen blurred and so did my mind.

49

"Get ready," said the nurse.

I held my beefy hands out, ready. Terrified of dropping her, my shoulders hunched, not blinking. More fucken terrified than any day on the job. Three blade-wielding triads finding me unarmed, taking a piss in a back alley, had nothing on this moment.

"Hu-rrrrrrrrrr," grunted Jian.

There was a gush of water, soaking me from the chest down.

I looked down at myself, my hands, wondering if I'd missed the baby in the burst.

The nurse laughed. "Your waters have broken, Jian," she said, placing her hand on my wife's back. "We're nearly there."

Jian was in no mood for laughter. She was on hands and knees, facing the other way. She screamed, guttural. The nurse rubbed her back and I kept my hands out, wired. Early in the morning, no sleep, not a wink. Baby decided to come the night before and I hadn't left Jian's side.

I'd watched videos of babies coming out, and in them they always stopped at the shoulders. This little squished baby head poking out, down there, and for a moment the mother looked like some two-headed creature out of Greek mythology, before that last push brought it free.

But that didn't happen with Kylie. She just came straight out, no stuffing around, into my hands and I kinda juggled her, my hands slippery and wet. Kneeling on the crash-mat they'd put on the ground behind my wife, and I fell sideways, like I was taking a slips catch at the cricket. But I held her and lay there on the wet mat, smiling, stupid smiling, and the nurse was saying *good good, you did it*. Jian was saying *where is she? Where is she?* And I looked down at my little girl with her tiny crushed features and her pink skin and something rose inside me, and I broke into tears. First time in my adult life, and they were a shock but there was laughter in them as well, and I cried, chest heaving, as I stared at the child in my arms.

There was a strange whirring sound. I looked up from the ground and the old man was there, again. That fucking peeping tom, standing there. His brow was creased, eyes quiet, watchful.

I understood.

"Not this," I pleaded. "*Not this.*"

The old man opened his mouth to say something, but no words came out.

"Just leave me this," I said, and I was begging. I was begging and I didn't care anymore. My voice cracked and it didn't shame me. I didn't care *I didn't care about anything* bar this. "Just leave me this memory. Just this one."

A shadow fell across the old man's face. "I can't, Endel." His voice came from far away, like he was down the other end of a tunnel. "It has to be this way."

"No," I said. "My heart."

I looked back at my hands and the child was gone. Just big hard empty hands that were not strong enough. Never strong enough to hold onto anything that mattered in my pathetic fucking life. I wasn't even strong enough to hold on to a memory. My fingers curled into fists.

"NOT THIS."

5 0

Your name is Endgame Ebbinghaus.

I groaned and rolled over in bed. I fumbled at the side table, found my cigarettes and lighter. I tapped out a Double Happiness and lit it, savouring the sigh of recognition my addiction gave to its drug.

It's Thursday, 13 October, 2101.

I got out of bed, wearing only shorts, and walked over to the broad windows. I looked though the morning gloom over the city, the mammoth, bulging structures of the casinos draped in their eternal neon and the hard, perpetual rain. Macau: that steaming, throbbing gambling mecca; the dark underbelly of the Chinese Dream.

You're head of security for Mister Long, boss of the Macau Syndicate for a drug cartel.

A soft footfall on carpet, I turned, and she was standing in the doorway watching me. Wearing short black shorts and nothing else, she walked over to me in a way that brought to mind the power of a panther, coiled, ready to strike. Lean and muscled, sleeve tattoos from wrist to shoulder to shoulder to wrist shimmering blue, head shaved save a short mohawk dyed metallic purple.

She looked up into my eyes as she snaked her arms around my neck.

Your partner is 'Chrome' Linh Phu. You have been living together for three years. She runs security, with you, for Mister Long.

We kissed, Linh's mouth hot against mine, and there was something fierce in it. In the kiss, and the look she gave me when she pulled her head away, eyes locked on mine.

We both turned and looked down at the city.

You're going to run this town together someday.

PART THREE
The Escher Man

"Past events, it is argued, have no objective existence, but survive only in written records and in human memories. To make sure that all written records agree with the orthodoxy of the moment is merely a mechanical act. But it is also necessary to remember that events happened in the desired manner."

– George Orwell, *Nineteen Eighty-Four*

51

The Omissioner was taking her imminent execution better than most. Tears in her eyes, sure; her knuckles white as she gripped the real wood desk in front of her. Otherwise, though, she was holding it together well in the face of certain death at the hands of two stone-cold killers.

I stood, the Type-107 casually levelled at the woman's chest. Chrome Linh Phu leaned against the wall behind me, arms crossed, very effectively impersonating someone completely indifferent to proceedings. Down the corridor, past Linh, an unconscious receptionist and a wood-panelled door with a CLOSED sign hanging on the other side of it.

The Omissioner took a deep breath and said: "Endel, I know you."

"That so?"

"You came here for treatment. I—I helped you." She almost managed to hide the tremor in her voice.

I glanced around. Large tai screens hung down near two of the four walls, black frames hanging empty. The walls themselves full of prints, rows upon rows in black and white. Simple icons: a clenched fist; a woman's lips; four-leaf clover with a line through it; the queen of spades; black Buddha on white; an assault weapon; an open palm; the gender symbols for men and women combined into one;

an uppercase C with a small c inside; a cowboy hat; a dragonhead; a double-edged blade; an Escher of a man walking up and up an infinite stair case; and on and on, filling the walls from floor to ceiling. The only variation to the rows of prints were the tai screens, and behind the Omissioner, a long hologram of a landscape: bucolic, green, a soft wind blowing within the picture, pushing low white clouds across the scene and silently rustling the leaves.

The woman wore an elegant, neck-to-calf *qipao* of blue silk. She was full-figured, with rich black hair and intelligent eyes. On the desk in front of the woman was a nameplate: *Om. Aletheia Milas*, glowing in soft green holotype across a black-backed plaque. A jade cigarette case and matching lighter lay on the desk, forgotten.

I said: "Got to say, not ringing any bells."

"Listen—"

"Seems to me," I said, indicating the room with a nod, "this is the kind of place I'd remember."

Despite her predicament, the woman found a reason to smile at that. "No, Mister Ebbinghaus. With the amount of neural trauma I saw in your scans, as a result of years of memory wipes, this is *exactly* the kind of place your masters would make you forget."

"Hmm. Normally when I kill someone," I said, "they either beg, bargain, or try to bullshit me. I guess you're going for the last one: claiming we're old mates."

"We're not old friends." The Omissioner spoke rapidly, trying to keep a grip on her terror. "But I did treat you, several times."

"That so?"

"Yes, you were desperate. You needed—"

"Shut up," said Linh, quietly, and the woman shut up. Linh said to me: "Finish it, Endgame, this bitch could have some high-tech alarm set up."

I pried a soft pack of Double Happiness out of the top pocket of my denim jacket, and pulled one of the cigarettes out with my lips. I found my steel cigarette lighter in my jeans and lit the smoke. I did it all one-handed, the other gently lay against the cool steel of the trigger. "Just a minute, babe," I said to Linh.

I took a drag, let out a slow cloud of smoke, and nodded at the Omissioner's desk. "Real wood. Nice racket, this memory business."

"Listen," she said. "You came in here about recurring dreams. You'd been taking memorybane. You were worried—" She hesitated. "You were worried about losing your soul."

"Soul? That doesn't sound like me," I said.

She took another breath. "No. No, you're right, that was me. That's what I said. You wanted out. Of Macau, of your current life. And I programmed that desire into your memory pin. The desire to leave."

I spread my arms wide, cigarette hanging from my lips, indicating I was still here.

She looked down at her hands and spoke quietly. "You told me to leave, as well."

"Solid advice."

I was about to offer the woman a last cigarette when she looked back up at me, something flickering in her eyes that I didn't quite catch. "And you spoke to me about your wife. You wanted to protect her. Her name is—"

Out of the corner of my hearing, a whisper of movement as Linh uncoiled herself from the wall. The next sound I heard was the Omissioner, gargling blood, blade buried in her throat. I felt a tic of irritation and shot Linh a look. She chose to ignore it, instead walking around the desk, pulling her blade easy from the Omissioner's throat, and wiping it on the woman's expensive dress.

Hope. That was the look the Omissioner had given me. Hope. Served her right, I supposed. People who walked around this city *hoping* usually all ended up the same way.

Aletheia Milas gave the long stare to the far end of her desk, bloodstain growing slowly down her front, dulling the shine of the silk. Chrome walked past me without a word. I took one more look at the woman, around the room. A thought lay there in my mind, resisting the remembering.

I blew a cloud of smoke at the dead Greek and followed Linh out the door.

52

The criminal gang bristled with weapons, the dull metal reflecting the lights of the blue-and-white Baosteel sign across the road. The word, in Mandarin and English, looked so benign. As did the lighted office front, snoozing at four in the morning behind wet, lonely streets.

"Ready?" whispered Linh. She was wearing a metallic black displacement mask – we all were – so I couldn't see her face. But I could hear the excitement in her voice. Top-of-the-line, illegal outside the military, the masks displaced memory feeds and nanocam recordings of anyone looking at the wearer; light-bending, sound distorting, and bulletproof to boot. We'd taken care of the cameras inside the offices, but not the myriad everyday surveillance here out on the street. I'd swapped out my regular double denim for black combat pants and vest, black gloves, all with a military-grade spideriron weave.

Ghost Machine Chan and Mei 'Five Klicks' Guo were with us for the raid. Ghost Machine was a square-headed techie from Guangzhou; Five Klicks a former sniper in the Chinese Special Forces out of Nanjing. She had synthetic green eyes and got herself a new tattoo with every kill. Small, laser-inked black butterflies covered her left forearm. Both were Long's people, completely loyal.

He wanted his eyes on this operation, and I assumed Ghost Machine and Mei – probably both – were streaming the raid back to him through their retinal feeds.

"Sniffers out?" Linh asked Ghost Machine, quietly.

Ghost closed his eyes, looking at something on-retina, refocussed on Linh. "[Still out,]" he replied, in Mandarin.

Baosteel was one of the biggest companies in the world, with a reputation as good as any globe-spanning corporate overlord could hope for: largely unnoticed. They permeated every aspect of modern life – memory pins, wind farm components, the rights to the PoV network for all the regional soccer leagues, a popular tempeh brand. The blue-and-white Baosteel signs were like jeans or glimmer trains: ubiquitous and unremarked. It was Linh who told me they weren't benign, weren't innocent. Three floors up was a lab where they produced a set of neural stimulants that could download via a memory pin. A trip for the mind's eye, Linh said, undiluted, producing phantasmagoria with a purity no chemical drug could rival. A huge threat to the Macau business.

The explanation didn't quite sit right with me. Askew.

Shadows, we flitted through the drizzle over slick bitumen. Through the front door, easy enough. Stolen swipe card, synthetic print attached to Linh's left thumb. Past reception, open plan workspace, back corridor, steel elevator.

Nanocams tricked temporarily three minutes before we entered, programmed to read every face in the elevator as a legitimate employee. Voice print, courtesy of a modulator stuck to Linh's throat, of someone with the right security access.

Easy.

A ping, the elevator opened. Security guard, black hat with a short brim and shining silver Baosteel symbol. He looked up from the glowing flexiscreen on his desk, cheeks red, and took a needle in the eye. The guard made a choking sound, hand halfway to his face, and collapsed backwards off his seat. Linh moved down the white corridor beyond, electric blue needle pistol in hand. I brought up the rear, as had been agreed before the mission.

I glanced down at the man's flexiscreen as we passed. A porn site flickered with its lurid colours and shapes and I looked away. I wondered if the last thing to flash through the man's mind was embarrassment. If his last thoughts were on the shame of watching Japanese futanari cartoons at his work desk. Not family. Not friends. Not a life lived. Just the humiliation of being caught watching two large-breasted chicks with giant dicks banging each other in a dungeon.

I kept moving.

Two guards walked around a corner further along; Linh shot one in the throat, Mei the other between the eyes with a small calibre pistol fitted with a long silencer.

We stepped over the bodies and ten metres later came to a vault door, meant to be the toughest part of our task today. It wasn't. It had the novelty of a manual code, typed into rounded metal buttons on a pad next to the door. We'd found an employee with a mah-jongg problem and bribed her to give us access to the system that generated a random code for the vault. Add to that another voice print verification and a confused nanocam system, and we were through.

The room on the other side had every appearance of a high-end memory pin storage centre. Sterile, shining cleansteel surfaces, gleaming, blue-lit instrumentation. Clear, slender flexiglass cases lined with rows of memory pins, their burnished points shining under the lights.

Four black silhouettes against a stark white room, we moved in.

"This is too easy," I said.

Linh glanced over at me, before letting her eyes range around the room. "They're complacent," she said, voice muffled by her displacement mask.

"This is just a storage centre."

She shrugged.

I clenched my jaw and was about to push it when Ghost Machine rushed past Linh, pulled a thin metal box from one of the many pockets of his vest, and snapped it open. He carefully opened one of the flexiglass containers, removed a single pin, placed it in the box, and returned it to his pocket. A glimpse of flickering in the box interior before it snapped shut.

"They look different," I said, nodding at the bronze gleam of the pins.

Ghost said: "[I hope so. They're the whole reason we're here.]"

"What do you mean?"

"Ghost Machine," warned Linh.

"[It doesn't matter,]" he said. "[Endgame will have the raid wiped afterwards. We all will.]"

I'd moved up so I was an arm's length away and to the back of Five Klicks Mei. "The fuck," I said, "is going on?"

Ghost pointed at the row of boxed memory pins. "[Next generation. Three times the capacity, more efficient recall, non-algorithmic processing, and an intuitive response framework. There have been rumours for months that Baosteel was close to a breakthrough in recall technology. Scientific feeds have been speculating that the new generation of pins could run the brain for Alzheimer's patients. They are saying it could be the first true form of artificial general intelligence, a hybrid model combining automatic brain function and mnemonic tech.]" Even through the mask, and the translation, I could hear the rising excitement in his voice. "[This will change everything]"

I paused, absorbing it all. Tapping the side of my head, I said: "My freewave connection is down. Some sort of jamming tech built into the room. You three all down?"

They all said *yeah* or nodded in reply.

I slipped the polished steel hand axe from under my jacket. The nano-sharpened blade clove into Mei's skull with little resistance; Chrome Linh Phu spun a smooth pirouette, her blade slicing the back of Ghost Machine's neck on the first pass, and plunging into the base of his skull on the second. Mei death-twitched three shots from her pistol as her knees buckled and she went down, the bullets *fizzzzzz*-ing off the ground. Ghost had the decency to die quiet, blood rippling over his neck and hair as he slumped to the floor.

Linh nodded at me, bent down over Ghost, and removed the metal case with the pin from his pocket.

"The fuck you didn't tell me the truth?" I asked.

Linh slipped the case in her breast pocket, then reached around and pulled two spherical nova grenades from the backpack at the small of her back. "Set your charge." The eyes that looked out at me were as expressive as the dull black metal of her mask. "Ghost was right. It's not relevant."

"The fuck, Linh. What we're planning, we're planning together. I need to go easy on the wipes, have as much history as I can muster when we move."

Linh knelt aside Ghost's body. Blood pooled around his head, red vivid against a pure white floor. She set the control and placed the grenade next to the man's left ear. Had to make sure the memory pin was completely incinerated. "History is overrated, Endgame. All you need to know is snapping necks." She looked up at me. "And I think you got that one covered."

From my thigh pocket I took a brick of C-6, walked over to the nearest wall and slapped in on angrily. Linh rocked back on her heels. "*Endgame*. Rather be on the outside when this place comes down."

I walked past her, pulled the second C-6 charge from the other thigh pocket, and attached it to the back wall. I set the switch to networked control, pausing by the open container of memory pins on the way back.

"Take them," said Linh. "I got an idea."

"Sure you do," I said, picking up the box. "A million fucking ideas. Not one of them shared with me."

I slid the container – holding maybe fifty pins – into the thigh pocket that had held the explosives. Linh, standing by the door, said: "We need to move." In her hand the slim black controller. When activated, the four explosives in the room would blow simultaneously.

"And I need information."

She paused, and with her mask still on I couldn't read the thoughts she was brewing. Though, mask or otherwise, it wasn't like she was an easy woman to get a read on. "Okay." She nodded. "Everything. We get out of here, and I tell you everything."

53

She told me everything. Well, everything she told me had the shape
of the truth, anyway, and that was something. That we weren't
part of a drug cartel, that we'd always worked for Chinalco, that
we'd been grinding out a corporate guerrilla war for five years,
and the pins represented the endgame of corporate power. The
Baosteel facility we hit didn't have more men protecting the
pins, she explained, because we'd never hit them like this before.
Never so hard, never so blatant. We'd just escalated the war from
cold to hot.

"Memory," Linh finished, "is control. Power does not flow from
the barrel of a gun; power flows from what the man holding the gun
is programmed to remember." Linh showed the rarest glimpse of
emotion as she spoke, eyes shining, leaning forwards on her seat.
"This is our moment, Endgame. If we have the will, we can take it.
The will and the act: those two will give us ultimate power. All we
have to do is finish Long. That dead-eyed ghoul is weak, now. His
regime is ripe for the taking."

We were sitting in an old tavern in Taipa called the Taffy Lewis.
Out of the way down a quiet alleyway, mainly locals, a grungy
brown wood beer joint drowning in cigarette smoke and the bad
language of its patrons. We sat on stools at a high round table at

right angles to each other, Linh facing one entrance, me the other. I sipped dark ale as a chaser to the whisky I'd started with. Linh had a tall glass of lime juice, we shared a plate of crisp tempeh egg rolls.

My on-retina display was busy, as usual. Facial recognition dialled to maximum in case anyone we knew walked in. My conversation prompt algorithm was set high as well, as these days I often found myself losing the thread of discussion. Sometimes I'd be faced with some reference to a common past event that – by the look in other person's eyes – I could tell I was meant to remember. So my visuals tended to be cluttered. Reminders of past conversations popped up, as did thumbnails of videos I could overlay on-retina to watch a relevant previous encounter.

It was confusing and I didn't like it. It made me feel weak. The only things that banished the slow-burning dual sensations of humiliation and paranoia were alcohol or violence. Alcohol dulled those sensations, same as everyone. Violence, however, was the one place in my fragmented life where I felt clarity, where I felt sure of my purpose, where I never second-guessed myself, and where the only thing I needed to follow was an instinct buried so deep no amount of wiping could touch it.

"Maybe too weak," I said.

"Too weak?"

"We've lost some of our best people."

"It had to be done."

"Five Klicks was a good soldier. And…" I paused and read the prompt on-retina, "and Ghost was considered the best feed rider and programmer in the Syndicate."

"Was considered," repeated Linh, with a smile that didn't touch her eyes.

"Fuck you. Baosteel hits back, we're going to need everyone."

"Everyone we can trust."

"Everyone. We take down Long, we won't need trust; we'll have fear. No more hits on our own people. All we're doing is weakening the Syndicate, and if we're found out before we make our move, any support we might have will disappear." I sipped my beer and said: "You can't just bomb everything, Linh."

"Ha. This from the man who laid waste to…" She trailed off.

"Laid waste to what?"

She paused and my memory prompt printed on-retina:

Reference unclear. Possibly 1: Baosteel Offices; 2: The Alegria Street Card Game; 3: The White Lotus Flower Shop.

My on-retina was sensitive enough to register if I stared at one of the choices for more than a couple of seconds. If so, it'd pull up the details and feed-shots of the incident.

I looked at Linh instead. The slender woman brushed the crumbs from her fingers. "What I mean is this: you're an atom bomb, Endgame. I drop you on this city, you'll reduce it to ashes."

"That so," I said. "Now who says you're the one holding the nuclear codes?"

"Ha." She leaned forwards so elbows were on the table. Like me she was wearing a denim jacket, I could see the glimmer of chrome from the handle of the blade sheathed under her arm. Her full lips were painted metallic purple, matching her mohawk. In isolation, they were sensual, her lips. In isolation. In combination with the woman around them, they somehow added to her menace. Like the *purr* on a panther.

"It's in your nature, Endgame," she said, huskily. "You're not a creature of restraint, or of subtlety." Her eyes glimmered with some inner knowledge I was not privy to. "You've got this abyss inside you. The only thing that fills it is the bodies of your enemies. But you're never sated. I don't need your codes; they were activated long before we met."

I drank my beer. Her words made me uncomfortable, so I talked about something else. "So. We're going to all this trouble for what? A world of pliant feed-zombies."

"Yes. That's exactly what it's for."

"I don't know."

"What don't you know?

"I don't know why I became a gangster when I started out, Linh. Maybe I needed the money. Maybe I liked busting heads. Maybe I watched too many movies about tough guys. I don't know. But I do know this: I didn't do it to give the world brain damage, including myself."

"Brain damage. You really think that's what this is?"

"The fuck else you call it?"

"Evolution," she replied, with a quiet certitude.

I responded with an eye roll that incorporated my whole head. "Fer fuck's sake."

Linh leaned back in her stool, looking me over, and crossed her ankles on the circular steel footrest at the bottom of the table. Her eyes flicked off into the middle distance for a few moments before they turned back to me.

She made to speak; I held up a hand. "Looks like a speech." I pulled my soft pack of Double Happiness out, lit one, and then motioned for her to start. "Now I'm ready."

Linh ignored my provocation, and began: "Through regeneration of the cell structure, the human body changes every nine years. Every nine years your genetic furnace melts down and rebuilds everything: every nail, every hair, every skin follicle. After nine years the human body is completely new, every component replaced. The neural pathways change as well, and a lot faster. Memory relies on the rewiring of those pathways – any of these people" – she indicated the others in the room with her eyes – "walks out of here and tomorrow remembers something about this night, it means the neural structure of their brains have subtly changed. Wiring and re-wiring day in and day out, all of us.

"More than the physical, that crude matter, our intangibles flow like the river: never the same in one point of time as another. We know this. Memories aren't fixed, they evolve. Sometimes we remember things that never happened, other times our minds block parts of our history that teem with inconvenient facts. Everything changes, physical and psychological. Always the flux, the only constant: the flux.

"You and I, we go further. Implants, strengthened endoskeletons, nanotech, advanced exo-mas. We've accelerated our own evolution, whether you care to admit it or not. The human condition has never been wedded to a fixed mark. I refuse to live that delusion." Her eyes bored into me. "I'm here to harness change to *my own will*. There is no essence, just the truth we choose each moment." She let out a long breath. "Fuck, Endgame, we're gangsters: power is why we're here. Why you overthinking it?"

"I feel like I've heard this speech before," I said, but my exo-ma didn't give me any prompts.

"You don't know what the fuck you remember."

"Yeah. True. But I don't believe it."

"What?"

"This *everything is flux* bullshit. The line of your ambition that runs through this, it ain't an accident. This motivation of yours can't exist without a past, without some history driving it down this bloody road. A history that you damn well remember."

Linh didn't say anything to that. She picked up her highball glass and put it back down without taking a drink. "Fuck," she whispered, "you do this every time."

"Every time?"

She shook her head, not looking at me. "So good at killing, yet such a terrible fucking gangster."

I finished my beer. "I just want to be human at the end of this, Linh."

She laughed; short, derisive.

"I mean it. What are we without them? Feed puppets, animated corpses dancing to someone else's tune. Where's the power there, Linh? For it to mean anything, I still got to be alive. It seems to me, if to remember is to be human, then remembering more means being more human."

Lips pressed together, she looked at me like I was drooling rather than speaking. "Bullshit. In the end, it's all just baggage. Lies from the past weighing us down."

I sighed out a cloud of smoke. "Jesus. Linh." I ran a hand through my thinning hairline. "Have a drink, unwind a little."

"I only drink when there's something to celebrate," she replied.

"Same here," I said. "I'm celebrating finishing this beer." I got the eye of a barmaid and made the signal for *again*.

The waitress soon brought me another whisky and beer, and Linh decided to stop speaking. I found that I liked that just fine. I drank my whisky, smoked my cigarette. Linh went back to her middle-distance stare, recycling in her mind her plans, her ambitions. Life passed on around us. In the Taffy Lewis, the real world moved on. People drank their beers and talked about food or job or family. A long-haired waitress spoke to a small table of older men she obviously knew, smiling; they looked up at her like she was some sort of angel, eyes gleaming. Next table along an ugly family of three with nothing to say to each other ate burgers. A Chinese man sat at the bar alone, chain-smoking and staring into an untouched bowl of noodles.

Linh looked out her exit, I looked out mine.

"The Omissioner," I said. "That woman. The other day."

Linh looked at me closely. "Yeah?"

"You were pretty vague on that one. How does—how did she fit in to all this?"

"She didn't," Linh said, without a pause. "Just some baggage needed to be cut loose. That's all."

I didn't believe her, but it didn't matter. Bullshit, so much bullshit, lies upon lies. It was exhausting living with so many. So many more piling up, day after day. Me without the capacity to see through even the most transparent. Just this gnawing sensation at the corner of my mind; just these words in my throat, never quite able to form. I sighed and finished my drinks. "So what's next, Linh?"

"Huh?"

"What's next? Say we do it. Take out Long, keep the Syndicate together, end up the king and queen of Macau – that the endgame?"

She smiled some secret smile. "No. It is only the beginning."

"I don't suppose you're going to share the next step?"

"Not yet. But I will." She leaned towards me and put a hand against my chest, an intimate gesture so out of character I flinched. "And when we take it, I'll need you by my side."

I looked down at her hand, still a little surprised it was sitting there. I picked it up and put it back on her lap. "Just point to the neck you want snapped," I said behind a cloud of smoke. "And I'll snap it."

54

We entered the suite at the Galaxy on Cotai Strip. Ha-Ha Poon, a surly Cantonese speaker with a shaved head, stood and nodded at us as we entered. At his table was a burger with one bite taken out of it, a bottle of dark Beer Lao, and a black metal Uzi with an enamelled gold grip.

We passed him without a word, through the open door into the lounge area. Linh and I kept the suite for special guests. I hadn't been introduced to this one. He was an old bloke, large grey eyebrows, European. Tailored grey suit, light blue tie, thin-shouldered, liver spots on his hands. He sat at a table with a flexiscreen and a personal tai screen. Even had the anachronism of real paper with actual *handwriting* on it spread out to one side. The chair he sat on was unusual, also something of a redundancy – among the wealthy anyway. A wheelchair, shining metallic, glassteel spokes on its wheels, padded blue leather armrests. When he looked up, the chair adjusted automatically, turning to face us. The chair's motor system was no doubt linked directly into his c-glyph.

When he saw me he made a thin line with his mouth, and his eyes glittered with some malignant intent.

"The fuck's your problem?" I said.

He sat up straight in his chair, drawing in breath to respond, when Linh cut him off with a gesture. She indicated him with her head. "Ladislaw Tauc. Omissioner. I mentioned I had someone to complete Ghost Machine's work on the pins. He's the guy."

Tauc's expression changed as Linh spoke.

"A pleasure, sir," he said to me, amused by something. "And what would your name be?"

"I doubt you'll be able to pronounce it once I've knocked all your teeth out. You give me that weird fucking smile one more time and that's exactly what I'll do."

He stopped grinning.

"We have the merchandise," said Linh.

I slipped the slender flexiglass case from the inside pocket of my jacket and placed it on the man's papers.

"Next generation," said Linh.

Tauc licked his lips, eyes fixed on the box. "Ah," was all he said, apparently lost for words.

"Yeah," said Linh, "*Ah*."

"You people have no idea," he said, with something approaching awe, "how this will change everything."

"We're the ones harnessing it, dickhead," I said. "You're the one doing our bidding."

He looked at me with contempt. "Really, Mister Ebbinghaus? Do you have any clue what happens next?" He was smart enough not to smile when he said it, which was the only thing that stopped me kneeing him right on the point of his chin.

"There can be worse things," I said, "than living in a wheelchair, you shrivelled old scrotum." Then I hesitated, something itching at my mind. "Did I tell you my name?"

He blinked.

"I told him earlier," said Linh, quickly.

Tauc, evidently decided he was done with me, turned his chair to face Linh. "When do I get my new spine?"

"You got a big brain, Omissioner," replied Linh, "I'll give you one fucking guess."

He made a thin line with his mouth again and looked down at his work. "How long do I have?"

"Twenty-four hours."

He looked back at her sharply. "Twenty—Look, really, I…" He composed himself. "These conditions are insufferable, your requests unreasonable, the workload unmanageable. I'm going to need at least—"

"Shut up," said Linh.

He shut up.

"Ghost Machine did most of the work, old man. On top of that, you now have the advantage of a pin with capabilities Ghost could only ever hold his dick and daydream about." She walked over and leaned on the table with her knuckles. "So, listen: you don't get this done, your screams will be indescribable, your agony incomparable, and the stain you leave on the carpet uncleanable. Got it?"

His dry, thin lips stayed pressed together, his eyes downcast.

I said: "She asked you a question."

His eyes tracked across the table, up Chrome's tattooed arms, to her face. "Crystal clear, Miz Phu."

55

Your name is Endgame Ebbinghaus. It's 11.12am, Friday 16 December, 2101. You're head of security along with your partner, Linh Phu, for Mister Long, the boss of the Macau Syndicate.

Long deceived you for many years, making you think you worked for a drug cartel. You do not. You work for Chinalco, and the crimes you commit, you commit for them. Their business is control through memory pins. You're not shedding blood for a profit margin. You're shedding blood to make people slaves.

Today you'll see Long; six days later you'll kill him.

A week from now you'll be the new boss of this town, or you'll be dead.

I groaned and rolled over in bed. I fumbled at the side table, knocking a glass and poker chips onto the carpet as I did so. Eventually I found my cigarettes and sat up in bed, smoking.

Linh's shadow appeared in the doorway. She looked at me with some distaste.

"Good morning, darling," I said, ironic smile.

She didn't smile back. Black leather pants, skin-tight spideriron

307

vest gleaming in the morning gloom, her blades holstered under each arm. Dressed for battle. "We got a war to win."

I rested my head against the wall, kept smoking.

"And you spend the night before drinking and playing poker."

"That's not true."

"Really."

"I also played blackjack."

"Don't fuck with me. I'm not some delicate, soft-handed wife you get to treat with contempt."

"Wife?" I said, "that escalated quickly. You getting clucky, babe? Looking to build a nest with me?"

Her eyes gleamed. "Call me 'babe' again, and the only nest I will build will be with your bones after I have flayed the flesh from them." She whirled and stalked out of view.

I laughed and shook my head. I guessed that meant I wasn't getting breakfast in bed.

I said: "Curtains," and the dark material along one wall parted, revealing a grey vista, high up from our hotel suite, of Macau in the pouring rain. I looked at the deep sill lined with thin cushions. We never really made love, Linh and I. That wasn't her thing. We fucked. And when fucked, she fucked angry, riding me, demanding, coming hard, her whole body shaking. Sometimes it felt like Linh treated sex as another battle to win. Afterwards, she wouldn't talk. She'd just get out of bed, walk over to the sill and sit on those cushions, lean a shoulder against the window and look out, naked flesh bathed in the neon of the city below. I didn't seem to make her happy, not with that or anything we did together. Except killing. Only after we'd run some bloody mission together, only then would her eyes light up, she'd be relaxed. Shit, sometimes even chatty.

I glanced over the on-retina message again:

One week from now you'll be the new boss of this town, or you'll be dead.

I finished my second cigarette, sighing out the last cloud of smoke, and got out of bed. Savouring that last few seconds before my feet hit the floor, from the lazy dream state of a half-remembered life, where I could be anyone and where every possibility was open. Including happiness. Until feet touched floor and the adamantium edges of kill or be killed resolved themselves around my mind's eye and there was one fate and one fate only, for I was a violent man.

I put on my jeans, boots, basic model skin-tight spideriron vest right on my skin, like Linh. On to the next room, my gear on the bar top: gleaming hand axe, dark-blue metal Chinese-made Type-107 machine gun; knuckledusters with 'Jonny Brass' stamped in the burnished metal; and a deck of cards backed with a golden dragon design.

I'd bought the hand axe from a pawn shop in Hong Kong a year or so back. Recently, at great expense, I'd had the nano-sharpened edge treated with an illegal, military-made anti-clotting agent. If cut, the wound would bleed and keep bleeding until you were in hospital, or dead. I'd claimed the 107 after a gunfight with the Alegria Street Girls; the knuckledusters after a bar fight with a jacked-up Brit who couldn't walk the talk.

Not knowing where I'd got the cards, some cerebral itch made me look up a 'Golden Dragon' casino. When I saw there were two casinos by that name in Macau, and seventeen scattered across Southeast Asia in Chinese special economic zones, I stopped looking. I mean, fuck, it was just a pack of cards. I put the deck in my top pocket.

Linh made sure her mohawk was straight with open palms, before rechecking the clip in her needle pistol and holstering it at the small of her back. She wore a new, large-collared jacket of the darkest green leather. The lining bulletproof. My denim had no extra protection, a mistake I'd have to remedy, given our plans.

She looked at me and nodded.

"You got it?" I asked.

She patted her top pocket. "Yeah," said Linh, "Now let's go talk to this cunt."

56

Long's suite, Grand Lisboa. The walls canary yellow stencilled with black elephants, the air smelled of cedar wood incense. Long sat at his round mahogany table, eyes fixed on me and Linh as we walked through the door. He wore a tight, stiff-collared shirt that accentuated the slender lines of his body, lips painted a striking red against the smooth pallor of his face. His hand rested on the table, nails the colour of his lips, tapping a staccato beat as we walked up to him.

Outside the door we'd been greeted by a large Singaporean named Desmond 'The Wall' Hung, a mixed martial arts champion who'd joined the Syndicate after Long's last doorman had disappeared in mysterious circumstances. We'd had to hand over our guns and blades, though he let me keep my knuckledusters.

Inside the room with Long were three people we'd never met before. Chinese, a man and two women, ex-military by the look of their stances and close-cropped hair. Black combat pants and vests; the man had a gleaming steel shotgun, the first woman both a needle pistol and katana on her belt, the second woman a compact machine pistol on a strap over her shoulder. The man stood behind Long against the wall; the first woman against the bar; the second came in from the next room, looked us over, and disappeared.

Linh's eyes flicked over them and then to me. In that brief second before she looked back at Long, I saw clear what she was thinking: *we can take them, easy.* I smiled at her philosophy of perpetual war.

"[You're late,]" said Long, "[Two days.]"

"Waiting for the heat to die down, Mister Long," said Linh, voice neutral. "Lot of attention on the Baosteel hit."

"[A failure.]"

Linh and I glanced at each other. "How do you figure?" I asked.

"[Two of your people died.]"

"Security was tighter than expected," Linh said, still calm. "A full squad of twelve was waiting."

"[Twelve peasants,]" hissed Long, using the Chinese term *xiāngbālǎo,* which my translator interpreted simply as peasant. It wasn't. The word was used a lot in my world and I'd come to know its layers. More than an insult, the equivalent of 'bumpkin', it implied irrelevance – people whose lives meant less than those of a gangster, people who eked out grinding, meaningless, and fleeting parts in the grand play. Those like Long, who'd squeezed another two or three decades out of life with longevity treatments, in particular liked to use the word.

"Ghost and Five Klicks were weak," said Linh. "Their deaths on the mission proves this. Battle is the great filter, Mister Long. It sifts out the feeble, the hesitant, those without resolve. It is good that they died; they were unworthy of their privileged place in the Syndicate."

Long stared at her with his old, unreadable eyes. I pulled my cigarettes out of the top pocket of my jacket and slid one out with my lips. I'd flicked on my lighter when the man behind Long said: "[No smoking.]"

My eyes danced over him, then back to the end of my cigarette as I lit it.

"[No smoking,]" he repeated, detaching himself from the wall.

I blew out a long slow white cloud. "The only way I'm putting this cigarette out," I said, "is in your right eye."

The man hesitated, swallowing.

Long held up a hand for him to stay. He did so, glaring instead, knuckles white on the grip of his shotgun. I smiled and made my way over to Long's bar to find some whisky.

Long looked at Linh. "[The prototype.]"

She slid out the slim metal box and put it on the table in front of him. He opened the lid, the snick loud in the quiet of the room.

Long looked from the box back to us. "[Your pins, as well.]"

"No," said Linh.

Long raised a pencil-thin eyebrow.

"A war's about to begin," she explained. "Endgame and I believe we need all the background we can get, if we're going to fight it right."

"[Miz Phu. I don't run my business based on opinions. From underlings.]"

Linh was silent. Long waited.

"Listen," I said, and pointed at him with my chin, glass of single malt now in my hand. "You're not going to believe what you see, anyway. Two days, we could have had it altered. Good enough so that no-one could tell the difference. So here's the thing: you're not asking to see our pins, Long, that's not what this is about." I said it all calm.

"[What, then, is this is about?]"

"Power. You just want to everyone to know you're the boss. Convince us all that you call the shots. Maybe you got to convince yourself of that, too. But all you really end up doing is questioning our loyalty. What you're doing is insulting your two generals just as hostilities are about to commence. And that, old man, is fucking dumb."

The third bodyguard in the other room reappeared in the doorway, hand resting on her machine pistol. The other two shifted their stance and looked at Long. But it was the slender old dragon that inhaled every ounce of my attention. All he did was wet his lips and let a black fire burn in his eyes, some dark excitement, before he shut it down. "[That is not what this is about, Mister Ebbinghaus. And you would be the last person I would trust to distinguish between what is and what isn't *fucking dumb*.]" He paused and continued: "[But I will deal with that, later. Now we shall see if you have actually done what you were told to do.]"

I took a drag on my cigarette. My hand was shaking, just a little.

He placed the bronze pin on his flexiscreen and I could sense, at the periphery of my vision, Linh changing her stance. She'd take Long and the man behind him, I could feel it. The woman at the bar was an arm's length away from me, I imagined using her as a human shield so the other woman with the machine pistol couldn't get a clear shot, hurling the first into the second, and following on fast, in close, with elbows and head-butts.

The flexiscreen glow increased in intensity. Long and the others were fixated on it. I downed my whisky and set down the empty glass, in reach of the soldier with the katana. I leaned against the padded wood railing of the high bar, eyes back on Long. Linh rubbed her fingers gently, slowly, against her thumbs.

There was a soft chime as the security protocols on the screen marked the pin as clear, and I let out a sigh disguised behind a cloud of smoke. Mister Long read the graphs and text scrolling down the screen and after an eternal half-minute said: "[Extraordinary.]"

To the naked eye, nothing seemed to change in the demeanour of Linh or the three soldiers. But still, the animus in the room ebbed and I found myself pouring another whisky. I was finishing my second glass when Long finally looked up at us and said: "[This changes everything.]"

Linh nodded.

"[Social order is impossible while minds roil with chaos. But now. But *now*, the mnemonic directives we'd been testing in Xuân Tăng…]"

"Can be supported by this system," Linh finished.

The name *Xuan Tang*, itched at my mind for a moment. I let it go.

Mister Long plucked the bronze pin up between red nails and gripped in in the palm of his hand. A slight sardonic smile crossed his features. "[*Generals*. Our war has begun. Best you rally the troops.]"

Linh nodded and left. I followed her out the door.

5 7

I was sitting at a table at the Blue Kafka café eating a late breakfast with the Pai Gow Brothers and Ha-Ha Poon when the grenade rolled through the front door. We'd met to eat before a weapons buy over at the Number 33 dock. I'd secured a line on six ground-to-ground missile launchers. We didn't have a plan for them yet, but there wasn't a whole lot of science to picking a target and blowing it up. We'd think of something.

The Blue Kafka was a lived-in-but-clean joint preferred by locals. Half full, with about a dozen people in it. Outside was a hard rain. I was facing the door, Ha-Ha Poon had his back to it, and the brothers sat shoulder to shoulder to my left. I was finishing my espresso when the *tink tink tink* of metal on a wood floor sounded, followed by a *roll roll roll* and a silver grenade trundling up to the right of our table.

I stood without thinking, took one step, and kicked it before it had time to stop.

The kick sent the grenade spinning back the way it came. It bounced once, clipped the doorframe, and spun on its side until it stopped in the doorway. A Japanese couple about to enter the café slowed and looked down, politely regarding the bomb at their feet.

My shoulders slumped. "Shit."

I hurled myself back over the lunch counter, my hip colliding with the chest of the surprised waitress just as the world bloomed white.

A wall of heat, my eyes shut on instinct, head pressed against the ground.

The heat abated, but only slightly, and the sound of falling glass and crackling fire filled the room. The waitress was behind me, pressed against the wall, her knees against her chest, eyes wide with shock.

The Pai Gow Brothers had made it into the narrow space behind the counter. They groaned. Twins, a mix of Portuguese and Chinese heritage, identified as Macanese. They dressed the same in knee-length dark red trench coats, and both were armed with long-barrelled revolvers and bowie knives at their belts. They did everything together, and didn't much like being treated as individuals. I'd been told they swapped memory pins regularly, absorbing their miniscule differences in personality into each other until they couldn't distinguish between themselves, either.

One Brother had blood on his forehead, the other a large coffee stain on his white shirt.

I said: "Ha-Ha?"

The Brothers shrugged as one.

The room on the other side of the counter was lit with a green, flickering tinge.

I eased the 107 out from under my arm and *clack-clacked* it. The Brothers pulled their guns. I held up three fingers and counted them down. After the last finger went down, the three of us popped up and—

The heat hit us again. The café was ablaze with fierce green fire, clumps of it on the walls, the roof, the tables, dripping from the broken glass of the thick front windows, engulfing the blackening husks of bodies in the shattered doorway.

—fired our weapons, overcoming that split-second of surprise at the carnage beyond.

Our fire was returned almost instantly. I flinched and ducked, on-retina a red arrow appeared, pointing upwards with `Target elevation 5 metres` printed underneath it. My understanding came too late, my gun barrel coming up as the line of muzzle fire from the second floor across the street found the counter. I swore and ran, chunks of brick and wood spewing out from the wall behind me, shouldered through the door leading into the kitchens, took three long strides, and dove through the rear door into a narrow alley behind the café. I rolled and came up, gun ready. The Pai Gow Brothers sprawled after me into the open air, one slipping down to his knees, the other standing, each facing opposite directions, guns drawn.

Empty. Steady rain, cobblestones slick with water, the smell of trash, twenty metres to either end. Iron doors, rusting, along water-damaged walls either side; windows high up, barred.

I took a deep breath. Behind us, the gunfire died down. Music was playing somewhere, real close. I looked around, trying to find the source.

"Do you hear that?" I asked.

"No," said the coffee-stained Brother; "What?" finished his twin.

"The music."

The Brothers looked at me strangely and returned their attention to either end of the lane.

A second later I realised the music was playing in my head. Some heavy, fast-paced song sung, real bad, by an old man. Or two people. One guy singing, an old man talking.

I wiped the water from my eyes. "Fuck it. We got to move."

I'd taken one step before stumbling and pitching forward; one of the Pai Gow Brothers caught my arm. As he hauled me back up, I looked down to see a hole in the top of my cowboy boot maybe an inch wide, blood oozing from it. I furrowed my brow. I couldn't feel a thing.

I shrugged off his hands.

"Lucky," I said.

"Why?" they answered.

"A sticky bomb and a thousand bullets. All we got to show for it is stained shirts and a ventilated cowboy boot." I found myself talking too loud, trying to speak over the sound of the music in the centre of my head.

"Ha-Ha Poon," said the blood-stained Brother.

"Oh," I said, hiding my embarrassment at forgetting. "Yeah. Yeah. Those motherfuckers."

"We going to get them, boss?" asked the coffee-stained brother. His twin nodded.

My eyes unfocussed for a moment as I read the tactical report on-retina. "No, gents. There are at least ten of them out there, and there's only so long they can shoot without hitting anything. I got no reports of other hits, but others may be coming for our people. We need to get to the Venetian, hole up with Linh, figure out the next part."

The Pai Gow Brothers nodded as one. I hobbled to the end of the alley with them in tow. We turned uphill, away from the café, into the gloom and rain.

58

Chrome Linh Phu stood with arms crossed while a blonde Scandinavian called Sorenson sprayed the cast on my foot. The bullet had punched cleaned through the bridge of the boot, exiting through the arch. I'd be out of action for a day or so.

Linh said: "Close the door when you go." Sorenson nodded and slipped away to the other room. The Pai Gow Brothers and a new guy, The Whistler Duh-Wah were in there, fidgeting with their weapons.

Linh waited until the door had closed. "What now?" she asked.

"Cigarettes'd be the first thing."

Linh's mouth parted to say something, but she changed her mind and walked over to my coat, slung onto a chair in the corner of the room. She picked it up, eyeing a large burn hole in one shoulder. "Time to upgrade."

"Yeah," I said. "Got an idea about that."

She chucked over my soft pack and steel lighter. I caught them and lit up.

"Baosteel?" asked Linh.

"Sure. Who else?"

"Did you take precautions on your way to the Blue Kafka?"

"Yeah. More than usual, even."

"Long knew about the meet."

I blew a cloud of smoke at the ceiling. "Maybe. Maybe he could have tipped them off. Risky, though, as he'd have to be certain about us. I don't reckon he's certain."

Linh pursed her full lips. She'd gone for a deep blue shade today. "Long's leaving town."

"What? Where?"

"Shanghai. Some big meeting. Taking the glimmer train up the day after tomorrow."

I smoked, considered. "Should give us enough time for it to work through the system."

"Yeah. Should."

"We need to get in the entourage."

"We already are."

I nodded once. "Good work."

"Not really. Long told us to join him."

I adjusted my posture to relieve the ache in my foot. "Did he now?"

We both thought that over, Linh staring at space, me at the smoke rising from my cigarette. "He doesn't know," I said finally.

"No," she agreed. "But he suspects."

"The meeting in Shanghai must be real big, then. Fucken huge."

Linh ran a hand slowly over the smooth scalp next to her mohawk.

"Don't worry about it," I said. "We've done all the prep we can. It's the best shot we're ever going to have. All we can do is take it."

After Linh left the room I took the cigarette from my mouth and stared at the glowing orange tip. Something sat there in the corner of my mind, something I could feel, but couldn't know. Something I could sense, but couldn't see. I laid my left hand flat on the arm of the chair, blinked at it a few times, and then put the cigarette out on it.

I flinched, the pain came, but I kept pressing the cigarette down. The pain passed in another blink, as the music started. A rock song, familiar and unfamiliar, guitar wailing, English man singing about an American woman. The volume ebbed, flattened, and another voice started over the top of it, at first singing along with the lyrics, then just speaking to something different entirely. Shadows flickered across my retina and I closed my eyes.

The ghost image of an old man appeared, standing in space. Faint, but against the back of my eyelids he was clear enough. Vaguely familiar elderly Chinese, face creased with wrinkles – especially laugh lines – a wispy grey beard and a shock of grey hair. He was wearing a black shirt with bold lettering on it, and apparently no pants. Just white jocks.

The old man held out his hands. "Endel Ebbinghaus, you mad cunt. Now, mate, we haven't much time, so here it is. You won't remember me, because your head's fucked. But I am an Omissioner and former comrade-in-arms. Right now, you're asking: *what's this old bastard doing in my head*?"

I grunted affirmation.

"Well, look, how do I say this? You're not who you think you are. You've been wiped, re-wiped, deleted, programmed, lied to, folded over yourself a dozen times until all that's left is a borderline Alzheimer's patient with an aptitude for cracking skulls. Now, we knew each other. We hung out, cracked some tinnies, and blew up some fascists. But, just so we're clear, the bloke I was hanging out with wasn't the *real* you, some essential Endel Ebbinghaus. In fact, you called yourself by another name back then. It was just an earlier version, no more authentic than you are now. So I'm not going to tell you who you are, because I haven't got a bloody clue.

"What I'm carrying on about is all the different people you can be. Right now, you're likely in Macau working for Chinalco, which means you are, to be blunt, an arsehole. I'm here to tell you that there are other possibilities. Now, you can't be anything, Endel, this isn't a self-help announcement and I am not your guru. But you can be a few different people, and all of them are better than the automatic killer you are today. Mate: all you are now is the *ghilman* of a corporate empire. If you want to live out a life that way, there's not much I can do about it."

The old man wet his lips. "But I don't reckon you do. So I'm going to help you. My end is this: I want to stop their plans for world domination. I can't put it any other way than that, mate. These blacked-hearted despots are aiming to subdue the entire population, turn them into sheep. Now, you're a bad human – this is true – but you're not *that* bad. The whole enslaving humanity thing is a tad too much, even for you."

The old man's eyebrows bobbled, and he smiled. "So I guess I'm asking you to save the world. That's all. Now," he said, rubbing his hands together with glee. "You're…"

The music faded, the dull pain in my hand returned, I opened my eyes. I rubbed at my eyes, thinking on it.

"Ghilman," I said aloud.

On-retina, the definition appeared. Ghilman: a slave-soldier.

"Oh."

I wondered if I was going mad. But I didn't wonder long. I lit another cigarette, took a couple of drags, then put that out on my hand as well.

"Now," he said, rubbing his hands together with glee. "You're carrying a program around inside your head, and it's a fucking cracker. This elegant little algorithm does two things. One: it strives to understand the conspiracy our friends at Chinalco are up to. And two: it desires, feverishly, to tell the world about it when the time

is ripe. And your part, mate, is so simple even you can do it." My
jaws bulged at that. He held up a hand. "What I mean is, regardless
of what happens to you – beyond, I suppose, your head getting
blown clean off – this little scheme of mine will come to fruition.
At some point, you're going to give that pin in your head to one of
your enemies. They'll be demanding it to provide you with an alibi,
or torture you some more, some gangster bullshit like that: business
as usual. And, well: *you're going to give it to them*. Sometime later –
months, more, after you've forgotten you even did it, the world will
know what these bastards have done.

"The place we met is where they were doing their experiments on
population control. Phase one is give everyone chronic memory loss.
We've known that bit for some time and it's more or less completed,
endemic now among pin users. Phase two is memory alteration
across the whole population. But they're not there, not yet. They can
do blunt force mnemonic directives – they've done it to you – but
that will only work on individuals used for specific purposes. Even
that can be *unreliable*. The key is to create a pin so powerful it can
include programming that allows for the organic growth of suitable
memories via the interface between the pin and the mind. That is,
to seed real memories with the lies these bastards want you to live."

My mind flicked to that crippled euro, Tauc.

"Now mate, I can't tell you everything about your wipe, but I can
tell you something that perplexed me. Your new set of memories
contains several mnemonic directives. Elementary instructions: stay
in Macau, be loyal to that angry Vietnamese tart who brought you
in, relish killing, don't fuck goats in public, that sort of stuff." The
Omissioner was clearly amusing himself, if no-one else. "Anyway,
the strange bit is this: you'd been given a new pin by these monsters.
Then you came to me. No surprises there. Can't just shove it in,
unless you simply want the victim to have a complete schizophrenic
breakdown. Nah, got to see an Omissioner. But here's the thing, the

brand-new pin had *already* been tampered with. My Kandel-Yu machine picked it up immediately. What I'm saying is: whoever the people you're working for, even they seem to be working at cross-purposes. So I don't know what the hell all that's about, but there it is. Anyway, I've done you a favour: activating this message should start to erode the mnemonic commands you've had implanted. The best I can do, mate, is give you back some of your own choices."

The old man looked to one side and scratched his head. "Hmm. Well. That's about it, I reckon. In summary: you're basically fucked, and you're probably going to wind up dead. I just wanted you to know." He stopped, rubbed his hand back and forth over his thick hair. He started again, voice more subdued. "I wanted you to know you loved your family. Never seen anyone driven so mad, seen anyone go to such limits, for family. You were like a cut snake. I don't think you're a great bloke or anything, misunderstood, something like that. But you loved them, and you would do anything for them. The last thing you said to me, before you went under and I performed the wipe, was *I can't ever remember them. It's the only way to keep them safe.* You're right, sadly. Quite right. I'm not telling you this so you can track them down and find them. I don't want that, and neither do you. I'm saying this because you have a right, mate. A right to know. These people you ride with are monsters. They took away the only thing that mattered to you. I'm just saying this so you know: your family, you kept them safe. Take that consolation."

He clapped his hands together, the sombre moment gone. "Now, you magnificent, mind-fucked, Aussie knee-capper, if you understand this, say *understand*, and this program will delete itself. I'll keep the music in your head though, mate. A rock and roll soundtrack to keep you company as you crack the skulls of your enemies, a gift from me to you." He pointed both hands to himself, then out at the imaginary me as he said *from me to you.*

He waved, fading from view.

I opened my eyes and stared at the twin burns on the back of my hand. Little black and ash eyes, staring back at me, unblinking.

"Understand."

59

The glimmer train swayed, gently, at eight-hundred kilometres an hour on its way to Shanghai. We had two entire cabins at the rear of the train. Private, owned by the Syndicate, taken out and attached specifically for the journey. In the second-last was a pool table, lounges, bar, and a gaming table set into the corner. Thick red carpet, the scent of leather, countryside flashing by outside. Bar and table manned by blank-faced Filipinos wearing white jackets.

The Pai Gow Brothers were at the table playing their namesake; The Whistler Duh-Wah was drinking coffee and watching something behind his eyelids. Desmond 'The Wall' Hung was sitting on a tall stool by the entrance to the rear cabin. Except for him, we were pretty sure we could trust everyone in the room.

Mister Long didn't trust us, apparently. We'd had to hand over our guns when we boarded. Stored in an overhead security locker that only he could open. We hadn't seen Long yet, either. His three new Chinese bodyguards did the taking. We'd started calling them the Southern Blade Three, after the name of the Guangzhou Special Forces unit they were rumoured to have belonged to. We still didn't know their names, just the city they were from and the fact they did everything together. When I pointed out we wouldn't be much use without our weapons if the glimmer train was attacked, they

T . R .   N A P P E R

said not to worry, that Long could open the locker with a verbal command in an instant.

We'd been allowed to keep our hand weapons, though, so I had my hand axe under my jacket and my newly purchased Norinco Bracer Number 7 gleaming on my left wrist. I'd noted that the Three each had pulse pistols. Linh didn't seem to care. She just shrugged and handed over her needle pistol. I knew what she was thinking: that with her blades she was the most dangerous person on the train, that no-one could stand against her. Chrome was probably right, which made me worry even more. Mister Long was no fool.

Linh and I sat away from the others, her thigh touching mine. I turned to face her, cigarette in hand, moving my leg slightly away. I took the smoke down deep in my lungs, savouring the bite. "Time?"

Linh looked from my face to the view out the window. Lipstick and eye shadow purple. Dark green jacket. Sunlight outside, the first we'd seen in months. It lit up Linh's face, smooth and young, so young. Something I'd forgotten about her, something I just didn't see any more, back in the underworld. Linh replied: "Past time."

We got to our feet.

"We need to see Long," I said to Desmond.

He shifted, uncomfortable. "[He said he wasn't to be interrupted.]"

"Then let him know we're here," said Linh, with a softness that made me flinch.

Desmond's eyes unfocussed as he relayed the request through. He seemed surprised when he said: "[Long said he's *happy* to see you.]"

I liked the welcome as much as I liked Linh speaking soft. Like a redback and funnel-web spider, thinking each other the fly. Too late to stop now, much as it is a little too late to stop halfway down, after you've thrown yourself off a cliff. I followed Linh through to Mister Long's carriage.

The final cabin was furnished much like the first, with red leather, thick carpet, and wood-panelled walls. No gaming table in this one, and a door at the other end that led to Long's private sleeping chamber. Outside the windows flashed Southern China and its soya and rice plantations, the towering black solar spires and the small, fenced-in modern communities of technicians and engineers that serviced the spires. Among the fields the sprawl of rural villages and their tiled roofs; bamboo outbuildings; slender but well-maintained asphalt roads; and rarely, a red-walled Buddhist temple.

Mister Long sat drinking tea from bone white china at the far end of the carriage. He wore an immaculate white shirt with stiff Mandarin collar and a richly patterned red-silk vest. I'd never seen him wearing the vest and took for granted it had a spideriron weave. His elegant fingers grasped his teacup as we walked in, and he sipped, watching us with old eyes over the rim. Two of the Southern Blade Three, man and woman, rose and approached as we entered. The third was sitting down the other end near Long, and made a show of putting her hand on the grip of her pulse pistol.

I smiled at the woman as she approached and hit her, a hard left jab, right on the chin. The bone crunched, her head snapped back, and she collapsed at my feet. Linh open-handed the man in throat; then drove her foot down on the outside of his knee. He fell, choke-screaming, one hand to neck, the other on ruined knee. The Southern Blade Three were no doubt very fast and very good. But there is something to be said for unannounced brutality. And we were, after all, Long's generals and their superiors.

I held up my hands, palms open, at the third soldier. She had the pulse pistol pointed at my head.

"We could have killed them," I said. "We didn't. We don't have to kill you, either."

Her eyes flicked from me to Linh, she swallowed. Long simply waited, unruffled, watching us as though we were some sort of point-of-view action channel program he'd happened across.

"We're here for Long, not you. After we're done, there will be no recriminations. Linh and I will run the Syndicate. You'll have an important place in it."

The soldier switched her aim between Linh and I, said nothing.

"Now, you're new, but I'm sure you know this: Chrome is the fastest and deadliest human in Macau. You get your shot in with that pistol, Linh here," I tilted my head sideways, indicating my partner, "will put a blade through your neck." I took another step.

She said: "[No further, Endgame.]" To her credit, her voice was firm, her hands didn't shake. Mister Long crossed his legs leisurely, face empty.

"The problem with that toy gun," I continued, "is it won't even take me down. Been shot by a few now, kinda gotten used to it. If Linh doesn't put the blade to you, I'll go ahead and snap your neck."

The train swayed slowly, the world passing by, oblivious. The man at Linh's feet groaned and rocked as he grasped his knee.

I tried it on. "We go back, you and me. You know you can trust me. You really want to die for the bloodless vampire sitting behind you."

Long raised an eyebrow.

The woman licked her lips. It would have been useful to know her name. "[You have my gratitude for helping my sister,]" she said. "[But...]"

Linh spoke, quieter than me, but somehow with more force. "You can't remember why you're with Long, can you? Your memories trickling away there, into the aether. No other reason any more than he's the boss, and you're a trained soldier. But you're not just a soldier anymore. You now live in a world where respect and personal connection weigh heavy. Endgame and me: that's who you respect – that's who everyone in the Macau Syndicate respects. Everyone knows us becoming the new boss is a matter of time. *Everyone knows*." Linh wet her lips. "Now that time has come."

The woman's shoulders and chest abated, like the air was going out of her. She holstered her pistol, and without a backwards glance at Long, walked down the aisle.

Long put down his bone china cup, noiselessly. Whatever surprise he had at losing his personal guard, he hid pretty damn well. He waited, legs crossed, watching. I could feel the tension growing in my fists, my chest, as he just sat there through it all. We helped the woman get her comrades into the next cabin and closed the door.

Linh pulled out her blades. They flashed as she turned them over slow, holding them down near her thighs.

I made a fist with my left hand and said: "Shield." The Norinco Bracer activated, and in an instant the thick, two-inch-wide bracelet transformed into a perfectly round shield two feet across, slightly convex, centred on my wrist. It was dull grey, opaque, military grade glassteel embedded with nanocarbon tubes and a heat-proof coating. No bullet or blade would even scratch it. With my other hand I pulled the gleaming axe from inside my denim jacket.

The carriage was around twelve feet across, but the lounges along one wall and two small dining tables along the other left an aisle of about four feet. Mister Long was twenty feet away, still sitting. He opened the gold cigarette case on the table in front of him, drew out a slender white cigarette, and lit it.

"Lot of equanimity," said Linh, "for a dead motherfucker."

Long regarded her for a moment, as though she were a type of insect species he hadn't seen before, a long curl of white smoke rising from between slightly parted lips. Like the tip of some fire, burning deep within him.

"[That time again,]" he said. "[Three stones in *ko*.]"

Linh started moving slow, down the centre, I followed.

"[Here again, doomed to fail. Though the fault is mine, as well. I thought slavery was better than death. I was wrong.]"

"What are you talking about?" I asked.

"[Poor, limited creatures.]"

Linh stopped moving. "Speak, cunt."

Long ran a fingertip over a fine eyebrow. He said: "[This isn't the first time this has happened.]"

We were silent. I wasn't sure if he was trying to buy time. He could be sending a distress signal to others on the train. Linh and I stood side by side in the centre of the carriage, where the space opened out between tables.

"[You two tried to take me three years ago. Plans hatched between squalid sheets in some gauche hotel in Cotai. The barbarian and the Vietnamese dirt baozi, peasants both. I expected you then, and I expected you now. Well, not quite now,]" he added. "[I did anticipate another month of indecision from your febrile but confused little minds.]" He turned his gaze to me. "[Ever wonder why Linh didn't simply kill you in the graveyard?]" I nearly asked: *graveyard? What graveyard?* But figured I'd shut up and let him give his speech, maybe learn something I wasn't meant to. When I said nothing he answered his own question: "[Because she wanted to keep you alive. I watched the whole encounter, through her feed. She wanted you alive, but also wanted you to suffer. Lingering jealousy and vindictiveness, I suppose, base emotions from a vulgar creature, wishing to punish you for leaving her for that Chinese broodmare. But she became arrogant during that graveyard battle, and you punished *her* for it. I quite enjoyed that, even if I didn't appreciate her failure.]"

Now I was really lost. *Chinese broodmare?* I glanced at Linh: she said nothing, deliberately ignoring me. But she didn't try to stop Mister Long speaking, either.

He said: "[It was she who convinced me to keep you alive after Xuân Tăng. This, I admit, was an error on my part. I let my desire for the humiliation of an enemy overcome the mundane practicalities of running the Syndicate. And curiosity, as well, arising from my former profession. Miz Phu managed a touch of forethought in convincing me, knowing she needed you if she was going to take another run at the throne. That's the way it works with you two: Chrome leads, Endgame follows. The wild savage led by the *húlíjīng*, the barbarian and the malignant seductress.]"

I looked at Linh again, longer this time. She wouldn't meet my gaze. This fight between Mister Long and I was a secondary matter. The main event had always been him and Chrome Linh Phu. The realisation should have stung a little, but none came; I'd known it a long time, part of some subterranean knowledge I carried around with me.

"[But here you stand before me again, not knowing that the battle is already lost. I will defeat you the way I did last time. You two have allowed yourselves to become so weak.]" He *tap tap tapped* the metal behind his ear with a red-painted nail. "[The socket here is merely for the freewave and communications. I have no slot for a memory pin. Only fools have them. Just the *peasants,* desperate to take solace, and to *believe* in some electric shadow from the past.]"

His face didn't change as he spoke. Just a young man's face, no more animated than if he was discussing what he had for breakfast. But still, I caught something. "This time it's different."

He raised a thin eyebrow.

"Unless you're saying you deliberately downloaded a virus from the prototype pin we gave you, and after that willingly let it be spread to every other pin you stuck on your flexiscreen. Unless you're saying you allowed us to take the mnemonic directive program Ghost Machine developed and Ladislaw Tauc finished, twist it, and make it so that every grunt in the Macau Syndicate now believes Linh and me are the best choices for boss. Remembers us maybe saving their lives once, or giving their families a kindness, helping them with a debt, whatever plausible bullshit that program finds in their head and tweaks. And you? Well, I reckon they've remembered a few things they don't like so much. Disloyal, spiteful, maybe fucked a few goats. That sort of thing. Your regime is over." I pointed the axe at him. "You're a fucking carcass. You just don't know it yet."

Long allowed himself a smile as he held his hands out towards me, palms inwards. From the fore and middle finger of each, blades emerged. Slender, metal so pure it almost looked white under the lights, until eight inches showed from four spots. He casually uncrossed his legs, stood, and took up a fighting stance in the aisle, side-on, feet apart, four blades flickering under the lights.

"[Well. We're all capable of surprises.]"

He came at us spinning. Literally: arms outstretched, a blur, a steel hurricane, faster than any man I'd ever seen. Faster than Chrome Linh Phu.

I flinched and took a step back, bringing my shield up. Scraping, sparks, Linh crying out and Long was out of reach, ten feet away, back where he started. Linh looked as shocked as I was, as she wiped the back of her hand across her cheek and stared at the blood on it. The cut – from next to her nose right around to an inch from her ear – leaked a film of blood that covered the face underneath.

My heart pounded, the black urge rose up and I roared and charged, shield and axe raised. He smiled in the split-second before

334

I hit and then he was gone, save his foot which tripped and sent me, arms sprawling, into the wooden door that led to his private quarters at the other end of the carriage. It shattered and I pitched forwards into the darkened room beyond.

In the few seconds it took for me to shake my head, get up, and jump back into the cabin, the two had likely struck a hundred blows. Linh Phu and Long were a blur of flashing metal and sparks, I glimpsed Linh's face, grim and set, among the slash and counter slash, spin kick and counter kick.

Long's back was to me. The combatants paused for a moment as Linh backed away. I took one step and heaved the hand axe at him, the blade sung as it spun, end over end, glittering through the air.

Whatever fucking combat tech was packed into Mister Long's head alerted him and he whirled out of the way, arms raised to the horizontal. The blade flashed past his upper arm, he twisted to backhand Linh, but she used the distraction to kick him in the ribs under the other arm. He rebounded off the strike, collided with a lounge, and gracefully flipped over it to land on his feet on the other side, back in his original fighting stance.

Linh didn't look great. Her chest heaved with exertion, green jacket was sliced up, cuts on cheek and legs, and she'd taken a blow to the mouth, her bottom lip split and bleeding.

Long, on the other hand, looked completely at ease. If he was breathing, I couldn't spot it. His only injury a drop of blood on his white shirt, under his right bicep. A drop of blood, then more, the stain expanding slowly, steadily. My blade – now embedded in the far wall – had nicked him under the arm. No matter what medical enhancements Long had, it was a wound that wasn't going to close any time soon. Not with the anti-coagulant that edged my blade.

Mister Long didn't seem to notice. He looked over us both with a relish that chilled my blood, and he chose me, double-pointing with the blades from the right hand. A flash of metal, pain, then the music started. I staggered backwards a couple of steps and looked down. Expanding streaks of blood on my right thigh from two wounds, a long gash on the inside and a second right in the muscle, the glint of metal within. Long had— he'd *fired* his finger-blades.

When I looked up, two more grew in place of those he'd shot at me, the rock song in my head was wailing, and Chrome and Long clashed again. I moved down the aisle, leg sluggish, inadvertently moving to every second beat.

bah-dup, bah-dah da bah-da buh-dadada

step – step – step

It was Linh who gave me an opening. She timed a violent lunge with her blades as I approached, Long was forced to take a step back as he parried, I drove a fist wearing a brass knuckle into his left shoulder blade. His hissed air and spun at the strike, blades aimed at my throat. But I was inside, still moving, still moving, leading with a headbutt. He ducked, the blow glanced the top of his head, he turned the momentum of the strike into a backflip, leaping over Linh's slashing blades and I pushed on, barrelling past Linh, deflecting his desperate blows with the shield and leading with it into his face. It hit him full flush this time, staggering him backwards, on instinct I grabbed his throat and lifted, slamming him with everything I had into the thick steel entrance door of the cabin.

The door cracked, right up the middle. Mister Long's nose was busted, blood flowing down over his slight chin. His right sleeve had darkened from white to red as blood leaked out an unsealable wound. His ribs battered, hip slashed open courtesy of Linh.

We'd given as good as he'd dealt.

But for all that, his eyes gleamed. Linh yelled a warning and I realised my error too late.

The muscles bulged in my forearm as I tried desperately to tear out his throat. All too late. He wrapped his hands around my wrist and yanked down.

His finger blades were no doubt constructed from some top-of-the-fucking-line alloy. Certainly one that didn't have a problem with dense muscle and hardened bones. The music roared into my ears. My hand and half my forearm were sliced from my arm. I staggered away, mouth a surprised O, as ropes of blood gushed from the stump. My back collided with something and my entire world shrunk to the wound. Nothing else in the carriage bar the roar of music as I yanked the belt from my jeans, wrapped it around the stump, and bound a tourniquet with teeth and shaking hand. Medical alerts flashed on-retina and a bout of dizziness dropped me to one knee. I tightened and bound until the black faux leather bit into my arm and the flow of blood slowed to a trickle.

I winced against the blast of a guitar solo and looked around the cabin, finding it hard to focus. Blood was sprayed across the long windows, seat cushions were sliced open, one of the dining tables smashed and toppled. Linh was standing a few metres from Long with her back to me, and I gritted my teeth as I tried to concentrate on her. Her blades were still up, the edges red.

Mister Long looked irritated. That was the entirety of the emotion that played across his face: *irritation.*

His jaw snapped down. Literally, like a snake dislocating its jaw before it consumes its victim. Something small glinted metallic deep in his throat and then he breathed fire.

Breathed. Fire.

His jaw snapped open and he breathed fucken fire.

I blinked, disbelieving. But I felt the heat, saw the thin jet of blue flame shot from his mouth, Linh half-turning as she was struck, trying to pull her jacket over her head.

She screamed.

My left hand, operating on some instinct my music-saturated brain couldn't quite follow, grasped for and found an object behind me. A bottle. I was leaning against the bar. I took a step and hurled it at Long.

Long didn't track it for a vital few fractions of a second, and when he did, flames licking back into his mouth, he casually batted it away with his hand. The bottle sliced in three and the liquid inside splashed against his outstretched arm and face. He and I realised the consequences at the same time, his eyes popping wide, my mouth twitching with the start of a grin.

He lit up like a beacon, engulfed in orange and blue flame from the chest up.

Lucky, I guess. Must have been overproof rum.

A piercing scream came from inside conflagration. My brief grin faded. I could hear it even over the music. It was the agonising scream of a child. My stomach turned.

Mister Long lurched towards the windows, leaving a sputtering trail of burning carpet behind him. Lengths of flame shot out from the human torch – it took me a second to realise they were his arms – battering against the train window, slashing at it. I grabbed the bar behind me just as the window burst and the flaming, screaming, flailing remains of Mister Long were sucked out into the sunlight.

An instant, a mere photoflash of his existence printed on my retinas, then he was gone. In his wake a cabin alive with blue flames, crawling up the walls, along the roof. Linh dragged herself along the floor towards me, hands and top of her head blackened, eyes fixed on me vivid with pain. Her jacket had been subsumed in the blaze somewhere behind her.

I stepped towards her, shaking, then took another, uncertain my legs would hold my weight, the wind whipping at my hair and clothes.

I reached for Linh and she grabbed me with both arms, fierce. Pressing herself against me as I staggered on, using the bloodied stump of my arm on the backs of the lounges to steady myself as I walked into the conflagration. I started coughing against the smoke, using whatever strength I had to keep walking, while Linh used whatever she had left to hold me.

The door opened at the far end, and the Pai Gow Brothers were there, stunned, waiting for us. So far away, too far away through the choking smoke and blue fire. They may as well have been on the fucking moon.

I choked and swayed with the train, past the flames eating away at the centre of the carriage, over the blackened patch where Long had stood. I coughed, lungs burning, stupid fucking song looping to begin again. My boots seemed stuck, melting maybe. My vision faded and I saw a man, large and bearded, crawling across richly patterned carpet towards his severed hand; somewhere outside myself I roared as edges of the abyss closed in, against death's inevitability.

Then I saw two girls, beautiful so beautiful, smiling up at me from the dark wood floor of our small apartment on the Rua da Gamboa. Sunlight bathed the room with its warmth and the two sisters – daughters, they were my daughters – smiled with identical, yet somehow different, white-teethed smiles: mischievous from one, wide-eyed and wondrous from the other. The light in the room faded and so did their smiles as they looked at me, some bloody apparition. Music and darkness blotted all and even the music started to fade.

I roared again.

I tore my feet from the carpet, two steps, three, four—

Screaming though I couldn't hear myself, five steps, six, seven—

—and thrust Linh at the Brothers. They caught her; each

grabbing her with one arm, while using the other to cover their mouths from the smoke.

I fell through the door to the other carriage. I closed my eyes. Hands turned me over. The music in my head tapered away.

I said: "Give me—give me a cig—"

60

"Cigarette?"

I groaned, wincing at the blinding light seeping through my eyelids.

"Cigarette," repeated the voice. Second time round I realised it was Linh. It took a few moments for the light to abate from blinding to bright, and for me to focus. When both happened, I found Chrome Linh Phu looking down at me. She had a soft pack of cigarettes in her hand, one smoke popping its head over the rest. I reached for it.

And ended up merely pointing at it with a stump covered in a hard, translucent membrane. I stared at the missing quarter of my limb for a few seconds before leaning across with my left hand, sliding out one with that, instead.

Linh reached over with a steel lighter. She looked exhausted, aged even. Fine wrinkles at the corners of her eyes I'd not noticed before. Her hand was a vivid red, as was the top of her head. Both looked to be smeared with some sort of salve. The shifting tattoo scales on her arms now dulled and lifeless. Her hair had been burned away.

"You look fucking terrible," she said.

"Says the barbequed Vietnamese woman."

Her eyes twitched with a smile. "I've had worse."

I took a drag and looked around to see where I was. Red roof, carpet, wooden panelled walls. I was lying on one of the leather couches, hooked up to an IV drip hanging from a steel stand. Out the windows, the world flew by at eight-hundred klicks.

"Not there yet?" I asked.

"On the way back," Linh replied, sitting down on a chair next to a small table that had been pulled over to where I was lying. On it was a green-labelled bottle of saké, a white ceramic *tokkuri*, and two small cups with the same green bird design as the *tokkuri* flask. She sipped her saké and said: "You've been out twenty-four hours."

"Oh. Where is everyone else?"

"Same place as last time." She indicated the room with her eyes. "We bought a new carriage."

"We?"

She finished her saké and poured another in one smooth, perfect motion. Burns, long scar on the face, a bunch of other wounds I probably couldn't see, and still she moved with clean fluidity. "We're the new bosses of Macau, Endgame. We got the confirmation at the Shanghai meeting."

I let that sink in. "Seems too easy."

"You call taking down that old dragon easy?"

I shrugged and smoked, looking up at the ceiling.

Out of my peripheral vision I saw her pouring another drink. She said: "Baosteel and Chinalco have come to terms."

I looked back at her, surprised. She passed me a cup of saké, I took it with the hand that held the cigarette, downed it, and handed back the empty cup, grunting a *thanks* as I did so.

"Regional bosses getting replaced," she said, "especially in Macau, that's just part of the business. All they care is the new regime can do the work. Endgame Ebbinghaus and Chrome Linh Phu, well, we got the right sort of reputation. They don't like it much when their man is taken down without permission, but Mister Long never came from the right family, wasn't in the Party, and never served military. Even if they did care, it's irrelevant."

I asked the follow up question with my eyes.

"It's irrelevant," she said, "Because the two biggest companies in the world just called a truce, entered into a partnership, of sorts. That's not a standard business day. It's the biggest thing to happen in fifty fucking years."

I groaned and turned onto my side. I felt pretty numb for the most part, sanguine. Good painkillers, I supposed. "Well, don't give me half a story," I said.

"A hot war was bad for our *commercial interests*, they decided, especially if the freewave got word that it isn't just gangsters, but two of the biggest companies in the world. Kill the share price. Even worse if the public heard the reason for the war was over memory pins. Chinalco has led the world on the dark arts of neurological change, of gradual memory decline, and most recently, on direct mnemonic directives. Baosteel, well, they developed a pin so advanced, so powerful, it will be able to take advantage of the weaknesses of the human mind to an extent we could have only ever dreamed on."

She looked at the window, cup of saké forgotten in her hand. "A revolution," she whispered.

"You sound like Long," I said.

"I'm nothing like him," she said, and didn't even bother looking at me while she said it. "Long is driven by hate."

"And you?"

"Rage."

If she'd told me what the fuck that distinction meant, I'd long forgotten it, and had no inclination to reacquaint myself. So I smoked my cigarette and let her contemplate, in her mind's eye, a dystopic landscape of barren, acquiescent human minds.

"How did Baosteel know what we were doing?" I asked, after my smoke was finished.

Linh broke off her glazed, middle-distance stare and looked back at me. She shrugged. "Oh, they figured it out a long time ago. They also figured that memory decline is good for business – shattering the faith of the people in the technology, not so much. No, they played the long game, waited until the dependence in the population got to critical mass, when there was no turning back. Maybe they planned to expose Chinalco, maybe not, but it doesn't matter anymore. They're going to rule the world, what matter if it is with a partner?"

Linh finished her saké and placed the cup gently on the table. The train rocked, I nodded for another cigarette. She pulled one from the pack, placed it in my mouth, lit it. It wasn't quite worth losing an arm to see her so strangely calm and, fuck, almost pleasant. Nice to have her lighting me a cigarette, though, rather than coming at me with one of her blades.

I blinked at the strange thought. Took a drag of my cigarette.

Linh continued her story before I could think on it much: "Mister Long needed us for a war. All the way up until the offer from Baosteel came in. When he'd been ordered by the Chinalco bosses to come to Shanghai, he knew what was brewing. He also knew that if an agreement was reached, you and I would become irrelevant. That's why he invited us on his little journey. Kill us after, if need be."

"Strange that he let us see him beforehand then."

"Hmm?"

"In his carriage, beforehand."

She shook her head slightly. "You're fucking dim sometimes, Endgame."

I smoked my cigarette. I was too high to get annoyed at her. "Huh?"

"Long was a lot of things. An Omissioner. A—"

"Wait – he was an Omissioner?"

"Of course. One of the best. He was ambitious, too. Believed he could win the war in Vietnam, through his experiments. Saw himself being raised up to national hero."

I shook my head slightly, not knowing any of this.

"But he was also a gangster. That's the thing, Endel. A gangster ain't going to show fear when his two generals ask to speak. He was arrogant, as any man in his position is. He figured he could take us, with or without his guards. He figured it because he *has* taken us before. At least once, that he admitted to. So yeah, he saw us beforehand, because he was on his way to a ceremony where he was to be crowned the king, and in his mind, we're still just two peasants. Despite everything, *peasants*. Two people so small, he figured, couldn't possibly overcome someone so very big."

I took on my smoke. Savouring it. Savouring the gentle rhythm of the train.

"Is my family still alive, Linh?"

Linh reached over to put her saké cup down, and missed the table by four inches. It bounced once on the carpet and came to rest on its side. I made sure to watch her response: surprise at first, quickly replaced by a film of controlled rage over the eyes; that familiar killer gleam.

"How—" she started.

"Just tell me whether they're alive."

She blinked at me, figuring her response. Eventually she kept it simple. "Yeah. Yeah, they are, Endgame. We had an agreement. You kept your end. I kept mine."

I breathed out a long sigh hidden in a cloud of smoke. A hard knot, twisting somewhere down below my heart, untwisted. A weight and tension I hadn't realised was there, dissipated.

"Why do you keep me around, Linh?"

"Necessity."

I indicated with my cigarette for her to continue.

"I'm not repeating myself, Endgame. I needed the black matter of your will to violence."

"It's more than that."

She tried to rub her scalp, but pulled her hand away gingerly as she touched the shiny red burn. "I owe you, for a few things. So I saved you. From a life lived as a civilian, as one of the nameless."

"That's closer," I said, after a pause. "But it's not everything. What Long was talking about. You and me. Did we have something, before I met my family?"

"We had everything," she said, quietly.

"We were together?"

Linh looked up at me with open contempt. "Is that what you think it's about? Pussy? Dick? God, usually I don't even like men. No." She shook her head. "No. We had the whole world. And you threw it all away for that Chinese bitch."

The gloom grew as the train drew closer to Macau. Drops of rain spattered the windows. With serpent tongue, lightning flickered over the far horizon.

"We got everything now, Endgame. Everything we dreamed about."

"I don't remember that, Linh."

"*You* wanted it just as much as I did."

"Maybe. But that sounds like someone else now. Another version of myself. I don't know if I want it anymore."

"Forget your fucking family. All you can bring them now is the reaper."

"Yeah," I said. "Yeah." I smoked and watched the lighting. "But I don't want you either, Linh. I don't want whatever it is you're planning. The last time we talked about it," I paused, waiting for the on-retina prompt. "The last time we talked you wouldn't even answer my questions. Even after all this."

"You want to know my plans, Endgame? You want to know what comes next?" There was something in her voice that made me look back at her. She leaned forwards in her seat, something building in her, like the storm outside.

I took a final drag on my cigarette, finishing it. I felt some sort of peace in the way the train rocked, in the way the smoke curled and thinned into a layer above me in the air, and in not knowing. Not knowing any more of this. "No," I said finally. "No. I don't want to know. I don't want any of it anymore."

She leaned back in her chair, flexing her jaw, bringing herself under control. "Then what the fuck do you want?"

"Another thing."

"What?"

"Something quiet, Linh."

"Yeah? Settle down, get an office job? I'd kill myself if I had to do that."

"You should settle down, Linh. Get an office job."

"Smart arse."

"But no," I said. "Shit, no. I don't want that."

"Then?"

"Money."

"That's it?"

"No. That's the first thing. How much did we make throwing that smouldering pig-fucker off the train?"

She shook her head, just once. "You've always been such a small creature, Endgame. Every *version* of you. Always thinking small, dreaming small. Money. The crudest of dreams for the smallest of minds. Money. The gremlin of ambition for the little people."

"Jesus, Linh. You're either sitting around sharpening knives and scowling, or giving these fucking summaries of your world view.

I prefer it when you're playing the role of mute enforcer. At least then I can pretend you're not some deluded sociopath."

With a whir of chrome her blade was buried to the hilt next to my ear before I had a chance to flinch. She smiled: "My sociopathy contains not one ounce of delusion. My goals are crystal clear."

I remained calm. It wasn't the drugs, I realised. I simply didn't care anymore. The tension in my chest had abated, knowing my family were alive. But as that faded I noticed another thing there. A lack. The Germans call it *Weltschmerz*. I was Australian, but had a German name, so perhaps somewhere in my past was a German relative who explained the word to me. I didn't have a shred of memory to back this assumption, and as Linh would say, it was irrelevant anyway. But this word, it bubbled up to my forebrain and sat there for me to inspect. 'World pain', is a rough translation. The mismatch between your hopes and the reality of the world; longing for universe that cannot be, and pain at the realisation it never will. My lack would forever remain hidden to me, which made that feeling more profound and at the same time, pathetic. I yearned for a world I *could not even imagine*, I felt loss for things I *could not remember.*

I turned my head and looked at the handle of the blade, ignoring Linh. Somewhere along the line something inside me had broken. And I had no fucking clue what it was. Linh was wrong about one thing though: money. Money was everything. That was the world we both lived in, the diamond-hard reality no amount of thinking or wishing would change.

My focus shifted from the knife to Linh's face. The default chill had settled over her features. She looked at me like she was trying to make a decision. Live or die, I supposed: the first thing that went through her head every time she met someone.

I said: "I want out of the loop."

"Loop?"

"This loop I'm stuck in. This fucking—this fucking staircase I can't ever get off. Up and up and up."

She waited, listening.

I sighed. "You got what you wanted. Long is dead, you're the boss of Macau. I helped you kill him and I saved your life. Now I want out."

"There is no out," she said, "of the business we are in."

"Bullshit. The tech we have with the new pins, that's exactly what we're able to do. You owe me this."

Linh paused for a few moments, thinking. She said: "So what do you want?"

"Retirement. And this is the package you're going to give me: one of the next-generation pins. I'm sick of being the kind of simpleton who doesn't know what fucking day it is. I want fifty million yuan sent to my wife. One day she looks in her bank account, and *snap*, it's there. Last, I want a nano-cleanse."

She was about to speak when something occurred to me. "Oh, one more thing," I said, and indicated my stump. "A new one of these wouldn't go astray."

"A cleanse," she said. "You're too young. You'd be wasting it."

"I feel fucking old, Linh. But yeah, sure, it's less effective right now. I'll get what, five, ten years? But I don't care about that. I want to be ten years younger and not even know I'm ten years younger. Complete wipe of everything after I arrived in Macau, keep everything leading up to that point. I want a new pin – clean, no hidden directives – so I can function out in the world again. Take my old one," I said. "Keep it as a memento."

"Mementos aren't my thing."

"Then why do you insist on keeping me around?"

She smiled, wryly. "Okay Endel. Sure."

"To make this work," I said, "You're going to need to slowly wipe me from the memories of your people. Take that little something extra from them as they come in to have their pins altered. Come to a point where they believe you and you alone killed Long. Come to a point where I never existed."

"A cleanse is expensive," she said. "There won't be anything left to send your family."

"There's that safe up in Long's suite. There'll be a little something something there. Enough change to help them out for a while."

"Maybe. Maybe he's just got a collection of porcelain dolls locked away." She blinked at me, thinking me over. "And who you going to be, Endgame?"

"I got an idea. Something far from what I am now, but not too far from my nature."

Linh reached out, withdrew her dagger from the lounge, and slid it back into its sheath under her arm. She looked small somehow, sitting there, alone.

"You're opting for obscurity," she said, still quiet. "When we could remake the world. Be as titans, standing astride it."

"No greatness in putting men in the ground."

She laughed without humour. "So stupid, Endgame, right to the end. Killing is the only greatness left in this world."

I gave her no response to that, just indicated the cigarettes with my chin. She pulled one out, placed it between my lips, fingertips lingering as she did so, and lit it for me.

"Out of the loop, Linh. I'm no good to you anyway. There's something wrong with my program, runs deeper than memory, ain't nothing going to fix it. I'm all used up. And if you're thinking about trying to brainwash me, make me your sock-puppet again, then—" I indicated the blade under her arm with my eyes, "—I'd rather you just end it now. The chasm inside me, it's—it's all closed up now. Without that I got nothing for you. No will anymore. No hate. No nothing." I exhaled smoke at the ceiling. "You owe me this."

She was silent for a few moments. "So you're breaking up with me?"

I smiled, wincing a little. "It's not you honey, it's me."

She smiled back: "Ain't that the fucking truth."

Chrome Linh Phu took a long, deep breath. Then she stood and stepped over, right next to me, and looked down into my eyes. She took the cigarette from my lips and replaced it with her mouth, kissing me passionate. I returned it, a heat rising in me that cut through the lethargy of the pain medication. When she broke it off, though, I was glad of it. The heat in me, it was of the other kind: a sickness, a fever.

Her lips glistened. "You're out," she said. "Goodbye, Endgame."

"Goodbye, Linh."

Linh walked from the carriage, swaying gentle, to the rhythm of the train. Somehow I knew I was never going to see her again.

61

Linh Phu was starting her breakfast of real beef phở, half a fresh baguette, and coffee with condensed milk, just before midday when the first reports came in. The Pai Gow Brothers – together coming to about half the man she needed, but as good as she was going to get – came in from the entry room when they heard her swearing. When they asked her what was wrong, she simply pointed up at the tai screen.

Half the screen was a headshot of the square-jawed Chinese anchorman on the English language channel; the other half had the Chinalco symbol. Underneath the words MEMORY PIN SCANDAL in bold.

The newsman gave the details with well-practised gravitas:

"...*from several anonymous sources, starting three hours ago and continuing as we go to air. The sources have pinpointed programming built into next-generation Baosteel Infinity Pins that implant 'suggestions' into consumers. Omissioners we have interviewed have called these suggestions 'mnemonic directives', a theoretical form of neural programming that has been discussed in the scientific community for many years. In further news coming to light over the past thirty minutes, more leaks – this time against Baosteel competitor Chinalco – point to disturbing and as yet unverified claims of brain damage inflicted by everyday memory pin use. We emphasise at this time that these are only accusations, and that—"*

Underneath, in ticker tape, updates were running in red holotype: `…Experts dispute authenticity of leaks — Baosteel denies any knowledge of mnemonic directives — Share prices plunge for major memory pin manufacturers — Zhang Wei Kardashian unfollows everyone on her Ego feed — Tianjin Teda defeats Arsenal 3—0 — Sources claim terrorist hacker group Jane Doe behind memory pin faults — Mass grave found near a church outside of Xuân Tăng may be related to memory scandal — Government sources implore calm, consider temporary market…`

One of the Brothers said: "That sucks. Hope I'm not infected."

The newsman continued:

"Further, we have a secret recording of a registered Omissioner by the name of Ladislaw Tauc, confessing these crimes to an unknown second person. We have verified the authenticity of what you are about to see."

The coverage flicked to a new scene. A cavernous room, shining cleansteel equipment, and in front of it all an older European man wearing a white coat and a look of contempt on his face.

"Before we get started," said a voice, familiar, rough as a chainsaw. *"Why'd you do it?"*

Ladislaw Tauc raised a bushy eyebrow. "Why what?"

"Betray your profession. Turn the population into docile cattle."

Tauc snorted. "Oh dear, really?"

"Yeah, really."

"Have you seen the world we live in? The population are already docile cattle. They credulously believe in the most venal of demagogues. They prefer the transparent lies of game simulations

over the hard truth of reality. They are known better by the giant corporations than they know themselves. They have no free will: they buy what they are told to buy, watch what they are directed to watch, hate who they are trained to hate. Any innovation I conjure through the science of memory will not change one jot the supine and pathetic stupidity of the common person. It will be merely a refinement, of all that has gone on before."

Linh muted the tai screen.

"Go get Tauc."

"And then?" asked the Pai Gow Brothers.

"Throw him down the memory hole."

They nodded.

"*Now.*"

They left quickly, closing the door behind them.

Linh leaned back in her chair and took a deep breath, rubbing a hand over her smooth hair. It'd grown out to about two inches now. Linh kept it dyed a dark green, flat and straight, with a part down the left side. The scar tissue underneath was almost completely healed.

She watched the report, remembering to sip her coffee after a few minutes. When the update ended Linh simply shook her head and whispered *motherfucker*. She broke the end of the crusty baguette, dipping it into her phở before chewing on it.

Her gaze slid over to the view through the broad windows opposite. Of Macau and its casinos draped in their glittering lights and neon lies, cutting through the rain and gloom of the truth, and offering something far, far better. Those gauche, unapologetic monuments to greed, built on the inevitable calculus of human nature. Money. Money had no memory, no loyalty, no feelings. All it cared about was itself, all it wanted was more. Such a crude god, but also the truest god. And a city that worshiped this crude and true god was a city that could be known. A city that could be controlled. A city that was now hers. She looked out over the weak and transient spirits that passed and lived and breathed and cried and wanted, all beneath. They were not slaves to memory and the remembrances she chose, not yet, but still they were slaves.

Linh Phu turned off the tai screen, and thought on the problem. Alone, she smiled at her vision, untouched by the breaking news.

62

Robert 'Iron Hand' König was drinking whisky and cokes with his fellow fighters from the Chang Tie Quan House at the floor bar in the City of Dreams when a Chinese princess walked straight up to him and asked him to buy her a drink. Told him, to be precise. Iron Hand's fellow fighters raised eyebrows and made approving shapes with their lips as he said *why not* and followed her over to a table, extra drink in hand. She'd ordered a beer. The big man smiled at her choice.

Iron Hand and the woman sat across from each other. She gave him an easy, familiar smile as he sat down. Something in the smile made him mirror it.

Robert was in his late twenties, clean shaven, with a full head of black hair. His piercing blue eyes were natural and, therefore, often a point of conversation. He had several faint white scars on his hands, his cheeks. One scar on his forehead went up into his hairline, parting the hair for a centimetre before disappearing under a thick, shaggy mane. When people asked, he told them he'd lost the hand and gained the scars in a glimmer bike collision with a Chinalco delivery truck.

The woman had perfect skin, save a small mole under her left eye. Almost perfect: on closer inspection, under the lights, the fighter noticed small lines at the corner of her eyes. For some reason he liked that even more. She wore a much-loved leather jacket and faded jeans, yet at the same time reeked of culture and sophistication.

"Don't usually get propositioned by uptown girls. The name's Robert."

"Jian," she said. "And I know yours, *Iron Hand*." She indicated his cybernetic limb with her beer glass. "You tough-guy types sure as hell aren't known for your originality."

"Oh, you watch the fights?" he asked, a little surprised.

"I watch *your* fights."

Robert smiled at that. A kind of confused one that said: *who is this woman?* He rested his hand on the table, the titanium alloy gleaming dully in the casino's lights. "You don't seem like the standard MMA fan."

"Probably because I'm not."

"Yeah. I can see." He looked her over. "You slumming it?"

"Well, Macau is the giant, glittering slum of the world, so yes. I guess you could say that."

"Not from around here?"

"You're giving me that line?"

"Lady, you're the woman dealing out the one-liners, I'm just tagging along for the ride."

The woman's eyes twinkled at that. "No, thankfully, is the answer. Not from here. Shanghai. I come here just to visit from time to time. You should come up and take a look around my part of the world sometime."

"Yeah," he said, a little too quickly. And then: "Maybe."

"*Maybe?*"

He reddened, just a little.

"You're so young," she said, more to herself rather than the man opposite.

"I don't feel it."

"No?"

"Try mixed martial arts for a couple of years, Jian. You won't feel so young." When he said *Jian*, he savoured the way it felt in his mouth. Something made him want to say the name again, and again.

"Ah," she said turning her beer glass slowly on the table. "Still, I'm too old for you."

"We're there already, Jian? In that case, this is the spot where I say: don't believe it for a second."

"I've also got two kids."

"Ah. Well, in Australia we have a term for someone like you."

"Enlighten me."

"Yummy mummy."

She rolled her eyes. "Yes. Well. There's a reason your country has a second-world economy."

"Hey," he said, with mock outrage.

"That's okay." She leaned forwards, conspiratorially. "I have a thing for barbarians."

"Yeah?" he asked. She smelled faintly of sandalwood, up close. He felt himself blushing, and her smile widened at his discomfort. He cleared his throat. "You really are slumming it."

"Hmm. Something about those rough edges, I suppose."

Iron Hand raised his glass to her, said "Well, cheers to that," and took a slug.

"One thing, though," she said, reaching out and fingering a button on his denim jacket.

"What's that?"

"This jacket has got to go."

"Woah there, *milady*. We're not married."

"No," she said, and winked at him. "Not yet. First things first: we go dancing."

Jian turned in her stool elegantly, stepped down and walked away. She paused when he didn't follow, turning back to look over her shoulder. "You coming, cowboy?"

Iron Hand's eyes dropped down at his drink. He rubbed his thumb on the side of the glass, slowly, before looking back up at Jian. "Have we met before?"

"Do I seem like a woman you could forget?"

"Ha. No. I guess not."

Her eyes never left his. "So. You coming?"

"Yeah," he said. He stood up, drink forgotten, friends forgotten. "Yeah. I am."

ACKNOWLEDGEMENTS

This book took ten years to write, so I'm going to have trouble remembering everyone that helped along the way. Apologies if I've overlooked you here.

I know that Louise B was one of my readers for this (because she reads nearly everything I write), as was Tina S, who received a wretched early draft over eight years ago. Thank you, both. My wife, Sarah, who had the unfortunate privilege of reviewing an even earlier version.

'In Search of Memory,' by Nobel Prize winner, Eric R. Kandel, was an invaluable resource for this book. If the science of memory interests you, I highly recommend it.

My agent, John Jarrold, as always, who saw the merit in the novel, and went out and got a deal for it.

I never thank the whole team at Titan Books, so it's about time I do. Thank you to Elora, Hannah, Paul, Fenton, Bahar, and everyone else behind the scenes. I should make special mention of Julia Lloyd here, who designed the phenomenal cover for *The Escher Man*. Brilliant.

My editor, George Sandison, who has a deft and precise touch, and who allows room for my idiosyncrasies and obsessions.

For every reader who has contacted me via email, or on social media, or in-person at conventions, thank you. Hearing (or reading) what my works mean to you is always welcome. I feel like I'm writing into the void sometimes. Even when I see one of my books on the shelf at a store, it still somehow doesn't seem real. It's only when someone reaches out, and talks about my work, that I can truly know it exists in the mind of another.

Thank you to Sarah, as always (and for the second time in these acknowledgments), and her unyielding support for my bloody-minded commitment to this unforgiving profession.

To my boys, Robert and Willem, who keep me on my toes by frequently ambushing me at my desk, whacking me with foam swords and throwing dirty socks at my head. The jury is out on how this assists the writing process, but it does make me laugh.

ABOUT THE AUTHOR

T. R. Napper is a multi-award-winning science fiction author. His short fiction has appeared in *Asimov's, Interzone, The Magazine of Fantasy & Science Fiction*, and numerous others, and been translated into six different languages. He received a creative writing doctorate for his thesis: *The Dark Century, 1946 – 2046. Noir, Cyberpunk, and Asian Modernity.*

Before turning to writing, T. R. Napper was a diplomat and aid worker, delivering humanitarian programs in Southeast Asia for a decade. During this period he was a resident of the Old Quarter in Hanoi for several years, the setting for his acclaimed debut novel, *36 Streets*.

These days he has returned to his home country of Australia, where, in addition to his writing, he runs art therapy programs for people with disabilities.

For more fantastic fiction, author events,
exclusive excerpts, competitions, limited editions and more

VISIT OUR WEBSITE
titanbooks.com

LIKE US ON FACEBOOK
facebook.com/titanbooks

FOLLOW US ON TWITTER AND INSTAGRAM
@TitanBooks

EMAIL US
readerfeedback@titanemail.com